Maggie Hope was born and raised in County Durham. She worked as a nurse for many years, before giving up her career to raise her family.

She is the author of A WARTIME NURSE, also published by Ebury.

D0729487

A Mother's Gift

Maggie Hope

EBURY
PRESS

357910864

First published as 'The Ironmaster's Girl in 2002 by Piatkus Books
This edition published in 2011 by Ebury Press, an imprint of Ebury Publishing
A Random House Group Company

The Random House Group Limited Reg. No. 954009

Addresses for companies within the Random House Group can be found at
www.randomhouse.co.uk

A CIP catalogue record for this book
is available from the British Library

ISBN 9780091952952

To buy books by your favourite authors and register for offers visit
www.randomhouse.co.uk

Penguin Random House is committed to a sustainable future for
our business, our readers and our planet. This book is made from
Forest Stewardship Council® certified paper.

Printed and bound in Great Britain by Clays Ltd, Elcograf S.p.A.

For my lovely grandson,
Jonathan Christopher Hepworth

Part One

Chapter One

It was just a muffled sort of sound at first but as it progressed down the row it got louder. Thump! Thump! Knock, knock, knock! Gran dropped her slice of bread and dripping on the table and rushed to the black-leaded range, picked up the poker and with the handle banged on the fire-back above the bars. Bang, Bang! This time the thumping rang metal on metal.

'Howay, pet,' Gran said to Kate, 'give us a hand, the man's on his way. Had away and tak' a peep. See how far he's got down the row.'

Kate nodded her head, went to the front door, had a bit of trouble getting it open because it was stuck with all the rain they'd had that summer and the threshwood was swollen and rotten and coming away in thin spelks, leaving gaps for the rain to get in. But she did get it open and stuck her head out to look up the row.

He was there all right, the Means-test man, him with his double-breasted suit and shiny shoes and his hair slicked back with real brilliantine not water. He was close an' all, too close. She pushed the door to and ran back through the Room to the kitchen.

'He's nearly here, Gran, he's just at Mrs Wearmouth's!' Mrs Wearmouth was only three doors away, Kate's heart began to beat faster with the dread of the Means-test man.

'We're here, Mrs Benfield, what have we to tak'?'

Billy Wright and his marra burst in the back door and glanced around at the meagre furnishings. There was obviously little to take from the kitchen, all it held was a table, a press which was propped up with an off-cut from a pit prop where Grandad had broken the leg one night when he came in bad with the beer and three chairs.

'The sofa in the room!' said Gran. 'Oh God, don't let them take me sofa will you, lads!'

'Not if we can help it,' said Billy, making a beeline for the connecting door. But he was too late and it was Kate's fault. She hadn't closed the front door properly and it had swung open and now, gazing at the opening in horror, she saw the Means-test man standing there, already writing in his notebook.

'Mrs Benfield isn't it?' he said, 'And who are these two lads? I thought there were just you and your man and the lass? Katie Benfield, isn't it?'

Kate stepped into the room and nodded her head, unable to speak. Not so Gran who pushed past her and stood, all four feet ten inches of her and with fists on skinny hips, confronting the Means-test man. The two boys melted away; they had other things to do, helping the other residents of the rows to hide their treasured bits of furniture and nick-nacks the Board reckoned could be

4

sold and the money deducted from the hardship allowance. Katie knew that they would be all up and down the back lane carrying precious bits out to hide in the back yards of houses that had already been inspected. She watched her gran, face red as fire as she glared up at the man.

'What the heck do you think you're doing?' Gran screeched. 'I'll have the law on you, I will an' all! Barging into decent folk's houses —'

'Aw, howay, Missus,' he said and pushed his glasses up over the bridge of his nose. 'You know full well who I am.' He looked mildly down at her and sighed. 'All right,' he said and for a wild minute Katie thought they had won. But no, he simply reached in his pocket and took out a card. 'There you are, Mr Thompson I am, see it there on the top? And I have full powers to have a look to see what you've got worth selling. So you'd best not get in me way or it will be the worse for you.'

He stepped forward and Gran turned on him, stamping her foot and screaming, 'Get out! Get out!'

Easily he took hold of her around her skinny shoulders and lifted her bodily to one side and then, as though nothing had happened, went over to the sofa and felt the plush covering and worn out springs. Calmly taking a piece of chalk from his jacket pocket he chalked a price on the back: 2/6. He was writing the amount into his note-book when Gran got her second wind.

'2/6!' she shouted. 'Two shillings and sixpence! Are you telling me my sofa's worth no more than 2/6?' Her expression reflecting her outrage she jumped at him, stamping her heel on his instep, grinding it in. When this made no impression, after all he has wearing good leather shoes and she was in flat-heeled plimsolls minus their laces, her 'house slippers' as she called them, she tried kicking him in the shins.

'Come away, Gran, please,' said Katie, grabbing her arm and pulling her as hard as she could.

Mr Thompson sighed. 'I'm sorry Missus,' he said, 'but if you are going to carry on like this I'll only call the polis. Now, howay, be a good lass.'

'A good lass! And you telling me my sofa that cost me four bob a week for three years is worth only two shillings and sixpence?'

'I'm trying to help you, Missus. Can you not see that if I say it's worth more it means you'll have more deducted?'

'Well—' Gran was brought up short, she didn't know what to say but not for long. 'Lad,' she tried in a softer tone, almost wheedling, 'lad, I only get four and sixpence for the bairn and fourteen and six from the dole for me man. I cannot keep the lass on two shillings, you can see that, can't you?'

Katie cringed as she saw the look on Mr Thompson's face, almost a smirk.

'I tell you what Missus, did you not go to school?' he asked. 'If you could but add up you would see you have nineteen shillings coming in, where do you think it comes from? Folk like me who's doing an honest day's work.' Sticking his chalk in his pocket he walked to the door. 'Good day, Missus,' he said. 'You'll be hearing from us.'

'Well, at least we've given the rest of them time to hide their bits,' said Gran. She was bending over the sofa looking at the numbers chalked on the back. Taking out a rag duster from her apron pocket she spit on it and rubbed at the chalk hopelessly.

'I might be able to get a job,' said Katie. 'I thought I could deliver groceries for the Co-op store. They want people.'

'They want lads,' Gran said flatly.

'Well, I can put my hair up in a cap and borrow Grandad's bike. I can—'

'Aw man, Katie, don't be a bigger fool than you can help. Nobody is going to tak' you for a lad, you're going on thirteen already though by heck, you don't act it!'

Katie looked down at her feet miserably. The toecaps of her boy's shoes were scuffed so badly the top layer stuck up in tufts. She had hoped they might be able to get a grant to buy her new school shoes but that wasn't likely now. And Gran would never sell the sofa, why should she? It was the only place she could get a bit of peace and quiet on a Sunday afternoon, when Grandad came in from the club and lay snoring upstairs in bed.

'Any road,' Gran was saying. 'Any road, if you got a job they'd tak' the other two bob off us an' all. I don't know. I might just have to ask your mam for a few coppers to help us out like.'

'No, don't, Gran!' Katie exclaimed. 'You know they cannot give us anything. I'll find something to do, I will.' Kitty Benfield sat down the sofa and gazed solemnly at her granddaughter. The granddaughter she loved and

Noah loved an' all, she knew that. Though sometimes she thought he loved the beer more. Ah, it was no good, men always had to have their pocket money for beer after working down the pit all the week. Though they weren't working down the pit at the minute and hadn't done for weeks.

There was no market for the steel from the ironworks in Middlesbrough so there was no demand for the coal from the pits because the pits were owned by the men who made the steel and they had closed them down. Not all of them but this one, the one at Winton, which was what mattered to her family. Because the Hamiltons owned the pits and the ironworks and most everything else she could think of. By, she'd like to see them worrying about where their next crust of bread was coming from. She'd laugh in their faces, she would.

Kitty roused herself from her bitter reverie and sighed. 'Aye, I know,' she said heavily, 'your mam's worse off than us.' After all, it was a fact that her Thomas and his wife had six bairns to think of without Katie. After all that was why she had taken Katie when she was but six months old, and a second child. Hannah had had to stop giving her the breast because she was already far on with a new baby. And Katie hadn't thrived on sugar water and condensed milk and Kitty had picked her up one day from the rickety pram which had been pushed into the furthest corner of the yard so her mam wasn't pestered by her weakly cry. By she had thought, the bairn was light as a feather.

'I'll tak' her,' she had said to Hannah and Hannah had

merely looked at her and nodded. Hannah had about given up, what with feeling sick and bone weary all through her pregnancies and this last one was the third in two years.

'It's no good you complaining, mind,' Kitty had said to Noah when she carried the bairn into the house. 'We've got this bairn now and we have to fetch her up.' To give him his due, Noah said not a word. Why, after all, it happened quite often that a grandmother took a bairn that was one too many. And there was no denying it was sweet to hold the little thing and Katie had been a good bairn, sleeping through the night once she had her belly filled with good milk. And look at her now, a lass to be proud of.

Katie looked like Noah an' all, a real bonny lass she was with dark blue eyes and wavy fair hair and straight limbs, not like a lot of the bairns in Winton where rickets was the scourge of the babbies. Her own younger sister, Ena, hadn't walked till she was three, her legs bent out in a bow.

'I just wanted to say, thanks for giving us time to hide the good tea service, Kitty, I'm ever so grateful.'

Katie and her gran glanced up. Dottie Dowson from next door was standing in the back doorway, hesitating for only a courtesy moment before coming in and standing before the range. She was a stout woman and her pinny was pulled tightly round her waist, straining at the thin strings tied at the back. She looked hopefully towards the kettle on the side but the fire was almost out and the teapot out of sight in the pantry.

'By, I'm fair clemming for a cup of tea,' she said.

'Aye well,' said Gran, who had come through from the room with Katie close behind. 'There's no coal and what's more, I've swept the coal house out, there's not so much as a teaspoonful left. So how I'm supposed to mak' a drop of tea I don't know.'

'Aye, me an' all,' sighed Dottie. 'I'll have to go to the soup kitchen again for a bit of dinner for the bairns.'

Kitty looked at her. So far the Benfields had not been to the soup kitchen which operated from a room behind the infants school. And she couldn't bear the thought that they might have to go now. She looked hopelessly at Katie and Katie caught the look and something shrivelled inside her. But if Gran wanted her to go to the soup kitchen then she would go, she decided, never mind if the girls from school saw her there. It was her fault the Means-test man had got in before the lads had the sofa hid and it was up to her to do something about it.

'I'll come with you, Mrs Dowson,' she said.

'Eeh, no, lass,' said Gran but her voice trembled unconvincingly.

'I will, I don't mind, honest,' said Katie. But half an hour later as she stood in line with a large bowl held before her and a paper bag for the bread in her pocket she minded all right. Especially she minded when a group of girls from the grammar school got off Radley's bus, talking and laughing until they saw Katie standing there, her back turned towards them in a forlorn hope they wouldn't see her. Not that they said anything nasty, oh no. After all, they had been her friends at the junior school and she had won a scholarship to go to the grammar school with them but Gran hadn't been able to afford the uniform.

'Hello, Katie,' June Wright had called and blushed and the girls had walked on talking quietly to each other and June had glanced back and away quickly when she saw Katie was still looking. Katie's throat burned and her heart beat sickeningly for she knew they must be talking about her. And it was then that she vowed to herself that she would get out of Winton, she would make something of herself. Oh yes she would if she died in the attempt.

Moving along with the queue Katie had her bowl filled with vegetable broth with bits of ham floating in it by Mrs Brown, the wife of the manager of the Co-op store.

'I've put some extra bread in for you, Katie,' Mrs Brown said kindly. Katie blushed and stammered thanks she could hardly get out because her throat was closing up tightly but at last she was free to go home as fast as the slopping broth would allow her to walk.

'Flaming hell, what's this muck?' Noah demanded when he sat down at the kitchen table to eat his share. 'By, our Kitty, you know damn well I don't like broth.' His face was red with anger and for a minute Katie thought he might chuck the lot out into the yard but he didn't.

'What do you expect when the pit's laid off?' Gran demanded. 'Do you know the Means-test man's been round this morning? Put a price on my sofa he did an' all.' Her voice quivered as she spoke, no anger there, just despair.

'You mean this is from the soup kitchen,' said Noah. 'Why man, is it any wonder a man turns to drink?'

'It's well to be seen you had the price of a pint!'

Noah sighed. He picked up his spoon and began ladling the soup into his mouth, swallowing fast and in between mouthfuls taking great bites out of a crust of bread in his other hand. The truth was he hadn't had the money for a pint, he had gone into the club intending to put the price on the slate. Only Les, behind the bar, had shaken his head.

'Nay, Noah,' he had said. 'The slate's full enough. You'll have to find threepence if you want a pint.'

Noah had stared at him in disbelief. 'Hey,' he had demanded, 'haven't I always paid me dues as soon as I could?'

'Aye, I know, lad,' said Les. 'But I can only sub you so far, be fair, man. I have the brewery to pay and I don't mind telling you they're getting a bit restless like.'

Noah had gone a fiery red with the humiliation but he held his head up and glared at the club steward. 'Well, by hell,' he'd said. 'If I go out now I tell you, I won't be back! I'll walk to Coundon first.' He glanced around the bar for support but as it happened the place was almost empty, only a domino-playing foursome of aged miners sitting in the corner nursing half-pints which had lasted them since the bar opened at eleven. They had looked up at the sound of the altercation at the bar but quickly turned back to the dominoes. Noah looked back at the steward. He was polishing glasses and whistling under his breath and obviously not caring if Noah and all the rest of the laid-off miners deserted for Coundon.

Noah strode to the door then glanced around once

again. 'Aye well,' he said. 'I could do with the exercise any road. I'm away then.' The steward didn't reply.

Now as Noah rammed bread into his mouth and washed it down with tea which was the colour of cat's piss it was that weak for it was borrowed from a neighbour, Noah felt the blackness of despair descending on to his shoulders and spread up into his head.

Chapter Two

'Will you be in for lunch today, Matthew?'

Matthew Hamilton glanced up from the letter he was reading, a faint frown of irascibility creasing his forehead.

'What?'

Mary Anne Hamilton bent her head over her plate quickly. What had she said to annoy him? It had been a perfectly reasonable question after all. The vague unhappy feelings that lurked as usual in the back of her mind moved forward a little.

Matthew caught the small defensive gesture and his irritation rose. Good God, why was she such a mouse? She acted like a mouse; she even looked like a mouse with her mouse-coloured hair and pale blue eyes. Her lips quivered timidly even as he watched. He fought down his feelings, made himself smile.

'Sorry, no, I won't be. I have to drive over to Auckland. I will probably be late for dinner too. You needn't wait for me.'

'But Matthew, we have the Dawsons coming!'

'Can't be helped. That fellow Parsons evidently cannot dot his i's or cross his t's without me.'

Why didn't Matthew sack him then, get himself an agent he could depend on, Mary Anne thought rebelliously. If there was one thing she dreaded more than another it was having to entertain Matthew's fellow ironmasters and other business colleagues on her own. That Henry Dawson could hardly be bothered to speak to her and he took very little trouble to hide it. He was a boor of a man who had worked his way up out of the gutter and had been too busy making money to learn the ways of civilised society. Mary Anne sighed. Not much different from Matthew, really, she reflected.

Matthew looked up as his stepson, Robert, came into the breakfast room closely followed by Maisie, his stepdaughter. Oh, Mary Anne had her uses, he thought, not least the fact that she had brought with her the controlling interests in Richards rolling mills from her first husband and mines on a very productive section of the Durham coalfield from her father. A pity then that she was so plain. He looked at her now, her face transformed by the smile with which she greeted her children. Her eyes glowed, there was even a little pink colour in her pale cheeks.

'Good morning, Maisie, morning Robert,' she said, her voice soft with love.

'Morning Mother, morning, Father,' said nine year old Robert. Maisie stood with her head hanging, her fine hair dressed in a thin mousey plait, the same colour as her mother's. Matthew felt the usual twinge of irritation. The child was either stupid or timid as a mouse before him. What did she think he was going to do to her?

'Where is Miss Morton?' he asked gruffly and Maisie stepped back. 'Shouldn't you be at your lessons by now?'

Maisie stepped back as though she thought he was going to hit her, he thought and his annoyance grew. Robert, however, looked him in the eye.

'She'll be down directly, Father,' he said. What he didn't say was that Maisie had wet the bed again and Miss Morton was changing the sheets herself instead of the laundry maid who was under orders to report such a happening to him. Matthew had decided that at five it was well past the time Maisie should have got over such a dirty habit.

'Come and kiss your mother, darlings,' said Mary Anne and the two children went to her. Matthew got to his feet and put his post into his attache case.

'Right, I'm away,' he said, before Mary Anne could suggest the children kiss him too. It always made him feel so awkward when they did. In any case he had told Lawson to have the Bentley waiting outside at nine o'clock and it was that time now.

It was one o'clock before the cream-coloured Bentley entered Bishop Auckland.

'Stop at the Queen's Head, Lawson,' said Matthew and the car purred to a halt obediently. Lawson got out and opened the back door for Matthew. 'I'll be half an hour, that's all,' said Matthew and disappeared into the hotel. Eddie Lawson watched him go and then went across the market place to get himself a pie and a half-pint of ale. It would likely be late before he got home for his tea. They had stopped off at the ironworks before setting off for West Durham and no doubt the gaffer wanted to visit his mines before he saw the mines agent. He liked to go poking around all his works unannounced, no doubt thought it kept the managers on their toes as well as the men. Woe betide anyone he caught slacking.

At least the strike was over, had been for a month. But by hell, he wouldn't like to be in the position of any of the pitmen this Christmas of 1926. There would be some pretty poor Christmas dinners. And some of the poor sods hadn't been taken back on at all, the owners were in a position to pick and choose.

Noah walked in the back door as Kitty was trying to boil the kettle on a fire made up of twigs from the elderberry bush in the garden and a copy of *The Worker's Chronicle*. It had been issued by Newcastle Trades Council for Action, way back at the beginning of the strike. He was just in time to see the headline, 'A FIGHTING LEAD TO THE WORKERS!' curl up and brown.

'What the hell do you think you're doing?' he shouted at her and shoved her out of the way. But he was too late to retrieve the paper. Growling with anger he turned to her and raised his hand.

'I wanted to keep them copies!' he shouted.

'Aye, go on, hit me,' Kitty shouted back at him as she squared up to the six foot of him and his powerful miner's shoulders. But instead of hitting her, Noah lowered his hand and sank into the wooden rocker by the fire. He felt for the half a fag he'd dumped earlier in the day and put behind his ear for safe keeping.

Kitty was nonplussed. She watched as he looked at the cigarette end before putting it back behind his ear. By, she thought, her anger changing to compassion in a second, he hasn't got any fags left. He must be saving that for the night. If she had three ha'pence she would have given him it to go and get a packet of five Woodbines at Meggie's shop in the wooden hut on the end of the rows. But she hadn't even a penny for the gas meter. Tonight they would sit in the dark with no fire or they could go to bed early.

Noah looked up as Katie came in with a bowl of broth covered by a plate in her basket. She gazed back at him apprehensively. This was the second day in a row she had had to go to the soup kitchen and she expected her grandfather to explode with rage. Her heart beat unevenly.

Noah did get to his feet. 'Put that slop down, lass and howay along o' me,' he said. 'I'll get something to burn on the flaming fire.' He grinned suddenly at what he had said.

'Flaming fire! That's one thing it's not! Not in this house, any road. But it will be, you wait and see. Whoever heard of a pitman without a bit of coal for his fire?'

'I don't know what the heck you're on about,' said Kitty.

'Sit yoursel' down and have a bite to eat, you daft ha'porth.'

'Nay man, me an' Katie will have it when we come back in,' Noah stated. 'Howay, Katie.'

'But where are we going, Grandda?'

'You'll see.'

Noah picked up a potato sack Kitty had begged from the greengrocer at the store; one she intended to wash and use as a backing for a proddy mat to go in front of the fire for the new year. (You always had a new mat for New Year.)

'Hey give that back!'

Noah shook his head impatiently. 'Don't bloody go on, lass,' he said. 'You'll get it back.'

He went to the door and Katie followed obediently.

'I expect you're not picked bits off the slag heaps,' Kitty shouted after him. 'You know they'll set the polis on you and then where will we be? Mebbe's better off without you, I reckon.'

Noah didn't answer, just set off down the yard and along the back alley, Katie having to give a little trot now and then to keep up.

They passed the pit yard and the towering slag heaps and Noah turned his head to look at the straggle of safety men coming through the gates, helmets pushed to the back of their heads showing a white line, stark against their coal-blackened faces. 'What cheor, Noah,' one of the deputies muttered and Noah nodded. 'I been meaning to see you, I could let you have a bucket or two of coal next week if you like. You know what it's like, the whole pit not working, everyone wants some.'

'Aye, I know, Tommy,' said Noah. 'Don't bother theesel' about us though. We can manage.'

Katie looked at him in protest. How could he say that? They hadn't a knob of coal in the coal house! But then, though it was usual for those in work to help out those not, a few safety men keeping the pit ticking over until better times and so getting their allowance could help out the hundreds out of a job, but not all of them.

'I appreciate the offer, lad,' her grandfather went on.

'Thanks.'

'Look lad,' said Tommy urgently. 'Just don't try picking off the slag heap. The gaffer's getting red hot against it an' he'll 'ave you for sure. You won't get taken on again any road.' He eyed the sack rolled up under Noah's arm.

'No no, I'll not,' Noah assured him and Tommy shrugged.

The safety men turned down towards the rows and Noah and Katie walked on through the colliery village and on through the older houses of Winton village. They were in open country now and rising slightly but soon Noah stopped and plucked a few handfuls of grass from near the hedge, grass which had not yet been frosted off. He climbed a stile into a field and set off down a footpath. Beneath them the ground was hard and the grass by the side of the path sparse and faded. There were pit ponies gathered under an oak tree further down, nosing about, looking for the odd blade. Though there was some hay spread about for them they loved the grass. It was something they didn't get much chance of underground.

They were the ponies from Winton Colliery, brought up until such time as the colliery should start working again. They whinnied and moved back out of range, wary that the day had come and their freedom would be gone.

All except for one, a sturdy grey of about ten hands, a Shetland pony. He stood about six feet away from Noah and nickered softly.

'Howay, lad, come away Peter,' Noah said quietly and held out a handful of green grass. Katie watched, fascinated as the pony's ears pricked and he moved forward to take her grandfather's offering. He stood champing at the grass, allowing Noah to fondle his ears, rub his neck.

'You're a good lad, Peter,' Noah whispered in his ear and the pony nuzzled at his pocket where, down the pit, Noah had always had a few sugar lumps. For this was Noah's pony, a good marra working with him in the pit. But there was no sugar lumps in the pocket now just as there had been none in Noah's breakfast tea that morning.

After a few minutes, Noah set off again down the field, making towards Eden Hope Colliery that had started up again after the strike and was working normally now. It was quite a long walk and the going was rough. The fields gave way to an ancient wagon way, still with bits of iron jutting out of the ground where they had held the tracks. Beyond there were slag heaps just as old, grey bits of slag showing through half-dead weeds and odd blades of grass. In summer time, only a few years ago, Katie and her friends had played along here, pretending the heaps were a moonscape, waging mock battles with kids from Eden Hope.

Katie sighed. She was older now, soon she would be earning her own living. In any case, children were chased away from the heaps since some of the boys had fallen through the crust just where a fire was raging beneath the surface and feeding on the bits of coal in the heaps. She shuddered, remembering the boys' legs, red-raw and blistered as they ran down the rows screaming for their mammies.

'Howay, Katie, you're all right, the fire's not in this part,' said Noah. 'Just follow me, where I put my feet you put yours if you're scared.'

'I'm not scared. I'm hungry, that's all,' said Katie and hurried to catch up with him. But surely the hardened crust of the heap felt hot through the thin soles of her boots? She was glad when they got to the other side and could slither down into the valley and the banks of a small beck.

'You'll have something when we get back,' her grandfather told her. Instead of turning right to Eden Hope and the pit, he turned left to where another, newer wagon way ran alongside the beck with a footpath beside it. They were going to the old coke works, Katie realised. Abandoned buildings stood at intervals along the line, windows broken and brickwork black with soot. Further along she could see tall chimneys and mineral wagons; small figures scurrying about. The sides of the valley were covered in dead stalks of rosebay willow herb and bracken. There were patches of black oil by the track and a coaly smell tinged with sulphur.

Noah was watchful, keeping his gaze on the figures up ahead except for quick glances up the line behind him. He stopped on the edge of a shallow black-filled hole.

'Pitch,' he said with satisfaction. 'By, I knew there was

a pitch lake around here, I remember it from when I was a lad. Sit down on the edge, lass, you won't stand out so much.' Climbing into the hole he began rapidly rolling balls of the pitch and throwing them to Katie to put in the sack. Fifteen minutes later they were back along by the stream, trying to wash the pitch from their hands and boots.

'Howay, that'll have to do,' said Noah, getting to his feet. He slung the sack of pitch balls over his shoulder and set off at a trot for the stile leading to the fields and home with Katie struggling to keep up. They were almost at the bend in the track with the turnoff just around it when Noah, bent over with the load on his back, almost bumped into someone coming the other way.

'Mind where you're going! Anyway, what are you doing here? Up to no good I'll be bound.'

Matthew Hamilton was making his way along the wagon way which led from Eden Hope Colliery through the derelict land of the old coke works to where the more modern works was coming back into production after the long strike and lockout. He wasn't in too good a mood either as he noted things that should be done to modernise the colliery, uses that could be made of this land. Now he looked at Noah suspiciously.

'What have you got there? Where have you been?'

Noah drew himself up. 'It's none of your business. This is a public pathway, it's always been a public pathway. We 'ave as much right as you 'ave.'

For the first time Matthew noticed the girl behind Noah as she stepped out to stand beside him. Wavy fair hair hung down her back and large, deep blue eyes stared at him, eyes only a little darker than the old man's beside her. Was it her grandfather maybe? A striking-looking pair, though he was dressed as though he was ready for entering the pit and she in a cotton dress and threadbare brown coat that could possibly belong to her grandmother. Her hands were stained black and there was a black smudge across her cheek. Seeing him looking at them she put her hands behind her back.

Pitch, that was what was in the sack and also liberally smeared over the pair before him. He stared at them, frowning, and two pairs of dark blue eyes stared back at him defiantly.

'Any road,' said Noah, breaking the small silence, 'you may be a gaffer but you're not the gaffer 'ere, are you? I know who the manager is and I know the agent an' all. Gan on and mind your own business, like I said. I know the gaffer 'ere, like I said.'

Matthew opened his mouth to contradict him but changed his mind as he saw the girl's expression become anxious. He'd always prided himself on being hard as nails but there was something about her that made him want to reassure her, tell her it was all right. He stood aside.

'Oh, go on,' he said. Noah and Katie were not to tell twice. Noah hitched the sack higher on his shoulder and they climbed the stile and set off rapidly up the field. They didn't stop until they had put a covering hedge between them and the wagon way.

'Who was that, Grandda?' asked Katie when she could catch her breath.

'Some bloody interfering toff,' Noah replied. 'Always wanting to rub your nose in it they are.' They set off up the field into the one where the ponies were now huddled around a gate. They were waiting to go into their warm stable, Katie thought, waiting for their feed of oats.

'They always know the time, them galloways,' Noah observed 'Won't work a minute after the shift ends. Aye but they're not used to being out in these winter nights.'

'They've been fed carrots,' said Katie. 'Carrots and turnips.' There were bits of carrots about where the ponies had been munching on them, the odd broken bit of turnip. Noah stooped and picked up a couple of whole carrots they had missed. 'Might as well 'ave these, I'm fair clemming,' he said. 'Bloody hell, what's the world coming to when we take the leavings from the ponies?'

Katie didn't care, she took her carrot and rubbed it on her dress before biting into it. Her stomach felt so empty the sides must be sticking together. An icy wind had sprung up and was stinging her legs through the thin cotton of her dress whenever her coat blew open at the front. She. chewed on the carrot and bent her head to the wind, striding out without thinking of anything but the need to get home. By the time they were walking down the rows it was dark, only a faint glimmer from the gas streetlamps lit the street and a rain mixed with sleet had begun to slant against them.

'There, now, Kitty,' said Noah. 'Didn't I say I'd get something better for the fire?'

Katie lifted her nose from the bowl of soup and

grinned. The kitchen was warm, as warm if not warmer than when the coal house was full of coal. She was in her nightie covered by an old cardigan and she had a pair of Noah's old socks on her feet in lieu of slippers.

In the grate a pitch ball flared and shifted and Noah added another to the flames. He sat in his rocker by the fire and stretched out his legs before taking the fag end from behind his ear where it had stayed since morning. Leaning forward he lit it from the fire with a scrap of paper and inhaled deeply. The heat from the fire made him remove his feet from the steel fender but he didn't care.

'Aye,' said Kitty. 'But I don't know where the heck I'm going to get a bit of good sacking for a new mat before Christmas now. You've ruined that tatie sack, it was nice and close-woven an' all.'

'By heck, woman, you'd find summat to grumble about in heaven!' Noah growled, but mildly. It was dole day the day after tomorrow, he'd have a few pence for himself, buy a decent pack of Woodbines. Twenty, even. It was cheaper to buy in bulk.

At least he got a bit of dole now. During the strike able-bodied men got nowt, only a bit of out relief for the wife and bairns. It was the single men who did the worst though. As long as they were able-bodied they got nowt at all. So it worked out that a man would get food for one day and not the next. A man was considered able-bodied if he'd had something to eat in the last twenty-four hours. Aye, but things would get better. They had to, they couldn't get much worse.

The oven shelf was hot, courtesy of the pitch balls and Katie lay in bed with her feet on the shelf wrapped in an old towel and it was lovely. She huddled under the blanket with her coat on top and the bedroom mat on top of that. Outside the wind howled and the rain pattered on the window. Sleepily she thought of the toff they had met on the wagon way down by the old coke ovens. She had been frightened he would turn her grandda over to the polis, he looked so cold and angry. She dropped asleep wondering why he had not.

Chapter Three

'Why man, I'm a hewer not a safety man,' said Noah. He stood in the manager's office where he had been summonded that morning by Billy Wright knocking at his back door.

'Me da says the gaffer wants to see you, Mr Benfield,' Billy had said.

'Me? Are you sure he wants to see me?' Noah was filled with foreboding. Had someone seen him take the pitch yesterday? But it wasn't stealing, not really, the pitch was no good for anything except burning, it had been left to the elements too long.

'That's what he said,' said Billy. 'As soon as you can get there.'

As Noah washed and shaved he went through what it could mean. Were they going to be put out of the house? Was he going to be told he'd never get a job in any of the company's pits again so he might as well emigrate? Leave his beloved Durham for one of those new-fangled car factories in the south?

'What's the matter, Noah? Why does he want to see you?' asked Kitty.

'Nay lass, I don't know, I haven't a crystal ball.'

Noah was in a right state inside when he finally stood before the manager's desk so that he never even saw the owner's agent (Parsons was he called?) sitting in the corner.

Mr Thompson gazed at the man in front of him. In fact he was as mystified as Noah. The man must be in his late fifties and past the time when he should be hewing which was a young man's job. Yet his back was ramrod straight and his shoulders powerful despite the low seams of the coalfield.

In the corner, Parsons uncrossed his legs and reached in his pocket for a cigar. Noah glanced across at him. Oh aye, he'd seen him before. The boss's lackey, wasn't he? Aping the boss's ways no doubt an' all. Not that he'd ever seen the boss or knew anything about him really. Except that he was an ironmaster from Cleveland, one who had supported the other owners in their demands for longer hours and less pay for the miners. Demands which led to the strike. Noah turned his attention back to the gaffer, dismissing bitter thoughts.

'Well, do you want the job or not?' Mr Thompson asked him.

'Why aye, I do, gaffer,' said Noah. After all, his pride in still being a hewer at his age didn't put meat on the table, not when there was no hewing to be done.

'That's it then, Monday morning, back shift.'

'What'll I be doing exactly, like?'

Mr Thompson sighed. 'Just generally helping the deputies, watching out for anything, you know, you've been down the pit long enough. You know what the dangers are in this coalfield.'

'Oh aye, I do that,' said Noah. He cleared his throat and forced himself to look humble. 'Is there any chance of a sub, like? I am a bit short an' I'll get nowt off the dole the morrow, not now I'm taken on again.'

'You're a cheeky bugger, Benfield,' said Mr Thompson. 'All right, see the wages man, he hasn't much else to do at the minute.' Noah grinned, his eyes crinkling in his ruddy face.

As Noah went out he started whistling, the sound surprisingly sweet and clear. 'Who were you with last night—'

'Are you sure you've got the right man?' Mr Parsons asked. "There'll be hell to pay if you haven't.'

'Oh yes, that's the right man,' said Mr Thompson. 'He's the only one I know to fit the description Mr Hamilton gave you. I hope the boss doesn't regret it. Noah wasn't one of the ringleaders in the strike but I'm sure he was right behind the ones that were.'

'I hope he learned his lesson.' Mr Parsons got to his feet and started for the door. 'I'll see you next week, Thompson. I expect you'll have someone keep an eye on Benfield. Let me know how he shapes up.'

'Oh, he'll shape up all right. He always was a good worker.'

'Well, I've still a lot to do. Good day to you Thompson.' Mr Parsons went out to the pit yard and got into the driving seat of his Austin saloon. He pressed the self-starter and drove in a circle round the empty yard before heading out of the gate. Hamilton coming had taken him by surprise today, usually he had advance warning of the owner's visits. The boss had been on his high horse too, criticising the way he had let some of the places on bank at the non-working mines get a bit run down. As if it was his fault, such things were up to the managers. But he'd sharpen them up anyway. They had very little else to do. Though after all, they were keeping things going underground right, weren't they? That was the most important thing.

Parsons' thoughts returned to his interview with Mr Hamilton that morning. A queer carry-on about the man Benfield, wasn't it?

'Do you know a man, in his fifties, worked at Winton, Parsons? A big man, red-faced, dark blue eyes? Not afraid to speak his mind?' Mr Hamilton had asked.

'Well, Mr Hamilton, there were nigh on 800 men worked at Winton,' the agent replied.

'Yes of course. This man has a granddaughter, same eyes as himself, blonde hair.'

'I can't say I do, Mr Hamilton.' Was the man going off his head? How was he supposed to know all the men that worked at Winton?

'No, but you can ask Thompson, can't you?' The boss sounded testy. What had the fellow done?

'I will, of course,' Parsons said hastily. 'Do you want Thompson to black-list him? Has he been impertinent?' (How the heck did you meet him? was what Parsons wanted to ask.)

'No, no, nothing like that. But if Thompson knows who it is I mean, I want him to give him a job.'

'A job? Do you mean at Eden Hope or are you intending to open Winton again? I don't mean to question your judgement but—'

'I'm sure you don't,' said Matthew with a hard stare. 'No, Thompson can put him on doing something till the pit opens again, can't he?'

'Yes, yes he can. Of course he can.'

'Right then, see to it.'

Matthew went out to his car and climbed in, sitting back with a sigh, content with his day. Though to be honest he didn't know why he had given that last order to Parsons. But somehow he couldn't get the picture out of his mind, he had kept thinking about it all day. The picture of the young girl coming round from behind her grandfather and standing shoulder to shoulder with him. The way she had gazed at him so directly with the old man's eyes, the uplifted chin and the smear of pitch across her cheek. Of course the sack was full of pitch, he had known it by the smell even before he had come across the pool of old pitch further along the wagon way. There was obvious marks on the surface where the man had been taking lumps out.

He'd never given much thought before as to how the miners got their heat when their concessionary coal was stopped. He looked at the window where sleet was pattering against the glass. It was snug in the car, thank God. Well, the old chap was showing some initiative going all that way for pitch balls.

The girl too, helping him.

'For goodness sake,' Matthew said, half-aloud. 'I'm going soft in the head in my old age.'

Lawson looked through the rear-view mirror at him, startled. 'Pardon, sir?' he asked.

'Take it careful, Lawson,' said Matthew. 'There's no rush.' He didn't want to get home before his dinner guests went home. One of the reasons he had come out today was to make the fellow unsure of himself. Dawson was in deep water and there may yet be the chance of picking up his works for a song. Matthew forgot about the old man and the girl as he turned his keen mind to the problems of working iron.

'What's that?'

Kitty stared as Noah strode into the kitchen and threw a ten-shilling note down on the table. He was grinning from ear to ear.

'What does it look like, lass?' he asked. 'I've been taken on at the pit. That's a sub the gaffer let us 'ave.'

Kitty slumped down on to Noah's chair. Suddenly her shoulders heaved and tears ran down her face unchecked, she who had never cried all during the ten-month strike and afterwards, when the miners had had to cave in and go back to work and the shock of finding that Winton wasn't going to open any road and they faced another long wait.

'Aw, howay, lass, I thought you'd be pleased,' said Noah. Awkwardly he put an arm around her shoulders.

'Eeh, I am, I am really. I thought the day would never come, I did. The pit's starting up then?'

'Nay lass, it isn't. I'll be working with the safety men. Until it does open, that is.'

Kitty looked up at him through swimming eyes. She opened her mouth to question it but closed it: again. It was enough that there was a wage coming in for the first time in so many long months. Katie came in the door and her mouth dropped open as her gaze was drawn to the note still lying on the table. She put the heavy bag of jam jars she had been collecting on the flagged floor.

'Katie! Katie! Hadaway down the store and buy half a pound of brawn and a couple of pig's trotters, pet. Oh, an' half a stone of taties an' a turnip. And a—'

'Kitty, Kitty man, what do you think the lass is a pit pony? She cannot carry so much, can she?'

Kitty nodded. 'No I wasn't thinking, was I. Just a quarter of taties then, Katie.'

'But what, what's happened?' Katie asked. She had been out for three hours collecting jam jars from all over Winton and beyond because the store gave a ha'penny each for them if they were washed and clean. She reckoned she had enough to buy a quarter of brawn and five Woodbines for her grandda. And here on the table was a whole ten-shilling note!

'Your grandda's been taken on, Katie! He's been taken on!' Once again Kitty Benfield dissolved into tears.

'Here at Winton? Do you mean here?' As her grandfather nodded, Katie was lit up with such an intense joy she felt she must be glowing like a gas mantle. 'Does it mean I can have—' Katie stopped abruptly as she realised she had been going to ask for new shoes already. By, her

34

granma would think she was so selfish, thinking only of herself.

But Kitty wasn't even listening, she was building the fire up with pitch balls so as to have a good blaze to cook the taties and turnip and heat the oven for the pig's trotters when she got them. She was bustling about in the old way, the way Katie vaguely remembered her doing so long ago.

Later, as her grandmother belched softly as she sat dozing in the heat from the fire, and her grandfather sat smoking a whole Woodbine, his legs stretched out on the fender as he inhaled deeply, Katie brought in the tin bath and filled it with water from the boiler at the side of the range and began to wash the jamjars. Maybe she could take two of them and go to the pictures on Friday night. The manager let them sit in the front four rows for a penny or two jam jars and Charlie Chaplin was on.

'We 'ave to pay the Guardians back for the out relief money we've 'ad,' Noah remarked suddenly. 'We're not going to be rich you know.'

'How much?' asked Kitty, waking up at the mention of money.

'A shilling a week, I've heard.'

'Flaming heck,' said Kitty. 'We'll be paying till Judgement Day.' But she wasn't going to let the thought of anyone or anything spoil the evening. After all, she wasn't going to have to sell the sofa now, that was worth a fair bit. More than 2/6 any road.

'Go and get yourself a pint, Noah,' she said and his eyes widened in shock. He jumped up with alacrity.

'Aye I think I will, Kitty,' he said. 'I was just thinking, a pint would go down nicely, like.'

'Aye, I bet you were,' Kitty said drily. 'Only the one mind.'

Katie reached for the tea-towel hanging on the brass rail above the range and began drying the jam jars. She couldn't stop herself from smiling as she caught her grandmother's eye.

'By,' Kitty said, shaking her head, 'when things are going all right there's not a nicer man than my Noah.'

Katie stopped smiling, remembering the times when he was not nice, how he could be harsh and even violent sometimes. Kitty seemed to read her thoughts.

'It's the drink changes him, Katie,' she said. 'He gets a black devil on his shoulder. An' then, it's not surprising he's had such bad moods this rotten year, is it? By, I'll be glad when it's a new year. But there's many a worse man than my Noah, believe me.'

'Then why tell him to go for a pint?' Katie couldn't resist asking.

'It's not for you to question your elders, cheeky monkey,' said Kitty, her tone changing. 'A man has a right to a pint, especially when he's working.'

He hasn't been working yet, thought Katie, but she didn't say it. It would be all right, she knew it. Any road, he'd only taken sixpence. He was starting back shift on Monday.

Down at the Working Men's Club and Institute, Noah walked in with his head up and rapped his knuckles on the counter, what was known locally as a ready money knock.

'I'll have a pint of the best, Les,' he called to the steward who was sitting at the other end of the bar, reading the Auckland Chronicle. There were two or three men in the bar, no more and they were sitting playing dominoes at a table by the door.

'Not till you pay your slate, you won't,' said Les, not even looking up. 'Not unless you have the tuppence ha'penny. To pay for it.'

Noah loosened the white scarf around his neck and pushed his cap to the back of his head. Then he felt in the top pocket of his waistcoat and pulled out a sixpence. 'There you are then, Les,' he said. 'There a tanner. Mind I want thrupence ha'penny change an' all.' He looked round at the domino players and grinned broadly.

'What's happened Noah, you come into a fortune?' asked one, then hopefully, 'You going to buy us all a pint then?'

'Nay I'm not, I cannot,' Noah admitted. He picked up the foaming glass which Les had put before him and took a deep, deep swallow. 'By, but it's bloody nectar, it is,' he said reverently. He put down the glass and picked up his change, putting it carefully back into his waistcoat pocket before he turned back to the men sitting at the table.

'Nay, lads,' he said, 'I've not come into a fortune but it's nearly as good. I've been taken on at the pit. I join the safety men on Monday's back shift.'

'Yer what? You never!'

'Aye, I have and I do,' said Noah earnestly,

remembering his own incredulity as he stood in the mine office earlier.

He could picture the scene perfectly, he knew he always would. 'Hamilton's lackey, you know, the boss's agent, he asked for me special like. It's because of the experience and knowledge I 'ave of Winton Colliery.' He turned back to the bar and took another swig from his glass of beer. At that moment he was as happy as anyone in the land.

Chapter Four

'By heck, Katie,' said Billy Wright, 'you shouldn't be doing that. It's too hard for a lass.'

Katie stopped shovelling coal through the coal hole to the coal house and leaned on her shovel, glad of a breather. She rubbed the back of her hand across her forehead, leaving a coaly smudge.

'I can manage,' she said. 'I didn't want to leave it for Grandda when he come in from work, it will be dark.'

'I'll do it for you,' said Billy, 'here, give us hold of the shovel.'

Katie hesitated. She was on her dinner hour from school and there wasn't much of it left. 'We cannot pay you,' she said.

'Did I ask you to? Howay, man!'

Billy took the shovel from her and began throwing in the coal, lifting a shovelful with an easy swing and making the coal piled on the pavement disappear rapidly.

Katie watched for a minute before saying something about getting washed ready for school and going inside.

'Who's that, then?' Her grandmother looked up from the pot pie she was preparing for when Noah got in from the back shift.

'Billy Wright.'

'Aye, he's a good lad,' Kitty observed. She spooned meat into the basin lined with suet pastry and covered it with a pastry lid. Deftly she tied the whole in a pudding cloth and lowered it into the pan of water already boiling on the fire. Sighing with satisfaction she stood back and watched it before drawing it slightly away from the heat on to the bar. By, it was lovely being able to cook proper meals again, she thought, it had been such a long time since she had had the chance.

'Tell Billy to fill a couple of buckets for old Mrs Scott,' she said as Katie came out of the pantry where the only tap in the house was. 'And tell our Betty to get Willie to come and get a couple of buckets the night.' Betty was one of Katie's younger sisters who lived with her own parents. The way they were giving away their concessionary coal would leave them short before the next load was due, thought Katie but she nodded. It was the way of the rows.

'Righto.'

Katie ran off down the row to the school. Only a year and a bit before she could leave school altogether and get a job. She couldn't wait for the day. It was the only way she was going to get on now that there was no chance of getting a secondary education.

Behind her, Billy Wright leaned on the shovel and watched her disappear around the corner. She was a bonny lass, he thought, a real bonny lass. If she was a bit older; if they were both a bit older and he had a job he might ask her to go out with him. Aye well, time would remedy that, wouldn't it? He walked up the alley carrying the two buckets of coal for Mrs Scott before taking Kitty's yard broom and sweeping up the dust left on the pavement.

He was due at the Technical Institute in an hour for his class in mining surveying. He intended to be ready when the pits went back to work. He wasn't going to work filling coal for long though. Nor even as a hewer on the coal face. No, he was going to be a surveyor and then maybe even go into management.

He climbed on to the bus for Bishop Auckland an hour later, washed and spruced up but with his dark hair uncovered for he had decided not to wear his cap. A cap was the mark of a miner or another lowly occupation and he meant to start as he intended to go on. And in good time he would marry Katie Benfield, he promised himself. After all, there was no hurry, they had all the time in the world.

'Gran says for you to tell our Willie to come round for a couple of buckets of coal tonight,' Katie said to her sister when she found her in the schoolyard during the break. Betty looked at her as she would at a stranger or at least someone she didn't know very well. She always did, all Katie's sisters did and it made her feel uncomfortable.

'We heard Grandda had got taken on with the safety

men,' said Betty. 'Me mam says he's got hair on his toenails, he's that lucky.'

For a brief moment Katie pictured Noah's toenails with hair sprouting from them and her lips twitched. She looked at her sister, noting her limp, straight hair, how thin and pale she was. She didn't look like a Benfield, she took after Mam's family. And they were mostly sickly.

Betty sniffed. 'We don't want any favours, like,' she said. 'That's what me mam says.'

'What do you mean, no favours? We're the same family, aren't we?'

Betty stared at her and sniffed once again. 'Oh aye, I suppose so,' she said as the bell rang. She went off, calling to a friend to wait for her, not even saying goodbye to Katie who was left feeling sad.

As she sat through the afternoon of needlework class at which she was hopelessly inept, followed by history, which she liked well enough, the thought kept coming back to her. Why did her sisters not count her as real family? That was what she wanted really, to be counted as one of them.

She had asked her grandma once why things were like they were but the old woman had only shaken her head. The truth was Kitty didn't get on too well with her daughter-in-law and when she had taken Katie, Hannah gave every appearance of having put out of her mind the fact that Katie was really her child. Hannah wasn't really fit to be a miner's wife, that was the truth of it. Kitty had remarked on it to Noah more than once.

'Why man, leave her alone, Kitty,' he usually said.

'She's our Tom's choice an' that's all about it.'

Katie would hear him and wonder. Why hadn't she been her da's choice, she wondered. She asked her gran once but Kitty had simply said she was *her* choice and that was all that mattered. And Katie did admit she would rather live with her gran than in the untidy, higgledy-piggledy house her mother kept.

Katie left school on her fourteenth birthday and went to work in the Meadow Dairy, a grocer's shop in Newgate Street in Auckland. But as she counted out eggs, sliced bacon and weighed out pats of butter, she dreamed of better things. One day, one day, she told herself, she would become a nurse. A proper nurse, trained, and for that she had to have a better education. So her evenings were taken up in studying and in attending classes in adult education. She hadn't time to go around with the other girls in the rows, she was determined to make something of her life. And that meant she had no friends. At least not friends she could call close.

'We will re-open the mines which are idle next week,' said Matthew.

'Will you, dear? That's nice,' Mary Anne replied.

Once again they were sitting over the breakfast table but now they were living at what had been Dawson Hall and which Matthew had re-named Hamilton Hall. For not only had the Dawson Ironworks been swallowed up by the Hamilton works, but Dawson's private property had been mortgaged to Matthew. Dawson had died the year before and Matthew had done what he considered to be the decent thing. He had provided his widow with a decent little house in Ormsby and moved himself and his family into the Hall. It was far away from the smells and dirt of the ironmasters' district of Middlesbrough on the North York moors.

He glanced irritably at his wife now. He was sure she hadn't heard a single word he had said. And if she had she hadn't understood, she was as dim as a Toc H lamp in his opinion.

'I said we were going to open up the pits, Mary Anne. Don't you know what that means? The business is picking up at last.'

Mary Anne glanced quickly up at him then returned her gaze to her plate. All he thought of was money, she told herself. That and begetting an heir. He wouldn't come to her bed but for that. Oh, God, how she hated it when he did. She lay there night after night, trembling with terror, going through the awful experience over and over in her mind until she heard him come upstairs and go into his dressing room. She would strain to hear the creak of his bedsprings as he climbed into bed and only then would she shudder and sigh and settle herself for sleep. It hadn't been like that with her first husband, dear Robert.

She had not been prepared for the rough way Matthew would take her with no preamble, thrust into her rigid body so that she had to bite her tongue to stop herself screaming out loud with pain.

She moved on her chair now, trying to ease the soreness in her vagina, the aching in her thighs.

'The miners will be glad, dear,' she said. Matthew snorted in disgust and got to his feet.

'Well, I'm going over there, I can't say when I'll be back,' he said. He went out into the hall and took his overcoat from John, his newly acquired manservant. Then picking up his hat and gloves before John could do it for him he strode out to the waiting car. A purposeful figure, Mary Anne thought as she watched through the dining-room window.

'Mama! Mama!'

Mary Anne turned, her whole demeanour transformed now that her husband had left the house. She opened her arms and Robert and Maisie ran to her; something they would certainly not have done if their stepfather had still been in the house.

'What shall we do today, darlings?' she asked, one arm round Robert as she kissed the top of Maisie's head.

'We have lessons first,' said Miss Morton. She was standing quietly by the door, watching the children with their mother. 'Well, until eleven o'clock at least,' she added as all three turned reproachful faces to her.

'I thought we could go into Whitby,' said Mary Anne. 'We could look at the shops and decide what Father Christmas should bring for Christmas. We can have tea there too, crumpets and butter and fairy cakes. Would you like that?'

No one was going to deny that they did indeed like the idea and well before lunch they were driving across the moors in the four-seater Austin that Matthew had bought for Mary Anne's use when they moved to the Hall.

Everyone in the house had been sceptical about it but Mary Anne had surprised them all by mastering the car within a week by driving round the estate during every hour of daylight she could.

They took a picnic basket and ate on the cliff above Runs wick Bay. Mary Anne wanted to make the day as memorable as she possibly could, for after Christmas, Robert was to go to a crammer in Barnard Castle before taking the Common Entrance. After that, well, his father had put his name down for Durham School.

As he usually did when in the town, Matthew lunched at the Queen's Head in Bishop Auckland. Afterwards he strolled through the market place towards the entrance to the bishop's palace. The gates to the park were open and he walked through, taking his time for he had a couple of hours to spare before his appointment with Parsons.

Today he felt a little less energetic than usual, not at all inclined to inspect his properties before the meeting; something he would normally have done.

A watery December sun shone on the trees sloping away from the path to his left. It lit up the few bronzed leaves still clinging to the branches. Below them he could see the occasional glint of the rain-swollen Gaunless on its way to meet the Wear. To his right he could see through the gates in the massive wall to the castle, old and solid, the mullioned windows glinting palely in the sun. He walked on to where the cow-catcher gate opened out the ride to the greater park behind it; the stretches of grassland and the old oaks from which the town got its name. It was very tranquil and beautiful, a world away from the smoking chimneys, whirring wheels and slag heaps of the mines. Yet he knew there were pit yards within easy walking distance. He stood leaning on the fence by the gate and smoked his cigar. Then he turned to make his way back to the town to where Lawson was waiting to take him to meet his agent. It was as he went out through the ancient arch which led into the market place that he felt someone was watching him. He looked up keenly. It was a girl, a book on her lap, an open packet of sandwiches on the bench beside her. A shop girl eating her dinner, he thought, taking the chance to get a little fresh air.

She did not drop her eyes as he caught them but returned his gaze steadily. He had seen her before somewhere he thought, puzzled. He walked closer.

'Do I know you?' he asked and immediately felt a fool. How could he possibly know a girl like her?

Katie reddened slightly, not knowing what to say. She remembered him and the occasion on which she had seen him and it was the memory of what a sight she must have looked with pitch on her face and her hands black with it that made her blush.

Now he had a close-up view of her unusual dark blue eyes, he remembered her too. 'You're the girl I met on the wagon way down by Eden Hope aren't you? You were with your grandfather. I'm right, aren't I?'

Katie hastily wrapped up the remainder of her sandwiches and got to her feet. 'I have to go,' she said and started to walk along by the market place to the entrance to Newgate Street. But Matthew was not so easily put off though for the life of him he didn't know why he was so interested in her.

'How is your grandfather?' he called after her and she stopped.

Turning to face him she said, 'It was you, wasn't it? You who got him taken back on at the pit? Thank you.'

'I don't know what you mean, young lady,' said Matthew.

She smiled and went off down the street to the Meadow Dairy. He watched her go in then turned and walked briskly to where Lawson was busily rubbing away a splash of mud from the bonnet of the car.

A nice-looking girl, that, Matthew thought and a picture of Mary Anne came into his mind unbidden. The contrast was stark. He wondered for a second what the girl would be like in bed. There was a spark of fire there, he could see it smouldering in her eyes. Not at all like Mary Anne nor that pale copy of her mother, Maisie. Good God, what was he thinking of, making such comparisons? The girl was just a kid, he told himself and climbed in the door held open by Lawson. But he didn't stop thinking of the girl. As he gazed out of the window he didn't see the lowering sky but her dark blue eyes as they looked steadily at him.

Chapter Five

Noah took a deep breath of the fresh, cold air as he came out of the cage with the rest of the safety men on his shift. It brought on a deep, rumbling cough and he stopped for a minute to clear his air passages. So he was a little behind the rest of the men as they crossed the pit yard to the gate. In spite of the cough, which was becoming a regular and persistent irritation to him, he was still an upright figure, striding out with a young man's gait. He glanced at the fancy car standing in the yard with a chauffeur in a peaked cap sitting at the wheel. (No sort of job for a real man, he thought fleetingly.)

'Wot cheor,' he said to the man as he caught his eye.

'Now then,' the man replied.

Briefly Noah wondered what sort of high-up boss was in the office of an idle pit but his curiosity was only slight, he was more interested in what Kitty had ready for his dinner.

Matthew, looking out of the window of the manager's office, watched Noah as he made his way down the yard.

'What's that man's name again?' he asked.

The manager was sitting at the desk making notes of the conditions under which they would re-engage the men with Parsons overseeing him. There had been no need for Matthew to be there and the fact that he was put both men on edge. They looked up from what they were doing. Thompson got to his feet and went over to the window.

'Benfield, sir,' he said. 'Noah Benfield. He's a hewer but he has been working with the safety men. He knows the layout of the mine like the back of his hand,' he added as though making excuses for having a hewer doing safety work.

The agent was gazing out of the window too by now. 'It's the man you wanted taking on,' he said. 'A couple of years ago.' He hoped to hell it was the right man, he had forgotten all about him until now. He glanced up at Matthew.

'A good man, is he? Satisfactory?'

'Reliable, yes. Never misses a shift,' replied Thompson.

'Won't be picking pitch then,' said Matthew.

The other two looked at each other. 'Pardon, sir?' asked the manager.

'Oh nothing,' said Matthew, 'Well, I'll be off now, good afternoon to you both.'

Both men felt a lightening of spirits as the ironmaster left the office. 'It's good news for the men, anyway,' said Mr Thompson. 'But how long do you think it will last, Mr Parsons?'

'For as long as Hamilton's Ironworks want the coke,

I suppose,' said Parsons. 'But the outlook is more promising than it was, let's just say that.'

Thompson knew he would get no more from the agent. Mr Parsons rarely discussed business with individual mine managers. Still, it was good to be starting up the pit after it had been lying idle for so long. He handed the notice to his clerk to be typed and pasted to the gate. By the following Monday he expected to have taken on all of the men needed for the work. Within a month or so production would be back to normal.

'Drive along the ends of the colliery rows, Lawson,' said Matthew. 'Fairly slowly, I want to see their condition.'

'Yes, sir.' Lawson was startled, the boss had shown no interest whatsoever in his workers' housing before now. He drove along by the rows at ten miles an hour. Matthew was just in time to see Noah Benfield disappear into a house two or three doors down West Row. He didn't even notice the condition of most of the roofs, most of which were awaiting the colliery slater to start repairs.

So that was where the man lived. Did his granddaughter live there too?

'Right, Lawson,' he said, leaning back in his seat. 'Home now if you please.' There was a couple of hours' journey back to the Hall on the North York moors and Matthew settled himself to have a sleep on the way. It had been a full and interesting day and he had to prepare himself for the night with Mary Anne. For he was determined that he would have a son of his own to inherit the empire he was still enlarging at every opportunity.

And opportunities there were, so many of his fellow businessmen, second and third generation ironmasters, had gone soft and slow, he thought. Too near-sighted to realise they were on the slippery slope and when they fell in over their heads unable to get out again. Ready for the picking they were and he was just the man to do it.

Matthew sighed, his thought returning to Mary Anne. Having sex with his wife, for he would hardly call it making love, was the hardest thing he had to do in his life. He couldn't enter her bedroom without a couple of stiff drinks. 'All cats are alike in the dark,' his father had once said to him but it wasn't true, not for him. Even with his eyes closed he couldn't imagine her being anything or anyone other than Mary Anne, his mouse of a wife.

Still, he thought, as they drove through Darlington and out into the blackness beyond on the road to Yarm, she had proved she wasn't barren at any rate. There were Robert and Maisie.

Later, about midnight in fact, when Mary Anne had been in bed for a couple of hours and was beginning to believe he was going to leave her alone that night, he entered his wife's room. She went rigid as she lay in the high bed listening to him taking off his clothes, felt the movement of the bed as he sat down to take off his shoes, heard the thud as they were thrown to the floor. The scent of whisky hung heavily on the air.

The assault, when it came, was swift and brutal with no preliminaries. She ought to have been used to it but still, it was always a shock. Grasping her meagre breast he parted her legs with his knee and thrust into her.

Mercifully it was over in seconds rather than minutes. He flung himself off her and lay on his back, panting. He felt her turn from him to lie with her back to him. She was still stiff and quiet; he could hardly hear her breath. Shame flooded through him, what was he putting this poor woman through?

'I'm sorry, Mary Anne,' he whispered and got out of the bed.

He put out a hand to her then decided against it. She would recover the sooner on her own, he thought. He walked across to the door and went out.

Mary Anne sagged down into the mattress as the door closed behind him. Her eyes stung with unshed tears but she didn't cry. Instead she got out of bed and went to the hand basin, newly installed in her closet. She would not go to the bathroom in case he heard her though she wasn't sure why. Instead she ran water into the basin, stripped off her nightgown and washed herself all over before putting on a clean gown. Then she gazed at herself in the mirror. Was she so repulsive? she wondered. Perhaps she was. Her front teeth were a little too long but they were white and regular. Her skin was white and rather dull, but that was because she hadn't got out in the fresh air as she ought, not these last few weeks. The children had both had measles but they were recovering now. Her hair was thin and refused to curl, she knew that. Even when she wore steel pins all night the curl lasted only for an hour or two in the morning. A Marcel Wave made it frizz, not wave. It was neither one colour nor another, she thought dismally. Wearily she climbed back into bed.

It had been different with Robert. Her lovely man. Robert. Aching, she turned over on to her side. Robert had loved her, really loved her, not what she could bring to the marriage. She had been able to conceive with Robert and she had two beautiful children to show for it. Oh, Robert, why did you have to die? The familiar ache settled on her, in her stomach, in her head. Robert was gone and in his place she had Matthew and Matthew didn't love her. It was her own fault, she could have refused to marry him, she had been a widow for goodness sake. She had wanted a father for her children and her own father had persuaded her that Matthew was just the man. And he had been kind when he courted her. In fact, he was kind to her most of the time. The exceptions were all in bed.

Dear God, she prayed, let there be a child. Then perhaps he would leave her alone. She lay awake for a long time, allowing the thoughts and memories of Robert to fill her mind. They were a comfort to her, she could almost forget the reality of her present life when she did that but sometimes they made her feel disloyal to Matthew. Tonight she didn't care.

Grey light was creeping around the edge of the curtains before Mary Anne finally got to sleep. She could hear movement in the dressing room next door, then water running. Matthew was an early riser. After a while the soft noises stopped; she heard his door close. It was only then that she relaxed sufficiently to drop into sleep and then she dreamed. The old dream, the one she loved. Robert was alive and they were living at Whitworth Hall and the sun was always shining and the children laughing. All four of them would go down on to the beach near Hart and they would search for shells and watch the sea coalers and their donkeys. Little Robert loved to watch the sea coalers.

Maisie was slow to walk and Robert would take her on his shoulders and they would walk along the beach to Crimdon and back to the Hall in time for tea. And then she woke up and the euphoria would fade.

Matthew never had time to spare to take the afternoon off from the business, she thought. And even if he did it wouldn't be the same. Wearily, Mary Anne forced herself out of bed. It was time to start another day.

Chapter Six

'By,' said Kitty as they sat by the sitting-room fire on the afternoon of Christmas Day. 'I reckon everyone in the rows will remember this Christmas all right. You should have seen the queue at the store yesterday morning, Noah. Ready money going over the counter an' all. Some folk could even afford to go into Auckland to buy the bairns a few bits. Radley's bus was nearly full.'

'Will you stop rattling on, woman? I'm trying to tune the wireless in,' Noah growled.

All that came from the accumulator set Noah had his ear pressed up against was a series of crackles and buzzes. Katie watched her grandfather excitedly, the wireless had been bought especially for Christmas with the dividend money Kitty had saved up in the store. All three had gone into Auckland to the main Co-op store to buy it, for the local branch sold little else but groceries and hardware. It had been a new experience altogether to see her grandparents walking arm in arm down Newgate Street for all the world like a young courting couple.

'Merry Christmas to all!'

A perfunctory knock heralded the entrance of Dottie and Jim from next door, Jim actually wearing a collar on his shirt and his braces on his shoulders rather than dangling down by the sides of his trousers. They were swiftly followed by Billy Wright, his mam and dad and his sister June. Before long the room was full to bursting. The young ones sat on the clippie mat leaving the sofa and the chairs brought in from the kitchen for their elders. Billy managed to sit next to Katie and was conscious the whole time of her thigh pressed close to his in the crush. All eyes turned to the corner by the window, where Noah still had his ear to the set. The crackling sounds were becoming longer and louder.

With an important though abstracted expression he fiddled with the aerial wire running from the back of the set out of a hole in the window frame up to the roof. He moved it slightly then went outside to gaze up at the aerial; came back in and twiddled with the knob.

'Can I give you a hand, Noah?' asked Will Wright, Billy's father, starting to get to his feet but Noah waved him back.

'Nay lad, I can manage,' he said.

Sure enough the crackling stopped and a voice came over the airwaves. Instantly there was an absolute hush among the listeners in the room. Noah sat back in triumph and looked round at the others with pride.

'We are here in Salisbury Cathedral where the Carol Service is about to begin,' the voice said.

'Hey! He talks funny, doesn't he?' Kitty demanded of Dottie. 'Do you think he's one o' them foreigners?'

Noah frowned blackly at her. 'By, woman, you don't half show your ignorance,' he snapped.

'I only thought—'

'Well, don't! He talks like that because he's a southerner, that's all. He can't help it,' said Noah. Then everyone fell silent as organ music filled the room and the choir began to sing. And they stayed silent for the whole of the programme which lasted forty-five minutes.

Afterwards Kitty served tea and slices of Christmas cake with Wensleydale cheese. Katie, handing round plates of food and cups of tea, was happy enough to burst. It was the first party she could remember since she was very small. By the time the visitors filed out of the front door rather than the back for it was, after all, Christmas Day it was already dark. Outside, she could see the lamplighter with his long pole over his shoulder walking down the row, pausing at intervals to light the streetlamps. The gas flaring up before dying down to a steady glow added to her enjoyment of the magical day.

'Eeh, it's a miracle all right,' said Dottie, lingering on the doorstep.

'What?' asked Katie, still watching the lamplighter.

'Tch,' Dottie chided. 'What do you think? The wireless of course. By, I don't know what my poor mother would have made of it. Merry Christmas, pet.'

'Aye, merry Christmas,' the others echoed and Katie went in and closed the door. The light from the gas mantle shone softly on the tinsel streamer wound round the brass rail above the fire and the red paper bell hanging from the ceiling. Oh yes, it had been a lovely Christmas.

1931

The memory of that day came back to Katie as she wheeled the trolley round F Ward. Christmas Day in hospital was so different from what she had been used to, it was a different world altogether. She certainly had not realised how different when she passed her entrance examination and received the letter of admittance. She had been euphoric about it and her gran had been so proud she had told everyone in the rows. But Katie had worked so hard at night school, she deserved to get in.

She gazed round the ward; there were some empty beds, their counterpanes lying smooth and green and with the sheet turned over them showing white for the regulation twelve inches. Everyone who could be sent home for the holiday had been but there were still patients who needed to stay. Women who had had emergency operations within the last week; a ruptured ectopic pregnancy case and three who had miscarried. Or had tried to abort their babies, depending on the way you looked at it, Staff Nurse had said caustically.

'A bit too heavy with the pennyroyal,' the senior nurse had muttered. A bit hard, they were on this ward, Katie thought. Especially remembering some of the young women from Winton Colliery trying to bring up three or four children born in as many years with next to no money.

For the hard times were back yet again, the men

working short time or not at all. According to the wireless, it was all due to something that had happened in America, the Wall Street crash they called it and it triggered off depression around the world. Three days' pay a week went absolutely nowhere, she knew that all right.

Katie had just started her probationer nurse's training and had been on the wards of South-East Durham General Hospital for only a few weeks yet she had dared to voice her opinion of the staff's suspicious attitudes to some of the unfortunate women once. Only the once had she done that for she had had her head bitten off for her trouble.

'What do you know about it?' Nurse Potter had snapped. Nurse Potter was a third-year nurse who would soon be taking her finals and so someone not to be argued with.

'Well, she has five children already and she is only twenty-two, I—' Katie had begun, referring to a recent emergency admission but she had shut up as she saw the quelling look on Nurse Potter's face.

'They deserve what they get,' the senior nurse had said as they walked down the corridor on their way to the breakfast break. 'She could have left those bairns without a mother, did you think of that? And any road, it's against my religion. It's murder.'

What Doris Teasdale, the girl in question had got was a night of appalling pain after the registrar had examined her. 'She won't die this time,' he had said. 'Let her stew for a few hours.'

'Arrogant pig,' Katie muttered, fortunately not close

enough for Dr Raine to hear properly. He had eyed her suspiciously however and after that ignored her presence completely, sailing past her down the ward as she stood, often with mop in hand cleaning the floor or coming and going to the sluice with bedpan in hand.

Doris Teasdale was one of the patients still in the ward. She lay against her pillow with a face so white it matched the pillow slip as Katie handed out the tea.

'There's a nice bit of cake, today, Mrs Teasdale,' Katie said as she brought round the tea trolley. 'Howay, I'll help you sit up. I've put two sugars in the tea and there's some nice bread and butter. It'll do you good to eat it.'

'I'm not hungry, Nurse,' Doris said, her voice thin and weary.

'Mebbe not but you have to eat it, man, it will get thrown into the pig bin if you don't. Anyway, think of the bairns,' said Katie and tucked her own arm under Doris's so as to haul her up the bed. 'The visitors will be here in half an hour, there's a full hour today, won't that be lovely?'

'I'm not expecting anybody,' said Doris. 'Just me mam and she can't stay long 'cause she has to leave the bairns with the neighbour.'

Katie almost asked where her man would be but bit the words off unspoken. She'd only seen Mr Teasdale once before and then he had stayed for all of ten minutes of the allotted half-hour. He was probably out getting a skinful, she thought.

Doris took a sip of tea, however, and started on the bread and butter. She just couldn't leave good food to get thrown in the pig bin. She'd eat it now, Katie knew, even if she had to force it down.

'Don't stand there talking to the patients all morning, Nurse Benfield.'

Katie jumped at Sister's voice, she hadn't realised she was in the ward. Sister was standing only a few feet away frowning heavily.

'No Sister.' Katie hurried back to the trolley and pushed it on to the next patient jerking it a little and catching it on the end of Doris's bed and making the cups rattle. Behind her she heard Sister's long-suffering sigh.

'And hurry up with the teas,' said Sister. 'Father Christmas will be in shortly.'

A merry Christmas to you, too, Katie muttered under her breath as she hurried round the rest of the patients. She took the trolley in to the ward kitchen and cleared it. There would be the washing up to do later for the maid had the day off on Christmas Day. The nurses and housemen were the only ones working today. All the nursing staff was because, as had been explained to Katie, it wasn't fair for only some of them to have the day off. So it was decreed that there should be no off-duty at all on this special day. With the number of patients down and empty beds on the wards it meant that the nurses spent a lot of their time avoiding Sister who was of the opinion that a good nurse could always find something useful to do.

Consequently, Katie was lurking in the sluice when the consultant, Mr Hobson, came sweeping into the ward, booming heartily. His cotton-wool beard and moustache clung precariously under his nose, rather in the way his theatre mask so often did. His red gown, the hospital's second best, for the best one was doing duty in the children's ward, barely fitted his rotund figure but the few patients hardly noticed. As usual they were struck with awe at his august presence.

The nurses were in a row with Sister at the head, ready to do Mr Hobson's bidding. All except Katie, that is, she was coming into the ward behind him. When she did manage to sidle round him and attach herself to the end of the line, she was rewarded with another of Sister's black looks.

She hadn't time to be apprehensive, however, for Mr Hobson was fishing in his bag and bringing out small parcels and handing them to the nurses to give out. So for the minute it was all bustle. And when the surgeon went off down the corridor, having done his duty so that he could go home to his own Christmas, it was time for the visitors to be allowed in.

Altogether, Katie thought to herself as she trailed off-duty at half past eight in the evening having been on the ward for thirteen hours, her first Christmas on the wards had been long and hard. For in the middle of the visiting hour there had been an emergency patient to be prepared for theatre who turned out to be a ruptured ectopic pregnancy. Mr Hobson had been called out to operate and he was none too pleased about that. Then old Mrs Turner, who had an prolapsed uterus sticking out between her legs, had had a touch of diarrhoea from a surfeit of Christmas cake her daughter had brought in for her. The daughter had also brought a quarter-bottle of navy rum to wash the cake down and the old lady had kept it under the bedclothes so she could take an occasional sip.

By six o'clock the odour of rum had begun to permeate the ward and Mrs Turner was complaining that she was feeling badly and a body could die in this hell-hole of a place. And other, worse smells got mixed up with the rum and there was a great deal of shouting when Staff Nurse found the almost empty bottle and tried to take it away. And Katie and the third-year nurse had the job of cleaning up Mrs Turner and stopping her from climbing out of bed. Then they had to make her comfortable which wasn't too difficult because the old lady fell asleep halfway through her bed being re-made.

The bed had to be made up for the patient returning from theatre and Sister wasn't satisfied with the way Katie had done her hospital corners and pulled them out so they had to be done again. Staff Nurse was doing the round of dressings and douches and when she woke Mrs Turner up to do her, once again there was pandemonium.

'What is all this racket?' demanded Sister coming out of her office, report book, in which she had been recording the happenings of the day, in hand. Her voice was so thunderous even Mrs Turner was cowed and peace reigned for a while.

Katie was too exhausted to eat much supper. In any case she had promised Billy she would pop out to see him if she got the chance. Billy Wright was staying in Middlesbrough over the Christmas holiday. He was staying with his aunt and uncle who had left the coal pits of South-West Durham to manage an iron mine at Eston.

Of course, his real reason for being there was so he could be near Katie for Billy was in love with her; couldn't remember a time when he was not. She knew that, but now that Katie had achieved her ambition of being accepted for nursing training, she was not about to give it all up to become a housewife. Maybe in three years' time when she had finished her training. Or better still, five years when she would be a qualified midwife with a bit of luck. Or even something higher? A ward sister? But usually her imagination gave up when she thought of that, a ward sister was altogether too exalted a position for a lass from Winton Colliery.

Katie exchanged her white nurse's cap for the outdoor regulation one and wrapped her cloak close around her before closing the door of her tiny room in the Nurses' Home and leaving the building. She hurried along the side path to the imposing iron gates at the entrance.

'Evening nurse,' the porter's voice came from inside the lodge where he sat muffled against the cold. 'Merry Christmas.'

'Merry Christmas,' Katie echoed, 'I'm just popping out for a breath of air.' She hurried along the damp pavement to the corner for it was strictly forbidden to have followers hanging round the hospital gates. Around her, mist from the river rose and curled as the tide ran in from Teesport. In the distance a ship's fog horn blew eerily.

Billy was there, stamping his feet against the cold and rubbing his hands together. Katie hurried up to him.

'I'm not very late, am I? Only Sister keeps finding something else for me to do—'

'Merry Christmas, Katie Benfield.' He interrupted her explanation by taking hold of her by both arms and kissing her quickly on the lips.

'Oh! Merry Christmas,' said Katie, rather breathlessly. She could still feel the soft but firm touch of his lips against her own and they tingled, confusing her. 'I – I can't stay long mind.'

'I thought we could go into the Station Hotel and have a drink though,' said Billy.

'I'm in uniform, I can't go for a drink.'

'Well, we can have a cup of coffee in the lounge, there's nothing to take exception to in that, is there?'

'No, I suppose not.'

So long as no one saw her, she thought. That was the trouble with meeting him so late in the evening. There were no tea shops open. Sitting in a deep, plush armchair in a corner of the lounge, half-hidden from the few other customers by an enormous Christmas tree, she felt a little safer. It was warm, and the coffee hot and milky though it still tasted bitter to Katie. She felt she would never get used to drinking coffee.

Billy felt in his jacket pocket and pulled out a small, square package and gave it to her. Katie looked at it, her heart sinking a little.

'What is it?'

'Why don't you open it and see?'

Slowly, Katie undid the wrapping and looked at the jewel-box. It was a deep blue and bore the inscription,

'Northern Goldsmiths'. Inside there was an engagement ring, three diamonds set in gold.

'I—'

'Don't say anything for a minute, please,' said Billy. 'I want you to know how much I love you. I'm a surveyor now, I'm doing well, Katie. We could be married, I'd get an official's house, they have bathrooms and everything. We could even buy our own house—'

'Billy, it's a lovely ring. But I have to finish my training. You know that's what I want. I can't marry you for years and years and it's not fair keeping you waiting.' She held the ring out to him.

'Katie, don't turn me down. I will wait, I don't want to but I will. Look, keep the ring, I'll get you a gold chain so that you can wear it around your neck, under your uniform. Please, Katie.'

Katie looked at him. By, she thought he was such a lovely lad. He deserved a nice girl, one who would be happy to stay at home and have bairns. His children would be good-looking like him, handsome and clever too, just as he was. For a moment, but only a moment she found her resolve weakening. But it was no good.

'I'll have to go back in a minute, Billy,' she said.

'Katie!'

She couldn't bear to see the hurt in his eyes. 'All right,' she said. 'I will keep it. But it's not binding, mind. Not for you. If you should meet someone else—'

'I won't,' said Billy. He picked up her cloak and put it around her shoulders. 'Come on, I'll walk you to the corner.' He felt he had to get her back before she changed her mind about the ring.

Curfew was at half past ten and they just made it to the gates. The porter, as he so often did, turned a blind eye as Billy kissed her good night then coughed discreetly as they lingered for another moment. 'Half past ten, Nurse,' he called hoarsely. 'Home Sister will be on the warpath, mind!'

'Thank you for the ring, thank you for everything,' Katie whispered then ran up the drive towards the Nurse's Home. Sister Jameson was sitting at a table by the door ready to record the times the latecomers came in. More than ten minutes late and you would be up before Matron in the morning.

In her own cubby-hole of a room she sat on the bed and gazed at the engagement ring. The overhead light made it sparkle and shoot off tiny shafts of colour, green and red. It was beautiful and she was an ungrateful bitch not to have shown more appreciation. It must have cost a fortune, maybe even twenty pounds. But she wasn't ready to give up her dream of a career, maybe she never would be.

Katie thought back over the years, the poverty and degradation of the strike. Poverty still evident in Winton Colliery because of the depression. The world didn't want ships so the shipyards didn't want steel so the iron and steelworks didn't want coal. Oh yes, she had learned all about the economy when she was attending adult education classes. She'd worked hard, she was going to escape and she was going to do it off her own bat, not rely on some man like all the rest of the women in her family had had to do.

She washed and changed into her flannel nightgown before snuggling down under the bedclothes. Not makeshift bedclothes these, not old coats with a clippie mat for an eiderdown but real wool blankets and a counterpane. This too was an achievement and she had brought it about herself.

Of course, she admitted to herself, Billy, though, was not any man but one who loved her and if she let herself she would love him. But she couldn't afford to let herself do that, not yet. In the future, maybe, when she had done everything she had set out to do. But oh, she couldn't help herself feeling for him but they had plenty of time, loads of time.

Chapter Seven

'Look, Maisie, a meccano set!' cried Robert. 'Look, Mummy do you see? It's exactly what I wanted!'

Mary Anne sat by the fire with her chair turned towards the Christmas tree in the corner. It was four o'clock and the children were allowed down to open their presents and have tea with the family because today was Christmas Day. She smiled at Robert's excited cries and nodded her head.

'Lovely, lovely, Robert,' she said. 'You'll make some great things with that won't you?' Oh, he was such a lovely boy; tall and straight-limbed just like his father had been, God rest him. Her back ached, she shifted her position in the chair, felt the baby move within her. Where was this one's father? she wondered. Was he really down at the ironworks overseeing urgent repairs to something or other as he had said? Or was he in Middlesbrough in that street where half-naked women hung around the mean doorsteps or beckoned from the windows? Oh, she'd seen them all right, one day when she had taken a wrong turn from Linthorpe Road and wandered on, trying to turn in a square to get back to the main shopping area.

'I'll take a little walk, Jack,' she'd said to the chauffeur, 'I need the air.' And what a shock she had got too. That horrible street with the unmade road, and the doors opening straight on to the filthy pavement. She had lifted her skirt to keep it out of the muck and a couple of men had leered at her and the women in the doorways laughed and jeered as she turned and fled back to the safety of Linthorpe Road. Did Matthew go there or somewhere like it? Certainly he didn't enter her bedroom, not since she had told him about the baby and for that she was thankful.

Yet men had appetites, she knew that, she had been married before hadn't she? Her darling Rob. The familiar stab of pain and loss shot through her. She sighed. She had to think of other things now, brighter things, happy; she had the new baby to think of. But this hadn't been a happy pregnancy, oh no.

'They aren't all the same,' her mama had said to her when she whispered her misgivings about it to her. 'You just have to endure it, that's all, Mary Anne. Think of happy things.'

The trouble was she couldn't always think of anything happy. Oh, how could she say that when she had these two lovely children? she reproached herself. Maisie was at her knee now, holding out the new china doll she had received from Father Christmas. Her eyes were lit with wonderment, she touched the porcelain cheeks delicately with her fingers; patted the nut-brown curls peeping out from under the straw bonnet.

'She's beautiful, isn't she, Mama?'

Mary Anne agreed the doll was indeed absolutely lovely. So it should be, it had been the finest in the catalogue she had sent for from Harrods and had cost a fortune . . .

'The girl's too big for dolls,' Matthew had said when she gave him the list of things she wanted ordering. 'You mark my words, some lad will see her playing with dolls and try to give her a real baby.'

'Matthew!' Mary Anne had gasped and he laughed coarsely. Why was he like that sometimes? Most of the time he was a perfect gentleman. But he hadn't quibbled at the price, he never did, she allowed him that. He had argued as to why she hadn't gone into Middlesbrough to shop.

'You'll get just as good quality in Middlesbrough as in London,' he had grumbled. But Mary Anne didn't go into Middlesbrough any more, not since that upsetting day when – no, she was not to think of that.

She put a hand on her back and rubbed it gently. The ache was getting stronger. Where was Matthew? He had promised to be back in time for tea with the children. This was Christmas Day after all. Was he at the works or was he in one of those unspeakable streets, in one of those hovels with one of those women? Sometimes when he came in there was a strange smell about him, sweet, cloying, an animal smell.

Mary Anne got to her feet and went over to the bell rope hanging on the opposite side of the fireplace. She would ring for Daisy to bring in the tea; her throat was dry and parched from the fire. Never mind that Matthew wasn't in. The children were probably happier in his absence anyway.

Matthew was, in fact, at the ironworks. He was looking at a giant overhead crane which, when working, lifted and slung the steel ingots to their allotted positions.

It was old, no doubt about it – 1901 this shed had been built and the crane too probably. If it hadn't been for the depression it would have been replaced years ago. It broke down regularly, no matter how much the mechanics tried to patch it up. Now that fresh orders had been secured at last it would have to be replaced. It might mean laying some of the men off for a while when the new one was being installed but they would no doubt welcome that. Welcome the chance to have a booze-up over the New Year.

Beside him, Jackson, the manager stood quietly, resentful that he had been dragged from his Christmas lunch for this. What was so urgent about it anyway? The boss was a bloody workaholic, that was what he was. Tomorrow would have done just as well. He stared morosely at the floor.

'Can you start it up for a minute?'

Jackson jumped; his attention had strayed.

'Me?' he asked.

'Do you see anyone else here?'

Sarcastic sod, thought Jackson. But he turned to the iron steps and climbed into the cab of the crane. He had to think hard before he could remember how to even start the monster but he wasn't going to let the boss see that. There was a minute's quiet but then he figured it out and the great machine burst into life.

'What are you doing?'

The crane drowned out Matthew's shouted question and he stepped back to look up at the cab. And fell over a small off-cut of steel that should not have been there and fell on his back, winding himself.

His first feeling was anger, even before he felt the crushing pain in his left ankle. He tried to rise and fell back, clutching at his leg, the pain was excruciating.

'Bloody hell, man!' Matthew roared but of course Jackson couldn't hear but he peered out of the cab anyway, his stare showing horror as he saw the prostrate figure below him. He started to climb out of the cab, forgetting to turn off the engine and Matthew rapidly made the signal for him to stop. Twisting on the top of the ladder, Jackson leaned forward to do so and the silence was deafening for a second. Only for a second, for as he moved he missed his footing on the iron ladder and fell to the ground, directly across Matthew. Luckily, the watch-man was already coming into the shed, having heard the racket.

'Bloody hell!' he echoed Matthew and ran to call an ambulance.

All the breath had been knocked out of Matthew when Jackson came hurtling down on him, so badly in fact that he lost consciousness. And when he did begin to come round he was in so much pain that he didn't open his eyes but tried his best to sink back into the blessed blackness. He heard voices in the distance, a workman's voice and then others, the weight was lifted from his chest and he in his turn was lifted. The pain made him black out again and when he came to he was lying on his back in a moving vehicle that certainly wasn't his car, yet Lawson was there, he heard him. Matthew opened his eyes.

'Hey up,' he heard Lawson say, 'he's back with us.'

'What happened?'

Matthew turned his head cautiously, seeing the dark windows of the ambulance, heard the klaxon blaring, felt every bump on the road with his battered body. 'My God!' he said.

'You had an accident, sir,' said Lawson, 'we'll soon be at the hospital. It's just your leg, I don't think there's much more damage. Not like the other fellow, he's in a bad—'

'Don't talk to the patient!'

Squinting past Lawson, Matthew saw an ambulance man in green overalls. He was glaring at the chauffeur and Lawson, suitably intimidated, moved back. Matthew saw that there was another narrow trestle across from him and Jackson was lying on it, his face very pale.

Thankfully, the ambulance took only a few minutes longer to reach the hospital and before he could even gather his thoughts together to demand to be taken to a private hospital, not the sprawling workhouse-like structure that was the South-East Durham, Matthew was being wheeled into Outpatients and Casualty.

He lay looking up at the ceiling which was adorned

with a few trailing streamers. A rather battered paper bell hung from the middle. It was a nasty red, contrasting with the faded streamers, thought Matthew drowsily. He was filled with a lethargy that was utterly strange to him, yet rather pleasant. He closed his eyes. What the heck, he thought, let them do what they willed.

The clock in the drawing-room struck eight, waking Mary Anne from a light doze. She sat up suddenly and her head swam; she swayed dangerously. She kept her head down for a few moments until it cleared. There was a persistent ache in her back; it was beginning to make her feel a little sick.

Where was Matthew? He should have been home long ago. It really was too bad of him not to let her know if he was detained elsewhere. The children had gone upstairs hours ago, he hadn't even seen them today of all days; it was after all, Christmas.

Mary Anne stood up cautiously and moved to pull the bell rope. She could wait no longer, she had to go to bed. Daisy would bring her a hot drink and she would ask the girl to rub her back. She sagged suddenly against the wall; her weight going on the satin bell rope so that it gave way suddenly and she fell heavily across the brass rail of the fender. When Daisy answered the summons, Mary Anne had rolled on to the hearthrug and was lying with her knees drawn up, moaning loudly.

'There was an emergency admission yesterday evening,' said Sister. The nurses were lined up in her office as she read the night staff's report and gave them their orders for the morning. Katie, being the lowest of the probationer nurses, was on the end of the line nearest the door. Which was just as well because she was half a minute late having had a fight with her newly starched cap to get it into the right shape and in the correct position on her head. Sister had noticed of course, she noticed everything. Thankfully she had made do with giving Katie a disapproving look before beginning the report.

'A Mrs Mary Anne Hamilton,' Sister continued. 'She is the wife of Mr Matthew Hamilton, the ironmaster. Incomplete abortion. She is in a side ward for the moment; she is to be taken down to theatre this morning at ten. Staff Nurse and I will get her ready for theatre. You, Nurse Benfield will attend us. Perhaps you may learn something.' Sister's tone implied that she thought this doubtful.

'Yes Sister.'

Katie had a small surge of panic at the thought of it. She was sure she would drop something and disgrace herself, her fingers felt all thumbs. But when Staff moved out to lay the trolley she fell in behind her obediently. Mrs Hamilton lay quietly under the covers, the dark circles around her eyes standing out against her white face. She said nothing but 'yes' and 'no' and 'thank you' in a faint voice barely above a whisper as Sister and Staff Nurse dressed her in a theatre gown and tied a white cloth around her head. They douched her with Perchloride of mercury 1-10000, and drew on long white stockings, all handed to them by Katie.

Mary Anne was drowsy as she had already had her pre-medication and made no objection to anything. But just as they were finished there was a small commotion in the passage outside. It was Matthew's voice, she thought, and even through the haze the drugs had brought to her mind she felt a twinge of apprehension.

Katie looked in wonder at Sister, who strode to the door and looked out on to the passage.

'What is happening?' she asked. She would have said a lot more if it were not for the fact that it was Mr Hobson outside together with Mr Caine and a patient in a wheelchair. A male patient in the corridor of the gynaecological ward! It was unheard of. But Mr Caine was talking.

'I'm sorry, Sister, but Mr Hamilton insisted, and I thought there was no harm—'

'No harm!' Sister ejaculated. She left them in no doubt as to her feelings on the matter.

'He wants to see his wife for a few minutes,' Mr Caine continued. 'You will allow the circumstances are extraordinary.'

This last was said in appeal to the gynaecologist. He glanced at Sister then back at his colleague.

'Perhaps a few minutes, Sister? The theatre will not be ready for another thirty minutes.'

Sister had to bow to the surgeon's wishes; she stood back. 'If you insist, sir,' she said. 'Though I hope the visit does not upset my patient.'

'Indeed. Yet it might be just the thing to settle her down.'

Matthew looked back impatiently at the orderly who was in charge of his wheelchair. The man was doing his best to show that the argument had nothing to do with him; he was gazing at the green-painted wall of the corridor.

'Come along then man,' he snapped. But Sister was not going to allow that at least. 'Nurse Benfield,' she called. 'Come and push Mr Hamilton in to see his wife.'

Hurriedly, Staff Nurse had covered the trolley and was pushing it out of the side ward. Katie went out to the corridor before the two god-like surgeons, for that was the impression she had got of surgeons, they were gods, almost, and pushed the man in to the side ward where Mary Anne was lying with her eyes closed. Not that she was really asleep but she hoped Matthew would think so. Sister came and stood just inside the door, watching suspiciously and Matthew turned to her.

'You can go now,' he said. 'I'll call you—' He stopped, having just noticed Katie behind him. Katie turned to go.

'Not you, girl,' he said. 'You Sister, I mean you.'

Both Katie and Sister gasped and the older woman turned crimson beneath her stiff white cap with the frill at the edge and the ribbons tied in a bow under the chin. But she could do nothing, she had perforce to back out into the corridor where the two surgeons were standing, talking lightly now.

'What's your name, girl?'

'Nurse Benfield, sir,' Katie managed to say.

So it was the same girl. Benfield, that was what Thompson had called her grandfather, why, it must be five years ago. Momentarily diverted from his intention of talking to Mary Anne, he studied Katie openly and she lifted her chin and gazed back at him. He looked somehow familiar, had she seen him before? He was a big man though not so big as her grandfather and he sat uneasily in the chair, dressed in a satin dressing-gown. One leg stuck out in front of the chair covered by a plaster cast from toes to mid-calf. He caught her gaze and smiled.

'Aren't you from Winton?' Matthew asked.

'Yes, sir.'

'I thought so,' said Matthew. He continued looking at her and she stood simply, waiting for him to stop. She had been striking as a young girl, he thought, now she was grown, she was beautiful, even in the ugly nurse's uniform with the mid-calf-length apron and striped dress, the black lisle stockings and sensible shoes. If she took off the silly cap that was tilted slightly to the right, she would be even more striking, he thought.

'Matthew?'

Though it had only been a minute Mary Anne had got tired of pretending to sleep and had opened her eyes and seen that her husband was in a wheelchair.

'What on earth happened?' she cried in alarm. He turned back to the bed and his wife. She'd failed him again, he thought, what a bloody Christmas this had been.

'Wait outside,' he said over his shoulder and Katie went out though inwardly she was seething. Who the heck did he think he was, coming in here and behaving like he owned the whole hospital?

Chapter Eight

'It's nothing, a slight accident at the works. I have a broken ankle and a few bruises, that's all,' Matthew said to Mary Anne. He didn't mention that Jackson, the works manager, had head injuries and hadn't come round yet. Mary Anne wouldn't know whom he was talking about anyway.

'What happened with you, madam? I thought you were going to carry this one. I suppose you've been lifting that great girl of yours, you never learn.'

Mary Anne laid still, the lethargy induced by the pre-medication drug creeping back over her now that the shock of seeing Matthew in a wheelchair was fading. Though she still felt the depressing ache of failure, she could read correctly the contempt in Matthew's expression.

'I didn't,' she said. 'It just happened. Sometimes it does, Matthew. It's not my fault.'

'Then whose—' Matthew began to ask then saw the tear that slid down Mary Anne's pink-tipped nose. He wasn't entirely free of compassion, it was simply that he was so disappointed in her. He hadn't only married her for the prospect of gaining her father's works; he needed an heir, a proper heir. She had produced two children, why couldn't she produce one for him?

'Oh for heaven's sake, don't cry, Mary Anne,' he said roughly, too roughly he realised but he couldn't think of anything else to say. Luckily they were interrupted by a knock at the door and Sister came in.

'The trolley's here to take Mrs Hamilton to theatre,' she said. 'I'm sorry but you'll have to go now, Mr Hamilton.'

Matthew looked at the officious little woman but didn't deign to reply to her. Instead he looked at his wife's white face. 'I'll see you later. You'll be all right,' he said. He meant it kindly so that it was a pity that Mary Anne took it as a vague sort of threat.

The girl from Winton was not in the corridor despite the fact that he had told her to wait there and this added to his irritation. But as he passed the open door of the sluice he saw she was in there, washing bedpans and that irritated him even more. She had nice hands, well shaped though a little red and with the nails cut very short and it was a shame to use them for such work.

'Wait a moment,' he ordered the man pushing his chair. He looked at Katie and, feeling his eyes upon her, she turned and he felt the full impact of her dark blue eyes.

'So you are nursing now,' he said. 'It's a long way from Winton Colliery rows, surely?'

Katie flushed. 'Not so far,' she replied and belatedly

added, 'Sir.' She stood, rubber apron covering the white cotton one and with bedpan in one hand and scrubbing brush in the other and he thought she looked delightful. She in her turn saw only the man, his dark hair swept back from his high forehead, his brown eyes, keen and seeming to take in everything at once. He looked about thirty-something to her, an older man though not as old as her grandfather. Why was he bothering with her? She was too lowly a nurse to be concerned with the care of private patients.

Matthew had been staring, he realised and now, recollecting, he glanced back at the orderly.

'Righto, man,' he said. 'Let's get on with it.'

Matthew forgot about his intention to have himself transferred to a private hospital. The chairman of the Hospital Board, who was a fellow member of the Board of Guardians and a friend of sorts, soon had him transferred to a private ward in the South-East Durham. Somehow he never thought of having Mary Anne transferred to the wing too, she was in a side ward anyway, wasn't she?

He hadn't exactly forgotten about Katie in the years since he had last seen her. But now he had nothing else to think about as he lay in the hospital bed and he amused himself finding out about her.

'She is a first-year probationer nurse,' Lawson reported to him. 'She's only been at the hospital for a month or two.' Her home address was still West Row, Winton Colliery; her next-of-kin was Noah Benfield, her grand-father. And she had a sweetheart. All this Lawson had discovered in the café outside the hospital gates and all for the cost of a few cups of coffee for the junior nurses who frequented it.

'I have a deep respect for your work,' he had told them. 'But I'll put my cards on the table. I really like that nurse on F Ward. Nurse Benfield, is it?' The first thing they told him was about Katie's sweetheart.

'I don't think the nurses should be encouraged to have followers,' Matthew said to Lawson and the chauffeur managed to keep his face expressionless despite his inward amusement. Matthew frowned at him. Logic told him that a girl as beautiful as Katie would have a beau but all the same he couldn't bear to think of it.

'I'm sure Florence Nightingale did not encourage them,' said Matthew.

'No sir,' said Lawson. 'Neither do the hospital authorities.'

Flaming hypocrite, he thought to himself. Being his chauffeur, Lawson was in a good position to know how Matthew Hamilton spent some of his time when out of the house and it was not always at the works. There was a certain house in Middlesbrough . . . Still, that was rich men for you. Liked to indulge their appetites.

Matthew was visiting his wife every day, first in a wheelchair and later, as his ankle improved, with the aid of crutches. It was very nice of him, thought Mary Anne, but not at all in character when she thought about it. But she was starved of affection and warmed to him as he showed her small kindnesses, patting her hand, insisting on bringing in the children to see her despite the scandalised opposition of Sister.

'Good morning, Nurse,' he said to Katie one bright frosty morning. It was the New Year's Day and once again he was on his way to F Ward ostensibly to see his wife. Somehow he was always there when Katie was on duty.

He was being discharged today and was dressed in a suit and crisp white shirt brought in by Lawson and had exchanged his crutches for a walking stick.

'It would have been better if you had waited a day or two more,' Mr Caine had said and Matthew had frowned.

'I tell you it feels fine,' he had snapped. 'I have work to do in any case.'

'I hope you don't intend to walk very far on that ankle,' had said Mr Caine. 'I'm warning you—'

'Oh never mind,' said Matthew and the surgeon had subsided. It was Matthew's opinion that the doctors kept you down as long as they could if only to inflate their fees. Scoundrels and charlatans, the lot of them. Though Caine was not so bad, he had to concede. He'd made a good job of setting his ankle, so why couldn't he leave well alone now?

The conversation with the surgeon was running through his mind as he walked along the corridor leaning heavily on his stick. Because, if he had to admit it, the ankle did pain him if he walked more than a few steps on the specially reinforced plaster. Seeing Katie outside the ward was a piece of luck, he'd hit just on the right time. It drove any thought of his ankle out of his mind.

Katie went pink. 'Morning sir,' she replied, hoping neither Sister nor Staff Nurse would come out and catch her talking to him, a patient and a private one at that. 'Er, how are you feeling?' she went on as he stood still and seemed to be waiting for her to speak.

'I'm going home today,' he said. 'I feel much better, thank you.'

'Oh, good.'

He gazed at her; she was so obviously uneasy in the way she kept glancing back at the closed door to the ward. She edged away.

'I have to go, I have a message for Matron,' she said. 'Goodbye, sir. I hope everything will be all right.' She slipped past him and walked rapidly away. He watched her and felt a small tingle of satisfaction as he saw her turn to glance back at him before turning a corner.

Katie left her message at Matron's office and went on to the nurse's dining-room for her break. She collected a cup of coffee and a biscuit and sat down at a table on her own, for she had things to think about. Mr Hamilton she thought about most of all. She realised now that he must be going out of his way to bump into her and she couldn't think why he should be so interested.

Now she remembered where she had seen him before. It had been years ago, during the awful, hungry times of the Great Strike and after she remembered the lake of pitch, the sack filled with pitch balls, the feel of the pitch on her hands. And walking along the path in the bitter cold with bare legs stinging and fingers numb. And the taste of the raw carrot left by the galloways, the pit ponies, she could almost feel the hard lumps in her mouth now. She looked at the biscuit on the plate before her; it was a digestive biscuit, plain and wholesome but she couldn't eat it. Then there had been the gentleman in his thick overcoat and felt hat and the striped trousers below the hem of the coat and his shiny shoes, only barely touched with the black mud of the path by the wagon way. How he had looked at her grandda, diminishing him somehow.

Now she knew who he was though she hadn't at the time. She doubted her grandda had known either. The big boss, the supreme gaffer. The owner of the ironworks that used the coal and coke produced at Winton Colliery and no doubt half a dozen other collieries.

Life was strange, thought Katie as she drank her coffee and rose to go back to the ward. Mr Hamilton lived in a different world and no matter how she worked and studied and tried her best she would never be in a position to enter that world. And she didn't want to, she told herself as she strode briskly along the corridor.

Now there was work to do, Mrs Hamilton was going home today too and the side ward had to have the bed stripped and made up again and she had to help the maid wash the walls and the furniture and polish it until it sparkled ready for the next patient. Not a private patient this time but one who was terminally ill with cancer of the uterus and permanently on morphine to keep the pain at bay.

When Katie returned to the ward there was no sign of either of the Hamiltons. The rest of the morning was taken up with scrubbing and making up the bed. And when she thought she had it right Sister came to the door.

'Strip that bed and start again, Nurse,' she ordered Katie. 'Have you learned nothing about bed making since you came? Turn the openings of the pillowcases away from the door if you please and straighten that corner. Both should be alike, you should know this. And don't forget to turn the bed wheels in—'

In the afternoon Staff Nurse instructed Katie on the proper procedure for administering morphine to the woman lying on the bed. 'Just in case, you understand,' said Staff Nurse. 'I expect Mr Hobson will increase the dose when he comes in after his theatre list. She is having a quarter of a grain now, every four hours but may need more.'

'But why me? Staff Nurse?' asked Katie, in surprise. She had not yet got as far as giving injections.

'You may be the only Protestant available. The Catholics refuse to give more,' said Staff Nurse. Katie blinked. She couldn't imagine refusing to do anything if Sister ordered her to. On the bed the woman, Phoebe Smith, moaned and it was the loneliest sound in the world.

Altogether, Katie was very thankful to go off-duty at six o'clock that evening. All she really wanted to do was go back to her room and to bed but it was her day off to-morrow and she had promised her gran she would go home to Winton.

As Katie alighted from Radley's bus around twelve o'clock the next day she saw Noah just turning the corner, evidently just coming off fore shift. He was in his black, his eyes gleaming through the coal dust, his helmet pushed to the back of his head. He was still wearing the leather knee protectors he needed for his work where the seam he was in was low and the only way he could swing a pick was on his knees.

Katie hadn't seen her grandfather for a few weeks and she got a cold feeling inside her now; she hadn't realised he was looking so old. He was bent over against the wind and though his coal-dust encrusted jacket was open he had an old muffler around his throat and he was walking much more slowly than she remembered.

'Grandda!' Katie called and waited for him to catch up to her. Noah grinned and straightened up, even quickened his gait.

'Katie, flower!' he said. 'By, you're a sight for sore eyes!'

She fell into step with him, not kissing him or touching him in greeting; he was too dirty for that. Not that she would have done had he been dressed in his Sunday best. That sort of thing was not done on the streets of Winton Colliery. Yet anyone watching would have known there was a bond between them as they turned into the back street of West Row, the studs of Noah's pit boots ringing on the cobbles.

Everything looked strange, Katie thought as she gazed around the kitchen half an hour later. She sat at the table spooning up a plateful of Gran's broth, which was thick with vegetables and bits of ham from the knucklebone she had put in it. It was hot and filling and just the thing for a cold winter's day, she thought as she broke homemade bread into it.

'Howay, then, tell us all about this fancy hospital where you're at,' said Gran. She had a half-pint mug of tea in her hand, laced with a generous dollop of condensed milk. And her hair looked thinner and greyer and her face more lined than Katie remembered. Yet it had only been a few weeks since Katie had gone away to train for a nurse.

'It's big,' said Katie. 'Very big. And I'm working on the women's gynae ward.'

'An' what's that when it's at home?'

'You know, Gran, women's troubles,' said Katie. 'Where they come with abortions and things wrong with the uterus – womb, that is.'

'That's enough of that sort of talk,' said Gran shortly but keeping her voice down. She nodded to where Noah was dipping bread into his bowl of broth and stuffing it into his mouth. He was pretending not to hear any of this women's talk.

'But Gran, you asked,' Katie protested.

'Aye well, mebbe I did. But it's not decent to talk about it in front of the men.' This last was said in a harsh whisper.

Katie bent her head to her plate. She tried to think of something else to talk about. 'Hey, Grandda, you know that chap we met years ago down on the wagon way near Eden Hope? The posh one? During the strike it was.'

Noah lifted his head now it was safe to join in the conversation. 'When we were after the pitch, do you mean?'

'Yes. Him. Well, I've seen him again. He must live near the hospital because he was in there. His wife an' all. He had a broken ankle and she—' Katie stopped before she said something indecent again. 'She had an operation,' she amended. 'He was in a private ward. Must have pots of money. Hamilton you call him.'

'Hamilton? Hamilton? Are you sure?'

'Yes, of course I am.'

'Why ye bugger!' Noah ejaculated. 'I thought there was something about that toff, I did.'

'Do you know who he is, like?' Kitty asked, curiosity lighting her face.

'Why aye, of course I do! Mind I never expected to see him round here and not walking along the wagon way neither.'

'Go on then, tell us,' said Kitty.

'Do you not know who the big boss is? The one who owns the pits and the ironworks and God knows what else?'

'Noah!' Kitty was becoming impatient with him.

'Hamilton! Hamilton Ironworks! You must have heard it woman, lest you go about with your eyes and ears shut.'

'Aye, yes, I have but I never thought it was a man,' said his wife.

Katie said nothing. Why hadn't she associated the name with the big boss?

Chapter Nine

Katie walked up the street to the Co-op store, Gran's shopping basket over her arm. 'I'll go for you, Gran,' she had said, glad of the excuse to get out into the fresh air and have a look round Winton at the same time. She smiled to herself, it felt as though she had been gone for ages but it was, after all, only a few weeks.

'Well, look who's back,' the girl standing by the counter with a clipboard in her hand said as Katie opened the door to the grocery department. There were only a few people in besides the two assistants but they all turned to look.

'Hallo June,' Katie said quietly as she took her place in the queue. It was Billy's sister who worked in the office at the store. When they had been at the Junior Elementary Katie and June had been great friends but June going off to grammar school had put a distance between them.

June smiled rather stiffly. 'What's it like in the big city then?' she asked. 'We didn't expect you to come back. Slumming, are you?' She smirked at the line of customers.

'Fine thank you,' Katie answered civilly though she had gone pink. 'I'm on my day off today.'

'Mind, you've done well, lass,' Dottie Dowson butted in and Katie smiled at her. 'You've worked hard to get there, I was just saying to our Jim. I hope you do well, pet.' There was a murmur of assent from the queue and it was June's turn to flush.

'Well, if you've come to see our Billy you've wasted your time. He's not coming home till the weekend.'

'No, I know, he told me,' said Katie and June's lips tightened. She turned on the counter assistant and snapped at her before flouncing up the stairs to the office.

'Get a move on, can't you? The line will be out of the door soon.'

The assistant pulled a face at June's disappearing back. 'She's not the boss, not by a long way,' she said, careful not to let her voice carry however.

'That one must be disappointed in love,' Dottie observed. 'It's a good job I can't afford to buy cream or her face would have soured it.' The women grinned.

When Katie came out of the shop she carried her basket of shopping along the top of the rows. It wasn't heavy; she swung it a little as she walked. Perhaps she would drop it in at home and walk on up the lane. It was a cold crispy day but the sun shone and up the lane she would get away from the all-pervasive smell of sulphur coming from the coke ovens. In the end she walked on, past the end of West Row, forgetting to drop off the basket. And there, just coming down from the bus stand, was Billy. Katie's heart lifted.

'Billy! I thought you weren't going to get here today. Your June said—'

'What does she know,' said Billy as he reached her and, after a quick glance round, kissed her on the lips. The touch of his lips was soft and gentle, his mouth closed. He smiled down at her, pleased because the pleasure of seeing him showed in her eyes.

'I was just going to walk up the lane to catch a bit of fresh air,' she said.

'Right. I'll come with you,' said Billy. He took her basket from her and they walked on up the rise, not touching, just side by side. Billy swung the basket a little and Katie grinned, imagining what some of his mates might say if they saw him. Dave Canvey for instance, Dave wouldn't be seen dead carrying a shopping basket.

Overhead the trees were bare and black against the pale, wintry blue of the sky, and when they reached the top of the bank and turned they could see the rows, wreathed in grey smoke and the older village of Winton, standing apart from the pit and all that belonged to it. The tower of the old parish church was not quite as tall as the chimney and winding gear at the pit or the slag heap by them. A wagon full of colliery waste went up the incline and tipped at the top. It looked like a child's toy from this distance. The pit hooter blew and Katie could just distinguish the winding wheel turning as the cage was brought to the surface. Behind the wheel and tall pit chimney the other side of the valley rose, brown and grey now and without the patches of green which showed in the summer.

They paused at a break in the hedge where a track led into a rabbit warren, the bunny banks as they had always called it. Up here there was a brick-built one-storey building which had once housed the engine which worked the overhead aerial flight; dragging corves of coal along a thick wire rope to the top of the bank where they could be dropped into wagons and run down the other side to the main railway to the coast. That had been years ago, nowadays the railway engines were of sufficient strength to carry the coal all the way themselves.

Katie shivered. The wind up here was so much stronger than down by the rows and the quality of her coat was poor. She'd bought it from the tally man before she had gone nursing.

'You should have got a club out at the store,' Gran had counselled but Katie didn't want any debt hanging over her when she started her new life.

Billy looked at her with concern. 'You're cold,' he said and drew her in the doorway of the building out of the wind. The door was ajar and Katie looked around curiously for she remembered it as always being locked up. Billy put his arm around her waist and drew her further in. It was strangely warm in there; leaves rustled on the floor, brown and sere. In the corner there was a coal sack – perhaps a tramp had taken shelter one night.

'Keep away from the middle,' advised Billy though how she could have gone anywhere without him she couldn't imagine, feeling his arm around her. It too was warm; he was wearing a good thick overcoat, dark blue and belted.

There was a square hole in the middle of the floor where the engine had been. There was nothing left now but a wire rope hanging from the overhead beam. The hole was about eight foot deep.

'Come here,' said Billy softly and leaned against the wall, drawing her to him. He opened his coat and enfolded her in it and it was warm and cosy and she leaned her head against his chest. She could feel his heart beating, strong and sure. Oh, Billy, she thought. I could just stay with you; forget about a career. When he kissed her his kisses became more demanding, her mouth opened to his and his tongue probed, sending hot shivers down her spine. His hand was inside her coat, feeling her breast through her jumper, then beneath it and touching her bare skin gently then more insistently and she felt her nipple harden in response.

Billy groaned, his knee was between hers and he was forcing hers apart. And with a last glimmer of rational thought she caught hold of his wrist; pressed back against the hard brick wall.

'Don't, Billy,' she said but softly.

'Why not? Oh, Katie—'

'No!' said Katie, louder now.

'But Katie, we're engaged, it'll be all right, really—'

'No!' Katie pushed him away.

Billy stood, breathing heavily now, his face flushed. He said nothing for a moment simply looked at her in anguish before seeming to take hold of himself and turning away. He stared into the corner where the brown leaves were rustling in the draught from the door; looked down the hole in the middle of the floor for a moment, blankly. Then he turned back to her.

'Sorry Katie,' he said. 'I shouldn't have tried to rush you.'

Katie felt awful. It was she who should be sorry she well knew. Either she wanted him or she didn't, wasn't that how it should go? And she did want him, her body cried out for him but it was the consequences she couldn't bear to think about. Supposing she had a child? Then all her plans, all she had worked for would be finished. She would be just another housewife, dependent on her man. She gazed at him and bit her lip. He looked strained, unhappy.

'I'm sorry, Billy,' she said. 'Oh, why can't I be like other girls?'

Billy smiled and took a step towards her. 'I don't want you to be like other girls, Katie. I love you as you are. Anyway, you're the one I want and I will wait if I have to. Don't worry about today, it was my fault.' He bent and kissed her lips again, chastely this time with his lips closed, a space between their bodies.

'Come on,' he bent and picked up the basket of groceries, 'we'd best get these back to your gran. She'll be fed up with waiting for them.' He paused and looked at her. 'You're still wearing my ring, aren't you? Even if it is on a chain round your neck.'

Katie fished inside the neckline of her jumper and brought out the ring. A shaft of light from the doorway caught one of the stones and it flashed brightly. 'Of course I do,' she said softly. 'I never take it off.'

Outside the wind had freshened; the short winter's day was already beginning to darken. She pulled up her collar, shivered, and Billy took off his scarf and wound it round her. It smelled of him, warm, masculines and with a hint of something else, bay rum was it?

He took her arm and drew her close to him and they set off down the bank towards the rows. A fine rain began to fall and they hurried on. A car came up: behind them with its lights already on and they lit up the first of the miners' rows and reflected on the slanting rain. It slowed for a moment and Katie looked at it, it seemed familiar somehow. And was that Mr Hamilton sitting in the back? No, of course it couldn't be, what would he be doing here on a night like this? Though it was a posh car and with a chauffeur.

'Where the heck have you been, Katie? There must have been some queue at the store the day.' Gran's words greeted her as she opened the back door. Billy had gone off to his parents' house, promising to call back for her at half past six.

'We'll go to the pictures. It's *The Singing Fool*,' he had said. 'You'd like to see it, wouldn't you?'

Katie had assured him she would. Now, she glanced at the clock on the mantelpiece and was shaken to see that it was already four o'clock.

'Sorry, Gran,' she said, looking contrite. 'I met Billy Wright and we went for a walk.'

'In this weather?' Kitty looked at Katie's flushed face and nodded her head. 'Ah well, there's no harm done. We can have a nice talk the night when we've had our teas.'

'I said I'd go to the pictures,' Katie admitted and her grandmother pursed her lips and spoke sharply.

'Oh well, that's all right. Just treat the place like a hotel, do.'

'Oh Gran, I'll tell him I can't go, I'm sorry, I never thought,' said Katie and Gran sighed.

'No, you go on, I'm all right,' she said. 'I want to listen to the play on the wireless any road.'

'Sure?' Katie looked doubtful but in the end she went off down the row to meet Billy. As she turned the corner she bumped into her father, striding along with his head bent against the wind, his hands deep in his pockets.

'Watch out, lass,' he said and stopped as he saw who it was. Tucker Benfield never said much to Katie on the occasions when they did happen to meet. To her he always seemed a silent sort of a man dominated by Hannah, his wife and Katie's mother. But now he gazed at her as though he were seeing her for the first time for years which wasn't strictly so. His mother and Hannah had always been at each other's throats and he liked a quiet life, which was why he usually had to sneak off if he wanted to see his parents. Which wasn't very often.

'Dad,' said Katie and she looked back at him. Tucker was like Noah to look at, she thought. But not at all like him in nature. If he had been he would have seen much more of her, she reckoned. Noah wouldn't have gone months without seeing his daughter, no, he would not. Thomas, the baby who supplanted her at home, had died at six months and Gran had said Hannah wanted Katie back and the two women had fought over her. For once Tucker had asserted his authority.

'Let the bairn bide where she is,' he had said and from then on there had been a coldness in the family. And Katie still didn't understand why she was the one who had been given away, as she called it. Even if it was to Gran and Grandda.

'Now then, Katie,' Tucker said now. 'I'm away to see me mother.'

'That'll be a surprise for her,' she answered. 'How long is it since the last time? Six months, is it?'

'Don't you be cheeky, lass,' he said but his face had reddened. 'Any road, I thought you were in Middlesbrough, learning to be a nurse.'

'I am. I'm on my day off.'

Tucker looked keenly at her. 'You seem well enough, like,' he said.

'I am. And the others, how are they doing?'

'All right, though your mother has a bad chest this cold weather.'

'Oh,' Katie replied. 'Sorry.' She waited but though he stood there he didn't say any more.

'Well, I have to go.'

'Be seeing you then.' Tucker turned and went off down the back street of West Row.

They talked to each other as though they were strangers, Katie thought, as she walked along the top of the rows to meet Billy. That's what they were, really, strangers. She forgot about her father as she and Billy walked to the Royal, the new picture house that had

opened at the other end of Winton. This was the first night
out she'd had for ages and she intended to enjoy it.

When the lights went down in the cinema and the
screen flickered and Al Jolson sang, it was warm and safe.
Safe because they were not sitting in the back row and
though Billy held her hand at first and then put his arm
around her shoulders, it was nice, unthreatening. And
afterwards they went to the fish shop and ate chips from
the bag as they strolled home.

'I'll be working at Winton from next week,' said Billy.
'Now I've finished my training I'm a fully qualified
surveyor and I could get an official's house with a bathroom and everything if I wanted to.' He glanced at Katie
to see her reaction. The future was good for him, couldn't
she see that? Why did she have to be so different from
other girls? Most of them would jump at the chance of
marrying a surveyor and living in a nice house. But he
was not surprised at her answer.

'I know, Billy,' she said. 'But in three years my training
will be finished too. I want to do it, Billy.'

Next day Katie was out for the eight o'clock bus to Bishop
Auckland. Though she had a half-day and didn't start on
the ward until one she had a lecture at eleven. As she
walked down Newgate Street it began to snow, big, soft
flakes that clung to the windows of the shops before
running down to melt on the pavement. Katie shivered in
her thin coat and pulled her hat further down on her head
and her scarf higher on her neck. It would be cold on the
bus. But the time would pass quickly. Her pages of notes

on the Theory of Nursing were in her bag and she had revising to do before she went into class.

The bus was not waiting in when she got to the market place as it usually was. There were a few people standing disconsolately at the bus stop, a few more huddled in the shop doorways as they tried to escape the snow. Katie stamped her feet, trying to bring life back to her toes. The cold struck through from the pavement, even though she wore rubber overshoes.

There were few people about apart from those waiting for buses; the sky was heavy over the town hall and the entrance to the bishop's castle on the opposite side of the market place. Katie waited and shivered. The town hall clock struck a quarter past the hour; she checked it with the clock over the castle gateway. It was indeed a quarter past the hour. It was too early to panic, she, told herself, and there was still plenty of time to get there. She wished she had taken the train, trains always ran. But the fares were so expensive compared to the bus . . .

Her thoughts were interrupted by the sound of a car hooter, piping away in the comparative quiet of the market place. She looked up, there was a large car standing just along from the bus stop; a familiar large car, the one she had seen yesterday. Mr Hamilton's car, she realised, as a man got out from behind the wheel and came over to her. The other people waiting for the bus looked at him curiously and then at Katie.

'Mr Hamilton says are you going back to the hospital? We can give you a lift.'

'No, I'll get the bus,' said Katie and the people looked at her as though she were mad.

'The bus may not come,' said Lawson. 'I heard the snow was heavier along by Darlington.' There was a chorus of groans from the people waiting.

Katie hesitated. She had to get to the lecture; it would be a bad mark against her if she did not so early in her training. Sister Tutor brooked no excuses, she knew that.

'Come on, lass, it's only a lift, it won't hurt you,' said Lawson. He glanced back at the figure in the back of the car. He didn't want to go back and admit he hadn't managed to persuade her.

Katie let out her breath. After all, what could happen in a car with a chauffeur sitting in front? And it was a lousy day and she was getting more and more wet and cold. She went with him.

'All right for some,' said a woman through the shawl that muffled her head. There was a murmur of agreement as the queue watched Katie enviously as Lawson held open the car door for her.

Chapter Ten

The interior of the car was warm and cosy with real leather seats and deep upholstery to sink into. Lawson closed the door after her and went round to the driver's seat. The car set off, gliding through the slush, down Newgate Street and out on to the Darlington road. Katie had murmured a thank you as she got into the car and Matthew had smiled and inclined his head but apart from that nothing was said until they were on the open road.

Katie began to relax. She might as well enjoy it, she told herself. Car rides were a luxury she didn't experience very often. And though the snow was beginning to lie out here in the country, it was not enough to cause a problem.

'You have been to see your family?'

He had been silent for so long that when he spoke Katie jumped.

'Yes,' she replied. 'At Winton Colliery,' she added. 'I'm grateful to you for giving me a ride, I have a lecture at eleven.'

'It's no trouble. I am visiting a friend in Bishop

Auckland and I have to go back to Middlesbrough anyway.'

'Well, thank you anyway, Mr Hamilton.' Katie had to stop herself from adding 'sir'. She glanced over at him; he was gazing at her, perhaps staring was the right word. She felt her cheeks redden; had she a smut on her nose? Did the scarf she had tied round her hat on the bus stand look common? She loosened it and laid it on her shoulders.

'It's warm in here,' she said.

'Not too warm, I hope?' He leaned forward as though to issue instructions to the chauffeur then sat back as she shook her head hurriedly.

'No, I like it.'

In fact her toes were at last beginning to thaw and she felt fine. Except that she would not be able to revise. She looked down at the bag containing her notes. Well, she would probably be at the hospital early enough to look them over.

'Your grandfather is Noah Benfield, isn't he? A good worker, according to Thompson.' He did not add that Thompson had also said, 'Though he takes Mondays off when he's on fore shift. But he works hard enough to make up for it during the rest of the week.'

'Yes.' Katie looked down at her hands. Had he been making inquiries about her? It sounded like it. 'How is Mrs Hamilton? Recovered, I hope?' The words sounded stilted in her own ears, what was she doing talking like that? But Matthew didn't want to talk about Mary Anne.

He nodded briefly, 'Quite well, thank you.'

The road was becoming a little bumpy and they could

feel the bumps even in this well-sprung Bentley. Outside the snow was falling faster. He saw her watching it anxiously.

'Don't worry we'll get there. It is not usually too bad nearer the coast,' he reassured her. The car lurched and Katie was thrown against him and he put out a hand to steady her, holding her arm. She looked down at his hand, it wasn't at all as she would have thought the hand of a gentleman to be. Though the nails were well shaped and manicured, there were calluses on the insides of his fingers and his palms as though he were used to working manually. She could feel the rough parts against the back of her hand. She looked at the hand and then up at his face. Matthew smiled and let go of her.

Katie looked out at the snow, feeling confused. It was all so unreal, especially after spending her day off at Winton Colliery. He was simply grateful to the nursing staff at the hospital, she told herself. Trying to pay something back. That was it.

They were through Darlington now and out on the road to Stockton. The snow was thicker and the car slid sideways but kept going.

'Lawson?'

'I'm sorry sir.'

He was very much the boss, Katie thought. Authority radiated from him. She wondered what her grandfather would think when she told him who had given her a lift. If she told him, that is. The car slid again and Katie gasped.

'Don't worry,' said Matthew. 'We won't turn over or

anything.' As if to prove him wrong, the car suddenly skidded into the side of the road, its nose deep in snow. 'Wait here, keep warm,' said Matthew. The two men got out, the chauffeur and the master surveying the situation. Then Lawson got a shovel from the boot and began shovelling snow away from the car. There was no other traffic on the road at all. They've got more sense, Katie told herself.

The front of the car was free now and Lawson got back in his seat and tried the engine. It started all right but the wheels whirred and stuck. Surprising Katie, it was Mr Hamilton who bent his shoulder to the car and pushed, and after a moment or two, succeeded in getting the car back on the road. He straightened and brushed off his coat and stamped the snow from his shoes before getting back in the car.

'We'll be in Stockton shortly and the snow will be wetter there,' he said as though continuing the previous conversation but he was panting a little.

Katie had had visions of them being marooned in the snowdrift miles from anywhere, just her and the two men; now she told herself not to be so silly. For sure enough within a minute or two they were entering Stockton-on-Tees and the road was practically bare.

It was ten past eleven when they drew up before the main gates of the hospital. The porter on duty peered out from the lodge, watching as the first-year probationer got out of the Bentley. His face was expressionless but even so Katie could imagine what he was thinking and went pink.

'We should go somewhere for a hot drink,' said Matthew. He was reluctant to let her go, like a young boy on his first date, he chided himself.

'No. Oh, I'm sorry but I have to get to my class,' Katie apologised for her abrupt reply. She began edging away.

'But surely you're too late for it now. You need something hot, it was a bad journey.'

'No, really, I'm fine. It wasn't cold in the car. Goodbye, Mr Hamilton. I'm really grateful for the lift. Really.'

'I'll be in touch,' said Matthew, admitting defeat and Katie sped away to change for her class. The paths around the hospital were clear of snow and it didn't take long for Katie to change into her uniform and, with her cloak wrapped around her, make her way to the Nursing School.

'Heat the upper half of the urine until it boils,' Sister Tutor was saying but she paused in her demonstration of how to test a specimen of urine and glared at Katie. 'You're late,' she said. 'Very late.'

'I'm sorry, Sister,' said Katie. 'It was the snow, I had to get in from Winton—'

'Please!' said Sister. 'I want no excuses. What good are excuses if you can't get to a patient in time? But perhaps you've already studied the subject? Come here and demonstrate to the class how to test a specimen of urine. From the beginning if you please.'

Katie picked up the holder with the test tube of urine and stared at it. She had done this, she had.

'Well?'

'First note the colour,' said Katie. 'Second take the

specific gravity.' She paused, seeing the page in her text book in her mind's eye. What came next?

'I'm waiting, Nurse Benfield.'

'Note the reaction. Blue litmus turns red—' Thank goodness it came back to her.

'Very well. You may sit down. Now as I was saying when I was interrupted—'

Was Mr Hamilton interested in her? Katie asked herself uneasily as she went back to her room to get ready for dinner and going on duty at one. No, not as a man was interested in a woman, he couldn't be, he was too old; he must be in his thirties or even forties. It was just coincidence that they had bumped into each other a few times and he remembered her. He was just being kind; he was a kind man. Though that was not how the miners thought of him, or the ironworkers either, at least not the ones who came into F Ward to see their wives. Some of them had seen him going into the side ward, talking loudly to the doctors as though he was their gaffer.

'Mean old bugger, tight as a drum,' was what one puddler had said of him and the man at the next bed had nodded his head in agreement. 'Wouldn't give a starving bairn the skin off his rice pudding.'

There was something about him though, thought Katie. He must have been good-looking when he was younger. Anyway, he was a married man and his wife was a nice woman, she was imagining things. And, she reminded herself, she had Billy and she loved him. She fingered Billy's ring beneath the starched linen of her uniform dress. It always gave her a warm feeling to touch it. Her future was planned; she would marry Billy. In a few years time when she was ready.

'The works, Lawson, if you please.'

'Yes, sir.'

Lawson sighed as the car pulled away from the hospital entrance. He had thought the boss would want to go home since he had been away twenty-four hours already but no, the damn man was like a robot, he just went on and on tirelessly. It had been freezing cold waiting in the pit yard at Winton half the night before finally being offered a bed at the manager's house. He was resentful of that too, the bed he had been offered was in the attic, partitioned off from the maid's room. He had barely warmed up before the boss was shouting for him and he had got up and shrugged into his damp uniform and gone out into a snow storm. And now it looked as though he wasn't even to get a break before lunch. Why the boss had spent so much time at the colliery he didn't know and didn't want to know. His job was simply to carry him around.

Matthew sat back in his seat and went over in his mind the happenings of the previous evening. He smiled slightly with some satisfaction as he remembered Thompson's surprise when he turned up at the pit-head offices and without Parsons, his agent. It seemed to him that Parsons had been too easily swayed by the manager, after all, it was his job to make sure the pit was economic, apart from supplying the ironworks' fuel. Not that the ironworks was going full blast in these depressed times but Eden Hope was lying idle again and it would be too much a strain on the resources to open it again unless the order book expanded a great deal more. No, it was better to run Winton to capacity. And he was not going to allow Thompson to close down a face in order to install new safety equipment, not yet. Next year perhaps, when the order book was full, he would consider it. Now there was time to make up, not to mention income. Parsons could be a proper old woman at times and besides, he was becoming too friendly by far with Thompson.

Was Parsons getting too old for the agent's job? He would have to look into it, Matthew decided. But they were turning in through the gates of the ironworks; he had an orderly mind, compartmented, and mentally he closed the compartment concerning the mines, just as earlier he had closed the one concerning the girl. Now it was time to consider the problems of the works.

'Put the car away, Lawson, said Matthew. 'You can have the rest of the evening off, I won't be going out again tonight.' As it was eight o'clock in the evening by the time they had arrived home Lawson's 'Yes sir, thank you, sir,' was slightly ironic though Matthew didn't notice. He got out of the car, opened the door for his employer and then got back in and drove round to the back of the house to what had once been the stables and was now a roomy garage.

His flat was above and there was a light shining from the window. Lawson smiled. She was here then. Forgetting his weariness he ran up the stone steps and into the warm room. Catching hold of Daisy he swung her off her feet and kissed her soundly on the lips. She felt warm and soft and smelled of warm pastry and rich meat.

'I brought your supper over,' she whispered in his ear. 'Put me down, do and I'll fetch it. I've kept it nice and hot.'

'I hope that's not the only thing you've kept hot,' he said and she blushed and giggled.

'Give over now, Eddie Lawson!'

'You don't really want me to, do you?'

He carried her to the old settee she had drawn up before the fire. The feel of her breasts against him had warmed him considerably.

'Cook will be looking for me,' she protested feebly.

'Well, this won't take long,' he replied and laid her down on the settee.

In the house, Matthew handed his coat and hat to John, his manservant. The hall was a little chilly as was the drawing-room when he walked in to greet Mary Anne. The room was much too big for the one fireplace, big though it was, he thought irritably. He would have to think about having radiators installed before next winter. After all, they were almost a third of the way into the twentieth century now.

'Matthew, you're back,' said Mary Anne and he felt a twinge of his usual annoyance at her habit of stating the obvious. She looked pale and even more colourless than usual and her hair looked lifeless. He walked over to her and kissed her forehead dutifully and was irritated anew as he felt her slight and quickly suppressed withdrawal.

He gave her no reason for his absence of the night before, he didn't even think of it.

'For goodness sake, get John to bring in more logs and fill the coal scuttle,' he said. 'It's bloody cold in here.'

Mary Anne winced at the swear word and wished she had the courage to reprove him as her mother would most certainly have done. But she had not.

'Sorry, dear,' she said and pulled the bell rope to summon the servant. She sat down and made an effort to show an interest in his work. After all, it seemed to be the major part of his life, meaning more to him than his family. Not like Robert – no she wasn't going to think of Robert. On the odd occasions when she had mentioned him to her second husband, Matthew had accused her of being morbid.

It wasn't true really. Thinking of Robert made her heart lighten and lift, not fall into the desperate melancholy she so often felt these days. Young Robert was like his father too, in temperament at least. She thanked God for it. Mary Anne made an effort to concentrate on Matthew.

'How was your day, dear?' she asked. 'Is everything all right at the works?'

Matthew stared at her in surprise. Mary Anne had never shown the slightest bit of interest in his work before now. And what could he say, anyway? Nothing that she could comprehend, she knew not a thing about any of it in spite of being married to two ironmasters.

'Mmmh,' he grunted in reply. Sitting down he picked up the evening paper. Hitler and his gang of posturing fascists were marching in Munich, looking for trouble. At home yet another shipyard had closed down on the Tyne. He threw the paper down on the occasional table beside him. 'I'm going into my study for a while,' he informed Mary Anne. I'll have my dinner in there. I don't want to be disturbed so make sure the children are kept quiet.'

Mary Anne stared at the door after he had gone, rebellion bubbling in her. She had never let the children disturb him, ever. The fact was he couldn't bear to see them; he would have liked to banish them from the house if he could. Maybe if they had one of their own it would be different. But then Robert and Maisie would really have their noses pushed out.

Chapter Eleven

The sun shone in through the high windows of the ward, the rays picking out hidden corners and causing dust motes to hover in the air. The women in the beds, those who were on the mend from acute surgery or even those older ones with chronic conditions were feeling bright and cheerful and basking in the warmth of the early spring. They chatted and laughed and pestered Mr Caine with demands to go home whenever they saw him. Yet it was still only early March, Katie reflected as she handed out bedpans from the trolley, then took them back to the sluice and emptied them and scrubbed them clean and put them on the racks along the walls.

'We will start extra cleaning today,' Sister had announced when the day nurses were gathered in the office to hear the night nurses' report. 'So all your normal duties will be finished by ten o'clock. Mr Hobson won't be doing any rounds this morning; he has an outpatient clinic so he won't be here until late this afternoon or maybe not at all. We have no acute patients at the moment. So come on staff. Let's go to it. Cleanliness is the only way to keep bacteria at bay.'

The nurses looked at each other as they filed out of the office. Their mornings were frantically busy on a normal day so how they were supposed to do extra cleaning, Katie had no idea.

Yet somehow, they managed it. At ten the beds were all pulled into the middle of the ward, the orderly was up a ladder washing the upper half of the dull khaki-coloured paintwork and the ward maid leaning over precariously on another as she washed the high windows. And Katie and the other probationers were washing the lower half of the walls or the floors or the bedsteads.

At twelve there was a short break while the patients were given their dinner though how they could eat it with the heavy smell of carbolic overhanging everything and getting up the nose and hitting the back of the throat, Katie couldn't imagine.

The women, however, were full of interest, they watched in comparative ease as the staff toiled, pointing out any spot they thought had been missed.

'There's a piece of fluff on that bed wheel, Nurse,' Doris Teasdale advised Katie as she stood up after wiping the legs of a bed with disinfectant she had made up herself in the prescribed manner, one part Phenol to twenty parts water. Katie sighed and bent down to look; there was indeed a minuscule piece of fluff on the bottom right-hand wheel of the bed. Though how Doris could have seen it she couldn't think, it being on the opposite side of the ward.

'I thought I'd just tell you,' said Doris, catching Katie's eye as she frowned at her. 'You wouldn't have liked Sister to find it, would you?'

'No. Thank you Mrs Teasdale,' said Katie as she removed the offending fluff. She glanced at the ward clock. Only two o'clock, the afternoon was dragging. She was warm and sweaty from the hard work. Though the sun had moved away from the windows the heat still lingered and, it being still considered to be winter, the porters had built up the fires in the central stoves. Katie moved on to the next bed. Only three more to go and then she was finished. Of course the beds were to be put back against the walls and the floor was to be polished and buffed up until the shine, removed by the disinfectant wash, returned. Katie sighed.

She lifted her bucket and went off to the sluice to empty and refill it. She measured out the Phenol carefully and added the hot water. While it was running she gazed ruefully at her hands, red and puffy from being immersed in the solution for most of the day. They were also numb; she remembered the lecture in which Sister Tutor had told them carbolic could have a slight analgesic effect. Tonight she would rub them with olive oil and sugar, her grandmother's remedy rather than the lanolin offered by the hospital.

'Don't stand there dreaming, Nurse!'

The voice from the doorway made her start. She hurriedly turned off the tap before the water reached the level prescribed and turned to face the voice of authority.

'You are very untidy, Nurse, your hair is coming down

out of your cap. Go and see to it at once,' said Matron. She advanced into the sluice and looked around critically. The enamel bedpans in their rows gleamed and the wooden benches were scrubbed and bare. Matron, however, did not look pleased or even satisfied. She looked at the rubber apron, which Katie wore over her uniform; the way her sleeves were rolled up above her elbows and the roll covered with white elastic cuffs and sniffed.

'Go and tidy yourself, Nurse,' she repeated and swept out into the ward.

Katie, in the little room with row of cloaks hanging along one wall, stood by the mirror on the opposite wall and took off her cap. She combed her hair up and twisted it into a roll and pinned it securely with hairgrips and replaced her cap. Then she sighed and looked at her reflection, taking a few seconds for herself. Her cap was a bit too big for her face, she thought, it did nothing for her looks at all. Her face was pale and there were shadows under her eyes, dear God, she was tired.

Outside she could hear Matron talking, her voice loud and commanding. Sister was answering, sounding so different from when she was talking to her nurses. Chain of command thought Katie and smiled at herself in the mirror. She wouldn't always be on the lowest rung. One day, she would be at the top. Squaring her shoulders she went out to the sluice and picked up her bucket.

'Mrs Jones needs a bedpan, Nurse,' said Sister as the main door of the ward closed after Matron. 'What do you think you're doing, wasting your time in the cloakroom?'

'Yes, Sister,' Katie mumbled and put down the bucket

and brought a bedpan, suitably covered with a lavatory cloth. In the ward the sun had disappeared and the sky through the newly shined windows was grey and menacing. Suddenly they were glad of the heat from the stoves and Doris Teasdale was calling for a hot-water bottle. By four o'clock the ward was restored to a gleaming, pristine condition and waiting for Mr Hobson to fling open the door and sweep in, followed by Mr Caine and the houseman.

At six o'clock, wrapped round with her thick cloak, Katie walked around the building before going inside for supper. She was happy, because tomorrow was her day off and tonight was her evening off and Billy was coming to see her. Not that they were doing anything in particular, just going to the second house at the pictures which she would probably have to leave before the end to get back into the Nurses' Home before curfew. But her heart lifted at the thought of seeing Billy. He was so good, coming all this way after his own day at work.

Billy was a fully fledged surveyor now, a figure to be looked up to in Winton Colliery, an official. He was talking of getting a car and not a second-hand one either but a new car, a Standard Big 9. 'Then I'll be able to pop over to see you often,' he had said. 'Would you like that?'

Katie had looked at him; he had a quizzical expression, almost, as though he wasn't sure if she would like it or not.

'Of course,' she had replied. 'You know I will. But . . . you know I don't have that much free time, Billy. And it's a long way just for an hour or so.'

'Maybe I'll be able to transfer to a mine closer to the hospital,' said Billy. 'Next year, perhaps.'

'That would be lovely, Billy,' Katie had replied.

Tonight he was staying at his aunt's house; tomorrow they were going to travel back to Winton together. Oh, it was grand, a whole twenty-four hours away from the hospital. And then, next week, she was starting on A Ward, which was men's surgical. That would be something new again.

Billy did not come. Katie waited by the telephone in the entrance for his call; he had said he would ring her; for her not to wait about outside in the cold. She went out to the front of the Nurses' Home and peered down the drive but there was no sign of him. She put on her coat and hat and wound her scarf around her neck for this evening, after the spring sunshine, there was a ground frost and the cold air was sharp and penetrating. She walked down the drive and said 'Good evening,' to the porter and he watched her go out of the gates and look up and down the road. She walked up and down a few times and then came back into the grounds and went past the porter and back into the Nurses' Home.

Katie hesitated in the hall of the Home and gazed at the telephone in the corner, partitioned off by a dark brown box with glass in the top and a brass handle on the door. She counted the twists in the cord that hung from the receiver to the handset, willing it to ring. She had a dread rising in her and it was silly, she told herself. What had she to dread? Billy had missed the bus that was all, he would be here soon. She looked at the clock on the wall, it was half past seven, and the next bus would be in soon. Then he just had to get out from the bus stop on Borough Road, that would take fifteen minutes.

The thing to do was go into the nurses' sitting-room and sit down in a comfortable chair, maybe read a magazine. She could hear the telephone from there couldn't she?

There was only one person in the sitting-room, a second-year nurse listening to a broadcast by the BBC. The ether crackled and hummed and the nurse fiddled with the knobs, trying to get decent reception. She looked up as Katie went in.

'You'd think you'd be able to hear this modern set better than the old one, wouldn't you,' she said. 'I particularly wanted to hear this programme, it's a concert from the Albert Hall.'

Suddenly the crackling subsided and a man's voice was heard.

'. . . death toll would have been more but it was the end of a shift and most of the men were on their way out of the mine. Consequently, there were only twelve miners killed in the explosion, which was confined to one face. We return you now to the concert . . .'

'What was that? What was it?' Katie demanded of the girl by the wireless. A Strauss waltz filled the room, the music light and lilting.

'What?' the girl looked irritated as she looked up but then she saw Katie's face. 'Hadn't you heard? There's been an accident at a colliery near Bishop

121

Auckland. Wilton, was it? No, of course not, Witton? No—'

Katie was no longer listening, she had run out into the hall. But then she didn't know what to do. How could she find out? She looked at the telephone but the only telephone she was aware of in Winton was the Post Office one and the Post Office would be closed. Though of course, there were the pit offices. She went into the dark wooden box and lifted the handset, getting close into the mouthpiece on the wall to make herself heard. The front door banged behind her and two nurses walked past, laughing and talking and she glared at them. But the operator was answering.

'I'm sorry caller, the line is engaged.'

Katie hung up the telephone and stared at it, trying to think. It might not be Winton, she might be imagining things. But why was Billy not here as he had said he would be? She tried again.

'Get me the number of Winton Colliery office please.'

And after a moment or two, the operator's voice told her again that the line was engaged.

'Can you get me Mr Matthew Hamilton, please?'

'What address is that, caller?'

Katie thought hard, the address of Mrs Hamilton had been on her notes, she had looked at it in curiosity really. Where was it? 'Hamilton Hall, North York,' she said hesitantly.

'There's a Hamilton Hall, Guisborough?'

'Yes, that's it.'

'Please insert tuppence, caller.'

Katie fumbled in her purse and found the coins and put them in the box.

As the telephone rang out Katie had a moment of panic and was about to put it down but it was too late, it was answered.

'Hamilton Hall,' a man's voice said and she pressed button A.

'Can I speak to Mr Hamilton?'

'Who wishes to speak to him?'

'Just tell him – never mind, he won't know my name,' said Katie. He probably wouldn't speak to her now. 'Tell him it's Nurse Benfield,' she said, 'I nurse at South-East Durham General.'

'One moment, please.'

A minute or two later she heard Matthew's voice on the other end of the line. He would help, she was sure he would.

'Mr Hamilton? It's me, Katie Benfield. I'm sorry to disturb you but I thought you might have heard something. I know I've no right to disturb you. I'm sorry . . .' (Oh, pull yourself together, she told herself. Stop apologising.)

'Nurse Benfield. You've heard then,' said Matthew. The message had been waiting for him when he came into the house at six; he had been out of touch before that.

'I have the situation in hand, Mr Hamilton,' Parsons had said when he phoned. 'Don't worry; the damage is limited to the one face. It was probably the miners taking risks anyway. We may even find one of the young boys took in cigarettes and matches. I will keep you informed.'

The conversation ran through his mind as he listened to Katie's halting voice on the line. But he couldn't tell her anything; he wouldn't get the list of dead and injured until tomorrow. When Parsons phoned in again. He had been looking forward to dinner and an evening spent before the fire in his study but he forgot about that.

'Mr Hamilton? Are you there?'

'Yes. Yes, I'm here, Nurse Benfield. There has been an accident, it's true. I'm trying to get hold of the casualty list. Look, give me the number of the telephone you are using and I will ring back in ten minutes. Can you do that?'

'Yes. Oh, thank you, Mr Hamilton,' Katie was filled with gratitude for his concern. She put the telephone back in its cradle and went out of the box to stand close by. Music from the wireless filtered through the door from the sitting-room. Outside, white frost glistened in the light that shone on the tarmac from the glass inlet in the door. She watched it unseeingly, her mind concentrated on listening for the telephone.

A staff nurse came and went into the box and picked up the telephone, asked for a number. Katie watched in agony, terrified he would ring back and find the number engaged and not bother any more. But the staff nurse came out of the box and went into the sitting-room.

Matthew had lost no time in calling the colliery office at Winton. This was his chance to put himself in a good light with Katie Benfield and he wasn't going to miss it. That would be where Parsons was he was sure. The agent would be engaged in preparing a statement for release to the papers, trying already to show that the management was not to blame for the accident. Yes, he would be there with Thompson.

'Thompson? Is that you, man? Parsons there, is he? Well, put him on, man and be quick about it. Parsons? You have the casualty list then? Is it complete?'

'I do,' said Parsons, swiftly recovering from his surprise in hearing the ironmaster's voice. 'And I have to report that preliminary inquiries suggest that the accident was the fault of the men, bypassing safety precautions—'

'Never mind that now,' said Matthew. 'Just give me the names, will you?' He tapped his fingers on the table impatiently.

Noah Benfield was halfway down the list of names, just before those of David Canvey and James Dowson. '. . . and there is one official, a young surveyor. William Wright.'

'Very well. Stay there, I am coming over. I'll be there in a couple of hours.'

'You're coming over, sir?'

'That's what I said, didn't I?'

Matthew rattled the receiver rest to get the attention of the operator. 'Hartburn 40,' he said when she answered.

Katie wrenched open the door of the box and picked up the telephone with trembling fingers. 'Yes? Mr Hamilton?'

'I'm afraid I have bad news, dear,' he said.

'Oh!' Katie didn't know what to say or think, there was a crashing and banging in her head and for a minute her sight dimmed to almost black. In the distance she heard his voice, the name of her grandfather.

'Katie! Nurse Benfield! Listen, do as I say. Go to the office; tell whoever is in charge what has happened. No, don't. I will call the office. You go to your room and wait. I will come for you and take you back to Winton. I . . . I have to go there in any case. Are you listening, Nurse Benfield? Will you do that?'

'Yes,' Katie managed to say before dropping the telephone and stumbling up the stairs to her room. She sat on the bed and waited obediently. After a while there was a knock on the door and she jumped up to open it, ready to rush out there and then and go with him to Winton. But it was not Mr Hamilton, it was Home Sister.

'I've heard what happened, Nurse,' she said. 'Are you all right?'

She handed Katie a cup of tea and Katie took it and drank it obediently though it was sickly sweet with added sugar. But she heard nothing of what Sister was saying; all her attention was taken up with listening for Mr Hamilton coming to take her home. And then, at last, she heard his footsteps coming along the corridor.

Chapter Twelve

Lawson had not been very happy about being ordered out on a cold dark night when he had already done a full day's driving. He was looking forward to sitting in front of the fire, listening to the wireless and waiting for Daisy to sneak out and up the stone steps to his rooms above the stable. It was cosy there and he stretched his legs out to the blaze and loosened his belt a notch after the supper Cook had sent over for him. It wasn't a bad life, he told himself. Though he had dreams of one day buying his own lorry and starting to work for himself. There was work to be had all right, he knew that. There were one or two owner drivers got in at the Cleveland Arms and he knew what they could make for themselves, hauling goods around the place and even further afield. Of course he would have to find his own accommodation.

Lawson's plans for the future were interrupted by a soft knock on the door and Daisy came in. Blimey, she was early tonight. He sat up and turned to her.

'Howay, lass,' he said and held out his arms.

'No time for that Eddie,' said Daisy. 'You're wanted. There's been an accident or something, his nibs is going over to Bishop Auckland.'

'Bloody hell,' Lawson swore. 'Just when I've got settled in. By, when I'm my own boss no one will call me out on a cold night, I tell you that.'

'Oh aye?' said Daisy. 'That'll be the day.' She grinned.

'Aye well, you need laugh but the day will come,' said Lawson. Reluctantly he got to his feet and fastened his uniform. Before putting on his cap he caught hold of Daisy and kissed her, one hand on her breast and the other holding her bottom. Groaning he let her go and went out to the car.

His employer was already coming out of the front door, tripping down the steps as though it was the beginning of the day not the end, Lawson thought sourly.

'We're going to the hospital first,' said Matthew. 'Hurry up, we have to go to Winton.'

Well, Lawson thought, that told him which hospital at any rate. He was shivering in the night air so was glad when the car began to warm up. He was not overly surprised when they arrived at the hospital and his employer rushed inside, coming out with that young girl. He reckoned the old man was going soft in the head but it was none of his business. He jumped out to open the back door for them then got back in himself.

'Winton?' he asked.

'Yes man, I told you. Winton Colliery to be exact, haven't you listened to the news on the wireless tonight?'

Oh yes, there'd been an accident, some miners killed.

Lawson could vaguely remember hearing something about it. But accidents at the pits were commonplace, it wasn't exactly on the lines of a major disaster. And even if it had been, the boss didn't normally rush to the scene. No, it was the girl. Lawson grinned to himself as he pulled away from the kerb and turned the corner out on tb Durham Road.

Behind him, Matthew Hamilton and Katie were barely aware of his presence. Matthew sat with a fatherly arm around her shoulders and with his other hand held hers. He said little but in the light of the streetlamps she could see the sympathy in his eyes. She did not question the way he had come so quickly, she thought he had to go to the colliery. He was the owner, wasn't he? So he must have things to see to. It didn't occur to her that his position at the top of the business empire meant this was not a thing he would normally do.

Katie felt numb, she hardly felt the weight of his arm on her shoulders or the occasional squeeze he gave her hand. Her grandda was dead in the pit. No, he couldn't be, it was a mistake, they had mixed him up with some other miner. Noah Benfield had worked a lifetime in the pit, he was too wise in the way of it to get caught. He used to say how you could hear the coal face working by tapping on the coal seam, 'Jowl, jowl and listen lad and hear the coal face working . . .' The old mining rhyme ran through her head. 'There's many a marra missing lad—' No she wasn't going to think of that any more.

'How do you feel?' asked Matthew.

How was she supposed to feel? she wondered. She

didn't know how she felt. She didn't believe her grandfather was dead, killed in the pit. Killed in the pit. The
phrase ran through her head, she couldn't stop it. She felt
it was being drilled into her skull. And in the back of her
mind there was another dread. What about Billy? But
she refused to believe Billy was probably dead too. She
should ask Mr Hamilton. But she dare not. Oh no, she
dare not.

'All right,' she said. 'Thank you.'

She stared out of the window at the lights of Darlington
as they sped through the town. The High Row was lit up
and people were walking about as though nothing had
happened. How could that be? Then they were out in the
country again, heading for South-West Durham.

There were lights in the pit yard when they got there.
The winding wheel whirred as the cage was brought to
the surface. A small crowd of people, women and
officials, pressed forward eagerly to see who or what was
coming to the surface. Katie stood up and was out of the
car before Lawson could open the door for her.

'Wait,' said Matthew and caught hold of her arm and
the women turned back from the entrance to the shaft and
looked at the posh car suddenly in their midst. One
stepped forward.

'Katie,' said Dottie Dowson and Katie shrugged off
Matthew's hand and ran to her. 'What am I going to do
without him?' Dottie asked her. But Katie had no answer,
just a hug of fellow feeling.

'Where's my gran?' she asked the woman who had
been their neighbour all Katie's life.

'They took her home. They've got Noah's body up, there's only the injured now. They're laid out in the lamp cabin.' She broke off as the crowd parted and the stretcher men came through with a man writhing under a blanket.

'Come away, Lawson will take you home.'

Katie looked up at Matthew Hamilton, the man who had brought her over from the coast in his car. It was like looking at someone from another planet, he looked so strange and out of place in his Crombie overcoat and his homburg hat. The pit folk were staring at him. But still she didn't ask him about Billy.

'I'll go home with Dottie,' said Katie. 'Thank you, very much for your help. Come on Dottie, you should be home now. There's nothing you can do tonight. Tomorrow maybe.'

Matthew watched as the two women went out of the pit yard in the direction of the miners' rows. A voice was raised among the people waiting by the pit head.

'What about the safety work that needed doing, eh gaffer?'

Matthew turned to the man who had shouted but he wasn't looking at him but at the door of the office. Thompson had opened it and was coming across. There was a murmuring in the crowd.

'Come in, Mr Hamilton, sir,' said Thompson. 'Mr Parsons is already here.'

The crowd hadn't even realised who he was, Matthew thought. He followed the manager into the office and Thompson closed the door on the yard. 'A bit nippy tonight,' he commented and the comment sounded ludicrous in the pit yard, that someone should actually be noticing the weather.

Kitty Benfield was sitting quietly by the fire when Katie opened the back door and went into the kitchen. The shock had diminished her somehow and she looked older, her hair more white than grey, her cheeks white and sunken. The sight of her was enough to break Katie's heart, bringing home to her finally that it was true, her grandfather had been killed.

'He's gone, lass,' said Kitty and held out her arms and Katie flung herself into them. Her grandmother looked down at her and stroked her hair. 'It's no good taking on, Katie, all the wailing in the world won't bring him back.' She took hold of Katie by the upper arms and held her and looked into her eyes. 'I'm sorry about Billy an' all, lass,' she said. 'He was a canny lad.'

The ensuing days were like a nightmare for the girl. She had a few days' compassionate leave from the hospital and the way she felt it didn't matter whether she had or not, she couldn't leave her grandmother. For there was another blow, Tucker, Kitty's son and Katie's father, had been injured and was in the County Hospital in Durham. Betty came round the very next morning to borrow the fare for her and her mother to go to see him. And Kitty did not say a word about Hannah not having a penny saved for emergencies but handed Betty a pound note from the Rington's tea tin which she kept on the corner of the mantelpiece.

'I'll come with you,' said Katie.

'No, I don't think so,' said Betty. 'I think he'll just want to see us just now.'

'I'm his daughter too,' said Katie and Betty gave her a funny look.

'Well, it's me and me mam he'll want to see,' her sister answered.

Katie forced her eyes open and uncurled from the foetal position she had been in all night in an effort to preserve body warmth. A faint light penetrated the thin cotton curtains so it was morning at least. The night had been icy cold. Stretching her legs out her feet landed on the oven shelf near the bottom of the bed. Her grandma had put it in the bed last night and then it had been lovely and warm but within an hour it was cold, bitter January weather. Katie shivered, her nose, stuck outside the bedclothes, felt numb.

Steeling herself, Katie pushed back the blanket and old coat and the new proddy mat that Gran had worked over every night for weeks ready to lay it down before the kitchen fire on Christmas Eve. Usually it kept out the worst of the cold but now the house hadn't been warmed by the fire in the range because there was no coal in the coal house to light a fire. And, as the miners had been forbidden to pick at the slag heap for bits thrown out with the waste slag and stone, the house just got colder and colder.

Katie jumped out of bed and pulled on her clothes, shivering violently. She thrust her feet into her shoes, no socks, as they had finally fallen to bits. More darns than sock they had been and now even the darns had disintegrated.

Downstairs, to her surprise there was a bit of fire in the grate and Gran was sitting over it, drinking tea from a pint pot. Even as Katie reached the ranges the fire collapsed in on itself and fell with a shower of sparks, dying in the ash can beneath. It had only been paper and a few twigs, how Gran had managed to boil a kettle was a mystery. But looking closely, Katie was horrified to see a hard, brown bookback, charred and almost gone.

'Gran! That wasn't my library book!'

'Eeh, lass, I was desperate,' said Gran, guilt making her cheeks red and mottled.

'But I'll have to pay for it,' wailed Katie. 'Where will I get the money?'

'Aw, don't be so soft,' said Gran, guilt making her angry now. 'How can they make you pay for it when you've got nowt? Nay man, they cannot make you pay.'

Katie didn't reply, what was the use? She sat down heavily on one of the hard wooden chairs by the table, close to tears.

'There's a drop of tea in the pot,' Gran said, coaxing.

'Bloody hell, this place is enough to freeze the balls off a brass—' Noah had come down the stairs, trousers at half-mast, braces hanging down. His collarless shirt was unbuttoned at the neck, the sleeves rolled up above the elbows. His feet were bare and white, the toes gleaming blue. He rubbed his hands together as he strode over to the range and stared disconsolately at the by now non-existent fire.

'Hey!' said Gran. 'Watch your language. I'll have no swearing inhere.'

Katie woke up with a start. She had been dreaming of her childhood, she realised. Well, if only Noah had still been here, he could swear as much as he liked, she thought. Even Gran would not object. But he wasn't here, and neither was Billy. She felt so full of pain she couldn't bear it. Wearily she got out of bed though she felt as though she never wanted to get up again. If only she could just burrow here, under the bedclothes and never come out. But downstairs she could hear the muffled sounds of her gran moving about: filling the kettle, settling it on the fire. Gran coughed a harsh, hollow sound. Gran needed her, she had to go downstairs and help her gran.

Chapter Thirteen

'Oh, it's you,' said June. She stood for a moment in the doorway before reluctantly standing back to allow Katie to go into the house. Billy's father and mother were sitting on either side of the fireplace. The curtains were drawn, denoting a death in the house and as a mark of respect and the gas mantle was burning, giving off a dim yellow light. The door was open to the front room and the middle of the floor had been cleared of furniture so that the coffin could stand there on its trestles.

The bodies were coming home today, the post-mortems were finished. The men had died from fractured skulls or crushed chests and most had suffered burns. Katie averted her eyes from the doorway of the waiting room.

'I'm very sorry, Mrs Wright, Mr Wright,' she said. The lump in her throat, which made it so hard to swallow, grew larger. She clasped her hands tightly, digging the nails into her palms.

'Aye lass,' said Mr Wright. 'I know you and Billy were fond of each other. I'm sorry for you an' all.' Mrs Wright held a hankie to her nose and stared at the drawn curtains, She sniffed.

'June will make you a cup of tea, Katie,' she said. 'Sit down lass.' June thrust the kettle on to the fire, looking very angry. Or was she simply grieving her brother? Katie couldn't tell. She sat down on the horsehair chaise-longue, which was at right angles to the fireplace.

'Billy and me—' Katie stopped as tears threatened then started again. 'Me and Billy were going to get married when I'd finished my training,' she said. She could feel the ring lying on her breastbone, could almost have drawn the circle of it against her skin.

June made a noise, choked off, derisory. She took down the tea caddy from the mantelpiece and spooned tea into a brown pot; poured boiling water on the leaves.

'What did you say, pet?' Mrs Wright asked.

'Nothing. But I was thinking, I can't help it, Mam, I was thinking that if Katie had really wanted to marry our Billy she wouldn't have put him off all the time, would she?' She poured tea into a fine china cup from the set kept for visitors and handed it to Katie, slopping a drop in the saucer as she did so. Katie kept her eyes on the cup. She pressed a finger hard against her upper lip to hold back the tears. She couldn't speak to defend herself.

'Now then, June, I'll have none of that sort of talk,' said Mr Wright. 'Our Billy will be coming home in an hour or so and we will show respect.'

'Why but, Dad—'

'Your dad said that's enough June,' her mother intervened. Katie took a sip of tea that scalded her tongue. She stood up and put the cup and saucer down on the table. She couldn't stay another minute, she felt, or she would die of it. Everything in the room reminded her of Billy. She could almost see him walking through the door from the front room.

'I have to go now, Mrs Wright,' she said. 'My gran needs me to help her.' Katie was amazed at how normal her voice sounded. There was barely a tremor.

'Aye, of course, lass,' said Mrs Wright. June made another derisory sound but Katie was past taking notice of her.

Katie walked to her parents' house in a haze of pain.

What was she going to do without Billy and her grandda? Oh, God, she didn't know.

Scrubbing down the stairs with the strip of oilcloth in place of a stair-carpet running down the middle, Katie welcomed the hard work. She concentrated on getting dirt out of the corners then left doors and windows open while everything dried out so that when Hannah came home from the hospital she complained loudly.

'Bloody, hell, Katie, it's freezing in here! Do you not know it's still only March?'

'Leave the lass alone, Hannah, she's doing her best,' said Gran. 'The house will soon warm up.' Gran sounded tired. She looked tired too, thought Katie, her face was red and sweat beaded her brow. She had just finished black-leading the range and polishing the brass and the fireplace twinkled in the light from the fire she had just relit. She should have taken Gran home before now; the old woman was using work to try to escape her misery just as she was herself.

The day of the funerals, the Methodist Chapel was packed. The Church of England had held the funerals for their two members in the morning and the one Baptist funeral was after the Methodists so that the whole day seemed to be taken up with them.

Men crowded round outside the chapel for the pit was idle as a mark of respect. So when Matthew Hamilton arrived in the Bentley, which was gleaming in the pale sunlight, they watched him sullenly for since the night of the accident most of them were beginning to know who he was.

'I've not seen him bother to attend a funeral afore now,' one man observed. 'Do you think he's seen the Light?' The others smiled; one even gave a guffaw, which was quickly suppressed.

'Nay lad, I reckon there's something else to it,' he answered. The men made way in silence for Matthew to enter the chapel.

He walked straight ahead, ignoring them. Inside he looked quickly around and then went down the aisle to the row just behind the rows reserved for the bereaved families. He sat down beside Parsons and Thompson who moved along the pew to give him plenty of room.

Parsons had been surprised to see him on the night of the accident but he was even more so now. What had got into the boss? Yesterday they had discussed the coroner's findings, 'death by misadventure' had been his conclusion as they had expected. And Parsons had put forward his opinion that the dead men had contributed to the unfortunate fall of stone by their own negligence and therefore were not entitled to full compensation. He had sat back, sure that Matthew would agree and instruct his lawyers accordingly but Matthew had not.

'Three hundred pound per family for every man lost will not break the company,' he had said and the other two men had gazed at him as though he was going off his head.

'I know that is the agreed amount,' Parsons had said after a moment. 'Agreed by the Owners' Association that is. But it will create a dangerous precedent. And the other owners will not like it. I would advise against paying out without a fight. After all, there is some evidence that the men may have contributed to the accident.'

'Nevertheless,' Matthew had replied and changed the subject, indicating that that was the end of the matter. He looked around the chapel built by the miners fifty years before according to the date on the stone above the door. It was an austere place, he thought with cheap boxwood pews and a floor of bare boards. A homemade black cover hung on the lectern especially for the funerals; in the corner was a pipe organ with an organist playing soft, solemn music. The organ was reedy, the music thin.

Then everyone was standing as the coffins were brought in preceded by the minister in a black plain gown. The coffins were covered with wreaths of flowers. They would have done better to save their money, he reckoned. But miners and their families were a superstitious lot.

'I am the resurrection and the life—' the minister intoned as the coffins were carried down the aisle and laid on the trestles. Then Matthew forgot about the others as he saw Katie coming in, supporting an old woman who must be her grandmother. For the rest of the service, while the minister delivered sentimental twaddle about the men who probably had been hard-drinking, work-shy scum rather than the saints he was portraying them as, at least in Matthew's opinion, he watched the back of Katie's head, occasionally glimpsing her profile as she turned a concerned face to her grandmother.

And more than one miner watched the big boss rather than paying attention to the service and a few of them came to the same conclusion as to what he was doing there when he should have stayed with his own folk and left them to their grief. Then the organ was playing 'Gresford', the miners' hymn and they were standing to sing the Twenty-Third Psalm.

'When are you due back at the hospital?' Matthew asked. The funerals were over, the mourners leaving the cemetery. Already the crowds were thinning out. Parsons and Thompson lingered on beside Matthew until he told them they could go, then Matthew had stood by his car waiting for a chance to speak to Katie. And of course she came over to him, as he had known she would, if only to thank him for coming.

Katie was still wrapped in a haze of grief, she hadn't even thought about the hospital or anything else except the necessity of getting over these few days, hoping and praying all the time that the heavy weight on her heart would lift, even a little bit. She had read the letter from Matron of course. An official letter giving her time off until the day after the funeral but no more. After all, the letter implied, a grandfather was not really a next-of-kin. Though it was very sad and the senior staff joined with Matron in offering Katie their every sympathy. But tomorrow, Sunday, she was to report for work on A Ward, men's surgical.

'Early tomorrow. I'll have to go this evening.'

'Then I will take you back,' said Matthew. 'Now, no argument, I insist.' He sounded like an elderly uncle bestowing a favour, he thought, so went on. 'Only if you wish it, of course. But it will be easier for you.'

'I can't go until after the funeral tea,' said Katie. She looked over her shoulder to where her gran was standing by the undertaker's car. 'Look, I'll have to go, thank you, Mr Hamilton,' she said swiftly, edging away.

'I'll call for you at seven, will that be all right? I have to go into Bishop Auckland in any case,' he added. It was all he could think of as a reason for hanging around for two hours. Two men walked past and glanced curiously at him standing by the Bentley, the chauffeur sitting behind the wheel, his expression impassive. Knowingly, they looked from Matthew to Katie but neither of the two noticed.

'What do you make of that, eh?' one said to the other.

'Nay lad, surely not,' said the other. 'And her lad hardly cold in his grave.'

'Nowt so queer as folk,' the first one replied.

Matthew got into the car. 'Home Lawson,' he said. 'I

won't need you tonight. I have decided to drive myself.'

'Yes sir.'

Well thank God for that, the chauffeur said to himself. He was absolutely fed up with hanging about miserable pit villages and damp cemeteries. It was enough to give anyone the hump, he said later to Daisy when she slipped into his cosy flat with his supper on a tray.

Once home, Matthew popped his head around the drawing-room door. Mary Anne was sitting on a hard chair by the fire, working away on her embroidery frame. She looked up at him and smiled. At last he was showing some feeling for his workers, going to the funerals of those poor miners. Perhps he was not so hard-hearted as he tried to make out.

'Are you staying in, Matthew?' she asked. 'If so, I'll order an early dinner. You must be hungry —'

'No, don't bother, I'm going straight back out,' he said. He looked at her, trying to hide his distaste. Her skin was sallow and beginning to show lines around the mouth and dark shadows under the eyes. She was breeding again, let's hope she would carry this one for the full nine months and deliver a healthy boy. Then at least he would not feel constrained to go to her bed.

'But Matthew, you've just come in, where are you going?'

'A meeting in the Royal, there's a chance of a government contract,' he lied glibly. 'Can't stop, I must go and change.' Mary Anne was left looking at the closed door. But the uppermost feeling in her mind was relief, she could have Cook prepare a tray with something light, perhaps a clear soup, a little chicken. She was prone to heartburn with this baby and that was something that hadn't bothered her with the others. Perhaps it was a good sign? Oh, dear God, she hoped so.

At ten minutes to seven, the Bentley glided to a halt on the end of the rows at Winton Colliery. Matthew sat behind the wheel, considering whether to go to the house and knock for Katie or to wait for her here for she would be bound to come out shortly.

Oh, for goodness sake, he was simply doing a girl a good turn, wasn't he? At least, that was what people would think. And come to think of it, did he care what these pit folk thought? Not at all he decided. He got out of the car and walked down the row to the front door of the house where she lived.

Katie had had just about as much as she could manage to take without screaming out loud. She felt weary to death and every limb ached. She fetched and carried for two and a half hours for the friends and neighbours who came in to offer their commiserations and stay to the funeral tea of cold ham, salad and pease pudding. She had buttered bread until her wrists ached and she felt her fingers might drop off.

Worst of all she had nodded her head and accepted the sympathy of everyone, the whole village perhaps. Her eyes were scratchy as sandpaper and there was a persistent throb behind her right eye that increased from simple pain to agony and back again every time she moved. All the time she kept a careful eye on her grandmother who was looking older and more frail by the minute. She feared she was reaching breaking point. Kitty sat in the Room in the rocker that had been Noah's and was now brought in from the kitchen to stand by the sofa. Kitty sat in unaccustomed idleness, she drank cup after cup of strong black tea.

Hannah was there. It was the first time she had been in her mother-in-law's house since Katie was small. She had not come to help Katie but then, no one expected it of her. She sat on the opposite side of the fireplace on the sofa with Betty by her side. 'Me and your gran would like some more tea, Katie,' she sang out at intervals. 'And mebbe a nice piece of that slab cake that's on the table there.'

'Leave the lass alone, I'll get it,' said Gran, suddenly noticing Katie's white face. She got to her feet and stood, swaying alarmingly.

'Now then, you sit down before you fall down,' Hannah advised kindly. 'Katie's a strong lass, she can manage. Can't you, Katie?'

Katie nodded and cut a couple of slices of the slab cake, the kind that was always supplied by the Co-op store as part of their funeral tea. The store had taken care of everything, arranging the funeral, cars, chapel service, minister and cemetery plot and also, the tea. For a discount, of course, in a sad case like this one.

Katie was trying not to think of the funeral tea that was going on at the same time in the next street in the Wrights' house. She had managed to slip in for a few minutes to pay her respects but it was all so unreal.

'Don't upset me mam any more than she is!' June had snapped when she saw Katie at the door. 'I thought you'd be busy with your grandda's funeral, any road?'

'I've just called for a minute,' said Katie.

'Aye well, I don't think you should go in, me man and dad are in a state as it is. I'll tell them you called, will I?'

Katie had stumbled back down the yard, her feelings too frozen even to cry.

She looked around the Room now as she handed over the slab cake. Most of the visitors had already gone, thank goodness. Soon Gran would be able to relax.

'Will you watch her while I get my things ready to go back to the hospital, Mam?' she asked softly so that Gran didn't hear, hating having to ask. 'Only I must go back-'

'Oh, aye, hadaway, get on back to Teesside,' said Hannah. 'I'm sure you'll be glad to leave all this misery behind you—' She stopped speaking, as there was a loud knock at the door. Everyone turned to look for it was the front door, unused for months until today when the coffin holding the remains of the master of the house had been carried out to the hearse.

Who was it? No one asked but the question hung in the air. No one went to the door until Kitty roused herself.

'Answer the front door, pet, will you?'

Katie put down the plate of cake and went to the door and opened it. It opened easily for she had oiled it especially for the day.

'Miss Benfield? If you're ready we will go now.' Matthew looked round at the gathering, most of them round-eyed and staring at him and stepped back on to the path. 'I'll wait in the car, shall I?'

The mining folk still left in the house were struck dumb. They stared at the big boss, for by now they knew him for the ironmaster who owned most of the pits round about. Mrs Wearmouth from up the street even held her cup halfway between her saucer and her mouth and the mouth was hanging open. Everything about the toff, his dress, his air of health and well-being stood out in contrast to them and in this mean little room the contrast stood out sharper than ever.

Chapter Fourteen

Katie sat in the front seat beside Matthew Hamilton and stared at the road stretching out before the car. Vaguely, in the back of her mind she was aware that she should have been overcome with embarrassment when he had shown up at her grandmother's house like that. But it didn't matter, nothing mattered now.

'Are you warm enough? I can turn the heater up.' Matthew took one hand off the wheel and moved it towards the dashboard.

'Thank you, I'm warm,' said Katie. She looked at his hand in the glimmer of light from outside. It was square and capable looking, the nails cut straight across and there was black hair protruding below the cuff of his shirt. Not the hands of a miner yet not the hands of someone who did no manual work either. If he could drive, why did he employ a chauffeur? Was it for prestige?

If she kept her mind on small unimportant things she found she could keep the deep, painful misery at bay, behind a mental wall, somehow. She was tired to exhaustion point and beyond yet she could not stop her mind working, restlessly ranging about. She closed her eyes but it felt as though there was sand under the lids and it scratched and stung so she opened them again. She hadn't noticed this was not the Darlington road until then. She roused herself to ask.

'Where are we going?'

'Why, back to the hospital, of course,' he said smoothly.

'But this is not—'

'Yes it is. This way we cross the North Road and go through Sedgefield. It's no further, just an alternative route. I like to vary my routes.'

'Oh yes.' She remembered the road now; they were passing Windlestone Hall, the home of the Eden family. Katie took no further interest in her surroundings but relapsed into seeming apathy. Her concentration had been breached and the agony threatened to overwhelm her yet again.

Matthew looked across at her. Her face was so white and set in the light from passing headlights. For a moment her head fell forward, and she trembled violently. She wasn't going to pass out on him, was she? He pulled the car over to the side of the road and stopped the engine. With a visible effort she straightened up and clamped her jaw against the trembling.

'Katie, Katie,' he said gently and leaned over to her and took her in his arms, pulling her head down on his shoulder. She was tense and unyielding though she didn't draw away.

'Katie, Katie,' he said again. His lips brushed against her hair. Beneath his hands he could feel her trembling increase. And then she cried.

She could hold out no more, her whole body relaxed, slackened and she leaned against him and wept. Silently at first, then with heart-broken sobs and copious tears which wet his chest through to the skin.

A surge of jealousy went through him. He kept perfectly still, holding her. Was she weeping for her grandfather? Or for the sweetheart he had found out she was meeting, the miner's get. A surveyor was all he had been! What could he have given a girl like Katie? Nothing! Nothing compared to what he could himself, wife or not. His grip on the girl tightened, he could make her forget, he could indeed.

Looking out at the night he realised they were almost to the turn-off for Hartlepool, it would only take a few minutes to get there. He gently eased her back into her seat and started the engine. Katie hardly noticed, she was beyond taking notice of anything.

Within half an hour he had them booked into a small hotel to the south of the town. The night receptionist did not query his entry in the book after he saw Katie, drooping against Matthew so that he had almost to carry her in.

'My wife is not well,' Matthew said anyway.

'I'm sorry, sir, I can send for a doctor if you wish it,' the man replied, sympathetically. Indeed the wife looked as though she might be at death's door, he thought, and very young too.

'No, she will be fine after a good night's sleep. She suffers from weak nerves.'

Oh that, the receptionist said to himself. Not anything dangerous then. The women from round the docks where he came from couldn't afford the luxury of nerves.

'What time would you like to be called in the morning, sir?'

'Eight. Goodnight then.' Tomorrow he had arranged to go over the books at the works.

Once in the room, he sat Katie on the side of the bed and took off her shoes. She promptly fell down against the pillows and closed her eyes. He took off his coat and shoes and lay down beside and took her in his arms again.

'I'll look after you, Katie, I swear I will,' he whispered in her ear and she murmured something. She didn't object or even open her eyes as he undressed her and then himself and pulled the eiderdown over them both. He kissed her eyes, and let his lips travel down, kissed her mouth, the hollow of her neck and the top of her breasts and cupped her bottom with one hand, drawing her even closer to him.

Katie did not open her eyes, she snuggled to him. She was dreaming of Billy. They were in the engine house of the old aerial flight and he had drawn her to the ground and, miraculously, the bed of leaves felt as soft as a feather mattress and as warm. This time, she would let him. The delightful thought floated through her dream. When he kissed her lips she kissed him back, felt his tongue in her mouth and it was sweet and exciting. There were strange sensations in the pit of her belly and they were swelling and rising and she felt the blood rushing through her veins and it was hot and surging.

'Billy,' she whispered.

'Billy be buggered,' said Matthew savagely. But yet he was gentle as he took her nipple into his mouth. Mary Anne would not have recognised him or his lovemaking.

Home Sister was knocking at the door. Through the woolly folds of sleep Katie could hear the knocking. And the voice calling.

'Eight o'clock, sir, madam.'

No, Home Sister would never have said that. She must have said it was six o'clock, that was it.

'Thank you Sister,' she called back though it came out as little more than a murmur.

'Righto?' It was a man's voice.

Katie turned over on her back and opened her eyes. This was not her narrow room in the Nurses' Home. Where was she? But that question didn't matter much as memory flooded back. Memories of yesterday and the funerals and worse. Grandda was dead. Billy was dead. They had been killed in the pit. What was that expression the Victorian coroners had used to put in the ledgers? 'Burnt in the pit,' that was it. Nothing else, that was enough, no investigation needed and it was neat and tidy at least. Katie closed her eyes and the agony washed over her again.

'Katie, come on, Katie, it's not so bad.'

Katie's eyes flew open. Mr Hamilton was sitting on the side of her bed in his shirtsleeves. Still disorientated, she stared at him. There were hairs coming out of his ears, she noted abstractedly.

'I won't let you down,' he said. 'I'll look after you.'

Katie sat up suddenly, clutching at the eiderdown. 'What am I doing here?' But she knew the answer. Memories of the evening before were coming back to her, fragmented and as in a dream. It wasn't a dream though; her muscles ached and her breasts were sore.

'Go away,' she said.

'Come on now, be sensible. I said it's not so bad and it isn't.'

'Not so bad? What do you mean not so bad when my Billy is dead and my grandda an' all! And you, all you wanted was to get me into bed. You took advantage when I was down, when I didn't know what I was doing—' Katie stopped for a moment, unable to go on. Then she said, struggling to keep her voice even, 'By, you might be the big boss but you're a rotten sod, Matthew Hamilton.'

'It was a terrible accident killed them, it wasn't my fault. But life goes on, Katie,' he said tritely. 'But be honest Katie. You wanted it as much as I did, you led me on.' Surreptitiously he looked at the gold watch on his wrist. 'I have to go, Katie, and so have you. I'll be in touch, never fear. We'll talk about this later.'

But the passion had gone out of Katie. What did any of it matter any more? Her future had died with Billy.

'Five past eight.' The voice of the chambermaid came through the door.

'Oh!' Katie got out of bed and began to pull on her

clothes. 'I might as well go to work. I was supposed to be on duty at seven-thirty.' Even her enthusiasm; for nursing had gone but she might as well get on with it.

Matthew sighed. 'All right, I'll drop you there.'

Within ten minutes they were in the car and driving out of Hartlepool. Katie was still in such a state of shock she couldn't think straight and she didn't even try. Everything was strange and unreal to her. She could only hold on to one thought at a time and at the moment it was that she was late reporting for duty on the ward. When they reached the hospital she got out without a backward glance and sprinted up the drive to the Nurses' Home and changed into her uniform. She walked swiftly along the corridor to the ward (running forbidden except in cases of fire or dire emergency), knocked at the door of Sister's office and went in when bidden.

'Yes Nurse?' Sister looked up from the notes she was studying.

'I'm sorry I'm late, Sister,' said Katie and Sister looked sternly at her over her pince-nez.

'Not only are you late, Nurse, you're on the wrong ward,' she observed. 'Or perhaps you have forgotten you have been transferred to A Ward.'

'Oh!' Katie gasped and turned to fumble blindly with the door handle. 'I'm sorry, Sister.'

Sister gazed at her. Of course she knew of the tragedy at Winton Colliery, everyone did. In her opinion, Katie should not have been expected back to work yet, she was obviously badly shocked. She got to her feet and went over to the girl. 'You look ill, Nurse,' she said. 'I think you should be reporting to the sick bay.'

'No, I'll be fine,' said Katie, managing to open the door at last. If only this white fog that surrounded her would go away, she thought.

'No, you won't, Nurse,' Sister replied firmly. 'Now sit down while I call Staff Nurse. She will take you there.'

It was a good thing he was blessed with the sort of mind which could keep things in separate compartments, thought Matthew as he sat back in his chair after a management meeting. For though his mind had been totally on the business in hand for the whole of the morning, as soon as the last man had left the boardroom his thoughts reverted to Katie Benfield.

It was almost one o'clock, he should go to lunch at home with Mary Anne, see how she was, for after all she could be carrying his son and heir. The trouble was he didn't want to, he wanted to go to the hospital and seek out Katie and take her to lunch. Surely she had a dinner hour like everyone else? No, if he remembered correctly from his days in hospital, the nurses had only thirty minutes. Damn. He fiddled with his fountain pen, doodled with his blotter.

It had been good last night, very good. She had responded to him in a way he hadn't dreamed she would. There had been that bad moment when she called him by another name, Billy, her dead sweetheart. Well, he would soon make her forget about Billy.

Matthew was slightly surprised at himself, usually when he achieved his objective with a girl like Katie he lost interest. Perhaps he would be making a mistake if he saw her again. There were plenty of other girls. But not like Katie.

He clipped his pen into his top pocket and rose to his feet. What the hell, he would go back to the Hall for lunch and see Mary Anne. There was no sense in letting a pit wench think she had a hold over you. No, the best thing was to forget about Katie, at least for a while.

'John, is the master in?'

The grandfather clock in the hall was chiming one as Mary Anne ventured out of her room and came down the stairs, holding firmly on to the banister. John, who happened to be crossing the hall at that moment, looked up at her. Heck, she looked pale and drawn and tired to death even though she had only just risen. But then, breeding took some females like that, he knew.

'No madam, not yet. May I ask if he is expected?'

'I think so.' Mary Anne almost asked if Matthew had rung to say he would be home but she stopped herself. The servants pitied her; she was well aware of it and was humiliated by it. Even now she thought she could see pity in John's eyes. 'Well, tell Cook I will wait another half-hour before starting. Perhaps he is delayed at the works.'

'Yes, madam.'

Mary Anne went into the drawing-room and walked over to the fireplace. There was a good fire burning but she shivered a little, she seemed to feel the cold so badly, especially since her last miscarriage. She put a hand protectively on her belly, oh God, she wasn't going to think of miscarriages, this baby she was going to carry for the whole nine months, and she was determined. She thought about Matthew as she held her hands to the blaze, he hadn't returned last night and staying out all night usually meant he came home for lunch. It was just a sort of sop to her feelings but still it showed he wasn't completely uncaring.

Mary Anne sat down on the sofa and picked up her embroidery. She was sewing a cross-stitch picture for the nursery, a picture of Peter Pan and Wendy, flying through the air under a starlit sky. She would have liked to be sewing a layette for the baby coming (and it would come, he would come, oh yes, he would), but she couldn't get rid of the superstition that having a layette all ready would offend the gods. She was well aware of the contradiction in the two thoughts but still . . .

She heard the front door open, Matthew's deep tones as he spoke to John and John answering. Quickly she put down her embroidery and rose to her feet though in truth she was hardly aware of it.

'Matthew,' she said as he opened the door and walked over to her, pecking her on the cheek and holding his hands out to the blaze almost in the same instant.

'Good day, Mary Anne,' he answered. She smelled a little of lavender water, a scent he had always associated with old ladies. Her breath was bad too, not exactly foul but unpleasant. Well, she had bouts of indigestion with this pregnancy of course. He should not be too critical; he didn't want to upset her. Poor cow, he thought. It was amazing how last night had put him in a more sympathetic mood.

'I'll ring for lunch shall I?' she asked.

'Yes, of course, I'm famished,' said Matthew.

'Where did you spend the night? I hope you had a proper breakfast,' she said and immediately his mood changed at the idea that she was questioning him.

'Where do you think I spent the night, Mary Anne? In the arms of some floozies? Have you forgotten that there was a mining disaster at one of my mines and it was the funerals yesterday? Or did you think I shouldn't bother about a few dead men, after all they were only miners,' he barked.

'Oh, no, I'm sorry, Matthew, I didn't mean—' she looked at his angry face. Of course he was upset having to witness the results of the accident, the distress of the mourners at the funerals too. But why had he had to spend the night there? She decided not to ask, after all, there must have been a good reason or he would have come home to his comfortable bed.

'Let's go in to lunch, Matthew,' she said. 'I'm sorry if I upset you. I meant nothing by it, I assure you.'

Oh dear, she didn't want him to be in a temper when the children came home from school at the weekend. It was the mid-term holiday and she had hoped they could be like a real family even if just for a few days. Of course, they weren't his children, she reminded herself. But if only he acted as though he was, especially to Robert. Her son was growing up, fifteen now and he needed a father to look up to. Why, Matthew didn't even like her son to bring a friend home, she had had to discourage him when he had asked to do that this weekend.

But that was the problem really, the boy was her son and not Matthew's. Sometimes she despaired of ever getting Matthew to really accept him as one of the family.

Dr Roberts, the Head Physician at the South-East Durham General Hospital, took his stethoscope out of his ears and nodded to Sister.

'Don't worry, Nurse, you will be fine,' he said. 'Sister and I will just have a word.'

Katie looked at him and quickly down again. This was the first time she had had anything to do with the great man and it wasn't in connection with a patient but herself. Yet she didn't care, she didn't care about anything just at the minute. Sister had administered a bromide to her on Dr Roberts's orders and Katie was sinking into a cocoon of warm, woolly sleep . . .

'Well, Sister,' the doctor said when they were both safely in the office with the door closed firmly. After all, this was the nurses' sick bay and one never knew if a patient heard and knew what they were talking about. 'Well, Sister, I don't know. I question whether the girl is of the right calibre to make a nurse. I know she has suffered a dreadful shock but it was just her grandfather, wasn't it?'

Dr Roberts had been an army doctor in the Great War to end all wars and he disapproved of any suggestion of lack of moral fibre. After all, where would they have been in the war if everyone had collapsed when a tragedy happened instead of stiffening their resolve and going on?

Sister murmured something that could have been agreement or not depending on what you wanted to see in it.

'Well, we will keep her sedated for a few days and then see how she is. She may pull herself together. I sometimes think we are bringing in girls who are not from the right sort of background, you know?'

Sister, who was the daughter of a docker but had been lucky enough to get her training in the war when nurses were at a premium, nodded again.

'I must be going now, my ward rounds wait. I can't spend all my time on one little probationer,' said Dr Roberts and went out. Sister went back to the four-bedded ward that was the main part of the sick bay and peeked at Katie who was the only bed patient. She looked pale and worried even in sleep. Her brows were knitted above the sweep of her long lashes, her lips parted as she breathed with quick, shallow breaths. Sister pushed back the lock of hair that had fallen over her brow and pulled the covers up over her shoulders.

It took a great deal of moral fibre or what ever you cared to call it to get from a poverty-stricken pit village in the depths of the great slump to being a probationer in a large hospital, she thought. Moral fibre be blowed. What the hell did high and mighty Dr Roberts know? She went out, softly closing the door behind her. There was a window in her office looking out on to the ward and she would keep an eye on the girl from there.

Chapter Fifteen

'You have a visitor, Nurse,' said Sister.

Katie looked up in surprise. Only one or two nurses knew she was in the sick bay and no one from outside that she knew of. Nurse Trotter perhaps? She had shown herself to be friendly.

It wasn't Nurse Trotter. She heard a man's voice outside the door of the ward saying something to Sister as she went out and Katie went pale.

'Mr Hamilton,' she said. She was overcome with embarrassment as scraps of memories from that awful night came back to her. She could feel the heat rising in her face as she flushed. She couldn't bring herself to look at him. During the first week Katie had been in the sick bay she had scarcely known or cared where she was. She had been plagued with horrible dreams and nightmares and was almost convinced that the scenes she remembered from the night after the funerals were all part of them. The drugs she had taken made everything seem vivid but somehow unreal. This second week the dose of bromide had been cut down and she felt more herself. All she wanted to do was get back to work, to some sort of normality. She wished with all her heart that Mr Hamilton would simply go away so that she need never see him again.

Matthew gazed at her. The flush, though fading now, had left her cheeks pink and her dark blue eyes were as striking as ever. What was it about her, he wondered, he couldn't leave her alone though he had had every intention of doing just that. Through his contacts he had found out where she was. When he had made inquiries, under the guise of being her father's employer simply asking on behalf of her family, he had been shaken when Dr Roberts had told him she was suffering from neurasthenia. And when he looked it up in a medical dictionary he hadn't come near her for a week. Yet in the end he couldn't stay away, she must be a witch he reckoned or at least she had bewitched him.

'Hello, Katie,' he said now, more for the benefit of Sister than Katie, 'how are you? I've brought you some flowers.'

'Oh, aren't they lovely? What a lucky girl you are, Nurse Benfield,' Sister enthused. 'I'll put them in water, shall I?' But she looked speculatively from Matthew to Katie and back again.

Katie looked at the sheaf of carnations in their artistically arranged greenery in disbelief. No one had ever given her flowers before. No one could afford such luxuries in Winton Colliery. In fact the only times she had ever seen flowers from a florist before had been at weddings or funerals. These reminded her forcibly of her grandfather's funeral and she was filled with unbearable sadness.

'Mr Hamilton, go away,' she whispered. She couldn't hide from it any longer, that night had not been a nightmare, it had been real. And this man, this old man had put her through it. Impotent anger rose in her.

'My name is Matthew,' he said as the door closed behind Sister and the flowers.

'Can't you call me Matthew? I'm very fond of you, Katie. I want to look after you.' He sat down by her bed and took her hand in his but she pulled hers away violently.

She felt so tired, weary to death and her weariness was compounded by the strong sedative she had been given. What did it matter? Her anger began to seep away. Her life was over anyway, she told herself. She felt as though she were fighting to escape from layers of cotton wool and getting nowhere. The feel of her hand in his lingered and it wasn't unpleasant, it felt strong and dependable. As he was himself a powerful man who knew what he wanted. Oh God, what was she thinking?

'You're a married man, Mr Hamilton,' she said and in her own ears the words sounded trite, like something out of a cheap B film. Everything was still so unreal, she thought wildly. In fact she was sure she had said those words in just the tone that Clara Bow had used in a picture she had seen once with Billy— Oh Billy, she had been determined not to think of him and her treacherous thoughts had betrayed her. Misery rose and threatened to overcome her. What did anything matter, now that Billy was dead?

'Not happily, Katie. My wife and I – well, we live separate lives really.'

Katie suddenly felt even more exhausted. She was still under the effects of the bromide she had been given the night before.

'Dr Roberts said you could come out in a day or two. Have a few days' sick leave at home. Would you like that Katie?'

'Oh! I thought I could go back on to the wards,' she said weakly. 'I don't want my grandmother to know I've been ill. I'm all right now, really I am. It was just the shock, I'm sure it was.' And even if she wasn't now, she would be all right, she would.

'Still, better not go back to work, dear.'

She didn't notice the endearment, being too wrapped up in her own thoughts. It meant Gran would have to know she'd been ill and she had had enough worry and sorrow since the accident. But what could she do? And in any case, she was longing to see Gran, find out how she was bearing up.

'I'll take you, Katie. If you want to go, that is. Or would you rather go somewhere else?'

'No, no, I want to go to Winton.'

Just at the minute all she wanted to do was sleep, preferably in her own bed with the warm oven shelf wrapped in a towel at her feet. She had woken in the middle of the night and she had been dreaming of Winton. She had been a schoolgirl again and the Means-test man was coming and Billy was calling, 'I'll save you, Mrs Benfield, I'll save you!' And the Means-test man had gone away and she had been happy. When she had woken up she had still been happy until memory flooded back and with it the desolation.

'Righto, I'll take you,' said Matthew. 'I'll go now and let you sleep.' He stood up and bent over her and kissed her gently on the forehead like a father would, like Noah sometimes did and she hadn't the energy to stop him.

Had she dreamed that night? Had she imagined him in bed with her when she had thought it was Billy? Maybe she had. She was so confused. Maybe he was just a kind man. Katie fell into a light doze. If only she could think straight . . .

'By all means, take her home,' said Dr Roberts. 'It will do her good, I'm sure.' He looked across his desk at the iron-master, wondering what his interest was in the probationer nurse. Was he a philanthropist then? Somehow he didn't think so. But then, he was a man of the world himself, he wouldn't ask questions. The hospital depended on the large donations given by the ironmasters. He couldn't afford to jeopardise that. Rich and powerful this man was reputed to be.

'Are you sure she will be able to return to her duties here? In time, I mean. Or perhaps not . . .' Matthew let his voice trail into silence.

Dr Roberts leaned forward on the desk and put on a confidential air. 'I do have my doubts, Mr Hamilton,' he said carefully for he was feeling his way, trying to decide

165

what Matthew wanted him to say. 'It may be that she is simply not strong enough.'

Matthew nodded, satisfied. 'Well, then, I'll take her to her grandmother tomorrow morning. I have to go over to Winton on business. Is that suitable?'

'Yes, of course. I'm sure that she will recover in familiar surroundings,' Dr Roberts said heartily. He rose to his feet in the same instance as Matthew and they shook hands in perfect understanding.

'I have brought you a warm coat to travel in, we don't want you catching cold, Katie.'

Katie looked at the coat that Matthew was holding open for her to put on. It was a deep blue, almost the colour of her eyes and a warm soft, expensive wool. She hesitated.

'Oh, I don't know, Mr Hamilton, I shouldn't take such an expensive gift,' she said. Gran would go mad if she took such a present from a man.

'Nonsense,' Matthew said briskly. 'You need a warm coat, you've been ill. Come along now, put it on, I want to be back in Bishop Auckland by twelve.' He shook the coat slightly, imperiously and Katie was silenced. It wouldn't hurt to try it on.

She shrugged her arms into the sleeves, stood as he turned her round and fastened the big buttons. It had a large fur collar and a low, draped waist and narrowed around the hips to the hemline just on the knees. Oh, it was a lovely coat. She buried her face in the high fur collar; it was soft and silky and the most beautiful thing she had ever had in her life. She could always take it off before they reached Winton Colliery.

'Whoever would have thought it of her,' Sister said aloud to no one in particular as she watched them leave, Matthew holding on to Katie's arm. 'Butter wouldn't melt in her mouth.' Staff Nurse said nothing, just went ahead with stripping Katie's bed. But she would lay odds they wouldn't see that one back here working as a probationer nurse even though she did look as innocent as a baby. No, Nurse Benfield had found herself a sugar daddy.

Matthew was driving himself again. 'You may have the day off today,' he had said to Lawson.

'Thank you very much, sir,' Lawson had replied but it was just as well that Matthew did not see the ironic gleam in his eye. The gaffer didn't want his chauffeur to see what he was up to. And Lawson was pretty sure what that was. Still a day off was a day off.

'I will drop you at the end of the rows,' said Matthew as they approached Winton. They had got there in record time for Matthew, unused to driving himself these last few years, had rediscovered his liking for speed and was indulging it to the full.

Katie hardly noticed how he drove until they swerved round the corner into Winton, still in third gear and there was a group of little girls, strung across the road and playing a skipping game. She was jolted into awareness as Matthew swerved again, brakes screaming, up on to the pavement and away from the children but almost into a boy who was leaning against a low wall on the opposite side of the road, hands in pockets and legs crossed nonchalantly. They were so close that the boy jumped and fell over the wall on to the rough ground beyond.

Katie had the door open and was out of the car in an instant. She vaulted the wall herself and bent over the boy.

'Are you hurt?' she cried. She felt his limbs and the back of his head, there was no blood thank goodness. He looked up at her, winded, and then shrugged her off.

'Leave off, will you, Katie Benfield,' he shouted. 'There's nowt the matter with me.' He got to his feet and dusted scraps of dead grass from his jacket. 'It's that fella there, he's blooming mad he is, driving like that. He oughter be in Sedgefield!'

Matthew was there by now, as were half the residents of the rows, all brought out by the sound of the car and the shouting.

'You're all right boy, aren't you?' he asked. 'Shall I take you to your mother?'

'No! What do you think I am, a baby?' The question enraged the boy even more. Matthew groped in his pocket and came out with a couple of florins and two sixpences. 'Here you are then, this will make you feel better.'

Magically, the boy's temper disappeared, he grinned and pocketed the money. 'Eeh thanks, mister,' he said. He'd never had so much at one time in his life before. But there were mutterings among the onlookers.

'Nearly kills the lad and then tries to buy him off!' Katie heard the woman's voice plainly and an answering man's growl.

'I am perfectly willing to take the boy to a doctor to be

looked over. Lady Eden's Hospital in Auckland if you like,' he said. He looked over the crowd, challenging them to make more of it but most of them dropped their eyes, some turned away, those who remembered who this man was from the day of the pit disaster. They wanted no trouble with a boss, they were still too close to the hard years of slump and dreaded their return. All except one, that is. Kitty Benfield had come out of her yard to see what the commotion was all about and when she got to the end of the alley, all she could see was that Katie was there with that flash man who had come to her door on the night of the funeral. And Katie was dressed up fit to kill.

'Katie! You come here, this minute, do you hear me? Get in the house!'

Katie remembered she was still wearing the coat and blushed fiercely as the neighbours began to notice her too.

'Thank you for the lift,' she said to Matthew and fled into the house with her grandmother, away from the avid curiosity in their eyes. The crowd was dispersing as mothers took their children away, smacking heads and uttering dire warnings about playing on the road. He got into his car and drove away. After all, he knew where she was, and he could come back when the incident with the boy was forgotten.

'What's that you have on your back?' Kitty asked as soon as they were in the house and the door firmly closed.

'Gran, you know what it is. I needed a new coat, you know I did and it was so cold and I've been badly.' Katie unbuttoned the coat and took it off, laying it over the back of a kitchen chair.

'Are you telling me you bought it yourself? 'Cause if you are you're a bloody liar, our Katie and that's swearing!'

'No I didn't,' Katie admitted. 'Mr Hamilton bought it for me.' Suddenly Katie was overcome by weakness. She sank into a chair, and began to shiver.

'What's the matter with you? Any road, what are you doing here when you're supposed to working at that hospital?' Kitty looked properly at her granddaughter's face for the first time and was shocked to see that it was as white as marble. 'Have you not been looking after yourself? Here sit in your grandda's rocking chair by the fire and get warm. You look as though you've got consumption! Hey, you haven't have you?'

As Katie shook her head, Kitty's anger returned, fuelled with relief. 'By our Katie, I don't know, you're nothing but a worry to me.' Kitty glared at her granddaughter. Even discounting consumption, she could see that Katie was definitely ill and it looked as though it was serious.

'I'm all right. But the doctor thinks I should have a few days off work,' said Katie. Her grandmother was bustling about now, sticking the long steel poker through the bars of the grate to stir the fire into life; settling the black kettle on the top when she had finished and reaching for the teapot and caddy; generally causing a great deal of banging and thumping in her anxiety. She put out mugs and brought stotty cake and a boiled ham shank out of the bread bin in the pantry.

'Have you been eating properly? You've not been missing meals have you, our Katie? I don't know, you're not fit to look after yourself, you're not fit to be let out—'

'Gran, I've told you, I live in a Nurses' Home, and we get three meals a day and a bit of supper.'

'Well, what's the matter then?' Kitty's voice was harsh in her anxiety.

Katie gazed at her grandmother and her eyes filled with tears of weakness. The old woman stood there, her arms folded across her thin bosom, and her mouth set in an angry line. But behind the anger there were other emotions; in her eyes there was a lost look like a wounded animal. Katie held out her arms and took Gran into them and held her and after a minute the stiffness went out of her and she relaxed as they cried on each other's shoulders for what they had lost.

'It's all very well, lady, but you still haven't explained how you came by that coat,' said Gran and Katie's heart sank. It was afternoon and Katie had eaten the best meal she had had in a fortnight. They sat by the fire talking about Noah and what a wild one he had been in his younger days drinking and playing toss ha'penny behind the pit heaps and being chased by the polis.

'Mr Hamilton bought it Gran. I told him I couldn't accept it but he insisted and he was bringing me back here and it was so cold—'

'Hmm!' said Gran. 'You shouldn't have put it on. What's folk going to think? They were all eyes and ears when he was here before. There's not something going on between you two is there? An' him a married man?' Kitty gazed at her granddaughter hard yet again. And when Katie didn't reply immediately her worst fears began to take hold.

'Katie Benfield, answer me!' she shouted and Katie jumped in her chair.

'No, Gran, there isn't,' she said. 'He's a kind man, that's all.'

'A kind man? A boss, a big boss at that? Who the heck do you think you're trying to fool our Katie? Has that lecher had his way with you?' she demanded. 'By our Katie I thought I'd taught you different from that! If your grandda were here he'd be mortified. As it is he'll be turning in his grave, I never thought to see the day.'

'No he hasn't, we didn't!' Katie shouted suddenly, unable to listen any more. 'I told you, he's just a kind man and I met him when I nursed his wife and he used to come to see her. I told you, Gran, I did.' Was she protesting too much? Even in her own ears it sounded as though she were.

'Aye so you did. Then you come walking in here bold as brass, wearing a fancy coat that would have cost a decent man a month's wages. I tell you, our Katie I don't know whether to believe you or not. He comes to the end of our street in that fancy car and you in it bold as brass, I could have sunk through the floor when I saw you, I could

Gran had sat down suddenly and Katie's eyes filled with weak tears as she looked at her, the old woman looked so sad and vulnerable once the anger left her.

'I didn't want to upset you, Gran, I'm sorry,' said Katie. 'I'll go to the store and get something nice for our tea, will I?'

'If you like. But don't you dare wear that flaming coat, do you hear?'

'No, Gran, I won't,' Katie replied. Just at that minute she would have agreed to go to the store in the buff if that was what her gran wanted.

'Well then,' said Gran, mollified a little. 'But are you sure you're fit for it now?'

'I am,' said Katie. 'It's not far is it?' She wanted to feel the wind on her face, smell the smells of Winton Colliery. She needed to.

Chapter Sixteen

Matthew spent the rest of the day going round the company mines in the area. He told himself he liked to keep his finger on the pulse of all his enterprises and that was the reason he was still here. There were a thousand and one things he could be doing back in Cleveland but they would have to wait.

The manager of Eden Hope Colliery was just sitting down to drink a cup of tea made for him by his secretary. He looked up at the door when Matthew walked in unannounced, angry at the intrusion but his attitude changed when he saw who it was. The tea slopped in the saucer as he put the cup down hastily and got to his feet.

'Mr Hamilton! Sir! Mr Parsons did not tell me to expect you today, I'm sorry I'm—'

'Stop babbling man, I was in the area that's all. Now, I want to check the books if you don't mind. I'm not satisfied with the production figures.'

By the time he left the manager, pale and sweating, in the pit yard, Matthew was into his stride. He went into

Winton, hesitated by the end of the colliery rows and went on to the colliery. Mr Thompson had been forewarned of his coming, however, and was somewhat better prepared and the agent Mr Parsons was there, so Matthew did not have to go into the town to see him. Consequently it was quite early when his business was finished.

He would go back to see if Katie was all right, he decided. To hell with what the old woman thought or any of the nosy neighbours come to that. So it happened that, as he turned the corner to the ends of the rows, he saw Katie just emerging from the back street, dressed in a shapeless coat of indeterminate colour somewhere between grey and brown. Even in the coat she looked beautiful, he reflected. Her large dark eyes contrasted with her fair hair and pale face. He wasn't used to this urge to protect, which swept over him when he saw her. He stopped the car and leaned over and opened the door.

'Get in,' he said. 'I'll take you wherever you want to go.'

Katie stopped where she was and stared at him in dismay. Oh, he should just go away, she thought. He caused so much trouble without even realising it.

'What are you doing here?' she asked.

'Just passing,' said Matthew blandly. Katie walked over to the car and leaned down to speak to him.

'Please don't come here,' she begged. 'My gran is going mad, you've no idea. I know you mean it kindly, but she doesn't understand, she doesn't understand at all.'

'Well, I'm sorry. But she's not here now, is she? And it's almost dark. No one can see much in the dark. Are

you going to the shops? I'll take you there, it's no trouble.'
Matthew spoke perfectly reasonably yet his tone was
insistent. He sat there, making no move at all to go away.
In the end Katie just got in the car, thinking it would at
least get him to move away from the rows. Besides she
was cold in the old, threadbare coat and weary. Her
grandmother's words rang in her ears.

Now as Katie sat in the car she glanced up at Matthew.
Had they really made love in that hotel or had she
dreamed it all? If they had, she should hate him, she
should be scandalised at him, she should be stamping mad
at him. Yet she wasn't. There was no room in her for any
other emotion than her despair and unhappiness at the
deaths of the two men across from the table to a chair and
was sitting prodding a ring of blue in the ham, a sort of
fine sacking.

'I got some pressed tongue, Gran,' said Katie. 'I know
you like a bit of tongue. It'll be nice with your homemade
bread and a bit of but—' She stopped and stared at the
ring of blue, already outlined on the harn. Gran was
beginning to fill it in, stabbing the prodder and cloth
through the harn over and over. She didn't look up at
Katie.

'What are you doing?' the girl asked.

'Don't be daft, lass, you can see what I'm doing,' said
Kitty. 'That blue was just the colour I had in mind for this
pattern. It'll look grand in front of the hearth in the
Room.'

Katie didn't answer; she was incapable of it for a
minute or two. She looked at the blue cloth on the table,

the front of the coat, the buttons still on it. The back of the coat was missing and the scissors beside the strips of cloth rolled into a ball told it all. Gran must have started to cut up the coat as soon as she went out of the door.

Gran leaned over and picked up the ball of cloth, peeling a strip from it. 'I'll just do this one before we have our teas,' she said. She spoke calmly but Katie could hear the underlying tension.

'Why? Why did you do it? You had no right! You hadn't Gran, no right at all!' Her voice rose, her heart beat wildly.

Kitty put down the prodder and stood up. 'What do you mean, I had no right? You're my granddaughter, I've had the fetching up of you all these years and I won't have you bringing shame on this house. What will the minister say? I won't be able to hold my head up in chapel, why I won't even be able to put my nose outside in the street if I let you take such presents from men like that Hamilton! He's the devil himself, Katie, can you not see it? What do you think your grandda would say? He'd put you out on the street, so he would!'

Katie took hold of the remnants of the coat and held the soft, fine wool to her face. 'You were sly, Gran, that's what you were. You waited until I was out, didn't you? You planned to do it.' She felt weak and weary and without the strength to shout though she felt like screaming and not necessarily about the coat.

'Well, you weren't going to wear it again, were you?' asked Gran, her tone hard and clipped. 'Not here you weren't not if you wanted to live in my house. And don't you call me sly, lady, you who've been carrying on with one of the bosses. Did you know the pit was going on short time again? No, I bet you didn't, you don't take any notice of what goes on with your own folk, none at all! Three days a week, that's what the men are going to be on from Monday next. How's a man supposed to keep a family on three days' pay? How, I ask you, tell me now. Go on, ask your fancy man, any road!'

'He's not my fancy man, Gran,' said Katie. She felt so tired. She felt as though her back would break in two at any minute. There, just between her shoulder blades.

'He's not, isn't he? Well, if he's not, he bloody soon will be! An' look what you've done now, making me swear!'

'Gran I swear to you—'

Kitty's fury suddenly erupted. There were bright spots of red on her cheeks, her eyes flashed and she practically danced as she screamed at her granddaughter.

'What do you think it's like for me when the women say you're a whore? I tell you, they don't believe you're working at that hospital now. Not when they've seen your fancy man and his flash car hanging about. Aye the word's going round the rows already! And your Betty an' all, poor lass, she says the folk at work are always making nasty remarks about you an' what can she say back? Because it's true, isn't it? Tell the truth for a change, will you?'

'All right, all right!' Katie suddenly shouted, desperate to make Kitty stop. 'Yes, it's true!'

Gran sat down with a bump. For a minute she couldn't

speak. Then she said, 'Get out of this house, Catherine Benfield and don't come back here again. Don't come near me again; don't even come back to Winton Colliery. 'Cause we don't want your sort here. You've broken my heart and all I can say is thank God your grandda wasn't here to hear you say it. Go on, get out.'

'Gran!'

Katie couldn't believe she was hearing it. Surely it was another dream, a nightmare, she would wake up soon and it would all be just as it was before, when her grandfather was alive, when Billy was alive. When there had been no pit disaster at Winton Colliery.

'Don't you Gran me, Catherine Benfield. You're no granddaughter of mine, indeed you're not. Nor your Grandda's neither. If I never see you again it'll be too soon. Hadaway out of my sight!'

Katie turned blindly for the door; fumbled with the sneck and finally managed to get it open. The cold air rushed in. She turned back to her grandmother in mute appeal.

'Gan on, I told you,' said Kitty, still riding on top of a wave of rage. 'An' close the door after you, I can feel the draught.'

Katie went out, pulled the door to after her and ran down the yard and along the back street to the ends of the rows. She didn't know where she was going, she simply knew she had to get out of Winton Colliery. The streets were deserted and the air damp and smelling of the gases from the coke ovens up by the pit yard. But it was a smell she had known all her life and it meant home to her.

'Good for the chest,' her grandda had used to say. The memory went through her mind as she stumbled into Matthew's arms. Matthew had got out of the car to stretch his legs before setting off back to Teesside and thinking himself all kinds of a fool for waiting here so long for nothing. Only now it wasn't for nothing, he told himself triumphantly, as she fell against him.

Kitty Benfield stared at the closed door, expecting any minute that Katie would come back and she would forgive the lass now. Katie would be sorry and after all the lass was not well and needed looking after, anybody could see that. She shouldn't have been so hard on her, losing her temper like that. She'd said things that shouldn't have been said, she had. Noah had always said she had a quick temper. She flared up easy, that was it but she soon got over it. When Katie came back in she would make her a nice tea with the pressed tongue.

Kitty took the black kettle from the bar and shook it; it was almost empty. She went out to the pantry where the single cold-water tap was in the corner with a bucket underneath to catch the drips. A nice hot, strong cup of tea would do them both good. She filled the kettle and carried it back to the range using two hands. By, she felt as weak as a kitten.

'Serves you right for getting in a rage,' Noah said inside her head. Kitty nodded, it was nowt but the truth. She leaned over to settle the kettle on the cinders and caught her foot on the chair supporting one end of the mat frame. She fell heavily, off balance and struck her head on the steel fender and the kettle fell too, spilling the water over her and the mat frame. The ball of fine blue wool strips rolled off into the corner leaving a trail of blue on the proddy mat and the stone flags of the floor.

Kitty was stunned, the kitchen swam crazily before her eyes. She closed them. She would just lie here a minute and collect herself. Any road, Katie would be back, of course she would be back and she would help her to get to the sofa for a lie down.

It was very quiet, she dozed for she knew not how long. She could hear the ticking of the clock but she couldn't see it. The gas mantle flickered and went out, the penny meter needed feeding. Katie would do that too. Kitty drifted off again. The fire settled down with a shower of sparks but she didn't hear or see it.

It was Betty who found her the next day. Betty, who had always been jealous of the closeness between Katie and their gran.

Part Two

Chapter Seventeen

Christmas Eve 1939

'You can wear your new dress tomorrow, Georgie,' Kate said. 'Now be a good girl and go to sleep.' She leaned forward and kissed Georgina on the cheek and the little girl flung her arms around her mother's neck.

'Is Father coming tomorrow, Mam? As well as Father Christmas?' The question was an appeal really. Georgina had waited and waited for Father to come home. She had stood by the landing window, which afforded a good view over the fell to the distant road, which led away to Middlesbrough in the north and Whitby in the south all the morning, and then again in the afternoon until the weak winter sun went down behind the rising ground to the west.

Kate gazed at her daughter's eager little face. Georgina's deep blue eyes, so much like hers, looked back earnestly. They were the only things that Georgina had inherited from her, the strong lines of her face were Matthew's as was the fine dark hair. It was the combination that made Georgie so beautiful, her mother decided. Poor Georgie, what would become of her?

'Goodnight, goodnight, mind the bugs don't bite,' she said, in the nightly ritual her grandmother had kept up with her when she was a child. She got to her feet and went to the door.

'Will he, Mam? Will he?' Georgina refused to have her query ignored. Kate sighed and turned back.

'I hope so,' she said. 'I can't promise though. But don't worry, he'll send a lovely present for you—'

'I don't want a present Mam. I want Father to come,' said Georgie, her lower lip turning down.

'Go to sleep now, Georgie,' Kate said. 'And if your father does come tomorrow you must call me mother. Mam is just a secret name, just between the two of us, isn't it?' Georgie nodded and Kate closed the door and went down the stairs into the little sitting-room she used when Matthew was not at home.

At home, she thought wryly. This was not his home though, was it? He lived in that great mausoleum of a house over by the Tees. With his wife and his family. His proper family. His very proper family, his wife was a lady. Katie remembered her vaguely, from the days when she had been a probationer nurse and his wife had been brought in, an emergency miscarriage. But her memory of Mary Anne was misty, it was so long ago.

Kate went to the cupboard in the corner of the room and brought out half a dozen ready-wrapped parcels which she carried through to the tree in the dining-room. She placed the parcels around the tree. Most of them were for Georgina but there was one for Matthew and one for Dorothy, the maid of all work.

When she had arranged then to her satisfaction she went out into the hall and listened in case there was any sound from Georgina's room. Satisfied there was not, she went through to the kitchen where Dorothy was just brewing the tea.

'By, I'm looking forward to that tonight,' Kate said. She slipped into one of the plain Windsor chairs that stood around the table. Dorothy poured two cups of tea and put one before Kate. She went to the cupboard on the wall and came back with ginger biscuits and arranged them on a plate. Then she sat down and watched Kate stir sugar into her tea.

Dorothy felt sorry for Kate. She had been with her since before Georgina was born, seen her change year by year. She had seen the eager young girl watching and waiting for him to come home; had seen the eagerness fade to disappointment on far too many occasions.

'Are you expecting the master home tomorrow, Mrs Hamilton?' she asked and Kate put down the spoon and looked up, smiling.

'Oh, yes, I am, Dorothy,' she said. 'He promised Georgie he would be home by dinnertime. Lunch,' she added. Matthew frowned when she said dinner instead of lunch and tea for dinner. Only sometimes it was easy to forget, especially in the rush of excitement she felt when he came home.

Dorothy pushed an errant lock of white hair back under her cap and took another sip of tea. She selected a ginger biscuit and bit into it thoughtfully. What the heck did it matter what a meal was called, that was what she always thought. And for why did he keep the family here, hidden away in a fold on a God-forsaken moor? Kate was a woman to be proud of, not one to be tucked away out of sight. Just because she spoke with a Durham accent she supposed and hadn't been brought up a lady. Dorothy had seen some of these so-called ladies and Kate was worth ten of them. By, if he let them down the morrow he deserved scalping, he did an' all.

How had a woman like Kate even fallen for a man like Matthew Hamilton? There was no denying she thought a lot about him. Only sometimes Dorothy fancied Kate wasn't so keen on him as she had been. Sometimes she saw her mistress looking at him strangely. Dorothy had come to know Kate well, very well in fact. No one else but she saw much of Kate anyway. Hamilton kept her well away from people; she might almost have been a prisoner on this lonely moor.

'He can't help it, you know, Dorothy,' said Kate. 'He has to keep up with the business. And . . . And there are other things.' She finished awkwardly; she didn't like to think of the 'other things' Matthew had to see to. They included his other family and no one here knew of them. Just as, she supposed, no one in his other family knew of her and Georgie. But Matthew knew best of course.

'This is the best way to do it,' Matthew had said when she felt her life slipping away and asked why it should be as it was. 'For Georgie's sake, I mean. She doesn't deserve to be looked down on as a—'

'Don't. Don't say it, Matthew,' Kate had begged. 'I don't mind, really I don't. Not when you come back to me whenever you can.'

Matthew had taken her in his arms and it was still good, so unbearably sweet. All her love, all her emotions were channelled into the feeling for Matthew and her baby. Oh, she loved him, she really did. He had been so good to her. Sometimes though, she felt really homesick for Winton Colliery and her gran; twice she had written to her and asked that the reply should be addressed to Dorothy but there had been no reply. The third time there had been but the letter hadn't been from her gran but from her sister Betty and it had been a wonder the venom in the words hadn't burned up the page.

'. . . Don't you dare write to any of us ever again,' Betty had written. 'Gran is dead and it's all because of you. The place was full of talk about you and your goings on. Gran couldn't hold her head up and neither could the rest of the family. You never were any good, Kate Benfield. Our mam will never forgive you, never. And our dad, he won't have your name said in the house. He's badly and all, I won't have him upset.'

Every word of the letter was burnt into Kate's memory. All she had now was Matthew and she clung to him. But still, black despair haunted her most days.

Those early days with Matthew were hazy in her memory; she had wanted nothing but to stay hidden away here. And now she had got used to it. All her emotions were channelled into her love for Georgie and of course her love for Georgie's father, for she found herself unable to think of anything else for so long. She thought for a while she was going mad: that was just before Georgie was born. Matthew had brought her pills until she found herself pregnant and then it was worse because she had to cut them out abruptly.

Kate sighed and drained her cup. She stood up and gathered the pots together to take them to the sink. What a weak, spineless thing she had been!

'I'll do that, ma'am,' Dorothy said. 'You shouldn't, you know what the master would say if he caught you.' The only time Dorothy called her ma'am was when Kate did some minor household chore or when Mr Hamilton was present. Kate's hands stilled, she looked down at the neatly stacked cups and saucers and bit her lip. Dorothy was more than double her age and it didn't seem right for an older woman to have to do all the work, servant or not.

'Yes, of course, Dorothy,' she said. 'Well, I think I'll go to bed myself now.' It was only half past eight but the sooner she got to bed the sooner it would be tomorrow and Matthew was coming, wasn't he? That would please Georgie. Anyway, Georgie would be up with the larks to see what Father Christmas had brought her. At seven, she was a firm believer in Father Christmas.

'Goodnight, Kate,' Dorothy said softly.

'Yes. Goodnight, Dorothy,' Kate answered. As she walked upstairs she thought how she loved the evenings with Dorothy when they shared a pot of tea and were just two women together. She couldn't imagine what she would do without Dorothy. She was the next best thing to having gran in the house. A familiar stab of pain struck her at the thought of her gran. Oh, she would like to see her, try to explain to her. But she could never do that, not now. Gran was dead. There was no one in Winton Colliery who would welcome her now. Betty had made that plain.

'You don't want to go back there, Kate,' Matthew said on the occasions when she had mentioned it. I don't want you hurt and you would be if you tried to go back. Believe me, don't I always know what's best for you?'

Kate had to agree. Even when Georgina had been so ill with pneumonia when she was a baby and Kate had thought she would lose her. Oh how she had longed for her gran to come and help her. Gran knew so much about children and their ailments and she would have known exactly what to do to nurse the bairn back to health. Kate had begged Matthew to go for her but he would not and in the end Georgie recovered. Kate thought about that terrible time as she undressed and washed in the bathroom Matthew had had put in last year.

She put on her nightie and filled the hot water bottle from the hot tap and put it into her bed. From downstairs she could hear the wireless playing organ music and carols. The kitchen door must be open, she thought and was comforted to think that Dorothy should brave any draughts from an open door so that she would be comforted by the music. Dorothy always knew her mood.

She had already filled a stocking with a tangerine and an apple, nuts and little chocolate animals and now she took it along to Georgie's room. Opening the door as quietly as she could, she went in and changed the empty stocking pinned to the mantelpiece for the filled one. Georgie slept on. Kate looked down at her in the light that came in from the open door. Oh, she looked so beautiful. Kate's heart filled with the remembered anxiety of thinking she would lose her. She pulled the bedclothes up around Georgie, kissed her cheek and slipped back to her own room. Downstairs the chimes of Big Ben rang out nine o'clock. Kate got into bed and hugged the hot water bottle to her chest. She curled up on her side and let herself go on remembering.

Matthew had been away when Georgie came to the crisis. He had gone despite the baby being so ill. He had said he would be back that night but the weather was bad and it was impossible. It hadn't been Matthew's fault that he hadn't been there, she said in her head. No, of course it hadn't. Snow had blown across the moor, blowing the opposite way to the prevailing wind, which came in from the sea. The sparse trees were all bent permanently to the west because of the wind. But that night they were twisted the wrong way with the blizzard which came in from the west. And the snow was piled up in huge drifts right across the road, stopping any traffic.

Kate had rung for the doctor at six o'clock. And again at nine but Dr Brown hadn't come. 'He must come,' Kate had cried into the telephone. Normally she did not use the telephone for she had no one to call. Matthew had had it connected in case of emergencies in the business but no one had the number but his solicitor.

Kate bathed the baby in lukewarm water to try to reduce her temperature for she was burning up with the fever. She no longer cried or made any sound at all, just lay there, panting for breath. The crisis had come just before midnight and the relief both she and Dorothy had felt when Georgie had opened her eyes and recognised them was indescribable. When the doctor came at one o'clock in the morning, Kate was sitting in the nursing chair Matthew had bought for her and rocking her gently in her arms.

'Put her to bed now, Mrs Hamilton,' said the doctor.

'No, she wants her mother,' Kate replied. It was as though she couldn't believe that Georgie was all right. In the end the doctor gave her an injection of bromide and Dorothy had put her to bed.

It was the following evening that Matthew came at last. Dorothy had called the solicitor first thing but Matthew was 'unavailable'.

'How could you let it happen?' Matthew demanded as he burst into the sitting-room. 'You can't have been looking after her properly! It must be your fault; she just had a bit of a cold when I left here. My God, even the wretched women in those hovels you came from look after their babies better than you did.' He was filled with the need to inflict hurt to assuage his guilt and Kate bore the brunt of it.

'I'm sorry, Matthew,' she said dumbly. The nursery was warm, a fire burning in the grate, but Kate shivered.

Matthew gazed at Georgie's face, calm now though pale, then turned and slapped Kate across the face. Kate stood with her head bowed while a red stain spread across her cheek. She felt she had deserved the slap and more for she had failed to give the right care to his daughter, hadn't she? A wail came from the cot; Georgina had been awakened by his raised voice and sensed the atmosphere.

'See to your daughter,' he snapped as though she had been going to ignore the cry. That was the only time Matthew had raised his hand to her. She had seen it happen before in Winton Colliery when a man took out his anxieties on his wife. It happened, men were sometimes like that.

Kate turned over on to her back. She had to stop this remembering or she would never get to sleep. Going over things that had happened did no good, you couldn't change anything that had happened no matter how you agonised about it. The only thing to do was to go on.

The house was very quiet now, Dorothy must have gone to bed. She had to get some sleep. She propped herself up on one elbow and reached for the bottle of sleeping tablets on the bedside table. She poured water into the glass from the pitcher there and took a tablet; hesitating whether to take two but in the end screwing the cap back on the bottle. One would have to be enough. She needed to get some sleep for Matthew coming home tomorrow but if she took two tablets she might be heavy-eyed and he wouldn't like that.

Chapter Eighteen

Georgina's seven-year-old heart swelled with excitement when she heard her father's voice in the hall. She dropped Emily, the doll she had got only yesterday from Santa Claus, on to the sofa and ran to meet him, dragging the heavy oak door open and flying out to the hall. He was there. All the disappointments of Christmas Day were forgotten because he was here now. She ran to him, her straight dark hair flying out behind her and stopped abruptly a couple of feet away from him. She looked up at him as he took off his coat and hat and handed them to Dorothy. He smelled of bay rum and the cigar he was smoking and suddenly seemed almost a stranger.

Matthew looked down at her and smiled. 'Hallo, little one, did you have a nice Christmas?' he asked and held out his arms and suddenly he wasn't a stranger after all. She jumped into them and he hugged her to him for a minute before putting her down.

'You didn't come yesterday and you said you would!'

she accused him. 'I waited all day; I watched for you out of the window!'

'I couldn't, Georgina,' he said, the smile disappearing. Really, he thought, he was very fond of her but it was time she was taught some discipline, some decorum. 'I'm here now though. Don't you want your present?' He stepped aside and revealed a large parcel wrapped in brown paper. 'Go on, open it.'

Georgie tore at the paper, breathless with excitement and at last revealed a big doll's pram. It was a splendid doll's pram with shining, deep blue sides and a fold-down hood and sparkling chrome wheels. She was lost in wonder at the sight of it.

'Daddy! How did you know it was just what I wanted? Now I can take Emily for walks in it!'

'Just in the garden, now,' he warned. 'If you go out on the moors you might get lost. Now go to your room, I want to talk to your mother alone.' He looked down at her and his smile returned. She was a pretty child, with her mother's eyes and translucent skin. She had dark hair like his and her chin was firm like his too. Now she lifted it and gazed up at him.

'I want to show you what Father Christmas brought for me. You didn't come yesterday and I've waited—'

'I couldn't, I told you,' he said sharply. He looked at the door of the sitting-room. Kate did not usually rush out to greet him, not these last few years. But she would be waiting for him in there. He felt the familiar rush of excitement that he always had when he was going to see her. 'Go to your room, Georgie,' he said and walked towards the sitting-room door.

Georgie stared after him, frustrated. Then she took hold of the handle of her pram and took it to the bottom of the stairs. She could hear sounds from the kitchen, water running into a pan, cupboard doors opening and closing. Dorothy was making a 'nice dinner' as she called it though Mam said she had to call it lunch. Georgie knew why that was. Father frowned when anyone said dinner when it was lunch. He frowned at a lot of things said or done by Mam or Dorothy and they all tried to avoid his frowns. For sometimes they meant he went away and didn't come back for days and days and days.

Georgie tugged and pulled at the pram until the back wheels were on the bottom stair. Pulling and panting she managed to heave it up another three stairs but it was very heavy and wobbly and she couldn't leave go of it to put back the hair that had escaped from her hair band and was over her eyes. She tugged and pulled with all her might because she had to get it upstairs. Father said that was where she had to go and how else was she to play with it, put Emily in it? At last she reached the first landing and sat down on the bottom step of the second flight to get her breath back.

The pram rolled back down the stairs. She saw it start to go and jumped up but she was too late, it was off, bumping on every step, bumping into the banisters, chipping the varnish on two and landing on its side at the bottom with a crash. Georgie ran after it, tripped and went head over heels to land beside it. She began to cry.

In the sitting-room Matthew was kissing Kate. He held

her close and nuzzled her neck and she clung to him, moulding her body to his. And Matthew's response was compelling; he wanted her *now*. He hurried back to the door and turned the key in the lock, he had no time to take her upstairs. He was half way back to her when the crash came, followed by the sound of Georgie crying noisily.

Kate's expression changed in a split second from sensuousness to alarm; she started towards the door. 'Georgie!' she cried. 'What's happened?'

Matthew hesitated, actually torn between going to see what had happened and carrying on with his lovemaking, the urge was so strong. But, of course, he had to follow Kate out to the hall. Groaning he followed her as she ran to Georgie who was lying on the parquet flooring red in the face but her weeping subsiding.

'What's the matter? You haven't fallen down the stairs? Are you hurt? Tell me where it hurts, pet.'

Kate had picked Georgie up and sat on the hall chair with her on her knee. Georgie nuzzled into her for comfort.

'For goodness sake,' snapped Matthew. 'The child is not hurt.'

'She's had a shock,' murmured Kate defensively.

'She should not have been playing on the stairs,' said Matthew. 'Georgina, go to your room at once. I told you before, now do it!'

Georgie knew that tone of voice. She climbed down from her mother's knee and walked up the stairs, holding on to the banister and sniffing as she went. Kate stood the pram up properly. At the bend in the stairs Georgie turned round.

'Can I have my pram upstairs?' she asked.

'No you cannot!'

Matthew's roar made her turn and run up the remaining flight and into her room. She looked around for Emily before remembering she had left her in her mother's sitting-room. Lifting her chin she turned to go down for the doll but half way down the stairs decided against it. She could hear her father's voice, the words clipped and decisive. She had meant to be so good when he came and she had waited so long for him. Her lip trembled for a moment. Then she walked to the window and stared out over the moors at the dead twiggy heather and clumps of gorse.

One day, she thought rebelliously, one day she would go out there and walk and walk and never come back. She would take Emily and live in a cave and drink from a stream and eat berries or something. And then they would be sorry when they couldn't find their lost girl.

In the sitting-room Kate lay on the hearthrug with her eyes closed so that she couldn't see Matthew's face as he thrust himself into her. When he was angry, and he was angry now for he didn't like his lovemaking to be interrupted by anyone or anything, he could be rough, sometimes very rough. Not at all like he was usually. It was as though he weren't really aware of her, of who she was.

He had pushed her down on the rug and pulled her dress down away from her breasts and grasped them so hard she gasped with the pain of it. He'd thrust her cami-knickers aside and forced her thighs apart. It was over in a minute and he rolled off her and got to his feet. He buttoned his flies for he hadn't even had time to take off his trousers. Then he sat down and crossed his legs and watched as she got to her feet and adjusted her clothing too.

Matthew felt a tinge of remorse when he noticed the bruise on her neck. Had he done that? He hadn't meant to.

'Are you all right?' he asked and she looked quickly at him in surprise. On the odd occasions when this happened he didn't usually inquire.

'Yes, of course,' she said and smiled to prove it true. Fleetingly she thought of Georgie, would Dorothy go to her? She would because it was almost time for Georgie's milk and biscuits. Dorothy would make sure she had no hidden bruises from her fall. She herself could give all her attention to Matthew.

'Would you like some coffee?' she asked him. He had sat down by the fire and crossed his legs and was swinging one leg as he gazed into the flames. It was hard to believe he was the same man as five minutes ago.

'If you like,' he replied and she went to the door and turned the key back in the lock.

'I won't be a moment, Dorothy will be busy upstairs I think,' she said.

'Yes.'

In the kitchen she saw that Dorothy had put on the coffee pot and laid a tray so it was but a minute's work to finish it off. Kate got out the biscuit tin and laid a selection on a plate; Matthew was usually hungry after sex. She thought of slipping upstairs to look in on Georgie, make sure for herself that she was all right but decided against it. Matthew would get restless if she was very long away and Dorothy was there with Georgie.

'I have decided that Georgie must go to school,' said Matthew. He spooned sugar into his black coffee and took a sip.

'School? But I thought you didn't want her to go to school. That's why Miss Whitfield comes isn't it?'

Miss Whitfield was a quiet middle-aged lady who came three times a week to teach Georgie her letters and numbers. She came promptly at nine o'clock and went away again at twelve, refusing all overtures of friendship from her or Dorothy and evading any questions about her life and family. All Kate knew of her was that she lived in another isolated cottage somewhere on the moors. Matthew had hired her when Georgina was five for he was against her going to the village school three miles away.

'How will she get there?' asked Kate, accepting his decision as she did all his decisions, until his next words, that is.

'She will board,' said Matthew and Kate gasped.

'No!'

Matthew looked at her as she sank down into the chair opposite him. He sighed and said nothing for a moment or two as he marshalled his thoughts.

'There is a small private school in Guisborough which

is ideal for her,' he said. 'She will mix with other children and have a proper education.'

'She can read well, and write an' all. And she is good at arithmetic, she can say her seven times tables. That's very good for her age. And I don't want her to go.' The flat vowels of her youth came to the fore in her agitation.

Kate was frantically trying to think of reasons why Georgie should stay at home. She had always thought that Matthew didn't want the world to even know she was there and this decision had taken her completely by surprise. What would she do on her own in this house on the moor with only Dorothy for company? She would go mad, that's what.

'Really, Kate you should not be selfish about this,' Matthew said smoothly. He was well aware that he would get his own way in this for what could Kate do? 'Georgina must be educated; I want her to be a proper young lady. I want her to speak properly,' he said pointedly and Kate was acutely aware that she had slipped back into a 'pitmatic' colloquialism with 'an' all' and forgotten to modulate her accent.

'I will arrange with the school that she comes home every other Sunday and of course for the holidays,' said Matthew. He finished his coffee and placed the cup and saucer on the tray.

'Why not every Sunday? Matthew I will miss her so much!' said Kate.

'It will be too unsettling for her to come every Sunday,' said Matthew. 'Come now, Kate, many of my friends and their sons went away to school at six years old, a whole year younger than Georgina. And if you are lonely, well I will contrive to be here more often. I will come for a few hours on Sunday afternoons, won't you like that?'

He said it with an air of bestowing a great gift, she thought and he was right. She knew herself; she would look for him eagerly, almost as eagerly as she would look for Georgie's visits. She loved him and he left her with no will at all. Sometimes she wondered at what she had been like in the old days, the days when it had all happened. But her mind soon shied away from that. He was her life now, him and Georgina.

'Come on then we will tell her she is going to school. I'm sure she will be really excited. She'll love it, making new friends, learning new things.'

Matthew put an arm around her and drew her to the door. He looked down at her tenderly, oh, he loved her. He was surprised that he did, he hadn't expected it to last this long but it had. His days of visiting certain houses in Middlesbrough were over, at least for the foreseeable future. He was besotted with Kate, couldn't keep his hands off her. And she loved him, he knew that. He hadn't meant to hurt her earlier on. He would take her to bed after lunch and make love properly to her, he decided. Georgina wasn't allowed in their bedroom so they would be completely private. And soon she wouldn't be much of a problem at all. Not that he didn't love Georgina, of course he did but she was not to be allowed to get in the way of his time with Kate. And school would do her good. The school in Guisborough was small and insignificant and the head mistress discreet. There would be no breath of scandal getting back north of the Tees.

'Daddy! Am I really to go to school? Really and truly? Oh, thank you, Daddy, thank you, thank you,' cried Georgina and jumped on him so that his arms went round her instinctively.

'Mam, did you hear Daddy say I'm to go to school? Isn't it grand?'

'What did you call your mother, Georgina?' her father asked but not sternly so that she wasn't abashed.

'I meant Mummy,' she replied. 'I'm sorry, Father.'

Matthew looked over her head to Kate. 'You see why she should go to school now, before she learns any other bad habits.'

From me, thought Kate. He means calling me Mam is common.

Chapter Nineteen

Georgina sat and stared at Miss High dumbly. Oh, she hated school and she hated the teacher and she hated the other girls who were sitting sniggering at her.

'She doesn't even know which is the capital of England,' Susan Jones whispered loudly. Susan Jones was the bane of Georgie's life. She always knew the answer to any of Miss High's questions.

'Stop that talking, girls!' snapped the teacher and Susan subsided into a giggling which enraged Georgina. She turned in her seat and glared at Susan; forgetting all about Miss High, she shouted at the girl.

'I do! I do!'

'What is it then?' Susan grinned. She was the daughter of a prosperous grocer in the town and had a group of friends always around her while Georgina was usually alone.

'York!' cried Georgina and the class erupted into laughter.

'Girls! Girls!'

Miss High raised her voice and cast a quelling glance around the class. 'Susan, Georgina, go and stand outside in the hall at once. I will not have such behaviour in my class.'

Georgina walked out to the front of the class and across, feeling every eye on her and her cheeks burned though she held her head high. Susan followed and they stood outside, one on either side of the door. They could still hear the teacher's voice.

'Now who knows the capital of England?'

'I do! I do!' There was a chorus from the children. 'London!'

'I knew that,' said Georgina.

'You're telling lies,' scoffed Susan. 'You don't know anything.'

'I do, I do!'

Georgina was so enraged she launched herself at her tormentor and the surprise of it pushed Susan to the ground with Georgina on top of her pummelling at her chest. All the frustrations of the first week at the school, all the loneliness and all the longing for her mother and home came out and Susan began to scream with fright.

Next minute Georgina felt herself hauled to her feet and shaken until she was breathless by the headmistress, Miss Nelson, who had come out of her office to see what all the commotion was about. Susan had subsided into the occasional sob, obviously her feelings hurt more than her body.

'Georgina, you will sit in my office and not move or make a sound until I tell you to,' decreed Miss Nelson.

Georgina found herself sitting at a corner of the desk in the headmistress's study, adding up columns of figures then subtracting one answer from the other. She did this in record time and perfect silence, forgetting all about the tribulations of the morning. Georgina was fascinated by figures, their relation to each other and the satisfaction of coming up with the right answer to a sum.

Miss Nelson watched her then marked her work; Georgina scored full marks. A fluke, maybe? Miss Nelson gave her more sums, more suitable for a nine-year-old and Georgina went through them smoothly, pausing only to lick her pencil once. Again her work was faultless. Miss Nelson gave her more, the work usually done by eleven-year-olds, the top class in the school. Georgina sucked her pencil a few more times and frowned but then her brow cleared and she came up with the correct answers.

When the bell rang for lunch Miss Nelson was convinced she had a mathematical genius on her hands. Of course, Georgina was abysmally ignorant about some things but with a mind such as hers she would soon catch up with her age group. Why, thought the headmistress, her school could one day be famous as the school that gave Georgina Hamilton her grounding in the mathematical sciences.

'You can go to lunch now, dear,' she told the girl. 'Afterwards tell Miss High that I want you back here with me for the first period.' She had it in mind that she would test her in other subjects.

'Thank you Miss Nelson,' said Georgie. She slipped off her chair then hesitated, she hadn't been punished yet.

'Run along then, Georgina.'

'Thank you, Miss Nelson.'

Georgina's smile lit up her face and her eyes sparkled. It wasn't so bad here after all. And she was going home on Sunday.

In the dining-room Susan, sitting with a group of her friends, smirked when Georgie came in. 'Here comes the dafty,' she said jeeringly to the girl next to her. 'Doesn't know anything.' But Georgie wasn't caring much, she hardly heard her. It was Friday and she hadn't to go back into class this afternoon, she was going to see Miss Nelson. And she liked Miss Nelson, she was lovely. *And* on Sunday she was going home and her man would be there (her mummy she had to remember to call her Mummy or Father would be cross again). He might be there too and it would be lovely. He loved her, she knew he did and he only got cross when he was disappointed in her. That was what Mam said. So she had to try her best not to disappoint him, she told herself. She would be good all day.

Sunday came at last and Georgie was on her way home. The school hired a bus to take the girls to their homes, a twenty-four-seater Dennis and Georgie sat at the front and waited impatiently as one girl after another was put down and she was the last one left on the bus as it climbed up from the village of Roseley to the point where the road met the track over the moors which led to the cottage.

'Isn't someone meeting you?' the driver asked as he opened the door for her. He was supposed to hand the girls over to someone and not let them out on their own.

He gazed along the track but it disappeared in the bends and folds of the moor. He was impatient to get back home to his dinner for he reckoned Yorkshire pudding and onion gravy spoiled for the keeping too long and bringing this kid up on on to this god-forsaken part of the moor had taken up more time than he expected.

'I think so,' said Georgie. 'But I'll be all right, it's not far, I just go along this path.'

'Hmm,' said the driver. But he couldn't take the bus along the track for in places it was little more than a sheep trail and narrow. But it was well defined and surely she couldn't get lost, she lived here, didn't she? 'Go on then, I'll watch you to the bend,' he said and Georgie skipped along the track, breathing deeply of the cold air. It was different from the air in Guisborough, she decided, it tasted nicer.

She took off her velour hat with the school badge on the front of the band and swung it by the elastic in one hand and her school satchel in the other. Though she was only here for the day she meant to find some time to read up on the capitals of the world and what's more, find out what an igloo was. Miss High had said they were to build an igloo next week and learn about the people who lived in them. And she wasn't going to be caught out letting everyone know she didn't know what the teacher was talking about again. Especially that Susan Jones.

At the bend in the road she turned and waved to the bus driver and when she turned back there was Dorothy, puffing and blowing her way up the bank to her. And it was grand to see her; she felt a wave of love for the old woman wash over her. Dropping her satchel she flung her arms around her.

'Hey, now, man, what's all this?' Dorothy demanded breathlessly but she smiled and kissed Georgie and picked up the bag and they went hand in hand down the track to the cottage.

The poor little lass was too young to be away from home all week, that was Dorothy's opinion. It wasn't normal. But then there was a lot about this family that wasn't normal, she reckoned. It was a good job she had come to them when she did. Kate and the little lass were so isolated here and completely under Hamilton's thumb. They hardly dared move without his permission. Mind, Kate hadn't been herself, anyone could see that. She had a lost look somehow. At least she was better now. One of these days she would tell Hamilton to go to hell and Dorothy was looking forward to that. Only the lass loved him, just like all children loved their fathers no matter what they were like. Dorothy sighed.

'I've made a batch of Yorkshire parkin,' she said. 'You can have some with your milk, it's still warm.'

'Is my father here?' Georgie asked looking up eagerly at the old woman.

'Not yet,' said Dorothy and the eager look slipped from Georgie's face. Bloody man, Dorothy said to herself. He's not human, that's what, letting the bairn down like this. 'Your mother would have come but she's expecting him any minute.' And I wouldn't put any fellow before *my* bairn, she told herself. Not that Kate usually did, she had to admit. Her thoughts strayed to her own daughter, in

Australia. In a way Kate and Georgina had taken the place of Prue, for she had been feeling lonely and bereft at the time.

'You can come with us,' Prue had said but Dorothy knew her too well. Prue was asking but hoping her mother wouldn't take her up on it.

'No, I won't leave the old country, not at my time of life,' she had replied and turned away in case Prue saw the anguish in her eyes. The truth was, Tom, her son-in-law, was jealous of any feeling Prue might have for her; he wanted it all for himself.

Ah well, she thought as she took hold of Georgie's hand, didn't it just show that there was a purpose mapped out for her? Here she was with this little family she had made her own. And there was Prue in Australia with two little boys she had never seen. Though maybe one day – Dorothy sighed, breaking off her chain of thought as it was so depressing. After all, she had a lot to be thankful for.

It had been a lovely day, Georgina thought as she lay in her own bed that night. For Father had been in a good mood and when he was happy everyone was happy. He had been home when she and Dorothy got there and had lifted her up in his arms and swung her round and asked what she had learned at school and she even told him about the capitals and how she *had* to learn them all before she went back. And what was an igloo?

'You see?' said Father, looking at her mother and Mam had nodded. 'Yes, I see Matthew.'

Matthew was in a good mood because he had just landed a lucrative contract with the government to supply steel to the naval yards. War with Germany had the country limbering up to full production and steel works were important again.

Kate peeped in to say goodnight and she sat on the edge of the bed and smoothed Georgie's hair back from her forehead.

'I've missed you so much,' she whispered.

'Me too, Mammy,' said Georgie and then, without much hope, 'do I have to go back tomorrow?'

'You know you do, petal,' said Kate and bent to kiss her. 'Now go to sleep, you have to he up early to catch the bus.'

Georgie lay in bed, listening to the muffled sounds from her parents' room, the murmur of voices. Well, she decided, if she *had* to go to school then she would make herself like it. What's more, she would do her absolute best to be the cleverest in the school, she would show that Susan Jones she was not to be laughed at, ever again.

The war was almost four years old when Georgina won a scholarship to The Towers School at Saltburn. The girls at the school didn't see much of the war apart from the fact that a lot of their fathers were away in the forces. They had to carry gas masks around with them in a box slung around their shoulders and they had air-raid warning drill once a week. Sometimes they heard planes flying overhead and tried to guess what they were and where they were going. And sometimes a girl was called out of class to go to the headmistress's study. They all knew what that meant, her father was killed or 'missing presumed killed'.

'They say she has a fine mathematical brain,' wrote Kate in a letter to Matthew in the summer of 1943. Her letters went to a Post Office box, he wouldn't have them sent to his home or works or even his flat in London.

He was away more than ever nowadays, but then a great many men were away in the armed forces. Some of them were away for years at a time and Kate knew she couldn't grumble if Matthew didn't come home for months at a time.

He was in London a lot, working with the government though what he did she hadn't the vaguest idea. But it was some comfort to her to think that he must see almost as little of his other family as he did of herself and her daughter. She tried not to think of Maty Anne and his other family; liked to pretend they didn't exist.

'I have taken a job as a nursing assistant at the cottage hospital,' she wrote then nibbled her pen, wondering how he would take it. Why shouldn't she though? She had actually applied and been accepted and worked at the hospital for more than a year and this was the first time she had told Matthew. She knew she would have to tell him when he came home and found her going off to work but somehow that never happened.

Kate was beginning to think more and more of her old life and ambitions. She had written to her mother without telling Matthew and received a very brief letter back from Hannah, giving only some stark facts of her grandmother's death and not asking after Kate or giving any other word about the family. Kate had wept buckets in the privacy of her room and come out with a hard knot in her stomach that never really went away.

This was her life now, she told herself. She had made her bed and now she must lie on it. That had been one of Gran's favourite sayings. She loved Matthew, she told herself as she did so often these days. But she felt she had come out of a fog which had enclosed her ever since the pit disaster when Billy and Grandda had died. She was ready to assert herself; Matthew had had it his way for far too long.

'I will work on weekdays only,' Kate continued in her round, unformed handwriting. 'I will be at home at the weekends when Georgina comes from school.' She paused for a moment, she never knew quite how to sign her letters to Matthew. Then she wrote, 'Your ever loving Kate.'

She put the letter in an envelope and addressed it then took it downstairs to the kitchen where Dorothy was making Woolton pie with vegetables from the garden. She was a bit short of lard for the pastry so she had added a bit of hard margarine and was having a difficult time kneading it in.

'I'll put the kettle on in a minute,' she said to Kate and wiped a floury hand across her cheek leaving a white, dusty trail.

'I'll do it,' said Kate. 'Then I'll go to the post box on the road.'

Dorothy started to mix the pastry with water ready to roll out for the top of the pie. She knew who the letter was for of course, who else could it be? And she had her doubts as to whether the master would let the lass go to a school in Saltburn; it was too near the industrial centre of Cleveland for him.

Dorothy had been with Kate for long enough to find out the whole story, even if it had been in bits and snippets. And she had her own opinions about it all. One of her opinions was that Kate was wasting her life in this cottage in the back of beyond. It was all right for *her*, Dorothy, she'd had her life and she had her memories. But Kate hadn't lived when Hamilton snatched her up. She'd only been a slip of a lass. She was still a slip of a lass, Dorothy reckoned, slim and a proper treat to look at with those marvellous eyes and translucent skin though Kate didn't seem to realise it herself.

Dorothy was tired. She knew that but for the fact that Kate did a lot of the work she wouldn't be able to manage. Anyway, if she retired she would miss Kate and Georgie almost as much as she missed Prue. Kate was like an adopted daughter to her.

Chapter Twenty

'You will give in your notice at once,' said Matthew. 'I don't want you to go back to the hospital.' He didn't raise his voice; simply spoke in the assured tone he used when he was absolutely sure his wishes would be paramount. Lately, instead of making Kate give in immediately, his attitude merely irritated her. More than irritated her, in fact, for she had become used to making her own decisions while he had been away.

'I cannot.' Kate was equally as certain.

Matthew gazed sternly at her. He was tired, these last few weeks in London working with the government had been hard, he was beginning to feel his age, he reflected. It was late in the evening after a particularly hard day. Travelling up from King's Cross even in First Class was an ordeal in wartime, the train being so packed with soldiers that the corridors were impossible to negotiate. Even the seats in his carriage were all taken by officers, tanned dark brown by the North African sun, who lounged about with their legs sprawled in front of them so that it was even more difficult to get out into the corridor. Worse, in one corner an officer had given up his seat to a young woman with a crying infant that refused to stop its caterwauling. They had reached Darlington before it fell into a snuffling sleep and he got out at Darlington in any case.

Thank God, he had thought as he strode up the platform breathing in the cold, sooty air. And thank God Lawson was meeting him with the car. He couldn't have borne the slow local train to Middlesbrough and then finding a taxi to the works.

Lawson had been classed as C3 when he went for his medical for the army in 1940 and so had remained in Matthew's service at the Hall. He was general handyman as well as chauffeur nowadays; it was so difficult to get servants of either gender.

The Hamilton Ironworks were going flat out as were all the steelworks on Teesside. But Matthew knew the war would end sometime and he also knew the political situation was most likely to change too. There were rumours of nationalisation in the air, not now of course as all efforts went towards winning this war. But later, maybe, should Labour get in. Now was the time to plan ahead or, if not that exactly, then the time to consider his options and be prepared.

Then there had been the meeting with Mary Anne. It had been four o'clock when he reached the Hall and Mary Anne was just finishing up a meeting of her Women's Committee for supplying comforts to the troops in Italy. The meeting had ended rather sooner than expected when

Matthew came home and the ladies had filed out, glancing sideways at Matthew as they did so and murmuring to each other that Mr Hamilton was still a handsome man; he was indeed, with his dark hair tinged witty silver and his dark eyes and air of authority. He was distinguished looking and his figure was so trim with no sign as yet of a paunch. Mary Anne was a lucky woman though there had been whispers about him at one time. He was not the man to let go to London on his own for weeks at a time. After all, there were a lot of young widows about nowadays.

Matthew did not miss the interest the ladies had in him; he smiled inwardly and looked them over openly to let them see he *could* have an interest in one of them but it was only a game he played, couldn't help playing. When they had gone he dropped his slightly flirtatious attitude as he shed his coat and hat.

Mary Anne was on her feet by the drawing-room door and Maisie stood a little behind her. Each woman offered her cheek for his kiss.

'I'll send for more tea, Matthew,' said Mary Anne. 'Did you have a good journey?'

'Don't talk rubbish woman,' said Matthew and strode towards the window and flung it open. Though there was a chill breeze outside the sun was shining on the summer flowers in the garden. The room smelled heavily of lavender water and attar of roses. The breeze was better. 'Train journeys are hell and have been since the beginning of the war.' He turned round to face them. Maisie was fast becoming a replica of her mother, he thought. Though she was only twenty-two she was already the archetypal middle-aged spinster. Mouse-like too, with quick nervous gestures. She had been practically engaged once at the beginning of the war to a man as colourless as she was herself, at least in Matthew's opinion. He had been killed at Dunkirk and she looked set on mourning him for the rest of her life.

'I have to go out again, Mary Anne,' he said. He had been going to stay at home tonight and to see Kate tomorrow but suddenly he couldn't bear to wait.

'Matthew! You've just arrived and we haven't seen you in so long!'

'There is a war on, you know,' he snapped. 'Anyway, where is that tea? A man could die of thirst in this house.'

'I can't get out of it now anyway,' said Kate, ending his reverie. 'I'm on the register for work. Besides, I enjoy it.'

Matthew turned over on to his back, away from her. They had just made love and the old magic was as strong as it had ever been but now it was satisfied for the moment, he could think more objectively.

'You know I can't afford to have our relationship made public. You are running the risk of doing just that,' he said.

'No, I'm not.' She was doing the work she had always wanted to do, nursing. Only as an assistant nurse but there was a shortage of trained nurses and she often had quite responsible jobs to do. Sister trusted her, even relied on her. She did not want to give it up. In fact, if she did another year's training she could take the examinations and become a State Registered Nurse.

'I am known as Nurse Benfield, no one is going to associate me with you. No one has in all these years,' she said. 'I'm on the register for work, I told you, I can't get off anyway. Matthew, I want to do this. I feel I'm wasting my life.'

'On me, do you mean?'

'No not on you. But there is a war on . . .'

That was the second time that phrase had been used today, thought Matthew. He turned his head on the pillow and looked at her. Hell's bells, he loved her, every bit of her. But he couldn't let her break up his marriage; the effect on his business would be catastrophic. It was essential that the Richards business which had come with his wife should remain with the Hamilton firm at least until after the war. Then Robert would be home from the army and he was at least titular head of the Richards side but nationalisation was a threat on the distant horizon. Matthew sighed. He was tired and sleepy as he always was after sex as he got older.

'We'll talk about it tomorrow,' he said and closed his eyes. Within a few minutes he was asleep and snoring gently. Kate lay awake for a long time, her anxious thoughts flitting back and forth from her own problem to Georgina's.

She still hadn't told him about Georgina's scholarship to Towers School at Saltburn-by-the-Sea. Oh, why couldn't she have had a normal family? she agonised. With a normal husband and father who would take pride in his daughter's achievements. One who didn't insist that they hide away on the moor like this? She thought about Mary Anne at home there in her big house and with her three children one of them born within a month or two of Georgina.

By, that had been a body blow to her, when she found out about Bertram. She had thought that he no longer slept with Mary Anne; she knew he did not love her. But then there was Bertram and Matthew hadn't even felt the need to explain him. Even brought the subject of his son up when he talked to her, comparing his progress with Georgina's. Well, Bertram was not so clever as Georgina, she knew that.

Kate turned over once again and Matthew stirred in his sleep, disturbed. She lay rigid until his breathing became deep and regular again.

She just had to go on, she thought. For Georgina's sake. But if it came to the stage where Georgina's future was suffering, well then . . .

'I have won a scholarship to the Towers School, Father,' said Georgina, making her mother's heart beat faster. The look Kate gave her daughter said plainly, 'I was going to tell him!'

'Have you indeed?'

Matthew buttered a piece of toast and spooned on marmalade. 'The Towers School? Where is that?'

'Saltburn, Father, you must know of it.'

'Oh yes. A pity.'

'Why? Why is it a pity?' Georgina's voice reflected her strained anxiety.

'Well, you can't go there, can you? It's too near the coast. It's dangerous.'

'There is no bombing now, Father. It's not dangerous in the least. In any case, Saltburn hasn't been bombed, has it?'

'Yes it has.'

'Well, at the beginning of the war maybe—'

Kate butted in at this point. 'I think she should go, Matthew. She is a very clever girl, you know she is. She deserves her chance. Miss Nelson says there is no reason why she shouldn't go to Durham University, or York. Even Cambridge or Oxford.'

'So, you are both determined, are you?'

Kate swallowed and she and Georgina glanced at each other. They nodded. 'We are,' said Kate.

Matthew got to his feet. 'Well, I can't discuss it now, I have to go.' He walked to the door before turning and smiling at his daughter. 'Em, well done Georgina,' he said and she was filled with delight at the scant praise. He did not say when he would be back and they knew it could be that night or next week or next month. They would just have to wait for his decision.

He walked to his car, a small Austin saloon, black and non-descript with a battered nearside wing where he had bumped into a lamppost one evening in the blackout. It was not so noticeable as the Bentley in spite of the battered wing. He had parked it off the road on the side of a dip but still had to walk a fair way to it.

She was clever all right, his daughter, he thought as he walked. A pity it wasn't Bertram who had the good mind.

It was just his luck that his legitimate son should have Mary Anne's brain while the daughter born the wrong side of the blanket should have his. He found his car and got in. This fine weather it started straight away and he drove off the moor towards the South Durham coalfield.

Today he wanted to check on his mining holdings. He had the balance sheets and they made good reading but he liked to see for himself, judge the atmosphere. And it didn't hurt to drop in on the managers as well as his agent. He might pick up an *Auckland Chronicle* for Kate. She would like that.

Aw, he might as well let the! girl go to The Towers School. No one of his acquaintance ever went near Saltburn he didn't think, not during the war. You couldn't go on the beach for one thing. And the alternative was to send the girl away, far away to a school in a part of the world where the Hamiltons were unknown. He had been thinking of an academy for young ladies in Edinburgh. But that would break Kate's heart.

The problem of Kate was different. He wouldn't have her working, especially not as an assistant nurse, she was too good for that. Well, he would have to see to it at once.

Later that day he made a discreet call to the Ministry of Labour office in Stockton and had a few words with the manager. It was a question of the lady's health, he was sure the manager would understand. Kate was duly taken off the work register.

Kate was aware that he had struck a bargain with her without saying a word. There was nothing she could do, for she was determined that Georgina should have the chance she had missed. One day Georgina would take her proper place in the world as Matthew's daughter she was entitled to it. She herself would just have to get used to the loneliness of living on the isolated moor again. But Georgina would not; she would have a life away from here. She need never come back, not if she went to Oxford or one of those other universities. In any case, she herself had Dorothy, she wasn't completely alone. And Matthew of course. She was bound to see more of Matthew when the war was over. Kate went down to the kitchen for her mid-morning tea.

'Is it eleven already?' asked Dorothy in surprise. 'I haven't set it out yet. Never mind, I made a cold tea cake from one of those Woolton recipes. I just couldn't get hold of any ginger in the village. And anyway, there wasn't any syrup for parkin either. The kettle is on the boil; it won't take but a minute. Georgina went out first thing, going to get heather to put in that brass vase in the hall, she said.'

Kate wasn't sure just when the mist came down, she had been making panacklty for their dinner. She liked to make it herself and Dorothy pretended she didn't know how to though she had watched Kate do it often enough. Kate loved panacklty, it reminded her of Winton and her gran and after all these years the hurt was blunted a little. She sliced potatoes and onions and cut up half the bacon ration with a reminiscent smile.

'By, many's the time I came in from school and could smell it as soon as I came in the door,' she said to

Dorothy. She arranged the food in an oven tin and brought the jug of stock from the pantry to pour over it. Dorothy watched and wondered yet again where it was exactly. Oh, she could tell by now it must have been a mining area in Durham but she had never asked questions about Kate's past and never would. She believed in minding her own business and Kate had never talked about it. Some things, of course, she let slip and Dorothy had pieced together a fairly accurate picture of Kate's story but she would have had her tongue cut out before she repeated it, she would indeed.

'I wonder where the lass is?' Dorothy said suddenly. 'I hope she's not gone very far, do you see the mist coming in?'

Kate had been putting the dish in the oven but now she straightened up, forgetting all about it. She had been living on the moor long enough to know the mists could be lethal, if anyone was lost in one.

'Georgina wouldn't go far,' she said uncertainly.

'I'll put the storm lanterns out though, just in case.'

Dorothy brought the lanterns from where they stood in a row by the door. She could hardly see the path as she carried one to the roadside and placed it on a flat stone in the low-lying wall. She stood there for a few minutes and called, 'Georgie! Georgie! Halloo!' But all they could hear was the bleating of sheep and a moorhen clicking softly. Dorothy went back to the house, still calling.

Soon they had a row of lights leading from the road to the house and one at each bedroom window. Now all they could do was wait and pray, it was no good going out on to the moor to get lost themselves.

Georgina wandered across the moor to an old abandoned smallholding she had discovered only a year before. There was a rowan tree growing by the broken-down gate to the farmyard; it was laden with fruit, which was not quite ripe and bent to one side a little with the prevailing wind, but it was a sturdy tree with the roots firmly embedded in the rock beneath the thin covering of poor soil. It would have been planted there to guard the place, keep away evil spirits.

It was a warm day even on the high moor and she was glad to sit down on a grassy patch in the shade of the tree and lean her back against the trunk. She gazed at the little farm, thinking of the families that must have lived there over the years. The father a lead miner perhaps, coming home only at weekends to help out on the farm, the mother would look after the animals all week and children would play under the rowan tree, stringing the red berries together to make necklaces. She wished the family had still been there, she would have had other children to play with then. Now she had no one.

Georgina smiled, she was being fanciful, and she had no idea what the people would have been like. Rough and ready, she supposed, the parents going to an early grave worn out by work; the father probably suffering from lead poisoning. Or they would have had to leave the moor when the lead mining gave out and the father would get a job in a coal mine. They had learned all about how most of the people had had to go away to work from Miss High last year.

Idly Georgina began to calculate how many stones had gone into building the cottage, you would have to allow for the different sizes in the stones but it was possible if you remembered there were two sides to the walls and only rubble in between . . .

She was deeply absorbed in her calculations when she suddenly became aware that she was cold. The sun had been warm when she came out and she was wearing a thin cotton dress and a cardigan, short white socks but the sturdy shoes she always wore when out on the fell. Now a thick mist had descended and was swirling around the broken-down buildings, even obscuring the top of the rowan tree. Georgina stood up and considered what she should do.

She could shelter in the farmhouse though if the mist lasted long her mam would be past herself with worry. Sometimes, though the mist lifted quite quickly and unexpectedly, she would wait a short while at least. She looked at her watch; the one Kate had sent for to reward her for winning the scholarship. It was almost twelve. Dinner was at one; she was expected home by then. Well then, she would go.

She pictured in her mind the layout of this particular bit of moor. It had taken her twenty-five minutes to get here and the sun had been behind her. She had come over the road and gone directly down into the dip on the other side and then to the right, along the sheep trail there. She would go back, she could do it. She drew a diagram in her mind and held it there. Left of the rowan tree to the clump of heather she had been going to pick on her way back. A right turn and up the bank to the road. It was very simple really. She might even pick the heather as she went.

It was ten minutes past two when Georgie saw the lights set out by Kate and a few moments later saw her father's car, just off the road. Daddy was here – a surge of joy made her forget how cold and hungry she was. She ran, stumbling over a root only once, down the path lit by the storm lanterns to the cottage.

'Father!' she cried, bursting in at the door. 'I didn't know you were coming today! I—'

Matthew caught her as she launched herself at him and hugged her close. He had got the telephone call when he was at the works and it had taken him two hours of crawling through the treacherous mists to; get here. And he had just opened his mouth to berate a trembling Kate and Dorothy hovering behind her for allowing Georgina out on the moor by herself and where was the search party for God's sake?

He was silenced; he hugged Georgina to him. 'Where were you? How did you find your way back? You could have been lost, died of exposure!' he cried, his voice trembling with emotion.

'No, no, I couldn't be, Father,' said Georgina. 'I worked it out how to get back. Only it took a bit longer than I thought it would.'

Matthew went away again and Kate wondered about

going back to the hospital. She longed to go, especially when Georgie went to school in Saltburn. She even went there and got to see Matron.

'I'm sorry, Mrs Hamilton,' that lady said with no preamble. 'You were becoming a very useful nurse and yes, I was thinking of putting you forward for further training. A pity you didn't tell me you had suffered from neurasthenia. I understand your mental health is still precarious.'

Matthew had done his work well, Kate thought bitterly as she returned to the cottage. She realised there was no fighting him, not at the minute. He was a powerful man, suppose he contrived to take Georgie from her? Or make her leave Saltburn? That day when she had thought Georgie lost on the moor had terrified her. She could do nothing that might make her lose her daughter. She just had to wait it out for a few years, after all she was not yet thirty.

Yet her treacherous feelings still betrayed her sometimes. She caught herself thinking of Matthew with love, felt her body missing him when he was away.

Chapter Twenty-one

Georgie ran along the beach with her friend, Julia Wentworth. They had been friends since starting at the Towers School on the very same day in 1943, almost five years now. Five years, thought Georgie and smiled at Julia.

'You'll miss the beach when you leave, Julia. Why don't you stay on and have a go at your highers?'

'Because I don't stand a chance of getting them!' Julia retorted. 'It's all right for a brainbox like you, Georgie. All I can hope for is a job in an office or something like that. You'll be going to Oxford.'

'I hope!' said Georgie and the two friends slowed to a walk as they approached Marske-by-the-Sea and trudged through the expanse of soft sand to the village.

'I do love the seashore though,' said Julia and Georgie grinned. 'I'll miss it.'

'We're like the little kids, aren't we?' she asked. 'It's because of the war.' All through the war the beach had been fenced with barbed wire to keep the public off and there had been pillboxes and gun emplacements, even mines in places. When the beach had been cleared it had been great.

'Everything is because of the war,' Julia said mournfully. They had reached the ice-cream shop and went in. Not that there was any ice cream, but there would be water ices if they were lucky. The post-war shortages affected just about everything.

Georgie paid for her lemon iced lollipop and watched as Julia got hers, then they went outside into the sun and walked together along the top of the cliffs high over the beach and descended into Hazel Grove at the beginning of Saltburn. Already there were trippers on the sands, families with hired deckchairs and windbreaks.

Further along by the pier the Victorian hydro lift slid down the rails to the bottom promenade and spilled out its load of excited children and their parents. A dog barked as it ran into the sea and out again, chased by a wave. It was Saturday and a perfect morning, the last perfect day of the summer term.

It was early on Monday morning and she was in the maths class when Miss Johnson, the headmistress, had sent for Georgie.

'But why, Miss Jordan?' she asked as the two of them walked along the corridor to the headmistress's study. But Miss Jordan just shook her head and looked serious.

Miss Johnson was sitting behind her desk but she stood up when Georgie came in and that was enough to alarm any girl. Had something happened to her mother? Miss Johnson's first words took that fear away.

'You are to take the train to Middlesbrough, Georgina; there is one at ten o'clock. You're to meet your mother; she will be waiting at the station for you. I'm afraid there has been a death in the family.'

'But who is it?' There was only Father; surely it wasn't Father. Don't let it be Father, please God.

Miss Jordan saw her settled in a carriage and stood until the train set off and Georgie was left to her fears. The train stopped at Marske and Redcar and seemed to take ages before it started up again each time. But at last it got to Middlesbrough. Kate was waiting on the edge of the platform anxiously peering along the line, moving impatiently to meet her as she stepped down from the train.

'Don't ask questions, Georgina,' she said before Georgie could open her mouth. 'We haven't time now; we'll be late. Come along now.' She walked ahead of Georgie with quick nervous strides so that Georgie had to almost run to keep up. She asked no more questions for Kate wasn't going to answer them.

Kate was lost in her own thoughts as she hailed a taxi outside the station and ushered Georgina into it. She gave directions to the driver in a low voice so that he had to ask her to repeat it and she was filled with impatience at the lost seconds and repeated herself much too loudly.

'All right, Mrs,' said the driver huffily and set off.

Kate was filled with anxiety. Why, she had almost missed it! Just as she had missed Gran's funeral and her father's. Her heart was scarred because of it, if she missed

Matthew's too, she would never forgive herself.

It was only because Kate had the special number that Matthew had given her for use in emergencies that she had discovered what had happened. Matthew had been away so long and she couldn't understand why; it was almost as long as had sometimes happened during the war. Matthew had had a heart attack and he had died. And she, his true wife though not his legal one, was not told. That had disturbed her deeply, she felt like a non-person. She and Georgina could have waited for him to come back to them for ever if she hadn't rung. She rarely got a newspaper so the death could have been in the paper one day and long forgotten and she wouldn't have seen it. Oh, she could so easily have walked into the village and got a local paper. She had withdrawn too much from the world.

'I'm afraid Mr Hamilton died of a heart attack,' the anonymous voice had said on the telephone and Kate had dropped the instrument. It was Dorothy who had picked it up and elicited the information that the funeral was today, at eleven o'clock. Today! And she had to get Georgie from school, they had to go to Matthew's funeral, they had to. He was, after all, Georgie's father.

Well, she had managed it though Dorothy had protested it was too much for her. 'Suppose you're ill?' Dorothy had asked. 'There will be no one to help you. If you insist on going wait a minute and I'll come with you.'

'No, Georgie and I will go by ourselves. We will help each other,' said Kate. So there they were at last and she had prayed they would be in time.

*

There were two opulent cars outside the cemetery. Georgie and Kate walked past them and through the wrought-iron gates and up the tarmac path towards a group of people standing around an open grave. They stopped a few yards away though, by a stand of trees.

'Behind here, Georgie,' her mother whispered and Georgie stepped on to the grass, her feet sinking in a little as the ground was wet.

'Why?' she asked. 'Why can't we just join them?'

'Because,' Kate said shortly and Georgie, glancing at her mother's set white face did as she was told.

There were two women, both swathed in black, and two men, or rather a man and a boy around her own age and of course, the parson. She stepped out to get a closer look.

'Georgie!' Her mother's hiss made her step back hurriedly.

'Why are we hiding?' Georgie asked. 'Is it Father? Tell me!'

'Sssh. Later.'

Georgie's thoughts raced and whirled. Her mother looked so ill, her deep blue eyes red-rimmed in her white face. Oh God, it was Father; it had to be. A deep dread welled up in her.

Robert Richards glanced up in the middle of the final prayer and his eye caught the swift movement over by the clump of trees. Someone was there, watching them, two women in fact. He felt a twinge of irritation, they had made it quite plain in the death notices that the service in the church was open but the interment was private to the family. Who the hell were they, anyway? Not one of Father's women, he hoped. But no, those sort of women wouldn't dare. Just some busybodies no doubt with nothing better to do than gawp at other people's misery. He stepped nearer his mother and put an arm around her shoulders.

The parson had finished and Robert led her forward to the small pile of earth beside the open grave. She took a handful and dropped it in on top of the coffin and the rest of the family followed suit. Then Robert, still with an arm around her shoulders, led her away towards the gates of the cemetery and the rest of the party trailed behind them.

'Come back to the Hall, Vicar,' Robert said. 'There will be a light luncheon.'

'No thank you, I won't intrude.'

Robert shook his hand and thanked him. 'A good service, Vicar,' he said. And a jolly good thing it was over, he thought, all his concern was for his mother.

Mary Anne shivered as she got into the car. 'Why is it graveyards are always cold?' she asked but she wasn't looking for an answer, it was just something to say.

'You can go now, Lawson,' said Robert.

Bertram gave him a resentful glance. He was the heir; it was for him to give the orders. But he said nothing for the minute; he would wait until they got back to the Hall.

Robert glanced back out of the rear window as they crested the small hill; there was a good view of the cemetery. He frowned; the two women were by the open graveside, one was even throwing a handful of dirt into the grave. The cheek of the blasted woman! If it hadn't

been for his mother being in the car he would have
stopped it and gone back and sent the pair of them
packing. As it was, he had to turn and face the front and
pretend there was nothing out of the ordinary.

The car turned into the gates of Hamilton Hall, crunching on the gravel. It pulled up before the Victorian gothic
entrance and Lawson jumped out and opened the door.

'I'll see to Mother,' said Bertram with a note of authority. He was first out of the car and offering his hand and
arm to Mary Anne. Robert looked at him with approval.
Perhaps the lad was going to be more responsible now his
father was dead. He certainly hoped so. Robert completely
missed the hostile gleam in Bertram's eye. He helped
Maisie out of the car and they walked together up the
steps and into the house after their mother and half-
brother.

A cold collation was laid out in the dining-room. There
were already a few people there, business friends of
Matthew's, Jackson, the works manager and Parsons, his
mine agent. And Mr Fox his solicitor. They were standing
around the great stone fireplace and sipping dry sherry.
Daisy and Benson the butler were handing round glasses
of sherry. There had been a buzz of conversation that
quietened as the family entered and the men all turned to
look at them.

'Come and sit by the fire, Mother,' said Robert and the
visitors moved away to make room. Though it was
summer, there was a definite chill in the air. Outside the
sky had darkened and rain threatened. Robert stood beside
his mother and sister as the company came to her

individually to offer their condolences.

'Mr Hamilton was a good man, a great loss,' said Mr Jackson as he held Mary Anne's hand for a moment and Mary Anne smiled briefly and murmured something inaudible. She lifted a lace handkerchief to dab at her eyes.

'Thank you, Mr Jackson. I'm sure my father thought a great deal of your abilities.' It was Bertram speaking, he had stepped in between Robert and their mother, giving Robert a cool glance as he did so.

Robert was taken aback, and then amused. Bertram was barely seventeen. His pale skin was smooth as a girl's, his narrow shoulders accentuated by the black mourning suit. But he had a look of determination, or was it defiance as he caught his brother's eye as though he expected Robert to push him back again. Of course Robert did not, he moved back himself to have a word with Mr Fox, the solicitor who was hovering near.

'Would you like another glass of sherry, Mr Fox?'

The solicitor's glass was almost empty and Robert lifted a hand to call Benson's attention to the fact. Daisy offered a tray of canapes but Mr Fox waved them away.

'Not at the minute, thank you, Mr Richards, I must get back to the office,' he replied. 'But I would like a word with you first.'

'Oh yes, I got your letter,' said Robert. In all the flurry of his stepfather's sudden death he had put the letter aside telling him that the solicitor would like to speak to all the family about the will on the Tuesday after the funeral. He had felt a brief surprise that Mr Fox wasn't going to read the will after the funeral but it was a very minor mystery. There were more important things to think about.

'I thought you would read the will this afternoon,' he said now. 'After all, it can't be very complicated can it?'

'I can't today. There is another major legatee who will have to be present. What I was going to ask was, could the family come to my office? No, no, that won't do, I can see you think it won't. Well, the only answer is for me to come to the house tomorrow. Which would suit you best, morning or afternoon?'

Robert sighed. 'Afternoon, I suppose. I must go to the works in the morning. There are so many things to see to in the run up to nationalisation.'

'Yes of course I—'

They were interrupted by Bertram; who had noticed them having a quiet talk in the corner. Now he came up to them and rudely butted in on the solicitor.

'Are you discussing business? You know of course that I am my father's heir, do you not?' he asked Mr Fox. 'Robert is only a stepson.'

Mr Fox looked embarrassed. 'Em, er,' he stuttered.

'Behave yourself, Bertram,' Robert said sharply.

'Don't tell me what to do! This is my house now, I'll do what I like and say what I like too. You have no authority over me!'

One or two people near turned to look at them for Bertram's voice was raised petulantly. They turned back quickly and carried on with their own conversations but a number of eyebrows were raised.

'I see we have joined in the airlift to take supplies to

Berlin,' said one. 'These communists have to be kept down, I say I—' Whatever else he had to say was drowned in a murmur of agreement.

'Bertram, come here, dear,' Mary Anne said quietly and Bertram, flushed and scowling, had no alternative but to go to his mother's side.

'It's only right, Mother,' Robert heard him say. He turned back to Mr Fox.

'Will three-thirty suit you?' he asked. 'I can be back by then. And I'm sure the others will be in. But what do you mean, another major legatee? How can there be?'

'I'm afraid I'm not at liberty to divulge the name of the person until tomorrow. I gave my word to Mr Hamilton. Now I'm afraid I must get back to the office. I'll just have a word with your mother, poor lady. Pay my respects.'

Robert was glad when all the visitors finally took their leave; the reception seemed to take for ever. When the last of the cars crunched over the gravel on its way out he breathed a sigh of relief.

'Thank God that's over,' he said to Bertram as they turned back into the Hall. 'Now what was the point of that little tantrum you threw earlier? Mother must have been ashamed of your behaviour.'

Bertram turned to him in fury. 'Don't talk to me as though I were a child! I am a man now and head of the firm, it is for me to take my father's place and I can throw you out if I so wish. So you'd better mend your manners when you talk to me.'

Robert sighed. 'Oh I can't be bothered,' he said tiredly. 'If you consider yourself an adult then act like one, especially where Mother is concerned. If you can't then keep out of her sitting-room until she retires.' He turned his back and walked into the little sitting-room that Mary Anne had made her own. She was seated in a chair by the window looking out over the rose garden. At this time of year the scent of the roses was heavy in the air coming in through the open window.

'How do you feel, Mother?' he asked as he went over to her and put an arm around her shoulders. 'If I were you I'd have an early night, I will send Daisy up to you with some light supper if you wish.'

'No no, I'm fine here,' said Mary Anne. Indeed, though there were shadows beneath her eyes and she was a little pale, she looked quite serene. 'I've sent Maisie upstairs though, she has a headache. Poor Maisie.'

Poor Maisie, that was how most people thought of his sister, Robert thought. When he had come home from the prisoner-of-war camp in Malaya in 1946 he had been as shocked at her appearance as she had been at his. He himself had recovered fairly well; he was lucky in that he had only been a prisoner for a matter of months. Maisie, however, still moped after her lover who had been an RAF pilot shot down over Arnhem in 1944. Geoffrey Walker had been the only man ever to take an interest in Maisie, so small and thin and mouse-like with her fine fair hair which just missed being blonde and which she kept in an old-fashioned bun at the nape of her neck.

'I'll go up and see her shortly,' Robert promised. He was fond of his sister but was beginning to wonder if she did not need professional help to bring her out of her melancholy. There had been some improvement lately; she had had her hair cut in a more fashionable style and, even bought a fashionable hat for the funeral. The death of their stepfather hadn't helped either, she had told him only that morning that she felt death was all around her.

'Now I'll ring for tea,' said Mary Anne.

They sat drinking tea from an exquisite china tea service, the cups almost transparent they were so fine. Mary Anne ate a sandwich and a slice of fruit cake with evident enjoyment, surprising Robert. But then, he told himself, she had eaten very little since Father died, perhaps it was just the relief that the funeral was finally over that had brought back her appetite.

'Where is Bertram?' she asked idly after sipping a second cup of tea. She replaced the cup and saucer carefully on the tray then looked up at Robert for his reply.

'I think he went for a walk,' he answered.

'The fresh air will do him good.'

'Yes.'

They sat quietly together, looking out at the roses. The weather had improved and evening sunlight shafted across the lawn and along the tops of the sycamore trees bordering the garden. 'Mr Fox is to read the will tomorrow morning. Eleven-thirty, he said. Is that convenient for you?'

'Quite convenient.'

'He did say there is a major legatee not in the family.'

'Oh?' Mary Anne sounded barely interested.

'Father asked him not to say who it was until the will was read.' Robert felt he had to warn his mother that there was something strange about the proceedings, but he didn't know what. He glanced anxiously at her now. Did she know about his women, his visits to a certain area of Middlesbrough? But surely it could not be one of them.

'That's not usual, is it?' asked Mary Anne.

'No. But it is no good speculating about it. We will all know tomorrow.'

'Yes. Well, thank goodness, the Richards part of the business is yours, Robert.'

'Yes. And evidently too small to be included in the nationalisation plans. Now that the coal interests have gone that way.'

'I think I'll go up now after all, Robert,' Mary Anne said suddenly. She rose and patted the back of her hair with one hand. 'I am tired, I have to admit.'

'Yes, you go up Mother. Goodnight.'

After his mother left the room Robert sat on, thinking of the business and what was going to happen. Everything was in a state of flux at the moment, the Labour government determined to nationalise. The electricity industry had gone in April, coal in 1946. How the miners had loved that, they had shouted for it long enough. Transport and gas had been nationalised, it was all one big new experiment. He was not like some of his colleagues, hoping it would prove disastrous, they didn't seem to realise that would bring the country to its knees. His stepfather had been going to be one of the executives to run the industry; he hoped they would ask him in place of the old man. It could all be very exciting.

His thoughts kept returning to the mystery of the two

women who had been lurking in the cemetery. But perhaps he was imagining things. They could have been visiting another grave and simply been curious about the funeral.

Chapter Twenty-two

'Why didn't you tell me, Mother?'

Kate and Georgina sat, one on each of the two couches which faced each other in the sitting-room. Kate was pale but composed, the shadows under her eyes accentuating her dark eyes. There were a few streaks of grey in her fair hair. Georgina noticed them for the first time and it gave her a small shock. After all, her mother was in her thirties, she wasn't old. The reality of death had been brought home forcibly to Georgina today though and she looked anxiously at her mother. 'Don't bother tonight Mother, I'm sorry I asked.'

'Oh, you might as well know it all, petal,' Kate sighed. 'You had to find out Matthew and me weren't married. Did you not suspect it?'

Georgie thought back over the years. Father had been away such a lot but then, during the war many of the girls' fathers had been away. In the forces, or on some sort of war work. And she had got used to it anyway. Still she had thought there was something different about her. The way her mother prevaricated when she asked for her birth certificate. The university had wanted it with her application.

'Won't your identity card do?' Kate had asked. 'All the details are there, surely? Anyway, there's no rush, you have a few months yet. I'm not even sure it is a good thing to go up a year early. Why not wait until you are eighteen? Have a year at home with me. I've seen little enough of you since you went to Saltburn.'

Georgie thought about this conversation now. For a supposedly bright girl, university material, she had been as dim as a Toe H lamp.

'Tell me then. But stop if you are becoming too tired. I don't want you to be upset either.'

'It all started, I think, just after the 1926 strike,' said Kate. She had a faraway look about her. She lifted her still slim legs and tucked them beneath her, holding her ankle with one hand as she talked. Her voice was low and matter of fact, it was almost as if she were talking of someone else.

'I was brought up by my grandda and grandma,' she began. 'And Grandda was out of work because the pit was idle; the pit at Winton Colliery. That was where we lived. And one day Grandda and me went to get pitch balls for the fire. We had no coal, you see, and a pit man's house with no coal is – well, there was no electricity, no other means of heating the house or cooking. And we bumped into a gentleman.'

Georgie sat as the shadows in the room lengthened and listened. It was a revelation to her. For so long she had wondered how her mother could be content to live in this isolated house in a fold of the moor, living only for her to come home from school. No, that wasn't right, she lived for Father to come home from his mysterious business. When Georgie had asked questions about it they had always been evaded, his work was very important, they had said, very hush-hush. It was an expression that was common during the war and immediately after it. And her mother also lived for her to come home from school, of course.

Georgie had idolised her father, she thought of it now as Kate told the story of how ambitious she was as a young girl, how she desperately wanted to become a nurse, how she had actually achieved her ambition in that she had managed to become a probationer nurse. And then how she had met Matthew Hamilton again. And his wife. How he had pursued her. And how that had been the end of her nursing, career. Then Kate sat silent for a long time. A single tear slipped down her face and she wiped it away angrily.

'Oh, Mam, don't get upset,' Georgie said, swiftly crossing to the other couch and putting an arm around Kate. 'Don't say any more now, there's no need. I know how you loved Father, I do.'

Kate looked sideways at her. She blew her nose and wiped her eyes and patted Georgie's hand.

'You're a good lass, Georgie,' she said, slipping back into the idiom of her youth. 'But you don't know the half.'

'I'm sure you'll tell me in your own good time,' said Georgie. 'I'll get Dorothy to start supper now, shall I? I think we could both do with an early night.'

As she opened the door the telephone began to ring in the hall, causing Kate to jump visibly.

'Who can that be?' she cried. 'No one calls here except your father!' And then she was overwhelmed by the fact that Matthew would never call again, never ever. She sat down suddenly, forced to confront the enormous hole in her life. Whoever was on the telephone didn't matter compared with that.

'I'll get it, don't worry it can't be anything important,' Georgina said, trying to reassure her mother. She picked up the telephone from the hall table feeling a little eerie herself.

'Miss Hamilton? This is Joseph Fox. I was your father's solicitor.'

'Oh. Yes?'

In that split second many things raced through her mind. Were they about to be evicted from their home? Had she and her mother any rights at all? Had her father made any provision for them? Surely he had! Such was the whirling of her thoughts that she missed what the solicitor was saying at first and had to ask him to repeat it.

'Go to Hamilton Hall? I don't even know where it is,' she said. 'Besides I don't think my mother would want to go and I don't want to leave her.'

'I'm sorry Miss Hamilton; I haven't made myself clear. It is very important that you both go. It is the reading of your father's will. You wish to know what provision he has made for you and your mother, do you not?'

'But how will we get there?'

Georgie glanced round to make sure she had closed the door to the sitting-room properly. She did not want her mother to hear this at least not until she herself had had time to think about it. Would her mother want to go to that woman's house? Mrs Hamilton, she thought and bitterness rose in her throat like bile.

'I will call for you,' said Mr Fox. 'At ten o'clock, I think. Then we will be at the Hall in good time.'

'You know where we live?' Of course he did, she thought. He probably knew all about her. Including the fact that she was a bastard. She made up her mind quickly as she heard her mother's footsteps. 'All right. Ten o'clock, yes. I will ring you back if there is any difficulty.'

'Until tomorrow, Miss Hamilton.'

'Who was that, Georgie?' her mother asked as she came into the hall.

'I'll explain in a minute. Go and sit down Mother, I'll bring the supper,' said Georgie.

'No. I'm not hungry, I think I'll just, go straight up to bed. Who did you say it was?'

'Go on up then, I'll bring you some hot milk and biscuits. I'll tell you all about it then, Mam.'

Kate was already trailing up the stairs. She couldn't summon enough interest to insist, in fact she had already forgotten what it was she was asking about. Her thoughts were in the past, her life in Winton Colliery. Grandda, Billy and now Matthew, all dead. And Gran. 'It will all end in tears,' Gran had said and she had been right as she always was.

When Georgie took up the tray her mother was standing by the window looking out over the darkening moor. She was still dressed.

'I thought you were going to bed, Mam,' she said. 'Come on, I'll help you get ready.' She hesitated to tell her mother of the reason the solicitor had called, maybe she would leave it until tomorrow. But when she was settled against the pillows and with the cup of hot milk in her hand, Kate looked up suddenly.

'I don't know what we are going to do, Georgie. We will have to leave this house. We have no rights, you know, no rights at all. I suppose I could go back to nursing . . .' Her voice trailed away.

'I think Father will have provided for us, Mam. I was going to tell you, that was a solicitor on the phone earlier.'

She told her mother all that Mr Fox had told her. 'We must be ready at ten o'clock,' she added. 'But if you don't want to go to the Hall, well then, we'll just say so, I'll ring him back.'

'No,' said Kate, surprising Georgie by the sudden strength in her voice. 'We'll go. And with our heads held high.'

She had thought she wouldn't sleep but surprisingly she soon drifted off, still thinking of the old days in the colliery house at Winton. Her thoughts carried on into her dreams, so vivid she was a child again.

Chapter Twenty-three

Mr Fox handed Kate out of the car before the entrance to Hamilton Hall. He smiled at her gently. 'Courage, my dear,' he said. He was a man of middle age with silver hair, which was receding so that his forehead seemed elongated. He was tall and thin and dressed impeccably in pin-striped trousers and dark coat with a silver grey tie. He had a kindly face, Kate decided, and she put her hand on his arm trustingly.

Beside her, Georgina stood, her hair clipped up on top of her head in an effort to make her look older. She wore a plain grey dress with a full skirt cut in the 'new look' fashion that was a reaction to the restrictions of the war years. Her shoes were grey and flat with wedge heels and on her head she wore a tiny hat of grey velvet and a wisp of lace.

'You must wear a hat, dear,' Dorothy had said. 'As a mark of respect at least.'

Georgie followed her mother and Mr Fox up to the heavy oak front door, and waited as he rang the bell.

Suddenly her stomach was full of butterflies, she fought down a feeling of sickness. Beside her she could feel her mother's tension, see the slight tremble of her hand on Mr Fox's arm. She took a deep breath as the door opened and they were ushered inside.

'The family is in the drawing-room, sir,' said John Benson, the butler.

'Thank you, Benson.'

Georgina barely had time to note the richness of her surroundings before they were in the drawing-room and there they were, Matthew Hamilton's other family. Only the women were seated, the men were in a group in the middle of the room, talking among themselves quietly. There was an instant hush as everyone turned to look at Kate and Georgina who stood uncertainly close together.

Mr Fox went forward and placed his briefcase on the table.

'Good morning to you all,' he said pleasantly. 'This is Catherine Hamilton and her daughter, Georgina. They have an interest in Mr Hamilton's will.'

Mary Anne gasped. 'I know you!' she cried. 'You're a nurse, aren't you?'

Kate stepped forward. 'I was,' she said.

'You had better sit down,' said Robert. He indicated two hard chairs placed side by side but made no move to help them.

'Sit down? Sit down? What do you mean? How dare you insult my mother by inviting them to sit down in my mother's house? She's a tart and the other one's a tart's bastard daughter! How dare they call themselves

Hamilton? I insist you throw them out, if you don't, I will!'

'Bertram! Watch your tongue!' Robert said sharply.

'Don't you tell me what to do! I am the head of this house now, remember. I'll say what I like.'

'No you won't, not in front to Mother,' said Robert. 'Now sit down and behave yourself.'

Bertram flushed a deep brick red. 'Don't talk to me as though I were a child, Robert! At least I am defending Mother. You don't seem to care.'

'Sit down, Bertram,' Mary Anne suddenly interjected. 'Both of you, sit down. In fact, we will all sit quietly and listen to Mr Fox.'

Taken by surprise, her two sons sat down and stared at her.

'Sit down, please, Nurse Benfield, isn't it? And you too, dear,' said Mary Anne. Everyone gazed at her in astonishment but she was perfectly composed.

Kate and Georgina sat down on the hard chairs. 'I wondered if you would remember me,' said Kate.

'You haven't changed,' replied Mary Anne. 'At least not much.'

'You know this woman?' gasped Bertram.

'Yes, indeed, I do. It was a long time ago, before you were born. I had a miscarriage. She was very kind to me when I was in hospital.' Mary Anne spoke in a very matter-of-fact tone of voice and as though Kate was an old friend.

'But Mother—' said Bertram but was interrupted by Mr Fox who cleared his throat and picked up a document tied with a red tape bow.

'Perhaps we can get on,' he said. 'I do have a lot to get through. If you don't mind, that is,' he nodded his head deferentially to Mary Anne.

'By all means,' she said and settled down in her chair.

'This is the last will and testament of Matthew Hamilton, ironmaster, of this parish,' he began.

Ironmaster? thought Georgina. But her thoughts were full of bewildering questions. Surreptitiously she looked at the family. Mary Anne, so calm though she had just lost her husband. She wore a black dress, very plain but with a diamond brooch at the neck. Her hair was fair and streaked with grey and she wore no make-up on her pale face. Beside Georgie's own mother she looked colourless. And her daughter, a younger edition of herself, though her dress was more stylish with a full, new-look full skirt which fell decorously over her knees. Her neat ankles were crossed and slightly under her seat. She seemed to take no interest in the proceedings but kept her eyes on her hands, which were clasped, on her lap.

Robert, the oldest son, looked like her yet did not. In him the fair hair had a natural shine to it and though it was cut in a 'short back and sides' he had it longer at the front and combed back in a quiff. He sat straight-backed in his chair; his long legs crossed one over the other. He wore a slight frown.

Bertram was different. He had dark hair just like Father's and the same dark eyes but there the resemblance ended. He still had the figure of a youth; his shoulders narrow and rounded and his skin had an unhealthy pallor except for his nose and ears. The poor lad had a cold, she supposed. He caught her gaze and treated her to a venomous look. Well, she couldn't really blame him, she thought. She and her mother must have come as a great shock to him. She looked away and tried to concentrate on the solicitor.

'My house on Fern Moor I leave to Catherine Benfield Hamilton together with an annuity of a thousand pounds a year,' he was saying and the whole company gasped.

'That's disgusting!' said Bertram, glaring at Kate.

'Shut up, Bertram,' said Robert. He sat stern and unsmiling, betraying no surprise or any other emotion.

'To my natural daughter, Georgina—'

'Natural daughter Georgina!' gasped Bertram.

'To my natural daughter, Georgina and my son Bertram, I leave the Hamilton Iron and Steelworks on the proviso that my stepson Robert shall have the overseeing of the works for the first five years after my death. I would like Georgina to attend Durham University rather than take up her scholarship to Oxford. She is to have two thousand pounds a year until she has finished her education at which time I would like her to enter the business.'

Georgie didn't hear much of the rest of the will. There was a pulse pounding in her ears, she clasped her hands tightly in her lap and stared down at them. Durham. She wanted to go to Oxford. She had her heart set on Oxford. The disappointment was overwhelming.

She was aware that there was some sort of a hubbub going on above her head. Gradually she could hear

Bertram's voice and then Robert's, not loud but commanding. Of course, he had been an officer during the war and was used to being obeyed. She looked at him. He seemed nearer her mother's age than Bertram's, but of course, Matthew had only been his stepfather.

Beside her, her mother was saying something to her. Georgie forced herself to listen.

'Let's get out of here,' Kate was saying. 'Howay, man, I cannot stand it.' They stood up and suddenly everyone else went quiet and turned to look at them.

'My mother and I are leaving now,' said Georgie, her head held high.

'You can't go yet,' Robert said.

'You can't just walk out of here!' shouted Bertram.

Mr Fox looked over his spectacles at them. 'There are things to agree upon, papers to sign,' he said mildly. 'I'm afraid I am not able to take you home just yet.'

'Then perhaps someone would be kind enough to ring for a taxi,' said Georgie and looked at the butler. 'Mr Benson, perhaps?'

For the first time that Robert could remember, John Benson looked unsure of himself. He looked at Robert for guidance as to what to do. It was Mary Anne who spoke.

'By all means, Miss Hamilton, if your mother is tired. This has been a shock to you too I know. And I'm sure the rest of the business can be seen to later. Benson, call a taxi please.'

'To go to the railway station please.'

'Yes. The railway station.'

Mary Anne was a polite hostess and she rose to her feet

to say goodbye, even walked a few Steps towards them.

'Mother! What are you about?' Bertram demanded.

'It's all right, Mrs Hamilton,' said Kate. 'We will wait outside in the fresh air if you don't mind. It will clear my head. I believe I saw seats there.'

Once in the outside portico Kate sank on to a seat, pulling Georgie down beside her. 'The old sod!' she said. 'He did this deliberately, do you know that, Georgie?'

'Who?'

'Your father of course, who else? I tell you Georgie, there was no need at all to bring us here today, we could have heard all about the will in the solicitor's office or even by letter. No, I bet Matthew was having a good laugh at us all this morning if he could see it that is. Well, I'm not playing his game any longer; I'm going home, that's what I'm going to do. Gannin' yam, as me gran would say, God bless her.'

'Mam, you sound so much better,' said Georgie. And Kate did, she had a becoming colour in her cheeks and her eyes sparkled.

'Aye. It was just what I needed to get over Matthew dying like that.' Kate laughed softly. 'After all the trouble he went to to keep the pair of us a secret from his family an' all.'

'He kept them a secret from me too,' said Georgie. 'I'm not sure I can forgive him that.'

Kate glanced at her. 'I know, pet, I know. But in the circumstances we thought it best.'

'You mean you had some say in it?'

Kate shook her head. 'No, no, I didn't have a say in

anything. Matthew was away a lot but he still had to have everything his own way, you know that. I didn't defy him until the war when I went back to nursing. And he soon put a stop to that.' The remembrance of how he had stopped it was still bitter.

Kate sighed and stood up, walking down the steps that led to the elaborate portico. She stared down the drive frowning.

'Where the heck's that taxi?' she asked the air. There were a few cars parked by the house and she glared at them. 'You'd think one of the buggers could have given us a lift to the station.'

'Mam! You swore!' said Georgie.

In fact, Kate realised, in this last ten minutes she had reverted more and more to the accents and idiom of her childhood. It had all been there underneath her polite way of speaking. Except of course that if she had sworn in front of her gran she would have earned a slap across the face. She smiled as she pictured her gran's face when she was angry. Oh God, what a mess she had made of things. Or Matthew had made of things. No, it had been her own fault, she had a will of her own, hadn't she, and she had Georgie, she wouldn't not have had Georgie, would she? She was worth it all.

A taxi was turning into the drive. 'Howay now, Georgie,' Kate said over her shoulder. 'Let's away. I can't wait to get home.'

As the taxi went down the drive, crackling and crunching over the gravel, Georgie looked out of the back window. There was no sign of anyone at the door or the windows. It was as if the house wanted nothing to do with them. She grinned and turned back to the front. That was probably right. Well, *she* wasn't going to be shrugged off so easily. She would make her mark and they would not be able to ignore her, oh no they would not.

It was not until that night in the privacy of her own bedroom that Georgie cried for her father. And her reasons for crying were all mixed up in her mind. There was the deep yearning to see him again if only once. She could ask him why he had done what he did. Spoiling her mother's life by keeping her on this isolated part of the moor, keeping her, Georgie, ignorant of her true position. It could almost have been a game, had he enjoyed it? It was a wonder it hadn't all come to light anyway.

She went over the events of the day. There was only Bertram who was related to her, she realised. And he'd acted like the spoiled kid he probably was. Robert and the girl, woman rattier, old maid probably, they had a different surname, Richards. They were her fathers step-children. And their mother, Mary Anne, she was a funny woman. Funny peculiar, that is, the way she had reacted to discovering her husband had another woman he had kept for years and years. It was almost as though meeting Kate was a bit of a relief to her.

No one was really grieving, she thought suddenly. No one in his first family anyway. Just her and her mother. And even her mother was perking up remarkably swiftly. She acted as though a burden had been removed from her rather than her beloved Matthew.

Georgie stood by the window, the tears drying on her

face. She sniffed and blew her nose on her hankie. She had a slight headache and her eyes prickled. She stared outside at the black dark of the moor. Only in the far distance, above the village hidden from the house in a fold of the moor was there a faint redness that showed there were lights there.

Durham, she thought. Well, it wouldn't be so bad and she would be closer to her mother. But she had no intention of entering the business when she finally got her degree, of that she was certain. No, she refused absolutely to work in a steel foundry or whatever they called the place. Anyway, wouldn't it be nationalised, anyway?

Cheered at the thought, Georgie drew the curtains and climbed into bed. In the bedroom next door she could hear small sounds that meant her mother was doing the same. There was the sound of a knock and a door opening, then Dorothy's voice. She would be bringing her mother hot milk and the comfort of her company for ten minutes as she always did. Thank God for Dorothy, Georgie thought sleepily. No doubt her mother would have gone off her head living in such isolation if it hadn't been for her housekeeper.

Chapter Twenty-four

'We will contest the will,' said Bertram. 'He had no right, no right at all.'

'It would do no good according to Mr Fox,' said Robert. 'No, Bertam, I don't think there is anything to be done.'

It was eight o'clock and the family had gathered in the dining-room for the evening meal. They were waiting for Mary Anne to come down. Bertram, as he had done since Matthew died, sat in his father's seat at the head of the table. He had looked up defiantly when Robert entered the room as though expecting a challenge but Robert had merely smiled and gone to his usual seat at the side, opposite Maisie.

'What does he know?' asked Bertram. 'I'm the head of the house now and I say we will contest the will. We can get another solicitor. I'm sure there will be others eager to take his place. In any case, Mr Fox is an old fuddy-duddy.'

If he expected an argument he was disappointed.

Robert merely smiled at him. In truth he couldn't be bothered with Bertram's naive utterances.

'Well, if you want me to leave I can do so,' he suggested. 'I have no wish to look after this estate, I have enough to do. My tenants in Whitworth Hall are going soon. Their lease is up and they have said they don't wish to renew it. I was thinking of moving out of here anyway. Now I have full control of the Richards works I want to live nearer.'

'I didn't say I wanted you to go,' Bertram mumbled, his ears going bright red.

'Go, who is going?'

The men got to their feet as Mary Anne came in and nodded to Benson. 'If it's ready you can serve now, John,' she said.

'I was saying that I wouldn't mind going back to Whitworth Hall, Mother. The tenancy lease is almost expired.'

'Oh?' Mary Anne looked a little alarmed. 'But who would look after things here?'

'I would of course,' said Bertram. 'It's my house, my land.'

'I understood that I was to have control until you were twenty-five, Bertram,' his mother said gently. Oh, how she wished this younger son of hers had as much sense as her older one.

'Yes, but that's only a matter of form. I didn't mean I would chuck you out. I just meant—'

'Never mind, Bertram, I understand,' said Mary Anne. 'In fact I was thinking how nice it would be to go back to

261

Whitworth Hall myself. This might be the perfect opportunity.'

'Mother! You're not going, are you?' Suddenly Bertram had reverted to a small boy frightened of losing his mother.

'No, I'm not going. In any case you have to go back to school. You have your highers to think of. Don't be in such a hurry to grow up, Bertram.'

'Oh no, I wasn't going to bother with that,' said Bertram. 'I will be busy won't I? What with the business and everything. And anyway, I am grown up.'

John came in and served the leek and potato soup followed by rissoles and vegetables from the garden.

'Is this all there is?' asked Bertram.

'Sorry, Bertram, the meat ration doesn't last the week. We're lucky to have this,' said Mary Anne. Rationing was still in force as the country struggled to help out ravaged Europe and at the same time cope with the huge debts from the war.

'What about me, Robert, will I go with you or stay here?' Maisie startled them all by speaking. She was usually so quiet.

'Oh Maisie, it's entirely your own choice,' said Robert. 'But I thought you would want to stay with Mother. If not I would love to have you at Whitworth Hall.'

'He's a right pain in the neck, that Bertram,' John said to Daisy as he brought the empty plates into the kitchen. Daisy was busy doling out plates of semolina and conserved apricots and John began to load his tray with them.

'Aye, I always said so,' she replied. 'By, if one of mine

and Eddie's had turned out like him I'd have murdered him. Though they wouldn't have done, we don't spoil our kids.'

Daisy and Eddie Lawson were married now and the flat over the stables had been enlarged to accommodate their growing family. She looked harassed as she dished up the sweet, her waist thickened and her ankles swollen. She was the only woman servant the Hamiltons had managed to retain and that was because Eddie didn't want to move, he was quite happy living over the stable and working around the place when he wasn't called upon to drive.

Now Eddie sat at the kitchen table wondering how he was going to get out of buying a cottage in the village with the two hundred pounds Matthew had left them. It had been Daisy's dream ever since they were married and now she was determined that it would come true.

'A turn up for the books mind, this tart and her daughter showing up, wasn't it, Eddie? I never guessed for a minute. Mind, I know he was one for the ladies, like.'

'Oh, I knew about her,' said Eddie. 'She's a pitman's brat from over Bishop Auckland way.'

'By, you old sod, you never said a word,' John said, pausing with the tray of sweets in his hand. Eddie laughed and tapped his finger on the side of his nose though in truth he had been as surprised as anyone by the revelations of the day. He remembered her all right, recognised her and her striking eyes and colouring but he hadn't known the affair was still on after all these years. The lucky old goat, he thought to himself with a twinge of envy.

'Aye well, the Hamilton mines are gone now,

nationalised with the rest,' said John. 'The miners are cock a hoop.'

'The steelworks won't be long neither and then what will happen to the Hamiltons?' said Eddie.

'Eh, folk like them'll still land on top of the heap, they always do,' Eddie answered.

'I hope so, else what'll happen to us?' asked Daisy. ''Cos you'll never shift to get another job, I know you.'

Upstairs, the meal finished, Robert excused himself and went off to his study but though there was plenty to do after his stepfather's sudden death he couldn't concentrate on work. He had kept his temper and said as little as possible all day for he didn't want to say anything until he had had time to think about what had happened.

He was filled with a cold fury. What sort of man was it that did what his stepfather had done to his wife? To keep a woman all those years, to have a child with her and bring her up hidden from his family? (Oh, he had known Matthew was fond of visiting the red light district in Middlesbrough but this was something altogether different.) He was furious for the sake of his mother.

Why had Matthew married her, anyway? Just to gain control of the Richards Steelworks, that was why, obviously. And he had had control, all these years; longer even than he would normally have done for when he himself had reached his majority he had been away fighting for his country.

Robert boiled with fury as he remembered all the times his stepfather had slighted his mother, speaking to her as though she were a servant sometimes, especially when

Robert was small. And Maisie, she was so timid and self-effacing because of Matthew, of course she was. He had belittled her and sneered at her all the time when what she had needed was someone to bolster her confidence. If only her fiancé hadn't been killed in the war she might have come out of it. If only he himself had been at home he could have helped. But there it was, Maisie was Maisie and there was no way of changing her now.

His stepfather had left his tart, for that was what she was, an annuity, well, he could afford it. He had come out well from the nationalisation of the mines. And made a fortune during the war too, all the ironmasters had of course. Even those that were bombed. That small one down the coast, at Skinningrove, it had been one of the first to be damaged, he remembered that. The Jerries had mistaken it for Middlesbrough which was a bit of a joke really.

Robert poured himself a whisky and added a splash of water before settling back in his armchair and sipping appreciatively. Most of the good stuff, the single malts was reserved for export only but Matthew had always managed to get the odd bottle. This was a Glen Morangie and very mellow.

He thought of that chit of a girl standing defensively beside her mother that morning. A girl who looked more like his stepfather than Bertram, there was no question of paternity there. Only her eyes were like her mother's, a striking dark blue which had darkened to violet when she felt her mother threatened. She had Matthew's thick black hair, his determined chin. Though somehow she wasn't quite so good-looking as her mother. But evidently she was clever, had won a scholarship to Oxford. If it wasn't for his mother's feelings, he would have welcomed her into the business, goodness knows Bertram wasn't exactly well endowed in the brains department.

Robert poured himself another drink, unusual for him. But then it had been an unusual day with the bombshell that Fox had dropped. He would like to have thought of the girl's mother as someone out for what she could get and not caring if she broke a marriage up in the process. But he knew his stepfather too well for that. Matthew had always had an eye for the ladies. Thinking of that Robert's anger rose again. His mother was better off without him but would she realise that? He drained his glass and got to his feet. It was past time for bed, there was plenty to do in the morning. He would just look in on his mother, say goodnight.

Mary Anne was in bed already, the great bed that had been her own since Bertram was born so it did not remind her of Matthew. He had slept in the dressing room next door every night and she had been grateful for it. She lay, propped up on the pillows with a book on her knees but she wasn't reading. She was thinking of Kate and her daughter, Georgina, and trying to puzzle out what it was that had attracted her to Matthew in the first place. His money? Mary Anne didn't think so, Kate hadn't struck her as the mercenary type.

Strangely, Mary Anne found she didn't hate Kate. She couldn't help liking her really. The way she had stood up to the family that morning, her chin held high. Her daughter's too. Kate had been a born nurse too, quick to anticipate the patient's wants and so very kind. At least she had been so with her. No, Mary Anne thought, Matthew must have been the one who did the chasing. He must have been very different with Kate Benfield than he had been with his wife.

Her thoughts were interrupted by a knock on the door.

'Come in,' she called and Robert stepped into the room.

'You weren't asleep, Mother, were you?'

Mary Anne smiled. 'No. I'm glad you looked in. You know I love to see you.'

'You will be tired though after today. I'll just say good-night and leave you to sleep.'

'Don't go for a minute,' said Mary Anne. 'I wanted to ask you something.'

Robert paused and looked down at her and she smiled. He was a lovely boy Robert, oh yes indeed he was, she thought. Her mind touched on her other son, Bertram, as it did so often when she was with Robert. Their natures were so very different. With luck Bertram would grow more like Robert than his father, she thought sadly but without much hope.

'When you go to live in Whitworth Hall would you mind if I came with you? I know men your age don't want their mothers living with them, but I could live in the cottage in the grounds, couldn't I? Once it's done up. I know building materials are in short supply, but—'

'Mother, of course you can. And Maisie too. You can live in the house as long as you wish. I'd like that. But I thought you felt you should stay here with Bertram.'

'I could come back during the holidays for Bertram, couldn't I? It's just one more year then I suppose he'll be off to university.'

'Mother, perhaps we shouldn't rush to make plans. It's early days yet.'

'Oh Robert, if you knew how much I have hated living in this house,' Mary Anne sighed as he bent to kiss her cheek.

'Goodnight mother. You need to rest,' he said. As he went out of the room he heard her murmur something else. 'What did you say, Mother?'

'Nothing, son. Goodnight.'

Now I'm free, he thought she had said. As he went to his own room he decided he must have misheard. He passed Maisie's room and paused, wondering whether to go in. But there was no sound so he went on.

Maisie was awake, however. She was sitting by the window looking out at the night sky as she did most nights since Geoffrey had been killed. In her nightie and robe with her hair down her back she looked different some-how, younger. Her hair gleamed a little in the moonlight coming in at intervals between the scudding clouds and, loose, it softened her face, emphasising her high forehead and well-shaped mouth.

'It's your money and position he's after,' her stepfather had sneered. 'It certainly can't be your beauty.' He had laughed as her face coloured up and her eyes prickled with tears. Oh, how she hated the ever-ready tears, they had been the scourge of her life. And no matter how she had tried, she couldn't stop them. As a child she had learned to keep in the background, especially when her stepfather was around. But Geoffrey had brought her out of herself. She had met him when she was walking in the park which surrounded the Hall. Her stepfather was home, so she had walked longer than she normally would and ended up sitting on the boundary fence for there was nowhere else to sit. And Geoffrey had walked by on the path on the other side. He was in his RAF uniform and incredibly handsome. She couldn't believe it when he stopped and spoke to her, treated her as though she were any young girl, attractive even. She began to feel alive in the following weeks.

Well, he had been killed, Maisie thought as she closed the curtains and climbed into bed. But at least she had her memories. Geoffrey had thought she was someone special, he loved her no matter what her stepfather said.

Chapter Twenty-five

'So you see, I'm going to Durham. It's all arranged,' said Georgina. Julia Wentworth looked at her in concern.

'But you were so set on Oxford,' she said. 'Is there no way you can still manage to go there?'

The two girls were riding along the firm sands at Saltburn at the head of a group of younger girls from school. Riding was part of the curriculum at The Towers School and Georgina usually looked forward to it. Though now, as the summer season got under way, there were more trippers on the beach and they had to take their lesson early in the morning.

Not that she minded that, especially not today. It was a bright morning with the sun causing the sea to sparkle like diamante. She nudged her horse into the waves until his feet were covered, that was what he loved. She; turned to her friend to reply.

'Oh, I don't mind, once I'd thought about it. I will be able to come home more and now that my mother is on her own, it's probably for the best.'

Julia was the only person Georgina had confided in, poured out everything to. She had been a; little hesitant about it but she had to tell someone or she felt she would burst.

The two girls halted and turned in the saddle to wait for the others to catch up before they led the way up the sands and off the beach to the stables. Georgina led her horse into his stall and worked silently rubbing him down, giving him hay. After the turmoil of the past week at home she was glad to get back to some sort of normality. Here she could pretend that nothing had changed, she would go home for the holidays and Father would come home from his business if only for a day or two. Only now she knew he was as likely to have come from his legitimate family as his business and that was why he was absent so often. And the knowledge made her boil with fury.

'You should have told me,' she had said to Kate. 'I should have known, I feel a fool for not realising anyway.' She *should* have realised what it was that was strange about her family. She hadn't been that ignorant of the world. She'd been a fool all right.

'I was going to as soon as you were old enough. And then it just wasn't the right time.' Kate had bitten her bottom lip. 'I haven't done right by you, have I, pet?' she asked.

Georgina gazed at her. 'Oh, I don't know. It wasn't your fault really.' Still, though she knew in her heart that was true, she felt some resentment towards her mother. But still, she was her mother and she loved her.

Kate had told her everything now. All about her grand-father and Billy being killed in the pit. And about her gran, how she had loved her gran. 'I was off my head for a while after the disaster,' she said sadly.

'And Father took advantage of it,' said Georgina bitterly.

'Well—' said Kate, looking unsure.

'Oh, Mam, you know he did,' said Georgina.

'Still, he loved me,' said Kate.

'He had a fine way of showing it. Keeping you hidden away, something he could take out when he felt like it, a favourite toy.'

'Don't talk about your father like that,' Kate said sharply. 'It was as much my fault as his. I was weak. I should have had more backbone.'

Georgina had left it at that. What was the point in drag-ging things up now? It was history, nothing could change it. And it hurt.

She went back to school for the last few weeks to sit her Higher Certificate of Education. Georgina had always had the ability to concentrate on whatever she was doing at the moment and she was reasonably sure she had done as well as was expected of her. Now it was the last week of term and she would be leaving The Towers School for the last time the day after tomorrow.

'I can't wait to be finished with school,' said Julia as they walked back to the main school. 'We're going to France in August for a whole month! And my cousins will be there for part of the time at least. I wish you could have come, Georgina, my cousin Maurice has taken a liking to you. He just needs a little encouragement.'

'I'm not interested in boys, there's plenty of time for that,' said Georgina. She had met Maurice at Christmas when he had stayed with Julia's family and she had gone over there on Boxing Day. He was a nice enough boy and she was interested in his stories of university life – he was in his second year at Cambridge. Oh yes, she had liked him, even been attracted to him but she had too many plans of her own to let a boy get in the way of them. She was going to be a great mathematician.

A picture of Robert Richards rose in her mind, she wasn't going to let him get in her way either. He was an arrogant sort of man and she had the feeling he would try to take over from her father. But she was determined not to let him. She was quite capable of managing her own future, thank you.

The last day of term came and for Georgina the while day was ruined at breakfast time. As she came downstairs she was startled to see some of the girls looking at her strangely. A group was huddled in a corner of the hall and when they saw her one held her hand over her mouth and giggled and the giggle was echoed by the others. Mystified, Georgina took her place at the table and the mystery was solved. There was a copy of a local newspaper on her plate and the headlines, two inches high, proclaimed 'LOCAL IRONMASTER'S LOVE NEST ON THE MOORS'.

There was a pounding in her ears; she didn't even notice the whispering around her as she read the text below the caption. It was all there but twisted nastily.

How her mother was from a mining village and a scheming hussy who had snared Matthew Hamilton while she was nursing his wife who had had a miscarriage.

'The astonishing fact is, Hamilton kept his mistress and illegitimate daughter hidden on the moors. It is understood that the girl is bright and is being educated at The Towers School where the governors and staff had no idea she was the daughter of *the* Matthew Hamilton, the successful businessman. His two families lived only a few miles apart yet he managed to keep the second secret from the first.'

A note was pushed into Georgina's hand, she took it automatically. Opening it she read, 'Georgina Hamilton, you're a tart's daughter. I bet you don't feel so high and mighty now, with your scholarship to Oxford.'

'A tart's daughter, a tart's daughter, is you a tart too?' someone said and the words ran round the table amid fits of giggles. Georgina picked up the paper and stood up. She tore it into pieces and flung them down and marched out of the dining-room and the giggles followed her.

'Georgie! Georgie! Don't go, wait for me. They're a rotten lot of cats!' Julia had come after her and caught her up just outside the door.

'You must have told them!' cried Georgina. 'You, it must have been you!'

'No, I didn't,' Julia said, 'I—'

'What are you two girls doing out here? Come inside at once, can you not hear the racket going on? You should be stopping it, I know it's the end of term and you're leaving but you are in positions of responsibility.'

It was Miss Johnson, just coming into the dining-room followed by the rest of the staff. Georgina looked at her dumbly then fled not looking back even when the headmistress called after her.

Her cases were already packed, her trunk had been sent on the day before. All she had to do was pick up the cases and leave. She ignored all attempts to stop her by the staff and Julia and ran down the stairs and out on to the street, making for the station. It was only a few minutes away and there was a train standing in. She flung the cases into an empty carriage and climbed in after them. As it chugged out of the station she saw Miss Johnson charge on to the platform and run after the train but she was too late. Georgina had left The Towers School and she was never ever going back.

Georgina walked up the track from Roseley. She felt she needed not only the fresh moorland air in her lungs but also the time to think of how she was going to tell her mother that their story was in the newspapers for all to read. Apart from her brief time working in the nursing home during the war, and that was a few years ago now, Kate had been isolated from the world. Would she be able to take being in the limelight? Oh it was true that the papers would soon forget the story, at least, something else would take its place.

Georgina knew from the newspaper story that there had been reporters at the cottage, asking questions of Dorothy and Kate. It must have been such a shock. Well, now she was here to fend them off, the interfering nosey parkers.

Her cases were becoming very heavy, she dumped them at the side of the track behind a clump of gorse. Not that there was likely to be any people about, no, they had been and done their worst, she thought savagely.

'I'll take them in the jeep.'

The voice seemed to come out of nowhere. Georgina jumped and whirled about. She hadn't even heard the jeep as it laboured across the uneven ground for she had been too engrossed in her own angry thoughts.

'They are all right where they are, thank you,' she snapped. But Robert Richards was jumping down from the jeep and striding over to her.

'Don't be silly, Georgina,' he said, as though she were a fractious child. He picked up the cases and swung them easily into the back of the vehicle. 'Come on, get in.' He got behind the wheel again and looked impatiently at her. 'Get in, I haven't all day to mess about in this godforsaken place.'

Georgina found herself climbing into the jeep though she had had no intention of accepting a lift. Robert Richards was that sort of a man, she thought. Well, he wasn't going to boss *her* about as he seemed to do with his younger brother, she told herself, treat her like a child. It was just that she was beginning to feel tired, that was all. It was a long hike to the cottage.

'What are you doing here?' she asked baldly as they bumped along to the rise where the track ran out. 'We'll have to walk from the road end,' she added.

'No we won't,' said Robert. 'I've tackled worse terrain than this in a jeep.' And so he had, he thought, a picture of the North African desert coming to mind. Sure enough he drove right up to the front gate of the cottage with no trouble.

There was a closed-up look about the place. Usually in summer the front door stood open but now it was firmly shut. But suddenly it was flung open and Kate came out on to the path, arms akimbo.

'I told you lot yesterday I had nothing to say to you! Now you'd better be ganning before I get the polis on you. Oh! It's you, Georgie, what the heck are you doing here? I wasn't expecting you till this afternoon. And you, what do you want with me?' This last was addressed to Robert as she suddenly recognised who he was.

'Well, that's a real northern welcome!' said Robert dryly. 'Aren't you going to ask me in Miss Benfield?' He couldn't help noticing how lovely she looked with her cheeks flushed with anger and her eyes flashing.

'My name is Hamilton; it was changed by deed poll years ago, Matthew saw to it. And Georgie is a Hamilton too, it's on her birth certificate.' Kate stared at Robert her chin lifted. He wasn't going to put her down, indeed he was not, and not on her own ground any road.

'Oh Mam, we may as well go inside,' said Georgie. She was weary of it all suddenly. And if there were reporters lurking about on the moor she didn't want to see them.

'Howay then,' said Kate. 'Let's hear what you have to say, Robert Richards. We might as well get it over with.'

Inside, Dorothy was hovering in the tiny hall, looking anxious. 'Will you make some tea, Dorothy?' asked Kate. 'It's all right, this is Mr Hamilton's stepson.'

'No tea for me,' said Robert.

'Oh, please yourself.' Kate led the way into the sitting-room. 'Now, as I said before, why are you here?'

'I want to know who is responsible for telling *The Recorder*,' said Robert. 'And if it was either of you, and I strongly suspect it was, do you realise what harm you may have done the family? Not to mention the business!' He didn't raise his voice but his tone was hard, cutting almost.

'You're a fool if you think it was me or my Georgie,' snapped Kate. 'I was pestered all day yesterday; I couldn't come outside of my own front door. Why should I speak to reporters, for God's sake? Did you read what they said about me and the lass? Did you? They pushed a copy through the letterbox this morning and were shouting through it, asking what I had to say about it. A tart they branded me, and my Georgie a tart's daughter. Do you think I wanted that?'

'I didn't think you'd care,' he replied. 'After all, that's what you are isn't it?'

Georgina snapped. 'Don't you talk to my mother like that!' she shouted. 'It wasn't her fault, *he* made her do it. He ran after her, he—'

'Oh? And how did he do that?' asked Robert. He looked mildly interested, as though he was asking about the weather. 'He didn't tie her up and kidnap her, did he?'

'No, but—'

'Oh, for the love of God, stop it!' said Kate. 'Georgina, keep out of this or you can go into the kitchen and help Dorothy. And you,' she rounded on Robert. 'You watch your tongue or get out of my house!'

'I'm going. I only came to say that if either of you talk to the press ever again, say one word to them, I'll blacken your names until you won't dare show your faces anywhere. And don't think I can't do it. What's more, we will contest my stepfather's will and make sure you don't get a penny, either of you. Now, have I made myself clear?' He looked from one to the other, Kate was livid, her face white as a sheet and Georgina was quivering with rage. But Kate put a hand on her arm warning her to stay silent.

'Are you finished?' she asked. 'Then get out.'

'Good day to you both,' said Robert and his tone was almost pleasant. It changed, however, as he went out into the hall and opened the door and a flash bulb exploded in his face. He strode up the path and grabbed at the camera and threw it down on the ground.

'Hey! What do you think you're doing?' the cameraman shrieked, 'I'll have the law on you, I will, that's expensive equipment that is.'

'Do that,' Robert snapped. 'See how far you get. This is private property in case you didn't know.'

'It's broken, look what you've done,' cried the cameraman. He was bending down on the path and picking up the camera. Kate, watching out of the window, couldn't see much wrong with it except that the flash bulb attachment had become separated from the camera. In spite of her rage at the way Robert Richards had spoken to her she gave an involuntary smile.

'Go on, get off this property,' said Robert, standing over the man threateningly.

'I'm going, I'm going,' the cameraman shouted. He got to his feet with the camera and bits in his arms and went off through the gate and up the path a short way, unsure where the so-called private property ended. Robert strode to the jeep and got in and started the engine. He reversed and turned back up the hill and drove straight up, making the newspaperman jump to one side.

'Watch where you're bloody going!'

Robert grinned and drove off, soon disappearing over the rise.

'The arrogant bugger,' Kate said. 'By, it's not often I swear but I've been driven to it today. I tell you, Georgie, I'll swing for that fella if he doesn't change his attitude to us. And mind, the next time one of those newspaper men come to my door he'll get a bucket of water on him.'

'Well, Robert soon shifted that one,' Georgie remarked. She gazed at her mother. Kate's face was more animated than she had ever seen it. And her cheeks were flushed slightly, a becoming pink so that her mother looked ten years younger. Georgie's heart lifted, let them say what they like, she thought. She and Kate would be all right.

Robert, driving along the road to Teesside, felt a bit ashamed of himself. Talk about kicking someone when they were down, he thought. And no matter what, there was no denying that Kate had had hard times these last few days. And Georgie too. Georgie was little more than a child, he should have had more restraint he could see that now. Poor kid.

He had been so angry though, so fearful of how all this publicity would affect his mother. And so sure that Kate or Georgina must have said something to the damned press. Now he reckoned they must have had some other source. He grinned as he remembered the cameraman and his broken camera. He would probably have, to pay for that. But it had been worth it. Kate had been so feisty when she opened the door but nevertheless she had had a haunted look, her eyes large and luminous in her white face.

She had looked so young, no older than he himself was anyway. For goodness sake, he thought angrily, Matthew must have got hold of her when she was still a child, the old lecher.

Chapter Twenty-six

'I'm going to Winton Colliery today. Will you come with me?'

Georgina, spreading marmalade on a slice of toast, looked up in surprise. 'Winton Colliery?'

'Yes, Winton Colliery. You know where it is, I've told you about it,' Kate said patiently.

It was the end of August, and in the weeks since her father had died Kate had not ceased to surprise Georgina. Kate had bought a small car, second-hand of course for she was not prepared to put her name on a list and wait for a new one, but a Morris 8 and in good condition. She had learned to drive and passed her driving test in record time and now Georgina was taking lessons.

'Are you sure you want to go back there?' Georgina asked. 'You haven't got very good memories of the place, have you?'

'Of course I have, I was brought up there,' said Kate. 'Now I've a fancy to go back. Howay, it's a lovely day for a ride out. You can drive if you like. At least some of the way.'

Georgina had been planning to go over the list she needed to take to Durham but after all, there was still plenty of time.

'Okey dokey,' she said.

'We'll take a picnic if you like. I'll have a word with Dorothy,' said Kate.

It was a good day for a drive. Soon they were rolling along the road east, driving across the Great North Road at Rushyford and on past Windlestone Hall to Coundon.

'I'll drive from here,' said Kate. 'I know the way and anyway you'll have the chance to have a proper look at the view,' she added as Georgina opened her mouth to protest.

They swept down Durham Road into Bishop Auckland, the castle and park on their right. There was a slight haze on the bottom by the river but when they swept up the road past the bishop's castle into the market place it gave way to bright sunshine. It was market day and the place was thronged but Kate wasn't fazed, she negotiated her way by the stalls and the buses standing in and turned down into Newgate Street, the main street.

'This is my home town,' she said.

Georgina was not impressed. The street was long, narrow, straight and dusty. The shoppers were mostly shabby and some of the shops could do with painting. There was still an air of austerity about the shop windows but then, she thought that was true of most towns in the aftermath of the war.

Kate turned left at the traffic lights and soon they were going through a succession of mining villages with their attendant slag heaps and winding gear and tall smoking chimneys making the air smell smoky. Periodically, along the long lines of tiny houses, there were heaps of coal, the miners' allotments, ready to be shovelled into the coal houses. There was coal dust in the air, shimmering in the sunlight.

'It's good to see the pits working,' said Kate. 'I know it's because of the war but even so. By, my grandda would have been over the moon if he knew they had been nationalised. It was always his dream. It all looks grand, doesn't it?'

Georgina looked at her in amazement. She tried to imagine what it must have been like for her mother when she was a little girl. If this was grand what must it have looked like then?

'It looks pretty dismal to me, Mam,' she said.

'Dismal? Dismal? Don't talk tripe,' said Kate. 'The bairns have shoes on their feet, haven't they? I know the government is stopping the rationing of shoes next month. Here the shoes were always rationed. Rationed by the lack of money to pay for them, not the coupons in the ration books. Mind, our Georgie, you don't know the half of it.' She shook her head to emphasise her point.

She was driving along the edge of the Winton Colliery rows by now and she slowed and pulled up by the side of the road.

'Are we here then?' asked Georgina.

'We're here. Come on, get out, we'll walk up the road

to the rabbit warren and have our picnic there before we look round.'

They strolled up the road past the houses, past where they could see the old village to one side, past the colliery yard and out into the country. Kate carried a rug to sit on and Georgina had the picnic basket over one arm. When they came to the track that was the entrance of the rabbit warren Kate changed her mind and walked on, up the bank to where there was a derelict building, its roof fallen in in one place and grass growing thick round the door.

'It was the engine house of the old aerial flight,' said Kate. 'Billy Wright and I sometimes came here when we were courting.' Memories of being here with Billy were rushing back to her. She had a soft, faraway look in her eyes as she spread the rug by the building and sat down, leaning against the old red bricks that were warmed by the sun. She looked so relaxed and happy that Georgina said nothing, not wanting to disturb her mother's mood.

They ate sardine sandwiches and drank dandelion and burdock pop, sitting side by side and gazing out over the valley. On the opposite side the bank rose steeply for about a mile, mostly farmland and woods. The view was hazy because of the smoke from the houses and mine workings but no less lovely for that. To Georgina it looked like an impressionist painting.

It was quiet, no one walked by for a while until a couple of miners coming off shift. They were still black and had their helmets pushed to the back of their heads so that the white line showed above the coal dust on their faces and their hairline. They still wore their leather knee protectors and as they walked coal dust shimmered on their clothes.

'Now then,' one said as they passed and both nodded their heads.

'Morning,' said Kate and scrambled to her feet. 'Do you mind, I used to live around here. Can you tell me if there's anyone called Benfield still living in Winton?'

The older one of the pair pushed his helmet further back until it was in danger of falling off the back of his head.

'Willie Benfield do you mean? Aye, he lives there. And there's Ethel, only she married Dave Canvey. Was it Ethel you wanted?'

'Thank you. Yes, that's right, thanks,' said Kate and sat back down as the men walked on.

'Ethel? Who is Ethel?' Georgina asked.

'My sister,' said Kate and picked up her sandwich and finished eating it.

'You didn't tell me you had a sister.'

'No. Well, I didn't tell you everything,' said Kate. 'When we've finished we'll walk down and see if Ethel Canvey is in.' As she ate, Kate was gazing out over the village and colliery. 'Look,' she said, 'they've put up some pre-fabs on that side, do you see? I wonder who has been lucky enough to get one of those? I read they have bathrooms and fitted kitchens. Even refrigerators.'

'We have a fridge, Mam,' said Georgie. To her the pre–fabricated houses looked tiny, smaller even than the houses in the mining rows.

Kate laughed and stood up. 'I know that. But somehow I never expected there to be one in Winton Colliery. Apart from in the manager's house, that is. Let's go down and have a proper look, shall we?'

They walked back down the road and put the picnic things in the boot of the car. Kate peered into the wing mirror, looking at herself critically.

'How do I look?' she asked.

'Oh Mam, you look fine, of course you do. You always do.'

They walked along the top of the rows, drawing curious glances from the few people about. So far, Kate had seen no one she knew. A few boys were playing in the middle of the street with a cricket bat and a tennis ball and wickets chalked on the wall of a coal house. Kate hesitated at the top of West Row, wondering whether to go down and look at the house where she grew up. In the end she walked down the back alley to the gate and looked over into the yard.

'Our Katie! What the heck are you doing here? Slumming it a bit, aren't you?' A woman had come out of the back door with a tin bath full of wet washing and she halted and stared at them.

'Mind Ethel, that's a grand way to talk to your sister,' said Kate, unfazed, though she had not expected to find Ethel so easily. She walked up to the woman and pecked her on the cheek. 'So you and Dave got me Gran's house, eh?'

Ethel sighed. 'You'd best come in,' she said and led the way.

The kitchen was different. There was a utility sideboard instead of Gran's press and a gas stove of all things in a corner. The walls were distempered a light lemon colour. The range was still large and black-leaded with a brass rail under the mantelshelf and on one side there was an old picture of Noah and Kitty and on the other a tinted one of Thomas and Hannah. A bright fire burned in the grate despite the warmth of the day.

'Sit you down,' said Ethel and picked up the iron kettle and shook it, decided there was plenty of water in it and placed it on the coals. Turning, she looked Georgina up and down.

'This is your lass, is it?' she asked.

'Yes, sorry. This is Georgina,' said Kate. 'Georgie, this is your Aunt Ethel.' She looked a little apprehensive, a child out of wedlock was not looked upon lightly in Winton Colliery. At least not as she remembered it.

'How do you do?' said Georgina, lifting her chin and holding out her hand.

'By, she's a fancy talker an' all,' said Ethel. 'How do *you* do, pet? You've got the Benfield eyes any road. Though you must have got that black hair from your dad.'

Kate beamed. Ethel was taking this altogether better than she had expected. She had always been such a shadow of Betty and Betty was a bitter sort of girl when they were younger. Now Ethel was different, more tolerant.

'I haven't got much in, it being washing day and I haven't been to the store,' said Ethel, putting out a plate of Yorkshire parkin.

'We've had our lu – dinner,' said Kate. 'We brought a picnic and ate it up by the old aerial flight engine house.'

'Mind, you needn't to have done that,' Ethel declared. 'We are family after all.'

'Well, I didn't know how things were now, I thought you might not want us in your house,' Kate said deprecatingly.

'Aye but we might as well let bygones be bygones,' said Ethel. 'Dave's in the back shift and the bairns get their dinners at school now, there never were such times. So I'm not rushed for time. I'll just hang these clothes out though, they could be drying.'

'I'll give you a hand,' said Kate.

Georgina was fascinated. She watched through the window as the two sisters hung out the lines of clothes in the back yard. The sheets were taken out of the yard and strung across the back alley. As they worked they talked about the days gone by, what an old devil Grandda Noah had been. How their father had lingered on for a while after the accident before he died and how Hannah had gone soon after. How the pit yard had been bombed in 1940 and nothing hit but the lamp cabin. How Betty had met and married a Canadian airman and gone to live in Canada from where she sent food parcels home with notes like she was blooming Lady Bountiful. How Dave, who'd been a Territorial, had gone into the army, the DLI, and been in Tunisia and Italy and come home unscathed. They were still talking when they came back in with the empty peg bag and while Ethel brewed the tea. Yet not a word had been said about Kate and Georgina and what had happened to them. Kate was talking in exactly the same accent as Ethel by now.

'An' what do you do, pet?' asked Ethel at last.

'I'm going to Durham University in October,' said Georgina.

'Eeh you're not, are you? That's grand! I don't think we've had anybody in the family going to university before. Mind, my lad Tom is bright, real bright. He's always top of the class at school. Get a scholarship he will, his teacher says.'

The afternoon slipped away and Tom and his sister Grace came in from school. They stood about silently, looking at the visitors with the striking dark blue eyes of the Benfields. It was plain to see they were all related.

Shortly afterwards Kate decided it was time to be on their way.

'Come again,' said Ethel. 'Eeh, our family used to be all over the rows and look at us now. Only me and our Willie. And his sour-faced wife.' She paused and looked hard at Kate.

'Did you know he married Billy Wright's sister? Well, he did. He's an overman now and she reckons they're too good for the likes of us. They've got an official's house over at the other end of the rows.'

They walked to where the car was parked at the end of the row, Ethel and the two children with them. Tom hung about the car, looking at everything; he even wanted to look under the bonnet.

'My dad's getting a car,' he said, speaking for the first time. 'He's going to get an Austin ten,' he told Georgina. 'Only the waiting list is too long for a new one, see.'

'I see.' Georgina nodded her understanding. 'This one

is second-hand too, of course. But it's all right, isn't it?'

'It's grand,' said Tom fervently.

'Come back soon,' Ethel was saying. 'Never mind what anyone else thinks neither. It was all so long ago, any road. I don't blame you for getting away from here neither. They were desperate times, before the war. So don't forget, come back to see us.'

'I will.' Kate and Georgina got in the car and Kate started the engine. Ethel leaned forward and spoke through the car window.

'You know, they *were* desperate times. Me mam had to let you go to our gran. She used to get dreadful headaches an' all, me mam, the megrims. An' the doctor used to have no time for her. Said she was just lazy and looking for excuses. But in the end it was a brain tumour took her. An' she had a hard time with me da before he died. She used to tell me all about it.'

They drove home with the sun behind them, lighting the fields and hedges. In places farmers were reaping and stacking corn, it was a beautiful early evening.

Georgina and her mother were quiet, Kate with a reminiscent look on her face and Georgina simply sitting there, digesting what she had seen and learned. On the way out they had stopped by the cemetery.

'Wait here, I want to go in alone,' said Kate. So Georgina sat and watched as her mother stopped by a sort of monument and stood for a moment, head bowed. It must be the monument to the disaster when her great-grandfather was among those killed, Georgina realised.

And Billy of course. Billy, her mother's sweetheart. Georgina waited ten minutes then went in and stood beside her mother. She took hold of her hand and felt it trembling. There was nothing she could say to comfort her, she knew. It had all been so long ago.

Chapter Twenty-seven

'I told you it would be a nine-day wonder,' said Dorothy. 'You see, they've forgotten all about you and Matthew Hamilton.'

She and Kate were sitting in the kitchen over a cup of tea and the papers. Now that Kate was mobile she popped into Roseley every morning and picked them up. There was a short piece concerning the ironmaster's will and Kate had feared they might have picked up on it and repeated the old gossip but there was nothing.

'Just as well now Georgie's away to Durham,' Kate replied. She paused for a moment before coming up with what was uppermost on her mind. 'I'm thinking of selling this house, Dorothy. I want to move back to Winton Colliery.'

Dorothy put down her cup so suddenly her tea sloshed a little into the saucer. She stared at it then got up and took it to the sink where she wiped it before sitting down again. 'Well,' she said. 'I suppose I could retire, find a little place for myself. They are building a few council flats on the edge of the village. Or I could go to Australia and see my grandchildren.'

'Dorothy! Won't you be coming with us?' Kate was shocked.

'You haven't asked me, have you?'

'Dorothy Poskett, don't be a fool,' said Kate. 'I shouldn't have to ask, you're part of the family. Unless . . . Maybe you don't want to go so far away? Oh, Dorothy, I'm sorry. I took it for granted that you would come with me.'

'It's not so far is it? I can always come back to Roseley for a visit if I wanted to.'

'You're a good friend, Dorothy,' said Kate and leaned across to squeeze Dorothy's hand. Dorothy smiled. 'And with Georgie in Durham it would be just as easy for her to come to Winton as it is to come here,' Kate went on. Her thoughts were racing; she had seen a house for sale in Winton old village. A lovely house, next to the chapel and with a large garden at the back. It was not grand enough to make Winton folk look askance at her but big enough with three bedrooms and a bathroom and a new kitchen. Or there was the one on the top of the bank on the way to Bishop, that was a lovely house too. And it would be almost as airy as the moors so Dorothy would like it. She wasn't so sure about Georgina. But then, Kate had resigned herself to the fact that Georgina would be unlikely to want to live with her in the future. She had her own life.

Georgina was almost twenty and in her second year at Durham. She was doing well and planned to spend the summer vacation in Europe with friends. All of which meant she was home less and less each year and though Kate knew it was inevitable she was lonely.

'I wouldn't hold her back,' she said, almost to herself.

'Who?'

'Georgie.'

'No, of course not,' said Dorothy. Then, ever practical, she went on, 'You couldn't if you wanted to.'

The letterbox rattled and Kate went through to the hall to pick up the post and skimmed through the few letters to see if there was one from Georgie. There was and her heart lifted. She took it back into the kitchen to read for Dorothy loved to hear the news from her beloved girl as much as she did herself.

'Dear Mam and Dorothy,' it began. All Georgie's letters began like that though it was understood that Kate read them first in case there was any private business.

'I'll be home this weekend,' Kate read aloud and looked up, smiling. 'She's coming home, Dorothy,' she repeated and Dorothy nodded.

'I'll make parkin,' she said. 'The lass always liked parkin.'

'I'll come on Friday. Mr Richards says it is imperative that I attend a meeting at Hamilton Hall. I'll tell you all about it when I come. Best love, Georgina.'

'Friday. That's today,' said Dorothy. Kate forgot all about her plans for going to Bishop Auckland to the estate agents. There was Georgina's bedroom to make ready and she would help Dorothy with the baking. And then there would be extra shopping to get in, she would do that now. With the car it was so easy to slip into the village.

Georgina turned east off the Great North Road and drove towards the coast. The MG was a little harder to handle than her mother's car but she had loved it since the day she was told it was ready to be picked up at the Morris garage in New Elvet. Normally diving it made her feel happy and carefree and since the end of petrol rationing in May she took every opportunity to get out in the car. But today she was in a bad mood. Had been since the day before yesterday and the telephone call from Robert Richards. Mr high and mighty Robert Richards, she thought savagely. Who did he think he was, her father? Sometimes she thought he had designs on her mother, the way he looked at her. Well, even if they worked and she would do her best to see they did not, that wouldn't make him her father.

There she had been a good obedient girl and told him her plans for the summer as he had told her she must and he had rung her up in college and told her they were out of the question.

'You must come here and spend some time getting to know the business,' he said.

'I don't have to do anything I don't want to,' Georgie had retorted.

'That's true, you don't. But then, you will lose your inheritance. Do you realise that?'

The upshot had been that she had agreed to attend the meeting at the Hall. 'I will bring my mother,' she said. That would upset him in case it upset his mother and

Bertram and that mouse of a sister of his, she thought. Bertram especially, he was such a child.

'By all means if you think you need her support,' Robert had answered, quite unruffled. In fact she could have sworn he was smiling at the other end of the line.

This wasn't the first time he had summoned her of course. He had insisted she go round the works with that toad, Bertram, and himself and spent a couple of hours explaining how these were the smaller works, the original Hamilton works which were being retained when nationalisation came into force.

'Father had it all worked out,' he had said. 'My little steel foundry and the Hamilton works too are both below the size when they would be nationalised. And meanwhile there will be capital from the main plant with which to diversify.'

'I will be in charge of the Hamilton works,' said Bertram. 'There was no need to bring in the tart's daughter.' He didn't look at Georgina as he said it and the tips of his ears were bright red.

'Watch your tongue, Bertie or I will wash your mouth out with soap,' said Robert. 'Now apologise to your half-sister. '

'I can take care of myself,' said Georgina feeling perversely put out that he should take her part. 'Do you think I care what a little boy says when he's having a tantrum?'

'I'm the same age as you, just about!' shouted Bertram.

'Then act your age,' said Robert. 'And you, Georgina, don't rise to it.'

Georgina fumed as she recalled it. He spoke to her as though she were as juvenile as Bertram. But she forgot about the incident as she turned on to the newly laid tarmac drive that ran from the road to the cottage. They could have had it laid years ago when Father was alive, she thought. But no, he had wanted the cottage kept out of sight. It was a wonder he had let her go to school in Saltburn, it being so near to Teesside and closer to Hamilton Hall. Yet no one had found out about her. At least not until after his death and then of course it didn't matter to him. Georgina's devotion to her father had taken some hard knocks in the last couple of years as she realised how she and her mother had been manipulated by him.

The door to the cottage opened and Kate came out as she climbed from the car. They hugged and Georgina could feel that her mother was no longer so thin as she had been up to and just after her father had died. In fact she looked really well. Her fair hair gleamed in the sunlight and her skin seemed to have a bloom on it.

Arm in arm they went into the house where Dorothy was waiting.

'I'll swear you look younger every time I come home,' said Georgina. 'Don't you think so Dorothy?'

'She looks naught but a lass,' Dorothy agreed. 'Now, I've laid out lunch on the dining-room table. You want to eat something before you go to that meeting. I always reckon you can't think properly if you haven't eaten properly. You haven't got a picking on you, Georgie. Do they not feed you right in that college?'

Georgina laughed. 'I'm fine, fit as a lop,' she said and laughed again. It was an old saying her mother said she'd picked up from her gran and had sometimes used though her father had frowned upon it.

Nothing was said about Robert's phone call until they were out on the road once again and on their way to Hamilton Hall.

'What's it all about, do you know?' asked Kate. She sat beside Georgina in the two-seater car feeling only slightly nervous as her daughter roared along the road. She sincerely hoped she would slow down as they got into heavier traffic but she would never say so. Anyway, Georgie was a brilliant driver. But Kate started the conversation to take her mind off the road.

'It's about my summer vacation,' said Georgina.

'I thought you were going to go camping in Europe,' said her mother.

'I was. I am,' Georgie replied. 'But *he* thinks I should stay and get to know the business better. I told him I wouldn't and he started issuing threats about me losing my inheritance. Anyway, he wanted me to meet him at the Hall today.'

'Then why am I here?'

'Because I said I was bringing you,' said Georgie, suddenly resembling the little girl she had insisted she was not. 'Why? Did you not want to come?'

'Why not? Mary Anne isn't there any more, is she?'

'I don't know,' said Georgie, sounding uninterested. She changed the subject. 'I want to make Robert understand that I don't want to work in an office. At least not the office of a steelworks. Why can't I do what I want to do?'

'And what is that, exactly?'

'Research into new technology, Mam, the coming thing it is. Computers. In a few years computers will be running the offices, you'll see.'

They turned into the drive of Hamilton Hall. The crunch of the tyres on the gravel reminded Kate forcibly of that day when they were summoned to hear the reading of Matthew's will. For a moment she considered asking Georgie to stop, to turn round and take her home. But she knew she couldn't do that. Instead she lifted her chin and forced her memories to the back of her I mind. Instead she looked out of the window at the smoothly mown grass, the tees of the avenue in the full leaf of summer and the view of the house just opening up before them.

'Hamilton Hall,' she murmured. 'Your father always did have a sense of his own importance. Anyone would think it had been passed down from generation to generation but it wasn't. He bought it.'

'Well, it doesn't matter now, does it?' Georgie didn't want to get into a discussion about her father, not when they were almost there.

'No. Not at all.'

They rang the bell and were ushered into the drawing-room by Benson. Mary Anne was there, Kate realised with a little jump to her nerves. She rose to her feet and came forward to greet them, her hand outstretched.

'Nurse Benfield!' she said as she took Kate's hand. 'No, I shouldn't call you that, should I? May I say Kate?'

'If you'd like to,' said Kate. She was taken aback. Mary Anne seemed so different, her manner easy, even friendly. And she looked younger somehow, her fair hair, now streaked with silver, was cut in a fashionable style and she was slimmer. She wore a pencil straight skirt in a warm brown with a coffee-coloured blouse and the colours suited her. And she wore makeup, lipstick and eye shadow and a hint of rouge on her cheekbones.

'And you, Georgina,' said Mary Anne. 'You are looking well, my dear. How are you getting on with your studies? You're so pretty too, the boys must be chasing after you!' She gestured towards the open French windows. 'It's such a lovely day we can have tea on the terrace. Come and sit down; Daisy will bring it directly.'

Mary Anne looked so well, so self-assured, Georgie and Kate could hardly keep their eyes from her. She had blossomed somehow, thought Kate. And the result was startling. Of course, the last time Kate had seen her was the day of the reading of the will. Mary Anne had been wearing black which was bound to make her skin look sallow for she had that type of skin, she mused, as Daisy brought out the tray and Mary Anne poured tea.

'I thought Robert would be here, he said it was a meeting,' said Georgie. She too was watching Mary Anne and not quite believing what she saw.

'Yes dear,' Mary Anne said smoothly. 'He asked me to apologise for him, he will be a little late.' She offered plates of tiny sandwiches, then sat back and looked from one to the other. Georgie took a cucumber sandwich and bit into it, she was hungry anyway, she may as well eat, keep her energy level up. She might need it for when Robert finally came.

'Maisie isn't here?' asked Kate.

'No, no she's at Whitworth Hall, Robert's place you know. It belonged to her father's family. When Matthew died I thought I would go to live there but I came back. I have Bertram to think of.' Mary Anne sighed. 'He left university, you know. Didn't finish his course.'

They sipped tea in silence for a minute or two. Mary Anne looked as though she were about to speak once or twice, her look of confidence slipping slightly. Georgie finished her tea and got to her feet and asked if she could take a walk in the garden.

'Of course,' said Mary Anne. The two women watched as she walked down the steps to the lawn and wandered away towards a shrubbery to one side. Then Mary Anne leaned forward towards Kate.

'I wanted a word with you,' she said. 'Robert isn't late, he is never late for anything, I've never known anyone like him for punctuality. But when he said about the meeting I told him I wanted to speak to you.'

Kate's expression was guarded; was Matthew's wife going to lay into her for taking Matthew away? The apprehension she had felt as she came here returned and she lifted her chin.

'Oh?' she murmured.

'I wanted to say . . . I don't bear you any animosity for what happened,' said Mary Anne.

'You don't?' Kate was mystified.

'No. I remember you when you were a young

probationer at the hospital. You were shy and naïve, gauche even. But you were kind. I liked you then. And I knew you had a boyfriend too, a boy from your home, wasn't it? You know how nurses gossip, even over patients' beds. Sometimes I got the impression that they thought all patients were deaf or slow-witted.'

Mary Anne sat back in her chair and glanced over to where Georgie had disappeared. 'I knew how Matthew chased after you,' she went on. 'How could I not? I'm sure even the other nurses saw it. And believe me, my dear, you didn't stand a chance once he had decided he intended to have you.

'I didn't care. By that stage I was only too glad for him to turn his attentions elsewhere. Though I never knew how far it had gone.'

Kate stared at the cold tea still in the bottom of her tea cup. She was acutely embarrassed, she didn't know what to say. Oh, that's all right, glad to do it for you? Her cheeks were bright red.

'Hallo! Where is everybody? We were supposed to be having a meeting.'

Robert came striding out on to the terrace. He bent and pecked his mother on the cheek and gave Kate a cool nod. 'I am never sure what to call you,' he said. 'But how are you?'

'Fine, thank you,' said Kate, feeling even more embarrassed than she had been a few minutes before. She took a hold of her feelings, however, as she had promised herself she would do on her way here. 'You can call me Catherine Benfield. Mrs, if you like, for Georgie's sake. I changed back to my maiden name legally last year.'

'*Mrs* Benfield. Where is your daughter? I asked her to be here. Does she understand that as executor of my stepfather's will I can hold back her allowance? I—'

'Robert, sit down and have a cup of tea. I'll ask Daisy to make more, though I don't know how the ration is holding out. And apologise to Kate, you know I hate rows. You sound like Bertie. Besides, Georgina is here, she is taking a walk in the garden while she waits for you.'

'I'm sorry Mrs Benfield,' said Robert looking anything but contrite. 'No, don't bother Daisy, I don't want tea. I'll just go and find Georgina.' He went off over the lawn with long, loping strides.

'It's because he is so protective of me,' Mary Anne observed to Kate.

'Yes. It's nice really.'

Robert saw Georgina as he emerged on the opposite side of the shrubbery; she was on her way back to the terrace.

'There you are,' he said impatiently, 'come along, we'll go into the study.'

His tone made her consider telling him to go to hell but in the end she followed him round the side of the house to the front door and into the study which turned out to be on the opposite side of the house to the drawing-room.

'I thought this was a meeting,' she said, surveying the empty room.

'It is. A meeting between you and I,' he replied. 'We are going to establish some ground rules.'

'For two pins I would tell you what you could do with the business. I could just get up and walk out and there would be nothing you could do about it,' said Georgina.

'Go on then, do that,' Robert replied smoothly. He glanced at her and smiled, an enigmatic kind of smile. She might look like her mother but there were some likenesses to her father, he thought. Matthew had hated to be crossed too but he knew which side his bread was buttered.

'And you needn't look at me like that, I mean it,' Georgina said crossly.

'I'm sure you do. But you are much too much your father's daughter for that. You want the money.'

'I have a right to it!' she flared. 'You know I want to go on, do research—'

'And there's no reason why you shouldn't.'

'How can I do both? Work in the office and at the university?'

'Isn't that why your father wanted you to go to Durham?' Robert got to his feet and walked to the window. Long shadows were beginning to creep along the lawn outside and the light had changed to that golden colour which comes just before sunset.

'I don't know why you wanted me to come here anyway. It wasn't much of a meeting,' Georgina went on, in a mood to grumble. 'And I might as well not have dragged my mother over either. She must be bored waiting for me. She was planning to go to Winton Colliery.'

'Oh yes, visit the old family homestead.'

'There's no call for sarcasm,' said Georgina with

dignity. 'Just because she came from a miner's family. There's nothing wrong with that.'

'Oh, don't be so prickly!' Robert turned his back on the view and walked back to the table. 'Of course there isn't. Your mother could have come in here if she had wanted to.' He lifted his briefcase. 'I have to go back to the office now. I have no more time, work to do. And I will expect you there on the first day of the summer vacation. That's next week isn't it? You can start by learning the routine. Learn from the bottom up. My stepfather was a great believer in that.'

She followed him to the door. 'Oh yes,' she said to his back. 'And no doubt you did that, slaving away as a junior clerk. I can just see it.'

He held the door open for her with exaggerated courtesy.

'I did as a matter of fact. Now, why don't you stop acting like the spoilt little girl you are and go and rescue your mother from her boredom? She will be in the drawing-room with my mother.'

'I'm not as it happens. I'm here,' said Kate. 'And I'll thank you not to speak to my daughter like that. You have no right.' She had been walking through to see if Georgina was ready to go when she heard the angry voices.

'I'm sorry,' said Robert who was already feeling he had gone too far. Especially the bit about the old family home-stead. 'You're right, I should not have said that. But the fact remains that her father wanted her to come into the business and I am simply trying to carry out his wishes.'

'I think we had better go now,' said Kate, her cheeks

red with anger though she kept her voice controlled. 'Before anything else is said. Goodbye. Please say goodbye to your mother for us.'

Taking Georgina by the arm, Kate swept out and round the house to the drive where Georgie's car was waiting.

Robert was left gazing after the car as it disappeared down the drive. Kate had looked like an avenging angel as she defended her daughter. She had looked magnificent, her eyes sparkling and with banners of colour on her cheeks. He shouldn't have talked to Georgina as he did, he thought ruefully. She was just a kid and it was natural for her to be resentful of him. And natural also that she would want to lead her own life. Of course, he would never do anything to take her inheritance from her. In fact she was more likely to be an asset to the business than Bertram was. His spoilt half-brother considered himself a gentleman and as such above working in the office. When he was there he played the lordling, throwing his weight about and treating the other workers with disdain.

Robert sighed. He liked Kate and now he had alienated her. In fact, his feelings came to more than liking if he was honest with himself. She stirred him more than any other woman had done. But he had his mother to consider. He couldn't hurt her; everything was such a mess of tangled emotions.

Chapter Twenty-eight

'But what did you find to talk about?' Georgina asked as she drove down the drive towards the main road. Kate had just been telling her how wrong she had been about Mary Anne all these years, she was such a nice, down-to-earth woman and she didn't appear to bear any resentment towards her.

'Oh, she must do, really!' Georgina exclaimed.

'No. I don't think so.'

They were silent for a while as the dusk deepened into dark and Georgie switched on the headlights. She glanced at her mother's profile but in the dark she couldn't see what her expression was.

'You must have resented her though,' she commented.

Kate sighed. 'Maybe I did, I don't know. I'm all mixed up. Anyway, let's forget about it. How did you get on?'

'Robert Richards is an insufferable man, really he is,' Georgie said savagely. 'I have to report at the works office at nine o'clock sharp Monday morning. So that's my trip off. I'll have to tell the others I can't go.'

Kate looked at her. 'Why didn't you tell him to get lost?'

'I'd lose my inheritance, wouldn't I? And I'm damned if I'm going to hand it over to the odious Bertie Hamilton just like that. Anyway, I need it for my real work. *And* it's mine! Why should I give it up?'

Kate gazed at her set face in the headlights of a car coming the other way. It was more than the money bothering Georgina she knew. More even than having to give up her plans and work in an office for three months or so. It was the humiliation of their position. Georgina had so much of Matthew in her. Kate's heart ached for her daughter. It was all her fault, she thought, yet again. She had tried to shield Georgina from it while she was growing up but perhaps it would have been better to have told her the truth from the start. She could have held out against Matthew if she had only tried harder, she thought sadly. But Matthew was so used to her doing what he wanted he had expected her to give in to him about most things. And she had been weak.

'It's all my fault,' she said aloud and Georgina turned sharply to her.

'Don't say that!' she almost shouted at her. 'Why do you always think everything that goes wrong is your fault? It wasn't your fault, it was Matthew bloody Hamilton's fault wasn't it?'

Kate was catapulted out of her introspective reverie as Georgina turned to her, her expression furious; plain to see in the light from an oncoming car. The car swerved and Kate saw the danger immediately.

'Watch the road, watch—' she screamed, and put a hand out to the wheel; the car swerved more violently then rocked and the wheels and brakes squealed as Georgina wrenched the steering wheel round to take the car out of the path of the one coming on the wrong side of the road and looking to be aimed directly at them. She never felt the impact, not even the blow as the car hit a tree by the side of the road and her head hit the windscreen and it shattered with showers of glass spraying over everything. Nor did she hear the other car as the driver reversed then sped away. She was spiralling down into nothingness.

Kate stirred and gave an involuntary moan. Her right foot was trapped in the bedclothes; it had gone numb. She tried to free it and a pain shot up her leg, an agonising pain, she'd never felt anything like it before. Her eyes were closed but she could see a light flashing through the lids; cautiously, she opened one eye and suddenly the pain was in her head, sharp and blinding. She quickly closed her eyes again.

There was something across her neck, affecting her breathing. It was warm and sticky and – it was Georgie's arm. Georgie was hurt! Full realisation came to her and Kate started to scream.

'Georgie! Georgie!'

'It's all right, pet, really. We'll have you out of there in a jiffy. Don't you worry, just try to relax.' The male voice was reassuring. She opened her eyes and tried to look to her right to where Georgie's head should be.

'Don't move your head!' he said urgently. 'Keep still. We'll see to you, don't try to move at all.' He turned away. 'This one is alive,' he said to someone. 'Give me a hand here, will you?'

This one is alive, thought Kate, uncomprehending for a minute. This one is alive. Did that mean the other one was dead?

'Georgie! Georgie!' she screamed, though the pain in her head intensified unbearably until suddenly it stopped and she sank into oblivion.

'Hit and run,' the policeman said savagely. 'By, I'd string them up by the balls if it was up to me. That young lass, just look at her, she was naught but a bairn.'

The fireman who was trying to free Kate from the tangled metal which trapped her leg nodded, his face grim. He stopped cutting and pulled the hole he had made wider. That should do it, he told himself and got to his feet.

'That's it, they can take her. Now for the lass. No big hurry there like. Just as well, she's going to take some getting out of that lot.'

'Is there nothing I can do, officer?'

'No sir,' said the policeman, not even looking at the man who spoke. 'It was a hit and run. Just go on, leave the road clear please.'

'My God! It's Kate and Georgina!'

The policeman looked closer at the man who had stopped his car a little way up the road and walked back.

'You know them sir?'

'Yes. They are . . . relatives of mine.'

By this time Kate was on a stretcher and being taken to the waiting ambulance.

'I'll go with her,' said Robert. 'At least I'll follow her to the hospital.' He started to walk to his car but was called back by the policeman.

'Just a minute sir. Can you give me the names and addresses?'

'Catherine Benfield Hamilton,' said Robert.

'And the deceased?'

The deceased. It had a horrible sound to Robert. Only half an hour ago he was talking to her, telling her off rather. Laying down the law to her, getting her into a rage. And now she had been killed in an accident that might have been partly his fault because he got her so angry.

'Sir?' the policeman prompted.

'Georgina Hamilton,' said Robert. 'Fern Moor Cottage, near Roseley.'

The ambulance set off, its bell clanging. Robert hesitated but there was nothing he could do for Georgina. Best leave her to the emergency services. He strode to his car, got in and followed the ambulance to the hospital. He was filled with pity for Kate. At one time he had thought he hated her but he hadn't really known her. And now? He didn't feel that way any more. And he wouldn't have wished this accident on anyone. Even if she survived herself it would probably kill her to know she had lost Georgina, she had idolised the girl.

Oh God, what a nightmarish thing to happen! Well, he would go to the hospital with her, stay with her, do what he could. Did she have any other relatives?

Blood relatives? He was ashamed to realise he didn't know.

Kate woke up in a small side ward where all she could see were white walls and a white shaded lamp hanging down above her. She lay there for a moment before the memory of the crash came back, crushing her. She could still feel the weight of Georgina's arm across her throat, see the impossibly small space on the driver's side of the car. A space that couldn't possibly hold a person. Her mind shrank away from it but the sight was burned into her brain. She lay with her eyes closed, not even wondering about her surroundings.

'Kate? Kate?'

She closed her eyes and pretended she couldn't hear. She didn't want to hear anything. All she wanted to do was sink back into the blackness again where she didn't have to think or feel.

'Kate, I know you're there, you can hear me,' the man's voice said. 'Open your eyes, Kate.'

No I won't, Kate answered him in her mind.

'Come on now, open your eyes.'

You're not going to bully me, thought Kate. Desperately she searched for the way back to the blessed blankness. But her foot had begun to throb; she tried to move it but she couldn't, there was still a heavy weight on it. Was she still in the car? Oh God help me, she cried but her lips didn't move and there was no sound.

Mr Bedford, the surgeon, looked at her intently. She looked distressed. He lifted an eyelid, her pupil was almost normal. She simply didn't want to come round, he could swear it.

'We'll leave her for a little longer,' he said. 'But she must be made to respond tomorrow.' He took Kate's notes from Sister and wrote a couple of lines on them.

Robert was waiting outside the side ward; it was he who had arranged for Kate to have a private bed, an amenity bed as they were called now.

'Well?' he asked as Mr Bedford came out followed by the houseman: and ward sister.

'Come into the office, Mr Richards.'

'I think she is close to recovering consciousness,' said the surgeon. 'Are you sure she doesn't have any blood relations left?' he asked. 'No one at all? Only I thought if there was someone it might help.'

'I don't think so. But her housekeeper might know. I thought she might help but I was disappointed, I thought Dorothy would have been able to get through to her if anyone could. They are friends though Dorothy is her housekeeper.'

'Well, I would try if I were you,' said Mr Bedford. 'I can't see any reason why she should be in this state. The police report said she spoke after the accident. Shock of course can do funny things. But it is dragging on too long for my liking, over a week now. I may have to bring in a psychiatrist next week if there is no improvement.'

Robert rang the number of the cottage from Sister's phone.

'Nothing's happened, has it?' the old lady asked in alarm. 'I was coming in to see Kate this afternoon. Oh

God, tell me nothing has happened!'

'No, nothing more, nothing has changed,' Robert re-assured her and could hear her sigh of relief loud in the receiver.

'I'm going out of my mind with worry,' she said. 'I don't know what to do. And then there's my poor Georgie, still not buried, it's time she was allowed to rest in peace.'

'There is one thing you can do,' said Robert, ignoring her remark about Georgina. As far as he could see it mattered little to the girl that she was ^till unburied. It had been on his orders. He was sure Kate would want to be at the funeral and if there was any chance at all of her re-covering shortly she should be there.

'Tell me if Kate had any family left in Winton Colliery. Do you know of any?'

Minutes later he was driving along the road to Bishop Auckland. He ought to have rung the steelworks and told them he wouldn't be in at all today. But they would manage without him, he told himself. He was expected at Hamilton Hall for lunch too, he remembered. Oh well, he would ring from the first call box he came to.

Robert crossed the Great North Road and entered Rushyford. There was a telephone box outside the post office. He put his sixpence in the box and pressed button A when Benson answered.

'Don't worry about me,' his mother said when he explained where he was going. 'That poor woman, my heart aches for her.'

As he got back in his car and drove along the Coundon road towards Bishop Auckland, he wondered at her. Mary Anne Hamilton was a wonderful woman, he decided. But he knew that already.

Robert drove to Winton Colliery and parked on the end of the rows as his stepfather had done a few times before him. A couple of boys were kicking a ball around on a piece of waste ground across the road from the houses. He walked over to them and they stopped playing and gazed at him.

'Mr Benfield?' he asked and held out half a crown. They stared at him and the money but didn't take it.

'Is that a Jaguar, Mister?'

'Yes, it is. Do you know a Mr Benfield? Please.'

'I might do,' a boy conceded. 'Can I have a ride in your motor?'

'Yes, all right. But tell me where Mr Benfield lives.'

'Can we have a ride first?'

'Oh, all right,' said Robert, exasperated. They whooped and climbed into the front passenger seat together. He drove them round the rows, through the old village and back to where they had started.

'Thanks, Mister.' They had the door open and one was already running away.

'Hey!' Robert shouted, and grabbed the other. 'Mr Benfield? I won't ask again, I'll just take you to the police station.'

'Aw, all right,' the boy conceded. 'My name is Benfield. We live up the street there, the house at the end.

Can I have the half-crown?'

Robert gave him it and he ran off. Robert locked the car before leaving it. Better safe than sorry.

It was Willie who answered the door. He was wearing a clean shirt and old trousers with braces dangling. His feet were bare and his hair damp from a recent bath.

'Mr Benfield. I'm Robert Richards. May I come in for a minute?'

Willie gazed at him then cast an apprehensive glance over his shoulder. 'Come in then,' he said and led the way into the kitchen where a tin bath was still standing before the fire. 'I've just come off shift,' he explained. 'If you wait a minute I'll see to the bath.'

Robert looked at the water in the bath which was scummy and glinting with particles of coal dust. 'Don't bother for me,' he said. 'I understand.' As he spoke a woman came down the stairs; a woman of about Kate's age.

'This is the wife,' said Willie.

'How do you do, Mrs Benfield?'

'Well, what do you want with us?' demanded June, her chin high in the air and her tone brusque. 'Slumming, are you?'

'June!'

Willie was embarrassed and his face flushed. To hide it he sat down on his chair and began to put on his shoes.

'Are you related to Kate Benfield?' asked Robert, ignoring the woman's rudeness.

'She's my sister,' said Willie. June made a derisory sound.

'The tart do you mean?'

Robert's anger rose swiftly but Willie butted in.

'June! Keep your mouth shut!'

June stared at him, her eyes glittering and her arms folded across her chest. She opened her mouth to speak but thought better of it. Then she turned without another word and went into the other room, banging the door behind her.

'Kate is my sister, Mister,' said Willie again. 'What has happened?'

Robert explained about the accident and the death of Georgina and how Kate was still in a coma. 'The doctors think if someone of her own came and spoke to her it might help,' he sighed.

'I tell you what Mr Richards,' said Willie. 'Why don't you go over and see our Ethel? I think the two of them have got friendly, like. At least, Kate came to see her. West Row, it is, number five.'

'Thanks, I will,' said Robert. The two men moved to the door and Willie walked down the yard with him. At the gate Willie paused.

'I would come but Ethel will be better. And the wife, her brother used to be Kate's sweetheart, you know. He was killed in the pit and for some reason June hated Kate after that. Seemed to think she was treating the memory of their Billy badly going off with that gaffer.'

Chapter Twenty-nine

'Howay man, Katie, pull yourself together,' said Ethel. She could have sworn that beneath her closed eyelids, Kate's eyes moved slightly. 'Mind, how do you think I feel? I've come all this way to see you and you won't talk to us.'

Ethel looked at the two men at the bottom of the bed, Mr Bedford the surgeon and Mr Richards, who evidently was one of the Hamiltons really. To be honest, she was a bit in awe of them both, especially the surgeon. He reminded her of the specialist who had looked in young Davey's ears last month. Very la-di-da he'd been. But he had promised he could do something for the bairn. Thank God for the new National Health Service. Davey would have gone deaf altogether without it. But the specialist said he could fix it with a small operation.

Mr Bedford smiled at her; an encouraging sort of smile. It made him seem almost human. 'Go on,' he whispered. 'Just talk to her.'

'What was that our grandma used to say? "When life

knocks you down you just 'ave to pick yoursel' up else it'll walk you into the ground." I remember her saying that. She meant it an' all. Me mam said it was all right for her, she never was bad in her life so she could talk.' Ethel paused and gazed at Kate's face. The skin was white except for her eyelids that had a bluish tinge. By, she was sorry for her though. Losing the lass, it was a terrible thing to happen. Those blasted motorcars! She hoped to heaven young Davey never got one. Tears pricked the back of her eyes and she blinked them back.

'Go on,' said Mr Bedford and she began again.

'Katie! Can you hear me, pet? Howay man!' Suddenly Ethel lost her patience. 'You don't want them to put you in the loony bin at Sedgefield, do you? I tell you that's what they'll do. An' another thing, they can't bury your Georgina till you come round. Leastways, they don't want to but they might have to. You don't want her to go without you to see her off, do you?'

'Mrs Canvey! Stop that at once!'

Mr Richards was shouting at her, he was angry. She looked up quickly, intimidated, her irritation dying as quickly as it had come.

'Sorry,' she muttered. 'But you said she just didn't want to come round. I was only telling—'

'Yes, well that's enough I think. Please wait outside if you don't mind,' Mr Bedford said smoothly.

Meekly Ethel stood up and walked to the door then she turned round defiantly. 'I *am* her sister, you know. I reckon I must be her next-of-kin. Not that fella there, *me*!'

Robert looked at her. It was true of course. Kate's sister had more right in here than he had.

'Behave arguing, Betty! You're always carrying on.'

In the short silence after Ethel spoke, they could all hear the weak, breathy voice from the bed and they forgot everything but the fact that Kate had come round. Mr Bedford's plan had worked.

Ethel moved back to the bed and looked at Kate, her eyelids were still closed but her face had relaxed somehow.

'It's Ethel not Betty,' she said. 'Eeh, Kate, are you not going to look at me? I'm that sorry, pet, I am.'

A tear ran down Kate's cheek; then another and another. Her eyes opened. 'It's true, isn't it?' she asked. 'My lovely, clever little lass is gone.'

'Aye, pet, it's true.'

Ethel put her arm around her sister and hugged her. From the bottom of the bed, Robert and Mr Bedford watched, unwilling to disturb them immediately. Then Mr Bedford stepped forward and Ethel, noticing, moved back.

'How do you feel, Mrs Hamilton?' he asked.

Kate wiped her eyes with the back of her free hand, the other was tied to a splint and had a drip into a vein feeding her a glucose and saline solution. How did she feel? She thought. It was a bloody stupid question. She wished she had died in the crash instead of Georgina. She felt absolute desolation. She felt like throwing herself out of the window of the side ward and ending everything. The future stretched ahead of her and it was barren, pointless.

She didn't think she could face it. She felt so bad she could never tell him it for it was beyond feeling.

'Mrs Hamilton?' he prompted.

'My name is Benfield,' she said. 'Catherine Benfield. And I want to go home to Winton. But first I will bury my bairn.'

'I reckon this must mean I'm the sole owner of Hamilton Ironworks,' said Bertram. He was bursting with satisfaction to the extent that his expression turned Robert's stomach. Well, on this at least he could prick the little squirt's bubble.

'I'm afraid you're wrong, Bertie,' he said. 'Georgina's holdings go to her next-of-kin and her next-of-kin is Kate. In other words, Kate is your new partner.' That wiped the smile off Bertie's face, he saw, holding back a grin himself.

'But she can't be! She was nothing but Father's tart. A whore!'

'Shut up, Bertram.' Mary Anne had entered the room unnoticed by her son. 'I don't want to hear language like that from you ever again, do you hear me?'

'But Mother—'

'Never again, I said. Is that what it meant to you, losing your half-sister? I am ashamed of you, ashamed. I ask you again, do you hear me?'

Bertie gritted his teeth. 'Yes Mother,' he replied. Then he lifted his head and went on, 'But did you hear what Robert said? The woman has half of the ironworks, it's not fair, it just isn't fair, Mother.'

'Well, fair or not it's a fact,' said Robert. 'She wants me to manage her share for her.'

Bertie gasped, he walked over to the window and stared out unseeingly. He had waited for years to get control of the business and now, just when he thought he had it in his grasp it had been snatched from him. Oh, he could bear with the bulk of it being nationalised, he had to, what else was there to do? When the Tories got in they would put things right, he was convinced of it. But this was different; this was letting his father's tart win. He'd begun to get used to the fact that Georgina had a share, for after all she was his half-sister just as much as Maisie was. But this, it was gall and wormwood. All his efforts had been for nothing. Worse, they had worked against him. Why hadn't he realised the tart would inherit? Now Robert, too-clever-by-half Robert who had patronised him all his life was in control.

'Flaming hell!' he said under his breath but Robert heard him.

'Don't swear in front of your mother,' he snapped.

Much worse expletives were running through Bertie's mind in a continuous stream but he hadn't the nerve to come out with them here. Instead he rushed out of the room and out through the kitchens to the stable yard and beyond. Once over the fence and into the woods he picked up a stick and thrashed an inoffensive bush and shouted his frustration in the filthiest language he could think of and he had learned a lot of that from his particular cronies at Cambridge.

For a minute he wished himself back there, he could

have forgotten it all in a pub-crawl. He could have got absolutely blotto.

There wasn't much chance of going back though, none at all in fact. He had been sent down and all over a bit of fun he and his friends had had with a girl from the town. Maybe they had gone over the top but she had been asking for it, they all thought so.

Aw, to hell with it, he could still get plastered. Bertie threw the stick away and headed back to the house for his car. He would drive into Middlesbrough; he could do a bit of hell-raising there and probably as good as in Cambridge.

'What do you mean to do?' Mary Anne asked. She and Kate sat in the garden in the late summer sunshine. Kate had taken lately to popping over to see her once or twice a week and Mary Anne looked forward to seeing her. She rarely saw her sons for Robert was too busy with the business and Bertie – well, who knew what Bertie was up to. She only hoped it wasn't something that would bring too much disgrace on to the family. And Maisie, well, Maisie spent most of her time in her room or wandering the woods at the back of the house, when she was there, that is.

'I'm going to buy a house in Winton,' said Kate. 'I've been dithering about it I know but I have decided. My estate agent is seeing to it for me.'

'Yes, but what are you going to do?' Mary Anne persisted. 'You are a young woman still Kate, only thirty-one or two aren't you?'

'Thirty-six, actually.'

'All right, thirty-six. You are not an old woman; you can't just sit at home and do nothing. Why don't you go back to nursing?'

Kate look startled. Nursing? That was an old dream. It had belonged to the young Katie. She had been another person then. There had been the short time during the war when she had thought she could take it up again but that had come to nothing. Matthew objected to it.

'It's different for me,' Mary Anne was saying. 'I'm fifteen years older than you. Besides—' She stopped, she had almost said she still had her family and she couldn't believe she had had such a crass remark on the end of her tongue.

There was silence for a moment or two broken only by the twittering of starlings that were on the lawn looking hopefully for crumbs. Then Kate rose to her feet.

'I must go now, I promised Dorothy I wouldn't stay out after dark.'

'Yes, of course.'

When Kate had gone Mary Anne walked slowly into the house. She shivered a little, the evenings were cutting in and were chilly after the sun went down behind the trees. She hoped Kate would do something with her life, she was a nice woman. Strangely, she had never resented Kate maybe because she didn't even know about her until after Matthew's death and by then it didn't really matter to her. She even felt a vague gratitude to her for she must have been the reason why Matthew left herself alone these last years.

Mary Anne had thought it was a prostitute in the town and dreaded him picking up some awful disease. But she had been thankful that he stopped coming to her room. She wondered briefly how Kate could have stood for Matthew's crude methods of lovemaking. Perhaps he had been different with Kate.

Mary Anne dismissed the subject from her mind as she switched on the wireless and settled down before the fire in the small sitting-room. It was time for the news. Robert had said something about footwear rationing coming to an end and she wanted to know if it was true.

Kate was driving along the road from Hamilton Hall to the bridge over the Tees where she turned off for Fern Moor. She stared fixedly at the road ahead and her fingers gripped the steering wheel tightly. Realising it, she began to breathe deeply, evenly, and forced her hands to relax.

She had thought she would never get into a car again and certainly not to drive one. It had been Robert who had persuaded her.

'It's like falling off a horse, you must get straight back on,' he had said. She had given him a hard stare.

'The crash was not like falling off a horse,' she had said. And he had looked stricken.

'I'm sorry, it was a stupid analogy,' he said.

'Never mind, I know you meant nothing by it,' she said. 'But I don't think I can ever drive again.'

'You will,' he insisted.

Kate didn't tell him of the nightmares she had every night and always she was in the car and the threat of what was going to happen hung over her, the terror engulfing her. Nor of the times she dreamed Georgina was alive and she never questioned the fact that Billy was there too, they were happy, eating a picnic up by the bunny banks at Winton. Then she would wake up and try to hold on to the dream but it would fade and reality came down on her like a heavy weight and there was no one there but herself.

'Come on,' Robert said now. 'I will take you out for a drive. The fresh air will do you good. I have to go to Whitworth Hall, I'll bring you back in good time for Dorothy coming home.'

'Very well, I'll go.'

For Dorothy had gone to Hartlepool where she had some second cousins and the house would be very quiet when Robert went away. Still it took a great effort of will. She had to fight down her panic, keep a tight control of it in order to get in the car, even to stay in the car.

'I just have to pick up something;' he said as they drove up to the house. It was a lovely old house, not at all pretentious like Hamilton Hall. It looked like a family home, she thought and should have children running about on the lawns or playing on the swings that hung from an old oak tree to the side. She looked at him, he was in his early thirties she surmised. He had time to marry yet.

'Will you come in for a minute or two?' he asked.

'No!' she cried then realised how emphatic she sounded. 'I mean, I'll just stay in the car if you don't mind. You said you just had to pick something up?'

If she got out of the car she might not be able to get back in. For a few seconds, looking at the old house she had almost forgotten where she was sitting and her rigid posture had relaxed very slightly. But now she stiffened, her back straight, not even resting on the back of the seat.

'Don't worry,' he said swiftly. 'Just sit there, I will be back in a jiffy.' And he was. That was one thing she had discovered about Robert Richards, if he said he would do a thing he did.

Over the next few weeks he had coaxed her and bullied her until in the end she had got in the driver's seat and driven. And she was grateful to him, of course she was. She needed to be able to get about, especially living on the moor as she did. But now she was leaving the moor and she couldn't wait for the day. Every day there reminded her of what she had lost. The place was thick with memories of Georgina, her lovely, clever girl.

Coming back from Hamilton Hall as the late sun slanted across the moor, picking out patches of heather with the purple fading fast by now and turning to brown, Kate felt so alone, despite that fact that Dorothy was home; she had lit the electric light in the hall and in the kitchen of Fern Moor Cottage. The light shone out in the gathering gloom.

Dorothy loved the electricity that Kate had had brought across the moor. She could hardly believe what it could do, the toaster and the electric oven, the small refrigerator and washing machine Kate had had installed only a year ago. A year ago, thought Kate. When it was another world from the grey, hopeless world she inhabited now.

She pulled up in front of the house and got out of the car, still with that feeling of relief and easing of tension she had every time. Inside the house there was a delicious smell of cooking. Dorothy must have called in at the butchers in Roseley and brought the meat ration back with her, it smelled like a beef casserole was in the oven. The smell even made Kate feel a little hungry – she might eat some of it without having to choke it down to please Dorothy. But no doubt that was Dorothy's intention in cooking it.

'I'm home, Dorothy!' she called and, slinging her coat on to a hook on the hallstand, went into the kitchen, pinning on a smile as she went.

Chapter Thirty

Kate decided on a house neither in Winton Old Village nor in Winton Colliery. It was built round about the 1880s when the first shaft was sunk and the Main seam found to be workable and had originally been the manager's house. It was about half a mile up the road from Winton Colliery, far enough to escape the most noxious of the gases from the pit and coke works, not to mention any fevers which at that time were prevalent in colliery villages due to the absence of clean water and sanitation.

Kate had always liked the house. When she was a child she would come with the Sunday School choir to sing carols on Christmas Eve and be given sweet mince pies to eat and ginger wine to drink.

The house was called Four Winds and stood on the brow of a hill facing over the valley with a medium-size garden surrounding and a stand of trees behind and to the north to protect it from the worst of the wind; a solid house, but not over large. The wind soughed through the trees, creating a singing sound and she found it soothing somehow. On the moors the wind had sung too, but it was not the same, there weren't the trees there for one thing.

The house had been modernised of course and one of its five bedrooms had been converted into a bathroom and there was a cloakroom with toilet and washbasin on the ground floor, both decorated with trailing leaves of bright green ivy.

'Do you think it's a bit grand for me?' Kate asked Dorothy the day they moved in.

'Indeed it is not!' she replied. 'And just look at the kitchen, with all the cupboards and a gas cooker and everything. Mind, I don't want any of those new-fangled kitchen cabinets, these will do me nicely.'

Kate had had the walls painted a sunshine yellow for the windows faced north. As she looked around now, Robert walked into the kitchen.

'I hope you don't mind, the door was open and so I walked in,' he said.

'No, of course not,' said Kate. But what was he doing here? she wondered to herself. He had got into the habit of arriving to see her unannounced, sometimes once or twice a week in spite of his busy schedule. And she was determined that she was not going to get to rely on him. She was not even going to get to be glad to see him. He was, after all, the stepson of her lover and the son of Mary Anne and she had wronged Mary Anne Hamilton, hadn't she? So why was it that her heart lifted when she saw him? She had no feelings for him, of course she hadn't. Anyway, she had sworn to herself that she would have nothing to do with any man ever again, at least not in that sense. What sense? For goodness sake, she told herself now, he was just being helpful that was all. If he thought she had read any more into it he would run a mile and who could blame him?

'Did you want something in particular?' she asked coolly. 'Only I am rather busy . . .'

Robert still wore a smile but not in his eyes. 'Sorry if I'm in the way,' he said. 'However I needed your signature on a few documents.'

There then, Kate told herself. He's only here for business reasons, of course he is. He took papers out of his briefcase and showed her where to sign.

'You should read them, perhaps,' he said formally.

'No, I'm sure it'll be all right if you say so. I haven't time in any case, I must get on.'

'Of course.'

He had been going to suggest that they have lunch together, maybe at the attractive-looking pub he had seen just up the road from here. Now he felt he couldn't. He gathered the papers together and replaced them in the case.

'I'll be off then, I am busy too,' he said brusquely. 'Goodbye.' He held out his hand and she shook it. 'Please don't bother to see me to the door.'

'Goodbye then.'

He went out to his car feeling very flat indeed for he had woken up that morning in pleased anticipation of seeing her again. But she had been so cool to him; made him feel a nuisance even.

Kate's enthusiasm for the day ahead had dulled too.

Suddenly she couldn't stand being in the house despite all the work there was to do.

'Come on, Dorothy, let's walk down the bank and I'll show you Winton,' she said, pulling off her overall. 'There's plenty of time to do this later.'

Dorothy looked at her. 'You go,' she said. 'I'd like to get on here. I'd rather get it done this morning. I'll see Winton another day.'

Kate couldn't argue, the black demon of depression on her shoulder was growing and sometimes only a brisk walk in the fresh air backened it.

'I won't be too long,' she promised. She started walking down the bank towards the colliery but on impulse cut off along a farm track. So far along was the footpath that led to the old line between Eden Hope Colliery and Winton. She walked down the path to the side of the field. It was empty now, evidently hay had been harvested and the stubble stood proud above a few straggly green shoots. There was no pit ponies in the field, no doubt they were all down the pits, for the mines were in full production now, coal was at a premium.

She climbed the stile and started walking along between the old rails. The line was overgrown with grass and bracken, yellowing now as the back end of the year drew ever nearer.

It reminded her of the time when she was a little girl and had come this way with her grandda, looking for pitch to make into balls for fuel. It was the first time she had seen Matthew, she thought suddenly. Oh God, why couldn't she stop her mind from working? All she wanted to do was not think about any of it any more, to walk and enjoy it all, even the smells from the coke ovens, coaly and sulphurous. So why had she come this way? It was opening old wounds, bringing back memories of her grandda and Billy. And if she had not met Matthew, there would not have been a Georgina and she would not have had this heartache . . . No! Kate was horrified at where this line of thought had taken her. She could never wish Georgina had never been, never, never.

And her misery at Georgie's death overwhelmed her again and she sat down on a mound by the side of the track and wept long and hard.

'Are you all right, Missus?'

Kate started and looked up at the man who had asked the question. She had stopped crying for a while and sat on until it must be midday or later, quiet, her knees drawn up to her chest and her arms resting on them and cradling her head. The shock of seeing the miner made her jump up and back away. For a minute she thought she had conjured him up, it was her grandfather!

'Eeh, Missus, I didn't mean to startle you,' he said. 'I just thought—'

'No, no, it's all right,' she said shakily. Now she looked properly at him she could see it was not her grandfather. He had the same eyes looking out of the coal dust which plastered his face, he had his helmet pushed to the back of his head showing the white skin above the black line but he was younger. She peered at him, her eyes were so sore from the weeping she felt she could hardly see.

'Willie? It is Willie, isn't it? For a minute I thought it

was me grandda! You're the spitting image of him! Don't you know me? I'm your sister Kate.'

'Kate? Eeh, Kate, you look like something the cat brought in. I heard you were coming back from our Ethel, like. But what are you doing up along the line here?'

Kate sat back down on the mound before her legs gave out altogether and after a moment her brother sat down beside her. He looked at her closely, his eyes, the same as Kate's, looking even more striking than hers from out of the blackness of his face.

'Are you all right, lass?' he said softly.

'Yes,' she answered. 'It was just the shock.'

She hardly knew this brother of hers, she thought. Her oldest brother, he had been down the pit since he was thirteen and passed the literacy test so he could leave school. He was a quiet man, his mother's boy she had used to think. He had stayed with his mother anyway when she had been taken by her gran and she had seen little of him since. It was Betty she had had more to do with. At school the girls were separated from the boys into different sides of the building and did not meet even in playtime.

'I heard you had lost your bit lass,' he said. 'I was sorry to hear that. When I see our Ethel I always ask after you, like.'

Tears pricked the back of her eyes again and angrily she fought them back. For a moment she could not reply.

'Thanks for that, Willie.' She stared along the line to where it curved round towards Eden Hope and gave an involuntary sniff.

Willie looked away before saying, 'I walk this way home sometimes. I'm at Eden Hope now, not Winton. It's not far though and it's nice to be out in the fresh air after the pit. I like fore shift, it gives me all of the afternoon.'

He picked a blade of grass and put it between his teeth, chewing on the end absently. 'That bloke, you know, the toff, Richards is he called?'

Kate looked at him inquiringly. 'Yes?'

'He came to our house, you know, looking for someone who belonged to you. He said you were in a coma. He was right bothered about you.' Willie paused and took the grass from his mouth and threw it away. He cleared his throat. 'I should have stood up to June and gone with him, I was sorry I didn't. June is so bitter though, I usually do what she says for the sake of peace. But I should have gone that day. Instead I sent him to our Ethel's.'

'It's all right Willie, I understand. Anyway it worked out all right, didn't it? Ethel came. And I'm fine now, aren't I?'

'Aye.'

He rose to his feet and held out a hand to Kate. 'Howay, we can walk along together. June will have me dinner ready.'

They walked along the line, Kate having to stretch her legs to go from one sleeper to the next. Strangely, she felt her mood lifting as she followed Willie until they came to where the line entered the pit yard at Winton. It was just a few yards from there to the colliery rows.

'Come and see us when you're settled,' said Willie. 'An' look lass,' he went on, moving close to her and bending his head, 'don't hold the grieving in. Best let it out. You'll get over it better you know.'

'I don't think I'll ever get over it, Willie,' she said.

'Aye you will. An' then you'll just have the good memories,' he assured her. 'I'll be seeing you then.' Touching his cap he strode off towards the pre-fabs just past the rows.

It was too late to go and see Ethel, Kate reckoned and besides, there was work to do at the house. She couldn't leave it all to poor old Dorothy. She set off briskly up the road to Four Winds. Dear Willie. It warmed her frozen heart a little to think of him and how waves of sympathy had flowed from him. She wasn't too sure about going to see him and June at home though. June had been so bitter towards her when Billy died, almost as if the disaster had been all her fault. Still, maybe she would change.

'It's not the same as living in West Row,' said Kate. 'I don't fit in any more.' It was a bright November day and she and Dorothy were sitting in the sitting-room at Four Winds. In spite of the sun, the wind was loud in the chimneys and they were glad of the blazing coal fire in the hearth. The room was small but the windows overlooked all of Winton, the old village, the colliery and the colliery yard and pithead. Kate could almost see the winding wheel turning as the back shift men were brought to the surface or at least she thought she could. What she did see were the tiny figures spilling out and moving down the yard and on to the road that led to the colliery village.

Dorothy, sitting on the opposite side of the hearth, with

some sewing on her lap and the workbasket on the small table at her side, looked up impatiently.

'Oh, Kate, don't be so daft, how could it be? You of all people should know you can never go back.' She held up a needle and tried to thread it with black cotton and failed. 'Oh, here,' she said. 'Thread this needle for me will you? I swear my eyes are getting worse.'

Kate took the needle and threaded it and handed it back. 'You should go to the opticians in Bishop,' she said absently. 'I don't want to go back,' she went on. 'But I thought I could make friends again among the people I know.'

'Aye, well, if you thought that you should have gone into one of them pre-fabs or mebbe one of the old pit houses. This one's over grand for them.'

Since they had come to live in Four Winds, Dorothy was much more a companion rather than a servant and she spoke as such. Now she looked round the room, newly decorated with pale flowered wallpaper that had only just started to come into the shops. The furniture had come from Fern Moor Cottage and was good quality and comfortable. Even though Kate had wanted to leave everything behind it wasn't so easy to buy good stuff new as it all went for export to pay off the National Debt. She hated the plainness of the 'utility' which was all that could be bought during the war and even now when the war had been over for almost six years.

'I wouldn't get one, you know that,' said Kate. 'Anyway, I like this house.'

'There you are then,' said Dorothy obscurely. She

rolled up the skirt she had been repairing and stuffed it in the basket. 'I'll go and make the tea, then, shall I?'

Kate sat on, watching the rows below her. There weren't many people about though, no doubt they too were having their tea. She sighed restlessly and got to her feet. She was thirty-seven years old, going on thirty-eight. That wasn't old, was it? She felt as though she was in limbo, waiting here until she died. Like those widows and spinsters left over from the First World War because their men had all been killed at the Front and there was a dire shortage of others.

Robert wanted her to take more interest in the works, she knew that. But she couldn't, oh no she couldn't. What she wanted to do was nurse but she had broken her training and would never get back in now. She was too old; she knew that. At thirty-seven she was on the scrapheap.

Dorothy came in with the tea tray but she didn't look round; she was off in a brown study of her own.

'Move the basket so I can put the tray down, please, Kate,' said Dorothy evenly. 'Or I will likely drop the darn thing.'

'Sorry.' Kate moved the workbasket to the floor and took the tray and put it on the small table.

'I was thinking, why don't you make an appointment with the matron at the hospital? She'll likely give you a job. I did hear talk that they were starting a nurse's training school there.'

'Funny, I was just thinking of that. But I think I'm too old,' said Kate.

'Oh, rubbish! Anyway, you'll never know if you don't ask,' said Dorothy as she poured out the tea.

'I might try,' said Kate though in her heart she thought it was useless. She felt useless herself, sitting up here with nothing to do but watch other people working. Tomorrow though, she would start work in the garden. She had hired a retired miner to work in it three mornings a week and he was good at his job. But she could help, prune the roses maybe, tidy up the greenhouse-cum-conservatory at the side of the house.

'If you go and see about it I'll go and see the optician,' said Dorothy, though she hated the idea of wearing glasses and had resisted it so far.

'We'll see.'

'Are you not satisfied wi' me work then, Missus?' Tommy Dacre asked gruffly. It was the following day and he had planned to turn over the vegetable patch so when the hard frosts came they would break down the soil, make it pliable. But neither the spade nor the gripe was hanging in their proper place in the shed. And when he went to investigate there was the missus going at the part he had set aside for growing leeks that could be shown in the leek show at the club in Winton. It was annoying, not to say downright maddening.

'O' course, it's your garden,' he conceded. 'You can do what you like wi' it.' He glared disapprovingly at the gripe, which was lying on the side, bending over a winter cabbage.

'Oh no, Tommy, I'm well pleased with your work,'

said Kate, standing up and putting up a gloved hand to push her hair back from her forehead and leaving a smear of soil in the process.

'Well then,' he said and bent to pick up the gripe. 'Mebbe you'll be leaving us to get on wi' it.'

Kate retired into the house defeated. She had forgotten the fierce pride most of the miners took in their gardens and the gardens of the Aged Miners' Homes where Tommy lived were minuscule.

'Dorothy,' she said after she had washed her hands and face and applied a little lipstick and face powder. 'Dorothy, I'm going to ring Matron now. So you can start to get used to wearing glasses.'

Both of them had an appointment for the following afternoon. Kate dropped Dorothy off at the optician's and drove on up to Cockton Hill to the hospital and parked in front of Block 1 where Matron had her office. Her heart thumped out of all proportion as she went in and along the corridor until she was outside the right door. She took a moment to compose her feelings before knocking and responding to the call to go in.

Matron Dobson was a small, dumpy woman with her hair entirely covered by the large, stiffly starched cap she wore. She gazed over half-moon spectacles at Kate, giving her the impression that the woman had read her character entirely in that one searching look. Then she rose from her chair behind the desk and held out her hand.

'Good afternoon,' she boomed. 'I understand you wish to join our nursing school.'

'Yes please, Matron,' said Kate.

Matron ruffled through some papers. 'You are how old?' she asked and Kate's heart sank.

'Thirty-seven,' she admitted. What a waste of time it had been coming, she thought.

'But you have some experience,' said Matron.

Eagerly, Kate told her of her time at the South-East Durham General and the short time as an auxiliary and then as an assistant nurse at the cottage hospital. It didn't seem to add up to much she thought as she watched Matron jot something down on the page befores her. Matron didn't seem to think so either judging by the expression on her face.

There were several more questions about her background, why she had chosen to come back to Bishop Auckland to live, had she any family responsibilities that could affect her work in any way.

'None,' said Kate and a shaft of the old familiar pain ran through her unexpectedly.

Matron looked down at her notes and came to a decision. 'Very well, you are accepted as a student nurse in our training school. I'm afraid you will have to start from the beginning again. The school begins next year, in the month of February.'

'I . . . I'd hoped to start sooner,' Kate faltered. She had somehow thought she would be able to start next week, not next year. The disappointment was crushing.

'Well, you can. The time until then can be useful to you,' Matron went on, 'I would like you to start work as an auxiliary nurse on the wards. I don't need to tell you what that entails, do I?'

'No Matron,' said Kate. It entailed doing most of the humdrum jobs on the ward, helping with the cleaning, doing bedpan rounds, clearing dirty dressing trolleys and a hundred and one other jobs. But she would be getting back into the right atmosphere and picking up tips from the rest of the staff, getting used to the ways of the wards again.

'Thank you, Matron,' said Kate. She'd got the job!

'Report here at seven-thirty Sunday morning,' said Matron, nodding her head in dismissal.

Chapter Thirty-one

'It's a pity they didn't both die,' Bertie muttered under his breath. He was standing by the window in Hamilton Hall, staring out at the dark, a few feet away from where his mother, Maisie and Robert sat round the table. Dinner was almost over but they lingered over fruit. 'I should have made sure of them both.'

'What did you say, Bertram?' Robert asked, pausing in the middle of peeling an apple to give his brother a hard stare. Mary Anne had just been asking Robert if he knew how Kate was, saying she hadn't heard from her in a while.

'Nothing,' said Bertram, 'I wasn't speaking to you.' He took a long swig of brandy and went to the sideboard to fill his glass. He was like a bomb waiting to go off, he was in such a bad mood.

'Don't you think you've had enough, Bertie?' Mary Anne asked gently. Bertram had been out all day, drinking in the clubs in the town with his friends no doubt. Oh, he was a wild one. It was hard to control him even though he was still a boy legally speaking. Robert tried, bless him, but of course he was not Bertie's father. He needed a firmer hand than hers, she knew well.

There was that trouble at university, trouble she had never got to the bottom of, and now he seemed to run wild for most of the time. Of course, the poor boy had lost his father and then the existence of Georgina had been a terrible shock to him. Maybe he would settle down soon, she hoped so.

'It didn't sound like nothing to me,' said Robert but he went back to peeling his apple, stopping again as Bertram lost his temper.

'Oh, get off my back!' he shouted suddenly. 'Both of you, leave me alone!' He turned to his mother. 'I'll drink whatever I damn well please and there's nothing you can do about it!'

Mary Anne shrank back in her chair and Robert put out a hand across the table and gripped hers. It was trembling and his own temper rose. She looked just as she had used to do when his stepfather shouted at her, which had been far too often. In fact, Bertram sounded like his father had then.

'Bertram, you will come here and apologise to your mother,' he said, his voice quiet but steely.

'Why the hell should I?' Bertram demanded. He took another drink and turned on his stepbrother, staggering slightly and waving his glass about so that brandy slopped on to the carpet.

'She doesn't care about me, she won't even advance me a few miserly quid.'

Robert rose to his feet and strode towards him. He was four or five inches taller than Bertram and well developed and he towered over him, making Bertram look like a spoiled little boy.

'Come and sit down, Bertram. And you will apologise to your mother,' he insisted.

'No I bloody well won't, you can't make me,' Bertram shouted. 'You are not my father!'

'No, but I have control of your money until you reach your majority and if you need an advance it is me you should come to,' said Robert.

'Oh yes, and you'll give me what I need, won't you?' Bertram shouted in an attempt at sarcasm. 'I don't bloody think!' He swayed dangerously and Robert put out a hand to steady him.

'Don't you touch me!' Bertram screamed.

Maisie stood up suddenly, pushing her chair back so that it almost tipped on to the carpet and distracting Robert's attention from Bertram.

'G-goodnight,' she stammered and rushed from the room. Robert looked after her, he should go after her and calm her, her nerves were so bad and she should not have had to witness this scene but he had to attend to Bertram first. As the thought ran through his mind there was a blow to his temple and he staggered, leaving go of Bertram and only just saving himself from falling to the floor. He put a hand up to his face and it came away wet with blood.

'Bertram!' his mother screamed, 'what have you done?' She ran to Robert and took his arm. 'Come on son, sit down, let me look at you,' she said.

'That's right, go to *him*,' Bertram said though he was no longer shouting. In fact he sounded a little unsure of himself now. 'Never mind me, he was threatening me.'

Mary Anne ignored him completely. She had taken the water jug from the table and was dipping a clean napkin in it to wipe the blood from Robert's face. 'There, lad, it's not so bad,' she said. 'Bertie must have forgotten he had the glass in his hand when he hit you.' She looked anxiously at him. 'You feel all right, don't you? I don't think it will need stitches.'

'Don't fuss Mother, I'm all right;' said Robert. The immediate shock of the blow was wearing off and he made to stand up.

'Stay still for a while,' said Mary Anne. 'Shall I get you a drink? It may steady your nerves.'

'No, no, I'm fine Mother.'

'Of course he's all right,' said Bertram. 'I hardly touched him. It was only because the glass broke, I bet most of that blood was from my hand, look, I'm bleeding.' He held out his hand, showing a cut along his palm but no one was listening to him.

'Anyway, he went for me first.' Bertram wound a handkerchief round his hand ostentatiously.

'I'm all right, Mother,' Robert said again. 'Please, go to bed, I'll deal with Bertram. I don't think he'll try anything else.'

'You're sure?' Mary Anne was hesitant. She glanced from one to the other.

'Oh yes, go to bed, Mother,' mimicked Bertram. He

had recovered his poise now he realised that Robert hadn't been badly hurt. Though it served him right if he had been, he thought savagely. Now he supposed he was going to have to listen to the Riot Act read to him. He turned to the sideboard again to fortify himself with another drink. Well, it had been worth it, he thought and grinned drunkenly as his back was turned. Sanctimonious sod, he should have been a vicar. Bertram chuckled at the idea.

'Put that brandy down and sit down yourself before you fall down,' said Robert. His contempt showed in his face and stung Bertram into retorting.

'I'm perfectly all right!' he said, swaying dangerously, but nevertheless he put down the bottle and sat himself. He was going to anyway, he told himself.

'Right then, what's this all about?' Robert asked. 'You haven't been near the office for days and you're in debt up to your ears. Don't try to deny it, I've made some inquiries of my own. Now, I won't have you pestering Mother for money, do you hear?'

Bertram attempted an ironic salute that nearly had him off his chair. 'Yes Sir Boss,' he said and leaned over and vomited on the floor.

It was well past midnight before Robert got to bed and then he couldn't sleep. He lay awake going over the events of the evening. He had had practically to carry Bertram upstairs where he had flung him ceremoniously on the bed and thrown a cover over him. Let Bertram sort himself out tomorrow, he thought. His own nostrils were full of the stink of vomit and he had yet to clean up his brother's mess in the dining-room, he couldn't leave it for Daisy.

He was going to have to do something about Bertram. His need for money seemed more desperate than usual so what had he done? Got himself into debt? Gambling? Women? The possibilities were frightening. People in Teesside must know who he was; they probably allowed him credit on the strength of his inheritance which he would come into when he was twenty-one. I must put word about tomorrow, stop him getting any more credit, Robert decided.

He blamed himself to a certain extent. He had not kept a close enough eye on Bertram since their father died. But there was so much else to see to. He would have to spend more time here in Hamilton Hall than in his own house at Whitworth. As it was, a lot of his time was taken up by travelling between the two.

Well, tonight he would sleep here, his bedroom was still ready for him at all times. He went there now and made ready for bed. Once between the sheets he put the problem of Bertram to the back of his mind. His thoughts turned to Kate as they did so often these days. And Georgina.

He had a feeling of guilt every time he remembered Georgina. Had he pushed her too hard? She had been little more than a child really for all her brilliant mind. He had tried to force her to take an interest in the business, knowing she had a lot to give, would have made a highly successful businesswoman. And it was because of him she had gone away angry on the day of her death. Was he responsible for the crash? He feared thai he was.

He had to try to make it up to Kate, at least as much as he could. Kate. Pictures of her vivid dark blue eyes flashed into his mind. Her eyes mirrored her soul, all right, as the old saying went. Full of tragedy when she allowed herself to know that Georgina really had been killed. So full of light and happiness on a few occasions before it had happened.

Restlessly, Robert turned over on to his side and tried to empty his mind of all disturbing thoughts, he needed his sleep, he had a busy day tomorrow. Apart from all his other appointments, he had to look into whatever it was that Bertram had got himself into.

'He's not really a bad boy you know, Robert,' said Mary Anne. She and Robert were sitting at breakfast. It was early, barely seven o'clock, so of course there was no sign of Bertram. In spite of Robert's efforts of the night before, there was a stale smell in the room and he had opened the windows to try to dispel it. Though nothing was said, Mary Anne had realised what had happened.

Robert smiled at her. 'No, Mother, of course not,' he replied.

'Only Matthew did spoil him, you know. He was away such a lot and when he did come home he wanted to make it up to Bertram.' She bit her lip and gazed at her plate, remembering the main reason Matthew had been away so often.

Robert got to his feet and dropped a kiss on the top of

her head. 'Never mind, Mother, I'll sort him out,' he said. 'Now I must run, I have a lot to do.'

After he had gone Mary Anne sat for a while over a second cup of coffee. It was true, she thought, Matthew had spoiled his son, but then he had also been over-strict with him sometimes. Matthew had been unpredictable and that was hard on a boy growing up. She sighed. At least Bertram was alive. Georgina was dead. Poor, poor Kate.

Robert put Brian Peacock on the job of finding out what Bertram had been up to. Brian was a retired detective inspector in Cleveland Police and knew the area well. He and Robert had become friends years before when Brian was investigating break-ins at the works during the war. There had been a small fire that could have become a major conflagration but for the vigilance of the security guard. There was suspected arson, documents missing from the office, foul-ups on the lines. Nothing very major but enough to suspect a fifth columnist in 1942. Robert had been home on leave at the time and had been keenly interested in the methodical way Brian had gone about discovering the culprit. Sadly, he had got away, but at least the sabotage had come to an end.

It was only a few days before Brian came up with some answers and the extent of Bertram's debts were enough to horrify his stepbrother.

'In hock to the hard boys,' was how Brian described it.

'But why did they let him get in so deep?' asked Robert. They were in the bar of the Durham Ox, talking over a pint of Cameron's Double Maxim and a meat pie.

Brian took one bite of his pie and pushed his plate away.

'I could have done the landlord here for false representation,' he murmured. 'Sometimes I'm sorry I'm retired from all that.'

'Yes,' said Robert and waited patiently for an answer to his question.

'It's obvious, isn't it,' said Brian. 'It's who he is, really. Don't forget, they knew your dada well. He wasn't a stranger to the sleazy side of Middlesbrough. Or Hartlepool for that matter. I daresay they knew what old Matthew was worth down to the last penny.'

'Yes, but—'

'Well, when his lad comes along and shows a taste for the things they have to offer, they are going to oblige, aren't they? They'll hand him the reckoning late, won't they?'

Robert had to agree with Brian's logic. After he left him he went back to Hamilton Hall. He was fairly sure he would find Bertram there. His half-brother had been strangely reluctant to leave the Hall these last few weeks. He found Bertram still in bed. Thankfully Mary Anne was spending the day at Whitworth so Robert had nothing to stop him from bursting into the bedroom and hauling Bertram out of bed.

'Get dressed,' he said. 'You and I have business to discuss and this is not the place for it. I won't have my mother troubled by it.'

'She's my mother too!' Bertram protested. 'And anyway, I'm not going anywhere with you. I don't have to, why should I?'

Robert sighed. 'I'm not arguing with you. Now, get dressed, we're going out. If you want to keep your neck intact I'd do as I say.'

'Are you threatening me?'

'No. But I know certain people who will and believe me you don't want to meet them. Not at the minute.'

Chapter Thirty-two

Life on the wards was hard, even harder than Kate remembered it to be in the South-East Durham General Hospital. Or was it just that she was older and not as strong as she had been? No, it wasn't, Kate told herself crossly as she walked along Escomb Road and hurried up the ramp to D Ward, which was, strangely enough, a gynaecological ward like the one she had first started work on when she was eighteen. She was tired. It had been hard to get out of bed this morning. Yesterday they had had a couple of emergencies and the ward was full to capacity;

'I am perfectly capable of doing this,' she said aloud. 'I am only thirty-seven, not eighty-seven.'

'What did you say?' It was Penny the cadet nurse on the ward. Penny was sixteen; even younger than Georgina had been when she died. Kate was did enough, to be the mother of most of the girls who had started in the same nursing school. A few more years and she could almost have been Penny's grandmother. She pushed that thought to the back of her mind. No, that was rubbish, she was exaggerating.

'Morning, Penny,' she said now. 'Enjoy yourself last night?'

Penny had been to a dance at the rink the evening before with the other students on the ward who were free. Except for Kate of course. Kate had said she couldn't make it and they hadn't pressed her; leaving her with the dismal thought that they thought her too old for dancing anyway.

'I met someone,' said Penny, all excited. 'He asked me to dance four times and then the last waltz.'

'Did he take you home?' asked Kate, immediately thinking of the dangers Penny could be in and that was another sign of her advanced age, she knew.

'No, he had to catch the bus home to West Cornforth,' said Penny. 'But he asked me if I would be at the rink next Saturday.'

'Well, that's great,' said Kate. The dance hall at Spennymoor was called the rink by everyone for it had once been a roller-skating rink and had a sprung floor, perfect for quickstepping and jitterbugging. It attracted the young people for miles around.

They went into the cloakroom and pinned on their hats and the morning's duties began. Listening to Sister reading out the report, doing the bedpan round, making the beds, doing vaginal douches, running for Staff Nurse who was doing the dressings, then clearing the dressing trolley and washing the instruments and putting them in the steriliser. There was supposed to be a twenty-minute break during the morning but it was usually cut short for one reason or another. But Kate had forgotten her tiredness.

She worked on happily though. She had been at the hospital for almost six months, first as an auxiliary and then in the training school and now on the wards. And she loved it. Even on a Sunday like today when the nurses had to do all the cleaning because the ward cleaner was off-duty. So they pulled out the beds from the wall to sweep and buff the floor then pushed them back to do the middle. She liked to buff the composition floor; it gave her a sense of satisfaction to swing the buffer backwards and forwards and see the deep shine gradually emerge. Besides it was undemanding, she could think of other things while she worked.

Today was Sunday and her half-day. She didn't always get a Sunday but today she did and it was a lovely late spring day and she planned to walk through the woods to the path along the top that led to Four Winds. She smiled in anticipation of the fresh air and the smell of the woods. Bluebells would be out; they always were at this time of the year. And there would be wild garlic and new grass and the newly half-unfurled leaves on the trees. Oh yes, life was treating her well just now even if there was still the awful open wound at the back of her mind which was the mourning for Georgina, not yet gone away. She doubted if it ever would. She had thought nothing could be worse than the suffering she had gone through when Billy and Grandda were killed but she had been wrong. The death of her lovely daughter was worse, much, much worse.

A porter came into the ward with a scuttle of coke to throw on the two potbellied stoves that stood in the middle of the ward. There was a rumour that they were going to install central heating but there had been no sign of it happening. Until it did, the patients were awakened at intervals day and night by the noise of the coke thudding into the stoves and the coal-tar smell of it. And the cleaner and nurses had to cope with the dust the stoves created. No one complained, most of the patients were used to the smell and were only grateful that they were having free treatment through Aneurin Bevan's magical National Health. These were the wards that used to house: wounded prisoners-of-war, they were mainly pre-fabricated but more modern than the main blocks. Those had been part of the old workhouse; there were still some patients there from that time. The flotsam and jetsam of life, Kate thought sadly. Oh, for goodness sake, she told herself, think of something cheerful for a change.

Kate finished the floor and helped Penny to give out elevenses, cocoa and biscuits. One o'clock came round in no time at all and at last it was Kate's half-day off. Going down the corridor to the cloakroom she almost bumped into Dr Blake, the Gynae houseman. He was just leaving Sister's office carrying a bundle of patients' notes.

'You're off then, Nurse,' he said. Dr Blake was a fresh-faced man in his late twenties and aiming to be a gynaecologist sometime in the distant future. 'Me too. If you hang on a minute I'll give you a lift, I'm going that way.'

'No thanks, Doctor,' said Kate. 'I've been promising myself a walk through the woods.'

'Oh, well, then—' he began but Kate interrupted.

'Bye, Doctor,' she said and hurried away before he could suggest anything else. It wasn't the first time Dr Blake had shown an interest in her and she didn't want to encourage him. She didn't want to encourage any man, she had finished with men, she told herself, as she put on her uniform gabardine coat and pulled on the nurse's outdoor cap. In no time at all she was walking down Escomb Road crossing through Cockton Hill to the path by the railway line that led to the woods.

Beneath the trees it was cool and fresh and the grass by the path green and damp. She strolled along, taking her time, revelling in being out in the fresh air, even picked a few bluebells to put on the kitchen windowsill.

'Kate! Dorothy said you would be walking this way.'

Kate, in the act of picking a particularly long-stemmed bloom got to her feet and looked round. Robert had just come over the rise in the path and was striding towards her. His smile lit up his face and Kate felt an unexpected surge of pleasure at seeing him. Dear Robert, he was always the same.

'Hello, Robert,' she said. Her hands were full of bluebells so he patted her arm and fell in beside her.

'I've brought my mother to see you,' he said. (Why did he always feel he had to give a reason for visiting her? he wondered.) 'It's a nice ride out for her on a Sunday afternoon. I rang Dorothy and she said it was your half-day.' Perhaps if he admitted it had been he who had wanted to see her, had come purposely to see her, she might shy away. She had been hurt so much. Not that he would hurt her, he would never do that. He loved her, he realised. He was simply waiting until he judged it was a good time to tell her. He had to be careful, he couldn't bear to lose her.

'It was nice of you to come to meet me,' said Kate. She felt ridiculously happy to see him and it *was* ridiculous, wasn't it? She was finished with men. Especially steel men, especially men from his family, especially . . . She turned her face away in case he saw the light in her eyes.

'Not at all,' said Robert formally, slightly rebuffed that she seemed to find the bluebells more interesting than he was. 'I wanted a bit of fresh air anyway.' She buried her nose in the bunch of flowers. She had been right to be cautious, she told herself. They walked on along the path at the top of the woods and the air seemed to her to be even sweeter in spite of the small rebuff, just because he was there.

All too soon they were crossing the road to Four Winds.

Mary Anne looked older, smaller and thinner. But her greeting was as warm and her smile as wide as it had ever been.

Kate took the bluebells through to the kitchen and put them in a plain glass vase and stood them on the windowsill.

'They look nice there,' observed Robert who had followed her through. He looked ready to dally and talk but Kate pushed past him.

'We will go in to your mother,' she said even though Mary Anne could be heard having a conversation with

Dorothy about the embroidered cushions Dorothy had started making as a hobby.

The two women spent a pleasant afternoon chatting and drinking tea and Dorothy came in and sat with them after clearing the tea things. Robert sat apart, watching them and listening and only saying something when his opinion was asked. Mary Anne glanced at him often, noting the way he watched Kate, his expression unreadable. And she looked at Kate too. For the first time it occurred to her that there was some sort of a spark there and she wondered about it. Were they falling for each other? It was a novel idea to her but not really unwelcome. Except that she didn't want Robert to be hurt.

'Perhaps we should be on our way, Robert,' she said, putting down her cup. 'You know I wanted to drive up Weardale before going home.'

'Oh, did you, Mother?' He couldn't actually remember her saying that but Weardale was a scenic ride out and why not go up there? His new pale blue Bristol car was a delight to drive anywhere. But it was a shame to leave Kate's so soon when he had been looking forward to seeing her all morning. But there was nothing else for it.

Once in the car after saying their farewells Mary Anne turned to Robert. 'Be careful, Son,' she said.

'What do you mean? I'm always a careful driver,' he replied.

Mary Anne shook her head. 'I didn't mean that. Never mind, it's probably nothing.' She had had few worries with this eldest son of hers, and if she admitted the truth he was her favourite among her children. She didn't want him to get into something that would only give him heartache.

'Let's go down by Winton Colliery,' she said on a whim. 'I've not seen it before.'

'OK.' Robert was quite willing. He drove down the hill and along past the old aerial flight engine house and the entrance to the bunny banks and on to the towering winding wheel and colliery buildings to the ends of the colliery rows. Turning the corner he parked opposite the back alley of West Row.

Mary Anne gazed at the little houses, each with a yard and coal house and earth closet with their iron sliding covers where the waste was shovelled out. Each cover bore the stamped imprint of Hamilton Ironworks. She gazed at the windows of the mean little houses, most of them shining clean and sparkling in the late sun and with dolly-dyed lace curtains hanging at them.

'Why don't we put flush toilets in them?' she asked Robert. 'For goodness sake, this is the second half of the twentieth century.'

'We can't, Mother; they don't belong to us any more. The mines were nationalised, don't you remember? The houses went with the mine.'

'A jolly good thing too,' said his mother. 'I expect the government will do something about them now.'

'Yes. Well, it certainly pleased the miners themselves. Seen enough?' he asked and she nodded. He started the car and drove along the road to the end of the rows and past the pre-fabs, each in their own little plot of garden. Most of the gardens were bright with flowers and though the little houses were pre-fabricated they looked as though they belonged to a different age altogether from the pit rows.

They drove up the dale in the long evening twilight as far as Wearhead and Alston then returned by Teesdale. They were quiet now, both of them, each occupied with their own thoughts as the moors stretched out on either side of them, seeming to go on for ever. Mary Anne was wondering if Matthew had met Kate before he saw her in the hospital, perhaps when he was visiting Winton Colliery? She remembered that she had thought there was some gleam of recognition in his eyes that awful day when she had lost her baby and Kate had been a young girl on the ward. An extremely pretty young girl, she had to admit.

She glanced at Robert's profile as he concentrated on keeping the car on the narrow road that went over the tops and down into Forest in Teesdale. Thank God Matthew was not his father. And the thought reminded her of Bertram and the usual niggle of worry that came to her every time the thought of her youngest son raised its ugly head.

Chapter Thirty-three

Kate and Dorothy decided to walk down to the village themselves after tea. Dorothy was getting slower and slower these days being troubled with her 'rheumatics'.

'I have to keep going though,' she said determinedly. 'Otherwise I'll just seize up altogether.' They walked slowly down as the birds sang their evening songs and Kate felt at peace with the world. At the entrance to the bunny banks they watched for rabbits and were delighted to see a couple nibbling at the grass before scudding for their holes as they noticed the intruders.

'I'm surprised there's any left after the way they were hunted during the war,' Dorothy observed and they turned away to continue their walk.

They weren't the only ones out on the road in the evening sunshine. Quite a few couples, some with young families, were walking up past the pit yard. As they passed the winding wheel whirred and the safety men spilled out of the cage. They were building pit-head baths, the building half finished already but for now the men had to walk home in their black as they had always done.

'Evening, Missus,' they said as they passed. 'Grand evening.'

'Lovely,' the women chorused. Kate felt suddenly happy and it was so long since she had felt so happy that she didn't at first recognise the feeling. But all that ended when a couple walking up the bank stopped in front of them.

'Don't June, leave it,' the man said.

'I will not leave it,' his wife replied. 'Why should I? I've been waiting long enough to tell the hussy a few home truths and now's me chance.'

Kate stood stock-still. A family with two young children brushed past her but she barely moved. This was the confrontation she had been expecting for a long time and it had finally turned up. The happy feeling slid away and disintegrated into nothingness. She lifted her head and faced her brother's wife.

'Hello Willie,' she said. 'Hello June. Do you know Dorothy? Dorothy is my friend.'

'Is she now!' snapped June. 'And there I thought she was your skivvy.'

'Hey you, watch your tongue!' Dorothy exclaimed. 'Don't you call me a skivvy.'

'Well, what else are you?' June demanded. 'An old woman like you slaving after madam here; you should be on your pension and the likes of her looking after you.'

'June,' said Willie warningly but Dorothy was well able to take care of herself.

'You don't know what you are talking about, lady,' she snapped. 'Get out of our way or old woman as I am, I'll make you.'

Kate had been frozen for a few moments but she suddenly caught hold of Dorothy's arm as June began shouting invective. Dorothy felt her trembling and saw the look of gilt on her face. Good god, the poor lass thought she deserved all this! Ignoring June and her demented shouting she turned and led Kate back up the road to the house, walking steadily and holding on tight all the way. Glancing back over her shoulder she saw Willie doing the same thing with June but June was fighting against him.

When Dorothy and Kate got to the door it was Dorothy who found the key in Kate's bag and opened it. She took her into the sitting-room and poured her a glass of brandy but Kate shook her head.

'Come on, Kate, get a hold of yourself now,' said Dorothy. 'The brandy will do you good. No? Well, I'll make a pot of tea. That'll set you right.'

Dorothy went into the kitchen and busied herself with the tea. By, she thought, she could kill that woman with her bare hands.

Afterwards Kate hardly knew how she got back to Four Winds. If it hadn't been for Dorothy she thought she might not have done. June had brought it all back: the horror of the pit disaster, losing Billy and her grandfather. How her grandmother had cast her off because of Matthew. When Dorothy made her a cup of cocoa she drank it obediently and went to bed though she was sure she wouldn't sleep.

She did though, restlessly, her sleep punctuated by vivid dreams of the past. The time when she had opened the back door of the house in West Row and seen her grandmother working on a new mat, the mat frames propped on two chairs. The beautiful blue cloth she was working into a circle.

'That's my coat, Gran,' she cried in her dream and Gran shook her head.

'No, it's not,' she said. 'It's my new mat.'

She worked the blue on and on until it filled the whole of the mat frame and Kate had shouted at her to stop and give her bonny blue coat back and Gran simply smiled and worked on, digging her prodder into the harn, in, out.

Kate woke with a start and turned over on her back. She glanced at the luminous dial of the clock on her bedside table. It was ten minutes past two. She had to be up at a quarter to seven to get to the hospital on time. The wind was soughing through the trees at the back of the house and whistling down the chimneys and it was almost as if it was playing a tune. And the branches of the plum tree at the front of the house beat a tattoo against the window in time to it.

Her mind returned to her sister-in-law's words. Wild words about how Kate had betrayed Billy and her family, what it had done to Gran, her going off like a whore with a married man because he was rich.

Had she done that? Kate wasn't sure. All her memories of that time were so hazy. She wasn't even sure what she had felt for Matthew. Had she loved him? Well, whether she had or not afterwards there had been Georgina and everything was worth it because of Georgina. And now she had gone. Sometimes she wondered if Georgina had been a dream. A lovely sweet dream that had turned into a nightmare that would stay with her for the rest of her life.

'Now you come here, lording it over the rest of us in your big house,' June had said. 'Playing at being a nurse until you get sick of it again; pretending you want to help folk no doubt. Well, we're on to your game, lady. Lady Muck, I don't think!'

Kate turned over on to her side and stared through a chink in the curtains at the clouds scudding across the sky. The wind had lessened now, the whistling in the chimneys stopped. It rustled softly through the leaves of the plum tree.

'Stop it, June! Do you hear me?' Willie had shouted as he grabbed June's arm and pulled her away. 'Stop making a show of yourself! Let the lass alone!'

June had struggled to free her arm but Willie was too strong for her, he dragged her away and down the road back to the village. Over his shoulder he had looked at Kate, standing there so white-faced and with her eyes dark and large and staring.

'Take no notice, lass,' he'd said.

'Oh no, take no notice,' June had shouted and he turned fiercely on her. What he had said then Kate couldn't hear as they moved away.

'Come on, Kate,' said Dorothy. 'I think you could do

with an early night any road.'

Kate didn't go into Winton much after that. She did her shopping in Bishop Auckland. Sometimes she met Ethel and asked her up to tea or something but even Ethel was not as friendly as she had been. There was nasty talk in Winton Colliery Rows; Kate knew it.

Chapter Thirty-four

Time went on, Kate entered her second year of training and it was hard.

'I don't know why you do it,' Dorothy said one morning. 'It's not as though you need the money. Two hundred pounds a year for goodness sake. You pay me more than that.'

Kate was rushing through her breakfast standing up at the kitchen table because she had overslept. She gulped a mouthful of tea and buttered a piece of toast. 'Well, I'm on holiday after today,' she said through a mouthful of toast.

She had planned to have a few days' rest and quiet, maybe go over to see Mary Anne. She had been promising to long enough. Dorothy was going to stay with her cousin in Hart. She liked to be beside the sea for a while. 'The wind off the North Sea blows the germs away,' she said.

Kate got into her little car and drove out of the drive and down the bank and up the other side. She was doing her three months stint in the operating theatre and she was thoroughly enjoying it.

Sometimes, lately, she forgot for a whole day at a time about Georgina. And then, when she remembered, the feeling of guilt was almost unbearable and she felt worthless, unfit to have been Georgina's mother and was that why she had been taken away from her?

Nonsense, she told herself, forcing herself to push the idea away, dismiss it from her mind. It was a natural part of the grief process, she'd read that somewhere. But she had to get on, keep her mind on her training. This time she was going to finish it, she was determined she would.

Kate parked the car in Escomb Road and ran up the ramp to the theatre. Today Mr Pierce was operating and he had a long list of patients to get through. There was one gastrectomy, two cholecystectomies and two appendisectomies. Kate put on a theatre robe and wound a white turban round her hair and put a mask over her mouth and nose. The operating table was to be scrubbed, the sterilising to see to and then she was to act as the anaesthetic nurse, helping Dr Gibbon in the anteroom to the theatre.

The day went by in a blur as she worked, hurrying to do as Dr Gibbon asked, then whatever Theatre Sister asked. Then, when the theatre porter and nurse from the ward went through the swing doors to the ramp that led to the wards with the patient on a trolley, there was the clearing up to do. The washing of the instruments ready for the steriliser, filling the drums with clean swabs ready to be sterilised in the autoclave, tidying the anaesthetic anteroom.

At half past five she was free to go home. She took off her gown and hat and combed out her hair that was sticking to her scalp with the heat in the operating theatre.

Then she could pull on her coat and hat and leave, for a whole fortnight. As she went out of the door she was followed by a chorus of, 'Have a good time!' and 'You lucky devil!' and the air was fresh and the wind cool on her hot face as she walked down the ramp to Escomb Road and her car.

There was a man leaning against the bonnet, it was too far away to recognise him at first. Then she saw it was Robert, his fair hair haloed in the late afternoon sun. As she approached he stood up straight and went to meet her.

'Kate,' he said and his pleasure at seeing her was plain to see. He took her hands in both of his. 'How are you, Kate?' he asked.

'Hello Robert. What are you doing here?' It was a while since she had seen him and then it had of necessity been a flying visit for she had been on a split shift and had to go back to the hospital for the evening.

'Oh, business,' said Robert vaguely. 'Let's go back to the house and I'll explain. Or would you like to go for a meal? There must be one or two places where we could go in a town like Bishop Auckland.'

'No, we'll go back to the house,' she replied. She got into her car and set off for Four Winds and he followed in his Bristol. She felt ridiculously happy to see him. It was just because Dorothy was away and she didn't want to face an evening on her own, she wasn't in the mood, she told herself as she turned into the drive and took her car straight into the garage to leave room for his on the driveway.

'Won't you stay for dinner? I've a couple of pork chops in the fridge and plenty of salad stuff in the garden,' she said. Thank goodness for Dorothy who had insisted on stocking up before she went off to Hart Village. There was even a bottle of wine. She had had it in since Christmas for though she had got used to drinking wine when . . . when she lived in Fern Moor Cottage (her mind skirted round the thought of Matthew), she still felt it was slightly wicked to drink alone.

They worked together in the kitchen, chopping lettuce and slicing tomatoes and cucumber still warm from the greenhouse and she took a breath when she shouldn't have while she was slicing onions and tears ran down her cheeks and he had to wipe them dry.

He was in charge of grilling the chops and they came out only a little charred round the edges.

'You'll still have to eat them,' Kate warned. 'It's a sin to waste the meat ration.'

'I like them like this,' he said. He had opened the wine and gave her a glass and they toasted each other. She sipped from it as she set the table in the kitchen and slowly the evening began to take on a magical quality. She didn't know whether it was the wine or Robert and she was having too good a time to care. It was so rarely that she had such a pleasurable change to her routine.

'Wait a minute,' she said as she put out the plates of food. She went into the sitting-room for the candle in the silver holder that normally stood on the mantelshelf in case there was yet another power cut. In the middle of the table it shed a soft glow as they ate and the shadows outside darkened.

This was the first time Kate had been alone with

Robert, really on her own. Always before there had been Dorothy or sometimes Mary Anne. In fact it was the first time she had been alone with a man since Matthew died. They finished the meal and moved into the sitting-room and Robert put a match to the already laid fire.

Afterwards, Kate thought it must have been the effects of the wine for she didn't move away when he took her hand and sat on the sofa and pulled her down beside him. He kissed her lips, lightly at first then with passion, his tongue probing between her lips and teasing hers. He touched her breasts under her blouse and felt the nipples harden in immediate response. He looked down at her face; her eyes were closed and a pulse beat at her temple.

'Kate,' he breathed and undid the buttons and pushed her bra out of the way. Her skin felt warm and inviting. He rubbed the base of his thumb over a nipple and she moaned as he took it between his teeth. Suddenly it became urgent and they stripped off their clothes and fell to the floor and he took her there, on the hearthrug before the fire.

Kate couldn't think, only feel. She was floating on a sea of exquisite sensation and her mind was carried along with it. Her body was afire with it. Her heart raced.

Afterwards they lay together quietly, his head on her shoulder, his ragged breathing slowing. She felt profoundly at peace.

Yet a poisonous thought niggled at her, shattering the peace. Did he mean to take over from his stepfather in this, too? No! Of course he didn't, did he? Kate sat up and fumbled for her clothes. He rolled away from her and smiled.

'What is it, Kate? What?'

'It's late, I must go to bed, I get up early in the morning,' she said.

Robert sat up too and put his arm around her shoulder. 'No you don't, Kate. You're on holiday tomorrow, remember?'

'Well, I have to—'

'Kate, Kate, what's the matter? Tell me.'

She was scrambling into her skirt and blouse, fastening the blouse lop-sidedly and having to do it again. He got to his feet and dressed, taking his time about it. Then he turned to her and took her in his arms and kissed her gently.

'I love you Kate,' he said. 'Don't send me away now.' And then, intuitively, 'This has nothing to do with Matthew Hamilton, Kate. I am not at all like him. I want to marry you.'

It wasn't true, thought Kate. How could it be? He was younger than she was. She had thought he was interested in Georgina. Surely he had been interested in Georgina?

'I'm older than you,' she said as though that made an insuperable barrier.

Robert laughed softly. 'So you are, Kate. All of three years I believe. A real old lady. I'm after your pension, how could you tell?'

'No, seriously, I mean it. I feel years older than you. After all that has happened—'

He put a finger to her mouth. 'Be quiet,' he said. 'Do you love me Kate? Because if you do, well then, that's all that matters, isn't it?'

'Your mother . . .'

'Come to bed, Kate, now. Don't say another word. I want to make love to you properly and I can't wait any longer.'

'I'm finished with men,' she murmured as he led her upstairs.

'Yes, I know,' he said. 'Now which bedroom is yours?'

Kate woke next morning feeling absurdly happy; she stretched her body like a cat and turned to the other .side of the bed. It was empty but she could hear sounds from downstairs so at least he hadn't slipped away.

She got out of bed and pulled on her dressing-gown and went along to the bathroom to freshen up. She was shy of meeting him this morning, she realised. She had practically thrown herself at him last night hadn't she? What with the wine and the candlelight and the sitting-room lit only by the firelight. Oh, she squirmed with embarrassment at the thought of it. Most of what she remembered of the evening was wrapped in a golden haze. All she remembered clearly was how she had felt, the deep feelings that had lain dormant for so long had betrayed her. It was the wine of course, it had lowered her inhibitions.

'I'm sorry,' she mumbled as she went into the kitchen. He looked round from the stove where he was cooking scrambled eggs.

'Good morning, Kate,' he said. 'I had a shower, I hope you don't mind. I'm cooking scrambled eggs, I saw you had plenty of eggs.'

He stopped and looked closely at her. 'What is it, Kate? What do you mean, you're sorry?'

'It was the wine,' she answered. 'I'm not used to it, I don't normally drink.'

Robert started to laugh but stopped as he saw her expression. 'The wine? Oh Kate, and I thought you loved me.'

She looked up quickly. Oh she did, she realised now how much. But she couldn't tell him so. A man like Robert would never marry her.

'I . . . it was a mistake, Robert. I'm sorry. I told you, I'm not interested, I want to finish my training, I want to go on, make something of my life. There's no room for a man in my plans.'

He was quiet for a moment. 'Well, you fooled me last night,' he replied at last and his voice had lost its warmth. A pungent smell of burning came from the stove and he turned and moved the pan away from the ring, turned the switch.

'I seem to make a habit of burning things,' he said, taking the pan to the sink.

'It doesn't matter, I'm not hungry.'

'I think I should go now. I have things to do.'

'Yes of course.'

He couldn't wait to get away, what a fool he had been. She gazed out of the window, her back to him so that he shouldn't see how she was holding on to her emotions.

Robert took up his jacket from the chair back he had hung it over and put it on. 'Well, I'll go then,' he said and waited.

'Yes. Goodbye Robert. I'll be seeing you,' said Kate. After a moment she heard the door close after him and she turned round. She wanted to run after him, stop him, but she did not. After a moment she heard his car engine start then the whine as he backed out of the drive.

Dumbly she went about the kitchen, cleaning up the mess of burned eggs; setting the kettle to boil up again and making herself a cup of tea that she forgot to drink.

'It was all a mistake,' she said aloud. Then she went back to bed and lay on the other side of the bed and breathed in the scent of him that was caught on his pillow.

Robert drove eastwards towards Hamilton Hall, his thoughts in turmoil. He couldn't believe she had turned him down flat, not after the way she had responded to him the evening before and in the night.

It was probably his fault. He had held back from telling her how he felt before now, knowing how she was grieving for Georgina. And the situation with the family was so complicated. He couldn't blame her if she wanted no more to do with any of them. But yesterday he had had an overwhelming urge to come to see her. And when he did see her coming out of the hospital grounds looking enchanting in her navy blue uniform coat and cap, he couldn't help himself.

Of course she didn't want to marry him, why should she? he thought savagely. He would keep away after this, indeed he would. Mr Fox could be his go-between if he needed to get in touch about the business.

Chapter Thirty-five

'I wish you'd find yourself a nice girl, Robert,' said Mary Anne. 'There are plenty about I'm sure. I worry about you, you know.'

'Well, there's no need, Mother,' said Robert. 'I'm perfectly all right as I am.' An image of Kate flashed through his mind and a stab of pain with it.

'There's Elizabeth Dawson, I've noticed the way she looks at you,' Mary Anne persisted.

'Have you? I'm sure I haven't noticed her being interested in me. Anyway, she's only a girl.'

'But old enough,' said Mary Anne. 'It would be nice to have grandchildren. And if you don't hurry up you'll be too old.'

Robert laughed. 'Oh Mother,' he said, 'there's plenty of time, I'm only thirty-six. And in any case, I'm too busy to think of such things.' He changed the subject to Bertram. Recently Bertram had entered his majority and as far as Robert could see was rapidly running through the liquid part of his inheritance. As soon as he could he had taken a flat in Middlesbrough and moved there.

'Out of the way so you won't be poking your nose in, dear brother,' he had said. 'I'm my own man now.' He rarely got in touch and when he did it was to demand why the dividends from Hamilton Ironworks were not larger. In fact Robert was expecting another Such visit any day now. It was time for him to hand over control of the ironworks to Bertram and then he could do little to save Kate's share losing value.

'Have you heard from Bertram, Mother?' he asked.

'Not in the last few days, dear,' said Mary Anne. 'Still, I'm sure he'll be in touch soon.'

'Yes,' said Robert, trying not to sound ironic. 'Well, I must be off. I've a lot to do today.'

He kissed the top of his mother's head and made for the door. It opened as he came to it and Maisie came in. Maisie looked different somehow. He realised with surprise that she was actually wearing makeup, lipstick and rouge. Her hair had been cut fashionably short and with a fringe and she was almost pretty. No, he corrected himself, she was pretty.

'You're looking well, Maisie,' he said. 'That dress suits you.'

Maisie looked down at the crisp navy blue dress with its full skirt and nipped-in waist and smiled. 'Thank you, Robert,' she said. 'I'm going out.'

'Oh? Can I give you a lift?'

'No thanks. I have passed my test. I bought a car yesterday. A Riley.'

Robert opened his eyes wide in amazement. How had he not noticed the change in his sister? It must have been coming on for some time. Surely it wasn't an overnight transformation. He recovered enough to congratulate her on passing the test and kissed her warmly.

'I'm glad, Maisie,' he said. 'Though to be honest you could have knocked me down with a feather!'

He went out to his car and got in. Today he wanted to go to Middlesbrough and seek out Bertram. He had to make a last attempt to get his half-brother to see what was happening, where he was heading.

The gutter, thought Robert. A rather melodramatic thought but it seemed to fit. Already he had heard that Bertram was looking for capital using Hamilton Hall for collateral. That meant a mortgage and if Bertram ran true to form Robert could see the house being taken from him. Oh, his mother would be all right, she would always have a home with him at Whitworth.

For a moment Robert even had a twinge of sympathy for his dead stepfather; he would be turning in his grave if he knew. All the years Matthew had worked and schemed to build up his empire, all the years he had longed for a son of his own and here was the son demolishing the lot in short order. Well, Bertram wasn't going to get his hands on Kate's share, that at least he could do for her. He felt the familiar twinge of longing for Kate and the bitter-sweet memory of that one night he had spent at Four Winds returned to him.

He was in Middlesbrough by this time, in that maze of

streets built when the iron trade was at its height. He drove on to where the streets had been of slightly better quality but were now run down. They were rebuilding on some of the bomb sites; he had to negotiate round tradesmen's trucks and even a pile of sharp sand. He parked a little further on and took a piece of paper out of his pocket. 12A Simon Street. It was over a shop with blacked-out windows and a small sign over the door. The sign was difficult to read because some of the letters had fallen off or worn off. PAR—SE C-U- they read. He looked at the door next to it, there was no name on it. But there was a bell and he pushed it.

There was no reply, no one came down to let him in. Robert turned the handle and pushed and it opened directly on to a flight of stairs.

'Bertram?' he called but there was still no reply and he went on up. There was a door at the top leading off a narrow corridor covered in carpet so dirty the pattern was hidden altogether. Robert opened the door and went in. It was a living-room with an old leather couch and dilapidated armchair, a wooden table surrounded by 'utility' chairs. A door was open to a kitchen with the sink piled high with dirty pots and a grease-covered stove. The other door must lead to a bedroom, Robert surmised. He crossed over to it, wrinkling his nose at the strange, sweet smell hanging in the air.

Bertram was lying face down on the bed and for a moment Robert thought he was dead. There was blood on the pillow, vomit in a pool on the floor by the side of the bed. But that wasn't the source of the smell, Robert was aware of that. He went over to the bed, holding a handkerchief over his mouth and nose.

Bertram was breathing. Thank God. The blood was from his hand, he must have cut himself on the broken bottle that was lying on the floor amid the vomit. Before he touched Bertram, Robert went to the window and tried to force it open. The sash was ancient and the rope frayed and worn. When it did open, it dropped suddenly and he had to snatch his hand back before it was trapped.

Going back to the bed he shook Bertram by the shoulder and his brother groaned and flung up an arm to ward him off. Robert lost his temper suddenly.

'For God's sake, Bertram, you'll kill yourself! Come on, pull yourself together!' Robert heaved Bertram's dead weight over on to his back and slapped his face. Bertram opened his eyes but they were slewing about, the pupils large and unfocused. He muttered something over and over but Robert couldn't catch or understand what he was on about.

He would have to get an ambulance, Robert realised. He didn't know a lot about drugs but surely the state his brother was in; his skin cold and clammy, saliva coming out of the corner of his mouth, his eyes rolling about, the awful smell made suddenly worse as Bertram wet himself. Robert ran downstairs and out of the door and stood looking round for a telephone box. There was one at the end of the road and he ran towards it praying that it hadn't been vandalised. It hadn't and within minutes an ambulance was on its way.

*

It was evening before Bertram was recovered enough to talk properly. He lay on the pillow looking like a small boy, his face deathly pale and his eyes shadowed.

'How do you feel?' Robert asked when he was allowed into the side ward to see him. Bertram's answer was barely above a whisper so Robert had to lean over the bed to catch what he said.

The policeman who was stationed by the bedside stood up to move closer but he wasn't close enough.

'It's all that tart's fault,' he said. 'I'd never have been on the stuff but for her.'

'Nonsense,' Robert said sharply. 'Kate has nothing to do with this, nothing at all, do you hear me?'

'I should have finished them both off that night,' Bertram went on. 'God knows I tried.'

'What's that? What did he say, sir?' The policeman tried to get closer.

'Nothing. He said nothing but a load of nonsense. He's not in his right mind, not yet, mixing up nightmares with reality.' The policeman looked from one to the other and then moved back. 'They do that, sir,' he said. Bertram's eyes were closed but he gave a pale imitation of his old, sardonic grin.

Robert did not get back to Hamilton Hall until late but his mother was still up. She had recently bought a television and was watching the end of a play in the small sitting-room.

'Robert! I thought you must have gone back to Whitworth. Have you had anything to eat? Daisy has gone to bed but I can soon get something from the kitchen.'

'No, Mother, thank you. I'm all right,' said Robert. 'Sit down, I have something to tell you.'!

He had debated with himself on thle way over to the Hall what he would say to her. In the end it was a strictly edited version of events. It was best if she knew nothing about Bertram's part in the accident when Georgina was killed. How would it help if she knew? Nothing was going to bring the girl back.

Bertram was suffering from liver failure; that she had to know. He told her as gently as possible and also how it had come about.

'I'll go to him,' she said. 'Oh, why didn't you call me? He will be needing me.'

Robert shook his head. 'No, Mother. He's asleep, he hasn't to be disturbed. I'll take you tomorrow, first thing. He is sedated in any case.'

'I knew there was something,' said Mary Anne. 'I could tell he wasn't himself. My poor Bertram.'

'Go to bed, Mother, he will need you in the next few days, they are not going to be easy for him.'

Robert rang Kate early the next morning, hoping to find her at home. He caught her just as she was about to go out of the door. At long last she had achieved her ambition to become a State Registered Nurse and was a staff nurse on D Ward.

'Kate, I must see you,' he said and her heart did a small flip as it usually did when she heard his voice. That wasn't very often these days because, true to his word, he communicated with her through Mr Fox in matters concerning the business.

'Oh?'

'Are you free this afternoon? I could come through to Auckland.'

Oh, she was free, but could she bear to see him? Just when she had finally got used to the idea that their brief affair was finished?

'Well—'

'Come on, Kate, I must see you,' he cried.

'I'm free from one until half past four. I have a split shift.'

'Well then, we can go to lunch somewhere. I'll meet you in that road by the hospital, is that all right? One o'clock and thanks, Kate.'

He rang off before she could change her mind and she went out to the car with her thoughts whirling in confusion. She wanted to see him again, she admitted it to herself. She thought of him often, especially when she was on night duty and sitting for any length of time on the darkened ward with patients sleeping around her. She had even taken to doing embroidery to take her mind off him. She had embroidered tray cloths and cushion covers to give to the chapel bazaar to prove it. Three months' night duty at any one time was a long stretch.

The morning dragged along even though she was busy the whole time. There were dressings to do and drips to attend to and an emergency came in, a girl with a ruptured ectopic pregnancy who had to be prepared for theatre. There were only two students on duty with her and a cadet and the main of the patients were becoming convalescent and querulous with it. Then the surgeon's round was delayed owing to the fact that he had been in theatre operating on the ruptured ectopic and it was ten minutes past one before she was free to leave the ward.

He was waiting there, just as he had been the time before. Leaning against her car, his long legs crossed one over the other. She was vividly reminded of that other time she had met him like this and of what happened that night. She blushed like a young girl.

'Hello, Kate.'

He straightened as she walked towards him. He looked just the same, she thought, until she got close and saw the strain in his eyes. He looked tired too but as he looked down at her his face lit up for a moment.

'Hello, Robert,' she said formally. 'How are you?' But she wanted to reach out to him, hold him.

'I'm fine,' he replied. 'You look well. Blooming in fact. We'll take my car, shall we? I'll bring you back in plenty of time.'

They went to The Eden Arms!at Rushyford. The hotel was quiet; there were only a few people in the dining-room. Robert had booked a secluded corner table in any case.

'What is this all about, Robert?' she asked after the waiter had taken their order. For surely after all these months he must have a compelling reason for seeking her out. She had hurt him that morning in Four Winds, she knew. And he was a proud man; she didn't think he would put himself forward only to be rejected again. In fact, she told herself, he probably had a girlfriend already. Probably he was even planning to get married and thought he should tell her. Oh God, was that it? Please don't let it be that, please, God.

'Let's eat first, it's a shame to let the food get cold.' The waiter had brought lemon sole in a delicious sauce but somehow, for all her busy morning, Kate didn't feel like eating. Nevertheless, she made herself swallow most of it. Neither of them wanted desert so they went straight on to the coffee.

'I'm sorry to bring this up, I know it's painful for you,' he began. Kate's dread deepened but for some reason she had no inkling of what it was he was going to tell her.

'It's about the accident.'

When she looked blankly at him he went on. 'The accident when Georgina was killed.'

'What? Why are you talking about it now, after all this time?'

'Something has come to light and I think you should know about it.'

Robert paused for a moment and drew in a long breath. He had gone over in his mind often enough how he was going to tell her but now she was sitting across the table from him and looking at him with her eyes wide he couldn't remember how he had been going to put it to her.

'New evidence? But it's been years!' she said.

'Yes. But I know who the driver of the other car was.'

He told her about Bertram, of going to see him in Middlesbrough, of the state he was in, everything. And what he had said about the night of the accident.

'He meant to force you off the road, and he managed it,' he said. Kate said nothing, simply gazed at him, her face white beneath her nurse's cap.

'I . . . Nothing will come of it,' Robert said. 'Nothing can. Bertram won't live long, his liver is failing.'

It was Bertram, she thought. In the back of her mind she had known it. Or suspected it rather and refused to believe it. There had been no accident, it was deliberate. Oh, Georgina, her lovely, lovely Georgina.

Chapter Thirty-six

'Kate,' said Robert. 'Kate, say something.'

They had come away from the hotel and out into the bright sunshine. 'Shall I take you home for a while?' Robert had asked. 'I know what a shock this has been to you. I could call Matron and say you were sick. You don't have to go into work, Kate.'

Kate had looked at him as though he was mad. 'I do have to go in,' she said. 'Of course I do. There will only be first-and second-year student on the ward if I don't.'

Robert looked at his watch. It was only half past two. 'Well, we can go somewhere else for an hour or so at least. Then I'll take you back.'

In the end they decided to walk in the bishop's park for a while. The gravel crunched beneath their feet as they walked through the arched gateway and along by the side of the castle to the entrance to the park. As Robert held the cattle-catcher gate open for her he made his appeal. She had been silent on the journey and he respected that, she had a lot to think about. His heart ached for her.

Perhaps he had not had the right to tell her and open the old wound. What good had he done? None at all, only harm, he thought.

She was doing so well now. She had achieved her ambition to train as a nurse, and he would bet his last penny she was a damn good one too. But he had to know what she was thinking.

Kate went through the gate and set off down the path leading to the Gaunless. It was shaded by tall trees and at the bottom the Gaunless tinkled along lazily, low at this time of year. They were halfway down before Kate stopped and turned to him.

'I just don't know what to say to you, Robert,' she said and her eyes were full of pain. 'My poor girl, my poor Georgina, she had her life ahead of her. She never had a chance. She was so clever, so talented. There was so much potential. Oh I'm still working things out in my mind.' She saw how troubled he looked, how concerned for her and despite her own pain she put a hand on his arm.

'I'm all right, really I am,' she said and turned and walked on. A great oak tree stood near the bottom, over-looking the river.

'Let's sit a while, shall we?' she said and they sat on the grass and leaned against the trunk of the tree. She closed her eyes and allowed herself to think of her lovely daughter.

Robert watched her, her face was still pale but com-posed, even her voice sounded composed. Yet he knew there was a lot going on behind the closed lids. He looked towards the water, not wanting to intrude on her thoughts.

Further along the bank there was a group of children paddling where there had once been a ford and the bottom of the stream was paved. Two mothers sat on the bank watching them and talking together! They could hear the children laughing and playing, happy and excited. The leaves of the tree above them rustled with a slight breeze. It seemed so peaceful, just as Kate's expression did. Were there traumas in their lives too? Of course there must be to some extent. He looked back at Kate and his heart melted with love for her.

'Kate,' Robert said suddenly, as though the words were forced out of him. They were, he hadn't meant to say them, not yet. 'Kate, I still love you. I know I haven't the right to say it. I know you have suffered enough from my family. I know—'

'Hush, Robert,' said Kate. 'Hush.' She put up a finger and put it over his mouth, tracing the outline of his lips. 'None of it was your fault, Robert. None of it, though some of it was mine.' She sighed. 'I have tried to get on with my life without you,' she went on. 'I was so determined not to get involved again, not with any man. After Matthew—'

'Forget him,' said Robert, taking hold of her hand. 'He has nothing to do with us. He can't rule your life, not now. He's dead, Kate. Put him out of your mind.'

'I know he's nothing to me now. But he was Georgina's father.'

'He's gone now, Kate,' Robert reiterated. 'He took advantage of you at a time when you were vulnerable.'

'I let him do it, though Robert. I think I needed

someone as strong as he was at the time.' Sadly she thought of that long ago sorrow, the deaths of Grandda and Billy. Now overlaid by that of Georgina.

They sat in silence for a while as the sun dipped behind the tall trees on the bank on the opposite side of the river. Mothers were taking their children from the water and drying them off, putting on socks and shoes and trailing them up the bank to the path out of the park. In the distance a clock chimed. It was four o'clock.

'I must get back,' she said and he stood and held out a hand to her to pull her up after him. He held on to her hand as they walked up the bank and along the path to the cow-catcher gate and she was content to let it lie. His hand felt firm and strong, and she looked up at him as they got to the gate where they had perforce to go round singly.

'There are so many things against us,' she said. 'What will people say? I was your stepfather's fancy woman and people know that.'

'Who cares? Do you?'

'No.'

But perhaps in her heart she did. Kate thought of how the gossip in Winton Colliery had hurt her. They were through the gate now and walking to the car.

'But Mary Anne, what about her? She was Matthew's wife. We are friends now which shows what a big heart she has. But will she not hate it, me marrying her son?'

'She'll be happy for me, for both of us. You must have realised she never loved Matthew Hamilton. She is fond of you, Kate, you know that. Don't worry, Kate. Everything will be all right.' They were silent for a while.

'I'll have to get back to the ward,' said Kate. What she really felt she had to do was put off the moment. They walked up the path and along the gravel drive to the entrance and his car beyond.

He drove up Newgate Street and turned right into Escomb Road, drawing to a halt behind Kate's car. He didn't get out straight away, instead he turned to her again.

'Kate?'

'I have to run,' she said and opened the door. He put a restraining hand on her arm.

'What time do you finish? I'll wait,' he said. He felt that if he left her now without resolving the issue they never would.

'Robert, it's hours yet. Eight o'clock.'

He's persistent, I'll give him that, she thought as she walked up the ramp and pushed open the double doors. The ward looked peaceful in the evening sunlight that streamed in through the high windows. Round a table in the middle, a group of patients in dressing-gowns sat talking quietly.

She got out the box of thermometers and the temperature book and went round the beds, tafing temperatures. There was nothing to be alarmed about. Mrs Hall, the woman who had been to theatre that morning, needed her drip changed.

'Can I have something for the pain, Staff?' Mrs James in the second bed asked. She was waiting to hear the verdict of the cancer specialist who was going to look in this evening and talk to her.

'I'll ring the doctor, see if you can have something

stronger,' Kate promised and went to the telephone immediately.

She helped the students to serve the evening meal then went into the office to write the report for the night staff during the visiting hours. She gave out the medicines while the students turned down the counterpanes ready for the night.

The thought of Robert was at the back of her mind all evening though she was too good a nurse to let it take over while she was in charge of patients. At eight o'clock she handed the report over to Night Sister and her responsibility ended.

In the cloakroom she gazed at her reflection in the mirror as she pulled on her outdoor cap. If she agreed to marry him, would he regret the fact that she was older than he was in the years to come? If she didn't, what then? Could she do without him? She was so confused, all her previous convictions were going for nothing in the face of her love for Robert. There was Georgina but Georgina would want her to be happy. She tried to think rationally but somehow it was impossible. She fastened her coat and picked up her bag. It might all be for nothing, she thought in sudden panic. He might, just might have changed his mind and gone while he had the chance.

Kate turned for the door almost bumping into Sister as she went past to the sluice.

'Still here, Staff?' Sister raised her eyebrows.

'Just going, Sister,' she replied. 'Goodnight, then.'

Coming through the gate on to Escomb Road she saw him immediately. Again he was half-sitting on the car bonnet, looking towards her, his expression unreadable.

'I would want to continue nursing,' she said as she reached him. She looked up at him anxiously.

'There are hospitals in the east of the county,' he answered. He returned her gaze and what he wanted to see in her eyes and relaxed tangibly. His smile bathed her in warmth and love.

'Well then, that's all right,' said Kate and he took her in his arms and kissed her.

A group of porters walked past, going off duty and they grinned and whistled; long low wolf whistles. 'Go on, there, Staff!' one of them called to her but she hardly heard, aware of nobody but him.

Robert had been sitting in the Wear Valley Hotel, watching the clock. The evening had been interminable for him but it had been worth it.

'Are you sure, Kate?' he asked. He couldn't bear it if she was not.

'I'm sure,' said Kate. She looked up into his face and smiled and his arms tightened round her.

'Good evening, Staff Nurse Benfield.' The voice sounded disapproving and she started but Robert still held her close.

'I will see you in the morning, Staff Nurse,' Matron continued. 'Perhaps now you should be on your way?'

'Come on,' Kate whispered in Robert's ear. 'Let me go. As it is I'll be hauled on to the carpet tomorrow morning. Acting in an indecorous way so as to bring the hospital into disrepute, it's called.' She giggled.

'Staff Nurse!'

'Yes Matron. Sorry Matron,' said Kate and pulled out of Robert's arms.

'Good evening, Matron,' said Robert with his most charming smile. 'I'm glad to say you are the first to know. Nurse Benfield and I are engaged to be married.'

'Emm,' Matron stuttered and for the first time in her life Kate saw Matron lost for words. She soon recovered, however.

'Congratulations to you both,' she said then looked to Kate. 'I hope this doesn't mean you will neglect your career, Staff Nurse. We will expect you to give your full attention to your work.'

'Of course, Matron,' said Kate. And Matron nodded and walked on along the road.

'Let's go back to Four Winds,' said Kate.

Turn the page to read an extract from

A WARTIME NURSE

also available from Ebury Press

Chapter One

'Don't go, Joss – please don't go. I don't want you to.'

Joss Wearmouth gazed solemnly at his sister, his eyes hopeless. 'I know, I don't want to go neither.'

They were sitting on a grassy bank speckled with wild strawberries and the tiny red fruit sparkled in the sun. A small, much-battered wicker basket which Theda had had as a child lay beside them, half-filled with strawberries. But now she had forgotten about the fruit altogether, for Joss had come down the garden path and out on to the bank beside the old waggon way and told her that he was 'surplus to requirements' at the pit.

'Well, don't go, you don't have to. You'll find a job here if you look hard enough, surely you will. There's the Railway Waggon Works at Shildon and there's Bishop . . . now there's bound to be something at Bishop Auckland.'

Earnestly she looked up at him, her Joss, the one who always looked after her and never talked down to her the way the elder brothers of other girls did.

Joss picked a blade of grass and rubbed it between his fingers, staring into the distance over the old waggon way and grassed-over mound which was an old pit heap really. Over to the ruined buildings of Old Pit, their harshness softened by distance and sunlight.

'You know we talked it all out yesterday, Theda. There is no other work,' he said at last. 'I'll get no dole, not when I'm living at home – not when Da's working anyroad. We should be thanking God his name didn't come out of the hat again like it did at Wheatley Hill. At least he's working.'

'Yes, but—'

'It's no good, Theda. There's you and Frank and Chuck and Clara to feed. You're only fourteen, but you know how it is. No, I'm sixteen, big enough to fend for meself. I said I'd go in the army and that's what I'm going to do.'

'I could leave school, I'm nearly fifteen,' she said. 'I can, I don't have to go till I'm sixteen just because it's the Grammar School. Everybody else leaves school when they're fourteen.'

Joss got to his feet and she scrambled up after him, looking into his face, her own so woebegone that he grinned and put an arm around her shoulders. 'What, and waste that scholarship we're all so proud of?'

'You could have had a scholarship, Joss. If you had, you'd have had a posh job in an office by now,' Theda countered. But she knew that Joss couldn't have taken up a scholarship, not when it fell in the year the family had had to move to Winton Colliery. He was the eldest and when he was old enough to go down the pit his money

2

was needed, that was how it always worked. And, any-way, Joss had wanted to go down the pit; that was what men did.

'Aw, howay,' he said now. 'I'll help you fill that doll's basket and we'll take it in to Mam and then go swimming in the reservoir. How's that sound?'

'I don't know about the reservoir,' said Theda doubt-fully, thinking about the amount of frogspawn there had been in the reservoir at Old Pit that spring. Not to mention what else might be lurking in the weeds that grew out ever further into the water from the bank!. 'Can we not go down the wood and paddle in the Gaunless?'

Joss laughed. 'Howay then.'

In the end, Frank and Chuck and little Clara trailed behind them down to the wood and the place where the bed of the Gaunless river was paved with large stones that didn't hurt their feet when they paddled, and just along from the paving a deeper pool where Joss could swim. They had pop bottles of water and slices of bread and fish paste and some wild strawberries for after.

'Keep an eye on the young ones, our Joss, and you an' all, Theda,' Mam had said. 'I don't know whether you should take them anyroad . . .' But there were howls of protest and in the end they all went. Mam watched them go from the gate of the back yard and Theda could see that her eyes and nose were red as though she had been crying.

'Are you sad, Mam?' Theda had asked. 'I wish Joss wasn't going, don't you? It's not fair, you know – I bet the gaffer cheated when he drew Joss's name out of the hat.'

'No, pet, Tucker Cornish wouldn't do that,' said Mam. 'No, I'm not sad, the army'll be the making of Joss. I'm just getting a summer cold, I think.'

Mam needn't have worried about the little 'uns. They never went near the deep pool, not even Frank. He was more interested in roaming through the wood than paddling in the stream anyway. So he wasn't there when Joss suddenly disappeared under the water. Theda, her woollen knitted costume hanging from her skinny body, was treading water when it happened. She blinked and rubbed her eyes with one hand – where had he gone? Panic rose in her.

'Joss? Joss?' she cried and dived under, for a streak of red was bubbling through the water at the spot where he had been diving. Taking a deep breath, she ducked under again. The water was brown and peaty but still clear enough for her to see that the top half of Joss's body was sticking out of a hole in the bed of the stream, his eyes wide open as he tried to move a rock that had rolled over, restricting the opening.

'Frank! Frank!' she screamed the moment her head was clear of the water, but there was no sign of Frank, only Chuck and Clara standing on the stones and staring at her.

'Stay there!' she shouted and swam to where she judged Joss to be before ducking under the water again. She heaved at the stone, adding her small strength to that of her brother, and for an eternity of perhaps two seconds she thought she couldn't do it. And then it moved and Joss shot up through the water and he was there, above her, and they swam the two or three strokes it took to reach the bank.

They hung on to the edge, gasping, until Joss summoned up enough strength to push Theda up on to the grass and then Frank was there, holding out a hand to his brother.

'What happened?' he asked, as they rubbed themselves down with the towels Mam had put in the carrier bag along with their picnic. Theda went behind a bush and changed into her cotton dress while Joss told the tale, for she couldn't bear to relive the horror of it. Then she bound up the graze on his leg with his hankie.

'Theda saved my life,' declared Joss, watching her.

'Well, I would have done,' said Frank, sulkily, mad that he had missed the excitement. And after a while they settled down and ate the sandwiches and drank the water out of the pop bottles and trooped away home for tea.

'Don't tell Mam or Da,' Joss warned the little ones, but of course Clara couldn't contain herself and the story came tumbling out as soon as she got in the door.

'No more swimming in the beck,' declared Mam. But Joss wasn't likely to; he was going away, wasn't he? thought Theda.

That night, lying in the bed she shared with Clara, Theda had a serious talk with God. She always talked to God rather than prayed as it was uncomfortable kneeling on the bare floorboards by the bed. She was sure God didn't mind her being comfortable when she spoke to Him. She told Him how lonely it would be without Joss and asked why they had been brought to Winton Colliery when there wasn't enough work to keep them all? And she asked a special favour: could He please look after

Joss for her when she was no longer able to keep an eye on him?

It was 1938 by the time the pit started working full blast again. Matt Wearmouth, Theda's father, came off the three-day week he had been working along with his mates and began working five and a half days and suddenly there was enough money in the house to feed the gas meter even on a Thursday night. The younger ones missed sitting in the firelight telling stories but Theda was glad because it meant she had more time to study for her School Certificate.

She had cried the day she had had to leave school to take up a job behind the counter at the Co-op store because she was doing well, and if only she had had another six months she could have done it. But Frank had left school and had been working on the screens at the pit for only a few weeks when he was laid off and times were desperate.

Theda had given up talking to God. There was Joss, thousands of miles away, in India of all places, with the army. And she hated her job at the Co-op; it was boring.

'I'm going to be a nurse, Mam,' she declared on the day she got the information on how to apply from Newcastle Hospital. 'If I have to have my School Cert, I'll work for it at night.'

'Aye, well, pet,' said Mam. 'If determination means anything, you'll make it.'

A year later, Theda had the certificate in her hand and sent it off to Newcastle along with her completed application form and a reference from the manager of the Co-op, given a bit reluctantly, for Mr Hodges thought she didn't apply herself sufficiently to her work. She was grateful that he gave it in the end, for she knew there was some truth in what he thought, but how can you apply yourself to tidying shelves and waiting while a customer decides between a tin of peas or a tin of beans? There was another reference from Miss Dart, the French mistress from school who had helped her out by giving her extra coaching.

'I wouldn't spend all my free time with my head buried in books,' said Clara as she sat on the bed the day Theda packed her cardboard suitcase. Clara was fifteen and already a machinist in one of the new factories the other side of Bishop Auckland. Safely out of sight of her mother, she was trying the new lipstick she had bought out of the five shillings Mam gave her back from her pay. It was a bright cherry red and contrasted well with her dark eyes and black hair. She pouted her lips and blew herself a kiss in her compact mirror, well pleased with the result.

'What do you think of that, our Theda?' she asked.

'A bit bright.' She looked up from her consultation of the list that the hospital had sent her: two nightgowns, three pairs of knickers, three vests, three pairs of black stockings (lisle, no artificial silk), and two pairs of flat-heeled black shoes. She had had to save up for weeks to collect them, together with the list of textbooks.

Clara pulled a face. 'At least I won't look a frump like you will in that lot. Anyroad, like I said, I think you're mad to go in for nursing. Emptying bedpans all day long, that's what you'll be doing. Or cleaning up other people's snotty noses. But don't take any notice of me, I'm just your little sister. You think I know nothing.' Clara jumped off the bed. 'I'm away now, going into Bishop to the pictures.'

'Better not let Mam see you with all that muck on your face,' advised Theda. 'You know she said you hadn't to wear make-up until you were older.'

Clara grinned and pulled her red beret over one eye, just like Marlene Dietrich. 'I won't,' she said, and winked. Theda heard her tripping down the stairs and going straight out of the back door, calling goodbye to the family in general as she went.

'Wait – Clara!' her mother cried after her, but she was gone, escaping down the street to the bus stop.

Theda hadn't given much thought to what would happen when she began working as a probationer nurse. But though the work was hard – she fell into her bed at night exhausted and slept straight through until six o'clock, and every afternoon when she had a split day and two hours off she slept on her bed for the whole time – she liked it. The girls she was with were friendly and the patients were ordinary people, some of them from the mining villages around and some whose fathers and brothers were among the men laid off work at the shipyards along the Tyne.

What she hadn't bargained for was how homesick she would be. Though she was only thirty miles away, she couldn't get home every time she had a day off as she didn't have the fare.

You're eighteen years old now, she told herself. Don't be a baby. How do you think Joss felt, going all those miles away?

Gradually, her body adjusted to the hard, physical work and she learned to stay awake when she had to after night duty to attend a lecture. And by the time she finished her first year and was studying for her first exams, she was coming up to twenty-one and there was a war on.

Of course, she'd known it might happen. She had been worried at the time of Munich, just like everyone else, and had felt a great sense of relief when Mr Chamberlain came home waving his piece of paper. But the war had crept up on her unawares, somehow. She had been sitting in her room with her books, as she so often was, for she had preliminary examinations coming up, when she heard the excited voices outside and went into the corridor to find out what was wrong. The door of the common room was open and some of the girls were clustered around the wireless in there.

'. . . no such undertaking has been received.' It was Mr Chamberlain's voice coming over the air.

'It's started then,' Nurse Lewis, one of the nurses in her year, said. 'I have a brother in the Air Force, I hope he's all right. I suppose the men in your family will be all right, being down the pits? A reserved occupation, isn't it?'

'My brother's in the army,' said Theda defensively and turned away. But for her the war was something that was happening in the background; apart from the normal stab of fear for her country, which she imagined everyone felt, she wasn't worried for her family. Though Joss was a soldier he was far away, out of harm's way, in the Far East and the war could be over before he came home. The hospital had been an enclosed world to her this last year or so; the patients came from the outside, it was true, but it was the world on the wards and in the nurses' quarters that had been Theda's reality.

Then she went home one day to find that Frank had been called up.

'But, Da,' she protested, 'Why? He was working again, wasn't he?'

'Aye. But if you'd been taking more notice of what was going on you'd have known he was in the territorials, had been for a few months. So he got his papers straight away.'

'He's just a bairn!' her mother had burst out and Theda had felt exactly the same way. It didn't seem right.

Then there was Joss. There were no letters coming through from India but she discovered that some of his friends had landed from a troopship somewhere in the south of England. It was all very hush-hush and there was no information of more of his unit coming.

'It'll be because of the U-boats. They don't want to let them buggers know where our troopships are,' Matt had said, nodding his head sagely, and fear gripped her heart once again at the thought of a torpedo hitting a ship with Joss on board and him floating in the water trying to swim to safety. It reminded her of the day he'd got stuck in the pothole in the bed of the Gaunless, and she went off on her own down the garden to the strawberry beds and had a good cry. Then she wiped her eyes and went back to Newcastle as she was on duty that night.

Sometimes she went out with the other nurses to the Brighton ballroom or the Majestic cinema; it occupied her mind and the town was full of soldiers and sailors who liked to dance. Sometimes she even met a boy and had a date but nothing ever came of it. No one ever quite measured up to Joss. She was gaining a reputation for being quiet and studious and not much interested in boys. She was studying when Nurse Lewis knocked on her door one evening.

'Come in,' called Theda, looking up from her work. Nurse Lewis popped her head round the door.

'Mind, you're a dark horse,' she said. 'Here, I thought you didn't have a boyfriend, weren't even interested?'

'I haven't,' said Theda.

'Then who's this smashing fella waiting downstairs in the lobby? Tall, dark and handsome, with a gorgeous tan. A corporal, an' all.'

Theda hadn't time to answer, she was pushing past Nurse Lewis and flying down the stairs, and there was Joss, home safe, and a great weight lifted from her shoulders. She flung her arms around him and he swung her off her feet and laughed exuberantly. It was the same old Joss, only older and with his skin tanned to mahogany and his body filled out to that of a man.

'Steady on there, our Theda,' he said. 'I didn't come all this way just to be knocked over by a slip of a lass like you.'

They had a lovely time, dancing at the Oxford Galleries in the town, and she discovered that Joss was a great dancer, swooping around the floor with dash and verve. But, of course, he had to go back to his unit.

'I have to catch the 11.10 train to King's Cross,' he said, and showed her his docket. 'I only had forty-eight hours' leave. But when Mam said she thought it was your afternoon off, I had to pop up and see you, hadn't I?'

'I'm so glad you did,' said Theda, and behind her eyes the tears threatened. 'I can't come to the station with you, I have to be back at the hospital.'

'Aye, well, I'll be back. I can't tell you where we're going but if I see our Frank, I'll tell him you were asking after him.'